PRAISE FOR *THE BUBBLE GUM THIEF:*
A DAGNY GRAY THRILLER

"There are lots of twists and turns here, and just when the case appears to be solved, it isn't. A gripping plot and a terrific cast leave the reader hoping that this is the first of a series; these characters are too good for just one book."

—*Booklist*, starred review

"Deliciously complex and entertaining. . . . Jeff Miller will be a must-read for me."

—*Deadly Pleasures Mystery Magazine*

"Brings a few new twists to the mystery genre [and] surprises us by pulling it together in the end."

—*Cleveland Plain Dealer*

"A terrifically entertaining novel. . . . The narrative is smartly written, the dialogue realistic, the actions on the part of all involved credible. . . . An amazing ride and a fine start to this series."

—*Mysterious Reviews*

BORDERLINE INSANITY

OTHER TITLES BY JEFF MILLER

The Bubble Gum Thief: A Dagny Gray Thriller

JEFF MILLER

BORDERLINE INSANITY

A DAGNY GRAY THRILLER

Published by Thomas & Mercer, Seattle

www.apub.com

Amazon, the Amazon logo, and Thomas & Mercer are trademarks of Amazon.com, Inc., or its affiliates.

ISBN-13: 9781503936812
ISBN-10: 1503936813

Cover design by Brian Zimmerman

Printed in the United States of America

Dedicated to my parents, Joel and Linda Miller,
for their endless support and love

PROLOGUE

·····································

Thirty-five years ago . . .

Sheriff Hal Dickens was patrolling the hills above the Rio Grande when he spotted a woman giving birth on the Mexican side. Ever the gentleman, he averted his gaze, until he heard her scream.

She was carrying the newborn across the river, and the frothy white rapids had pulled them under. The sheriff ran down the hill, jumped into the water, and pulled them to the surface. Holding them to his chest, he carried them to the banks on the American side.

Dickens leaned the woman against a boulder, and she brought her baby boy to her face. *"Tu nombre es Pedro,"* she whispered. Then she moaned and began convulsing.

"Gemelos," she said, but Dickens didn't know what that meant until a second baby started to push its way out of her.

It wasn't something he had done before, but the good sheriff muddled his way through the delivery of the twin. The woman looked into the eyes of the younger son and said, *"Tu nombre es Diego."* She gave her baby a kiss and looked up at the sheriff.

Dickens smiled at her. *"Me llamo* Hal," he said.

"Me llamo Maria."

She was bruised and cut and dirty. He wasn't sure what kind of journey had taken her to the border, but he could tell it wasn't an easy one.

"Let's get you well," he said.

He took Maria and her boys to the town's only doctor. Over the next four days, the doctor monitored them, while his wife fed and cared for them. Each day, the sheriff brought clothes, diapers, and other supplies and checked to see that she was healing and that her boys were fine.

On the fifth day, the doctor pronounced Maria well. Dickens told her it was time to go.

"*¿Adónde?*" she said, smiling.

"Back home," he said. "Back to Mexico."

Her smile vanished. "*Mis hijos son estadounidenses.*"

He shook his head. "I saw you give birth to the first boy in Mexico."

"*¡Y el segundo en los Estados Unidos!*"

"You aren't a citizen, Maria."

"*Pero Diego es!*"

"It's the law, Maria."

She began to cry. "I thought you were good," she muttered in English.

"It's the law, Maria."

As tears poured from her, she told him she had a cousin in Corpus Christi who could take the American baby.

"No, no," he pleaded. "Don't split up your boys." But she would not agree.

Dickens drove Maria and her boys eight hours to Corpus Christi. They arrived at sunset. He walked her to the doorstep and pushed the doorbell. A small Mexican woman answered.

"Soy tu prima," Maria said. A flurry of Spanish flew between the women, and Dickens didn't understand much of it. Both of the women started crying.

"Por supuesto," the aunt said. *"Por supuesto."*

After twenty minutes of conversation that he couldn't follow, Dickens announced, *"Es el momento."* He didn't like rushing her, but it was getting late.

Maria lowered her head. "Okay," she muttered. She looked back and forth between her boys, and her face went blank. Dickens realized that she couldn't tell the twins apart. One of them was an American, but she didn't know which.

"You have to pick," he said.

She gave the aunt the boy in her right arm. *"Esto es un regalo, Diego,"* she whispered to him. In English, she added, "For the love of God, do something good with it."

The sheriff drove Maria and Pedro to Brownsville and across the border into Mexico. Parking at a bus station, he opened his wallet, pulled out $138 in assorted bills, and placed them in her hand. "To get home," he said. She folded the money and shoved it into her pocket, held Pedro to her chest, and walked to the platform, never looking back.

CHAPTER 1

There were twelve anorexic women sitting in a circle in Room 4A at the Shirlington Community Center, but only one of them was fingering the phone in her pocket, waiting for the vibration of a text identifying the location of a serial killer.

Dr. Colleen Childs had a strict no-phone policy, but Dagny Gray didn't care. She probably had a no-gun policy, too, but Dagny's was strapped under her jacket. FBI special agents were always on the clock, even in group therapy.

At Dr. Childs's signal, two women walked to the center of the circle, joined hands, and stared at each other for seconds that felt like minutes. Then, upon command, each traded compliments that escalated in uplift and hyperbole until both women collapsed in a tearful hug.

Another pair took their place. As they traded words like *powerful* and *magnificent*, their voices tumbled under the hum of the air conditioner, which kept the room uncomfortably chilled. It was wrong to cool any room on an autumn day, Dagny thought, but especially wrong to cool a room full of slight and underweight women. Dr. Childs should have informed management to shut it down. She was too focused on emotional feelings and not enough on real ones.

"Dagny and Elizabeth."

Dagny looked at Dr. Childs.

"It's your turn," the doctor said.

Dagny rose and took a couple of steps to the center of the circle. Elizabeth stood opposite her. Although she was only twenty-seven, Elizabeth looked and dressed like a much-older woman. Plaid sweater, covered in balled lint. Long pleated skirt. Glasses with a black frame and big lenses. Underneath it all, rail thin and worn. The girl took Dagny's hands and stared into her eyes. Dagny averted her gaze.

Dr. Childs motioned for Dagny to speak.

"Elizabeth, you are a strong, fierce woman, and there's nothing you can't do."

"Louder, please," Dr. Childs said.

Dagny raised her voice. "I've only been here for a few weeks, but in that time, I've seen you grow." She looked over at Dr. Childs, who was waving her hand to prod Dagny to continue. "You have the power to do anything you want. You need not let anything have power over you."

Elizabeth smiled. "Thank you, Dagny."

"Now, Elizabeth, tell Dagny what you see," Dr. Childs said.

Elizabeth looked at Dagny and smiled. "You are an ocean breeze on a summer day. You are a delicate flower—"

Dagny blurted out a laugh. "I'm so sorry," she said, and then despite her best efforts, she laughed again. The more she tried to suppress it, the harder it came.

Dr. Childs rose from her seat. "We are here to support one another—"

"I'm so sorry," Dagny said. "I'm so sorry. But . . ." She surveyed the scowls in the circle around her. "This was a bad idea." She grabbed her backpack.

"Wait!" Dr. Childs yelled, but Dagny was already out the door. She jogged through the hall and ducked into the women's room, and leaned against the sink.

At thirty-five years old, she was fighting the same battles she had fought as a teenager. She grabbed a tissue from the dispenser and dabbed her eyes. Looking up at the mirror, she saw only sadness, and then Dr. Childs, standing behind her.

Dagny turned. "I'm sorry." She sniffed and wiped away a last tear.

"Come back to group and tell them."

"I can't talk about myself in front of other people. I don't understand why anyone would want to. It seems like the whole point of this is to get us to say things in front of others that we wouldn't want to say even to ourselves."

"Yes, that's the point." Dr. Childs was in her forties; her graying hair was pulled back in a bun that was neither too tight nor too casual. Her posture was good. She was fit but not thin and wore a professional suit, tailored to her build. Her glasses were stylish, and she wore just enough makeup that Dagny wasn't sure she was wearing any. Her cadence was clear, and her sentences were concise. She never stumbled over words or changed course midthought. Her confidence unnerved Dagny.

"I feel lost and confused right now," she said. "I don't think it's a good time for therapy." She realized the absurdity of the sentiment as soon as she expressed it.

"What about your boss?"

The Professor had insisted that Dagny attend counseling sessions as a condition of her continued employment. "I'll talk to him about it. He'll give me a reprieve."

"I doubt that. He calls me to make sure that you're attending. It seems quite important to him. You seem quite important to him."

That was news to Dagny. "He calls you?"

"With a regularity that borders on intrusion."

Dagny smiled. "Despite the tears, you know, I'm fine. I've maintained my weight for—"

"Three months."

"It's been four."

"And you think that means you're doing fine?"

"My last relapse came at a difficult time. I'd lost someone important to me. It was an aberration."

"Losing people isn't an aberration, Dagny. It's a part of life. And if you can't get through it without starving yourself, then you've got a problem."

"I have a system in place now."

"Anorexics are great with systems."

"I'm serious. I'm eating now. I always will."

"The fact that you think your problem is eating tells me you don't have the slightest handle on it."

"That's a powerful assessment of a person you barely know." It was also, Dagny knew, spot-on.

"So, let me get to know you." Childs put her hand on Dagny's shoulder. "Forget the group session. Try me one-on-one."

"Why do you care?"

"Because you've got a good insurance plan."

Dagny laughed.

"Will you let me try to help you?"

She didn't have a choice. It was a condition of her employment. "Okay."

Her phone buzzed against her leg. She pulled it from her pocket and glanced at the text from Victor.

"I have an opening on Monday."

"I can't," Dagny said. "I'm going to Chicago."

CHAPTER 2

Father Diego Vega was naked, still wet from the shower, and dripping water onto his bathroom rug. "I was sick, and you took care of me. I was in prison, and you visited me." He grabbed a towel from the hook and tied it around his waist. "And the people to his right said, 'We didn't do any of these things.'" Diego grabbed a can of gel and pumped some into his hands, then lathered his face. Looking into the mirror above the sink, he saw short, dark hair; a strong chin; and weary eyes. There was nothing boyish about him anymore. When did that disappear? "'We didn't feed you. We didn't clothe you.' But Jesus stopped them. 'When you did these things for the least of you, you did them for me.' That's what he said. And that is what it means to believe."

After shaving, he gathered his uniform: boxer shorts, black socks, black clerical shirt, black jeans, black belt, white collar insert, black shoes, and his watch. At one time, such garb made him feel special, but now it felt constricting and uncomfortable. Grabbing an apple from a bowl on the kitchen counter, he ran out to his car, a 1969 cherry-red

Corvette convertible. Clenching the fruit in his mouth, he unlocked the door, started the engine, and headed toward town.

A painted wood sign at the border announced: **WELCOME TO BILFORD, OHIO'S FRIENDLIEST TOWN**. The billboard forty feet behind it featured the full, round face of the county's sheriff, who hiked a thumb over his shoulder under block letters declaring **GO ON HOME!** Diego took a bite of the apple.

Downtown Bilford looked like America, at least the way it looked in the 1950s. A four-block grid of three-story buildings housed glass storefronts and apartments. American flags hung from telephone poles. There was a post office, a barbershop, and a statue of a man riding a horse in the middle of a fountain, surrounded by a square patch of grass. At the center of the town stood the county courthouse, built tall like a mountain, casting its shadow everywhere.

But it wasn't the 1950s. The storefronts were mostly empty. The fountain rarely ran. The barber pole didn't spin. Some artists had moved in and opened galleries; each seemed to last a month or two before another took its place. A theater company had taken over the old movie house so they could show Beckett to small, appreciative crowds. A handful of daring souls had opened restaurants, since the rents were cheap, and at least two of them had attracted a loyal clientele. There was some life in old Bilford. But of all the buildings in downtown, only the courthouse saw steady action.

Diego worked the apple with one hand and turned the wheel with the other. "Sheep and the goats. Sheep and the goats. And lucky us, we live in the goats' town," he said. Or was it a ghost town? Lots of people lived in Bilford's city limits; most of them didn't go downtown, absent a summons. All of the new construction in Bilford was five miles west, next to the interstate that took people to Cincinnati, Dayton, Columbus, and other places that were bigger and better. The schools were out by the interstate now. So were the library, the golf course, and a shopping mall. The local newspaper was there, and the local radio station, too. The jobs were there. They called it New Bilford, but it was still Bilford.

Diego's people didn't live in downtown Bilford or New Bilford—they lived in the nooks and crannies in between. They lived one town over, in Cleves, and one town up, in Rhodes. They couldn't afford to join the country club, but they fixed its roof. They did their best to avoid the courthouse, but they also cooked the lunch that the judge had delivered to his chambers every day.

Diego passed by the statue and the fountain and the courthouse, and he turned onto Alpine Drive, which wound its way over a hill and along a river. He pulled into the gravel lot in front of Barrio Burrito and checked his watch: 9:28. "Faith comes slowly," he said. He stepped out of the car and tossed the apple core into the woods next to the lot. Ignoring the CLOSED sign on the restaurant door, he walked inside. A plate sat on the counter; there was one tamale left, and he took it.

They were gathered in the stockroom. The oldest were sitting; the younger were standing among piled boxes and supplies. A few were dressed in their Sunday finest; most were dressed in T-shirts and jeans. The children were chasing one another. Angel and Cesar, as expected, but also the twins, and Jorge, who usually sat looking glum. The men were talking to the men and the women to the women, and nobody noticed that he'd entered. Diego ate his tamale and listened, but it was all cacophony, and louder than usual.

He squeezed his way through the crowd to the front of the room. As he passed through, the noise subsided. Parents shushed their children and gathered them close. He stepped onto a wood crate and began.

"Today, I would like to talk about faith. And why faith isn't enough." He always led with his sermon, since the congregation seldom had the patience for much more than that. "In Matthew, we find the parable of the sheep and goats, which teaches us nothing about running a farm." No laughs. He had hoped for a laugh. "It's a parable about faith and works, and their intersection. For Matthew tells us that Jesus will divide the people like a shepherd divides the sheep from the goats. And he'll turn to the people on the right—to the sheep—and say to them, 'I was hungry, and you gave me food. I was thirsty—'"

"Father, there's something important we need to talk about."

The interruption came from Juanita Valquez, a petite, gentle woman. It was not her habit to interrupt the services; the fact that she spoke now told Diego that it was a serious matter.

"What is it, Juanita?"

She rose from her seat. "Father Vega, my brother is missing."

"From church?" He scanned the congregation.

"No, I mean he is missing. I haven't seen him in seven days."

That wasn't unusual. Much of the Mexican population around Bilford, like much of the Mexican population in the rest of America, was transient. "I'm certain he will call, Juanita. Sometimes it takes a little while to settle in."

"He's not the only one missing."

Miranda Delgado stood. She was a lovely, round woman who brought Diego baked treats nearly every week. "My oldest boy, Javier, is missing, too. Also for seven days."

It was his instinct to provide comfort to these women. "Perhaps they left together. To find some place where it is easier to find work. This happens, Miranda, and then a few more days pass, and you get a call and everything is okay."

Juan Sanchez stood. He was a large man with a booming voice, and one of the few legal residents who attended services at Barrio Burrito. As the owner of a Ford dealership, he was by far the richest man in attendance. "Father, there are times that those things happen, but this is not one of those times. Three of my boys are gone, too." Sanchez was not referring to his sons but rather to the stable of illegal immigrants he employed to clean cars or cut grass—jobs he doled out as charity to help the community. Lest anyone challenge his motives in hiring them, he paid these men the same wages he paid his legal employees and footed the expense from his own pocket, without deducting the wages as a business expense. "I've heard of at least four others who are missing, which would make nine young men in the past week. Most of these boys were close to their families. They wouldn't leave without telling anyone. When you call their phones, it goes straight to voice mail. Something has happened."

Diego surveyed the congregation. There were about fifty people in the room—almost all of them illegal immigrants or their family members. They were not looking for comfort. They were looking for help. "Who else knows someone who is missing?"

A few hands flew into the air.

"Let's make a list." He tore an invoice from the side of a box of paper cups, turned it over, and scratched down the names as they were called. Lino Fuentes. Hector Morales. Gabriel Diaz. Emilio Garza. Diego added Miranda's son, Juanita's brother, and Juan's boys. In all, there were thirteen names on the list—all men in their late teens or early twenties. Diego read their names aloud. "No one here has heard from any of these young men?" Silence. "Does anyone have any idea what might have happened to them?"

Roberto Soto rose. He was a mechanic without a garage; if you needed your car fixed, he came and fixed it. "It's got to be Sheriff Don." This generated vigorous agreement, so much so that Diego had to quiet them.

"Please, please. If it were Sheriff Don, he'd be bragging about it on the news. And he's not. So it's not him."

The crowd stayed silent until Juanita stood again. "If it's not Sheriff Don, then it's something worse, isn't it?"

Diego wanted to tell her that it was not worse, but this would have been a lie, and he never lied to his parishioners. "Let me make some inquiries and see if I can find out anything. In the meantime, I think we should proceed with Mass and pray for these young men." But his mind was elsewhere as he began again. "Let's talk about the sheep and the goats."

We live in the goats' town, Diego thought. We live with the goddamn goats.

CHAPTER 3

Dagny Gray grabbed the next rusted rung of the fire-escape ladder on the east wall of the sixteen-story Tandoor Apartments building on the west side of Chicago. Special Agent Brent Davis followed behind her. "You first," he'd insisted. "That way I can catch you when you fall."

Dagny had seen Davis interview people, charm them, even disarm them—but she'd never seen him confront an actual danger. So *you first* could have been general chivalry or just plain cowardice. It didn't matter. Dagny was fine with going first. As a general rule, she didn't follow anybody. Not even up the side of a building, in the dark, on the west side of Chicago.

The ladder rose straight up the side of the building. There was a platform to the left at each floor. When Dagny got to the sixth platform, she looked down. This was a mistake. "Don't look down," Brent said.

"The view's terrible," Dagny replied. "All I see is you." Queasy and chastened, she looked back up and realized the climb ahead was bigger than the climb behind.

Martin Benny had killed thirteen young women at nine colleges in five states over the course of three months. They had been chasing him for weeks, and now they had him. The serial killer was staying in a two-bedroom corner unit on the thirteenth floor. It belonged to the estate of Harriet Swinton, the aunt of Benny's grandmother's friend. Harriet had died four months earlier, but the estate was in dispute, and the apartment remained furnished but vacant. Special Agent Victor Walton Jr. had traced through connections and pegged it as Benny's hideout. The twenty-five-year-old forensic accountant was great at that sort of thing, and maybe not much else that the job required. Dagny loved him like a little brother and prayed he wouldn't blow this mission.

An old man's voice barked in her earpiece. "Can't the two of you go any faster?"

"Easy to say from the comfort of a couch, Professor."

"I'll have you know, I'm standing at the window."

Dagny looked at the building across the street and counted the windows up to the seventeenth floor, where Timothy McDougal was watching Swinton's apartment through parted curtains. In McDougal's younger years, fellow agents tired of his didactic lectures and mockingly referred to him as the Professor. To their dismay, he embraced the nickname. These days, few called the crusty octogenarian-ish Bureau lifer anything else.

"What do you see?" Dagny asked.

"The shades are drawn, but I can see the flickering light of a television around the edges of the master bedroom window," he replied.

"Looks like the rent on your unit there is really paying dividends." She heard Davis chuckle below and hoped Victor wasn't laughing from the thirteenth-floor stairwell in the Tandoor.

The plan was simple and reckless. When Dagny and Brent reached the thirteenth floor, Victor would walk to Benny's door and knock. With his attention drawn to the door, Dagny and Brent would break through the windows. Then, Victor would burst through the front door, and somehow the three of them would apprehend the nation's most feared killer.

Anyone with any sense would have sent a SWAT team to do this job, but the Professor had long advocated that a small team could do a better job than a big one, and proving the point was more important than trifles like personal safety. So Dagny, Victor, and Brent, along with the cozily ensconced Professor, were the entire operation.

As Dagny scaled the building, she noticed the wind, and the sound of the cars below, and the whine of a distant siren. She noticed that the birds would fly away from the bricks jutting from the building's walls when she got within two floors of them. She noticed the cigarette butts that littered the platforms and the tangles in the cords of the cheap venetian blinds that covered some of the windows. She did not once think about things she hated about herself, the losses she had suffered, or what she hoped to accomplish in life. And so she smiled the closer she got to Benny's floor.

"Where are you?" Victor whispered through the earpiece.

"Tenth floor," Dagny said. "Nervous?"

"Yes."

"You've got your Glock?"

"Yes."

"Safety off?" It was an inside joke.

"Funny."

"Eleven."

"What?"

"I'm on the eleventh floor now."

"Oh. I thought you were making a Spinal Tap reference."

"I'm heading to twelve."

"Wait a second," Victor said.

"Why?"

"I need a few moments to breathe."

"No breathing," the Professor barked through the earpiece. "Just do it."

"Says the man in the building across the street," Dagny replied. She stepped onto the platform at the twelfth floor. Brent joined her. "Victor, remember, when you knock, don't knock too softly, because he needs to hear it over the TV. But don't knock too loudly, because it's a casual knock, right? Not a panicked one. The knock of a neighbor who wants to borrow an egg. Not quite the knock of a pizza deliveryman, because Benny hasn't ordered a pizza, and if you knock like that, he'll be on guard."

"They didn't teach knocking at Quantico, Dagny."

"One more thing, Victor."

"Yes?"

"Please don't shoot us." She was more worried about this than anything Benny might do. "Now go."

She heard Victor's steps through the earpiece and climbed up the ladder to the thirteenth floor, crouching on the platform under the left living-room window. Brent joined her on the platform, crouching down beneath the window on the right. The steps stopped; Victor's breathing did not. He was at the door. They waited for his knock.

"It's time, Victor," the Professor said.

Three quick knocks, like a neighbor who needed to borrow an egg. Dagny unzipped her backpack and withdrew a crowbar; Brent did the same. She nodded to him, and they swung through the windows. The first bash shattered the glass; a second helped clear the shards. They barreled inside, guns drawn. Once the glass settled, it was quiet, save for the sound of a television in the other room. Dagny looked around. A green-velvet couch. A console television. Maroon lampshades with tassels. Scenic watercolors on the walls.

There was a bang at the door. Victor had tried to break through. Another bang. Dagny moved backward toward the door, keeping her eyes on the hallway, feeling blindly for the deadbolt. She flipped the lock and opened the door just as Victor was making his third attempt at an entry. He tumbled to the ground.

The three formed a triangle, each facing out. Brent checked the kitchen; Victor, the dining room. Dagny opened the entry closet and pushed the coats to the side. Nothing. She headed down the hallway and ducked into the bathroom. There was a man's razor and an open can of shaving gel on the counter, a pile of hair in the sink. She heard a drip behind the shower curtain and pushed the curtain aside. The shower was empty. She opened a small linen closet—nothing but towels and medication. Dagny walked out to the hallway; Brent finished with the guest bedroom and joined her. He motioned to the closed door of the master bedroom. They could hear the television playing a potato-chips jingle. Victor joined them in the hallway.

"What is happening?" the Professor said through their earpieces. No one answered him. Not yet.

Brent raised his foot and kicked the door, knocking it open. Dagny tried to enter first, but Brent nudged past her. The television sat on a dresser. An Indiana University sweatshirt was draped over a chair in the corner. There were framed pictures of grandchildren on the walls. An envelope sat on top of the neatly made bed. Brent kicked in the door to the master bath. Dagny checked under the bed and tore open the door to the closet. Victor shifted from foot to foot.

Benny was gone.

Dagny took a pair of nylon gloves from her pockets and put them on, picked up the envelope from the bed, and tore it open. She unfolded the note that was inside. In large script, it said:

I'm too tired, and you're too late. —Martin Benny

The commercial ended, and a news anchor appeared on the screen. "To repeat the breaking news, serial killer Martin Benny turned himself in to Chicago police earlier this evening. Benny will be housed at the county jail until law enforcement determines where he will be detained and which jurisdiction will try him first." The screen showed a half-dozen officers loading a handcuffed and clean-shaven Benny into the back of a police van.

"For the love of all that is good, will someone tell me what is going on?" the Professor barked.

"We're too late," Dagny said.

They took a booth in the back of a TGI Fridays. The Professor sat next to Dagny. He was a short, shriveled man, with slight patches of white hair above his ears but bald on top. In moments of considered contemplation, he would stroke his short white beard to its fine point, but this was not such a moment.

Brent and Victor sat across from them. Under different circumstances, the sight of the two tall men stuffed uncomfortably into the same side of a booth would have brought Dagny some measure of joy. Apart from their size and job, they had little in common. Brent was a handsome black man; Victor was a pale redhead. Brent was fit and athletic; Victor was a little doughy and a lot clumsy. Brent was in his mid-thirties and looked like a man; Victor was in his mid-twenties and looked like a boy. Brent worked people; Victor worked paper. Dagny valued Victor's skills more highly, but the Bureau rewarded Brent's.

When the waitress came, Brent ordered a coffee, Victor, a piece of apple pie, and Dagny, a cheeseburger with extra cheese. The Professor ordered nothing. They all looked glum.

The Professor had leveraged the success of their last case to achieve unprecedented independence within the Bureau. For the time being, they operated with virtually no oversight. They could choose their cases and commandeer whatever resources were necessary to solve them.

Bureau protocol, rules, standards—none of that applied to them. They appeared on no FBI organizational chart. Every facet of the operation was an experiment—the culmination of the Professor's entire career in the Bureau, and a test of everything he believed. And so far, they were failing that test.

Victor broke the silence. "I'm a bad person."

A minute passed before Dagny finally asked, "Why?"

"The guy turned himself in. He's going to jail. He won't kill anyone else. So I should be happy, and yet I'm not. And the only reason I'm not happy is that we didn't get to catch him."

"That's a perfectly fine reason to feel sad," she said.

"I don't know," Victor replied. "It's just selfish."

The Professor turned to Victor and pounded his fist on the table. "You're damn right it's selfish, and thank God for that. That selfishness that makes you want to be the one to catch a criminal—that thing that drives you crazy when you don't—that's the very thing that makes one a good agent. We spent two months tracking this fool, and he shows us up by turning himself in. I'm not sad—I'm furious. I feel rotten and low, and I wouldn't want to work with anyone who didn't feel the same way." He paused as the waitress set their orders on the table. "Your pride, your greed, your vanity—they can either undermine you or make you great. You choose how to use them. I use them to catch bad people."

Dagny agreed. Although she had no appetite, she picked up her cheeseburger and took a bite.

CHAPTER 4

Marcia Bell's law office was on the floor above a Quiznos. Diego pressed the intercom button and announced himself. The door buzzed, and he opened it, climbed the steps, and turned the knob of a glass door marked by the painted words **LAW OFFICE**. The receptionist's desk was empty; he walked past it and down a hallway. Marcia shared her space with several other solo practitioners; he passed their offices and found hers.

Bell was forty-six years old and looked exactly that and nothing more. She wore a white blouse and a dark-gray skirt; her suit coat hung from the back of her chair. Years of coffee stained her teeth. Her dark hair was only partially contained by the large barrette at the top of her head, and she swiveled back and forth in her chair in apparent synchronization with her thoughts. She waved Diego in, and he took a seat in front of her.

The phone on her desk rang. She silenced the ringer, but the lights kept blinking. Manila folders were piled on her desk in irregular stacks.

Her diploma and bar certificate hung on her wall, which was otherwise bare. A picture of her husband and teenage daughter sat on the
second bookshelf from the top. The rest of the shelves were filled with
immigration-conference materials and various iterations of the United
States Code and Code of Federal Regulations.

"Don't tell me . . ."

He wasn't sure what he wasn't supposed to tell her, so he waited.

"I know you from somewhere."

"I don't think so."

"I never forget a face."

There was nothing familiar about her. "If we've met, I'm sorry to
have forgotten it, Ms. Bell."

"My face isn't as memorable as yours. Please call me Marcia. What
can I do for you?"

"I need you to relieve my fears."

"That sounds ominous."

"Perhaps. Members of my congregation are worried about family
members who have disappeared."

"It's not unusual for the undocumented to disappear."

"Thirteen of them? In the span of a week? Without any warning
they were leaving, and without any contact since their disappearance?"

She leaned back in her chair. "That's a lot."

"Have you heard anything? Maybe Sheriff Don?"

"He picked up a couple recently. I'm representing one of them."

Diego opened his notebook, pulled out a piece of paper, and
handed it to Marcia. "Anyone on this list?"

She put on her glasses, picked up the paper, and scanned the names.
"No."

"Would you know if Sheriff Don picked them up?"

She laughed. "Don Marigold puts their names and faces on the
Internet between fingerprinting and holding. He considers it a high
achievement, and he's not quiet about his achievements. I check his site

every day, and I haven't seen any of these names. Plus, he gives them their phone calls. Word gets out—he likes it that way. Gets everyone all scared."

Diego sighed. "I was hoping you'd have the answers, but it sounds like you don't. Any idea who I should talk to next? I know Marty Feldstein does some immigration work."

"Are you looking to make a fair effort and then report back to your people that you tried? Or do you really want to find these folks?"

Diego was not used to people challenging the sincerity of a priest. It was refreshing. "I want to find them, of course."

She tilted her head and leaned forward. "You need to think about that, because once you climb into this cave, it's going to be awfully dark."

"I want to find these people, Marcia."

"Well, if you're serious about all this, you'll probably want to talk to Ty Harborman."

"Who is Ty Harborman?"

She shook her head. "How long have you been out here, preaching at the burrito stand?"

"Two years."

"Two years, and still a tourist?"

He wasn't sure how to respond, and was relieved the question was rhetorical.

"Ty Harborman runs an employment agency for illegal immigrants. Nothing legitimate, mind you. But he helps them settle and gets them jobs. Makes his way on finder's fees and commissions. He might know the names on your list."

"How can I find him?"

"You'll need an introduction. Are you sure you want to do this?"

"I am." He wasn't sure why she kept pressing him.

"Then I'll get you an introduction." Marcia started to return his list of names but then pulled it back. "Let me add two more." She picked up her pen. "Rico Chavez," she said, scribbling. "He lived in Cleves. He was supposed to meet me two days ago about a deportation hearing, but he didn't show. No answer when I call his phone. I'll write down his number for you, in case it helps."

"Okay."

"And David Fisher."

"David Fisher?" Diego said.

"I know, not quite like the other names."

"Is he Mexican?"

"American, mostly."

"I don't understand."

"You still won't when I tell you the story."

"Try me."

"David was a good boy. Not too bright but graduated from Bilford High. Worked restaurant jobs, never for too long. Smoked pot and started selling it to the college kids. Got arrested. Agreed to thirty days in jail and two years' probation. And then, on the day of his release from jail, an ICE agent showed up at his discharge hearing. Told David he wasn't an American citizen and that he was being deported to the Philippines."

ICE was the US Immigration and Customs Enforcement Agency. "He wasn't American?"

"Oh, he was as American as they come. But he was not, technically, a citizen. His mother was Filipino. When she was fourteen, her parents sent her to live with her grandmother in Manila. The grandmother rented her services to American GIs. One of them got her pregnant."

"David's father?"

"Not the one that raised him. ICE had documents showing that Harold Fisher didn't arrive in the Philippines until three months after David was born. Some other GI had to be the actual biological father. Mr. Fisher, however, seemed to think the kid was his and that he had been born early. Brought the mom and the kid back home to the States a few weeks after he was born. The couple married, and when the mom died later, the guy raised David as a single dad."

"But if his real dad was another GI, then he's an American citizen, right?"

"We can't prove who the real father is. Even if we could, the spawn of an unmarried American male overseas is not considered to be an American citizen."

"They would really send this kid halfway across the world, to a place where he doesn't know anyone?"

"They would if they could find him. He's missing."

"If he's hiding, I don't blame him. But if I find him, I'll let you know where he is."

"I don't want to know where he is. Just let me know that he's all right." She slid Diego's list back to him. "Now, Harborman." She picked up the phone and dialed. Diego listened as she explained the situation and vouched for his credibility. Twice, she explained that he was a priest. There was some back and forth he couldn't follow, a kind of familiar laugh, and then she hung up the phone.

"He'll talk to you, but the conditions are pretty specific." She relayed them to Diego. It required a trip he didn't really want to make.

It was a beautiful autumn day, so Diego put the top down on his Corvette. The car had drawn its share of remarks, and he felt self-conscious driving it, even though he'd salvaged it from a junkyard and restored it over the course of several years. There was some work left to do, but there always was with a car like that. It was worth something now. Perhaps he was obligated to relinquish it once he'd brought it value. Or perhaps a man who'd given up sex was entitled to a nice car.

Dayton was an hour's drive from Bilford, and he spent that hour thinking about what Marcia Bell had said to him. "Two years and still a tourist," was the way she'd put it. She barely knew him and had pegged him to the core. When he'd asked the church for permission to move to Bilford, he had promised big things. Establishment of an English-language program. Creation of an after-school center. Organization of a law clinic. He'd delivered none of these things, not that the church was asking.

And there was that other thing Bell had said: "Once you climb into this cave, it's going to be awfully dark." It did not feel like he was driving into a dark cave, at least not until he pulled into the parking lot behind Saint Paul's parish.

At one time, he'd been king of the parish, greeted by everyone with smiles, handshakes, backslaps, and the like. Now, he felt like a trespasser. His departure had been blessed by the archbishop, but it had been cursed by everyone else. He'd given them all the best of reasons for his departure. The charitable impulse was fine in theory, but it was not always appreciated in application.

When he pulled into the parking lot, he noticed that the sign marking his space had been removed. Fair enough—the infrequency of his visits no longer warranted it. Still, it stung. He parked the car and entered the church through the back door. Hurrying through the hallway, he hoped to escape detection. Father John Barton, however, saw him scurry by his office. "Diego, nice to see you."

He backed up and stood at Father Barton's doorway. "John, it's good to see you." Diego waited to be invited in, but an invitation was not extended.

"It's been a while."

"Too long, I know."

Like Diego, John was in his thirties. He looked older. His hair was receding; his waistline, expanding. The lines on his forehead had deepened. His color seemed off.

"How is your congregation?" Barton asked. "Growing?"

It hadn't grown the way Diego had hoped. "Holding steady."

Barton smiled, and Diego tried not to read too much into it. "Still meeting at the taco truck?"

"In the back of the restaurant. Yes."

"Communion with tortillas and sangria, I imagine."

Diego laughed politely. "I am lucky to be part of them, John. They fill me with spirit."

"Yes," John said. "Though for some of us, the Lord does that."

"These people are a gift from the Lord."

"All people are a gift from the Lord, Diego."

Yes, Diego thought, but some are a better gift than others. "It's been good to talk to you, but I must go. I have another appointment." He left before John could respond.

Diego pushed through a few doors, crossed the cathedral, and made his way to the middle confession box. When he slipped inside, he felt better. It occurred to him that he could stay here until everyone else left and only then make his way back to his car.

A man slipped into the other side of the box. The voice called, "You Father Vega?"

"I am."

"Marcia told me you were on the level. I'm Ty Harborman."

He was a big man. That's the only thing Diego could tell from his shadow. "It's a pleasure to meet you, Ty."

"I'm not Catholic, so I don't know how this thing works."

"You mean confession?"

"Yeah. If I'm going to talk to you, I need it to be confidential. This is confidential, right?"

"It is."

"Even though I'm not Catholic?"

"It's still confidential. Anything you say is between us."

"So if you were called to court, they couldn't ask you about what I say in here?"

"That's right."

"I'm only here because of Marcia, you know. She's a good lady."

"She is. I know."

"Okay, so what's going on? What are you looking to find out?"

"Thirteen men have disappeared in a couple of weeks. Fourteen, actually. Maybe fifteen," he said, remembering the names Marcia had added to his list. "Families are worried."

"Who's missing?"

"I have a list." Diego handed it through the slot between them.

It took Harborman a few seconds to review it. "Jesus Christ. Yeah, I know some of these guys. They're missing?"

"Yes. How many do you know?"

Harborman counted six.

"Can you mark them?" Diego passed a pen; Harborman marked the paper and returned it and the pen to Diego. "How do you know them?"

"Do you understand what I do?"

"Not really."

"People come here lots of ways, right? Sometimes they overstay a visa; sometimes they slip across the border. Sometimes someone smuggles them in."

"A coyote?"

"I call them recruiters, and I have an arrangement with some of them. I let them know what my employment needs are, and they try to bring me people to fill them."

"You instruct them to bring you people?"

"No. This isn't slavery. I'm an employment agency. When people are coming here, they want jobs. They don't always know where the jobs will be, so they may not know where to go. If I have jobs that need to be filled, they want to know that, so they can go somewhere there is work. There're people like me all over the country."

"So, employers tell you what they need, and you pass it along to the coyotes?"

"Or sometimes families are trying to bring up their relatives. They'll give me some money to give to a recruiter, and I'll pass it along to cover the cost of transportation."

"You act as a middleman in the negotiations."

"Not just a middleman. A lot of jobs are temporary. While someone's job is winding down, I might be finding him his next job. I keep tabs on law enforcement. I help people acclimate—find lawyers and doctors and relatives. I help them figure out the schools."

"You do some of the things I've been hoping to do."

"I do it better than you ever could."

"How do you get paid?"

"Ten percent of earnings goes to me for a year, plus any finder's fee I can get. More than fair, considering the services I provide."

"How many folks do you have working under you?"

"Six fifty when things were good."

"Six hundred and fifty?"

"Yeah."

"In Ohio?"

"Southwest Ohio, from Northern Kentucky up to Columbus. Dayton, Wilmington, Middletown, Bilford, all the way over to Portsmouth."

"And do you own the area?"

"You mean like the mafia? It's not like that. That's as big an area as I can reasonably handle. Anyone else who wants in is free to compete. A handful of others place people in the area, too. But it's hard to break into the business. Employers want to work with someone they can trust."

"You said six of these guys used to work for you. Why don't they anymore?"

"I couldn't get them any work. Businesses aren't hiring now. Things are too tense, thanks to Sheriff Don."

"Sheriff Don has only one county."

"But he's got everyone all riled up. The feds have stepped up enforcement, since he was making them look bad. You've got politicians in other counties having to explain to voters why their county isn't as tough as Bilford. It's a frightening time."

"So, did you let your workers go?"

"I told them I couldn't place them right now, and that they should look for day labor. Hang out at Home Depot, hope to get picked up."

"Have you talked to any of the guys you marked on my list?"

"Not for a few months. No idea where they are now."

"Could they have gone back home?"

Harborman reached for the list again. "Lino, maybe. No, I mean, he had family here. These guys all had family here. No way Gabriel leaves without saying good-bye. No way Emilio leaves, period—his mother is sick. Manuel, he's not leaving. Maybe Hector. I don't know. Honestly, all of these guys had family here. I can't see them leaving without saying something to them."

"Any chance the feds swooped them up?"

"I would have heard about it. Someone at ICE keeps me updated."

"Why does he do that? Kickbacks?"

"We have an arrangement. Suffice to say, if they'd been picked up, I would know."

"Sheriff Don?"

"I don't have any insight there, other than you'd think he'd be holding a press conference if he rounded up thirteen more illegals, right?"

"I'd think so."

Harborman let out a big sigh. "Talking to you, I kinda hope Sheriff Don got them."

"Why's that?"

"Because if he doesn't have them, I think they're dead."

There were eleven cities in Bilford County: Zakes, Harrison, Cleves, Madison, Hanes, Rhodes, Silverton, Chester, Adams, Tylerville, and the largest, Bilford. Bilford police had jurisdiction over the city by law; they also provided service to Zakes, Harrison, and Rhodes by virtue of intra-municipal agreements. The Bilford County Sheriff's Office policed the noncontiguous, unincorporated areas of Bilford County, as well as towns not served by the city police, save for Cleves, which had its own small force. This meant that Sheriff Don Marigold had clear authority over more than half of Bilford County, and he often tried to exert authority over the rest. Using county funds, he'd purchased billboards just within the borders of the city of Bilford to make sure everyone knew the city was in his county. Diego passed another one of these signs on his way to the Bilford County Sheriff's Office. It read WE WERE HERE FIRST.

Marcia Bell's words had challenged Diego to step up his game; Harborman's had clarified the stakes. Instead of asking others if Sheriff Don had swooped up the missing men, Diego was going to ask the man himself.

To get to the sheriff, Diego had to drive past the tents. There were at least a hundred of them behind an eighteen-foot-high, electrified chain-link fence. Unless the temperature dropped below freezing, this was where the male prisoners worked, ate, and slept. Diego slowed his car and watched as a group of men dug one of the sheriff's infamous holes. Every day, prisoners dug a large hole, filled it with dirt, and dug it again.

The holes were infamous, but the pink brassieres were genuinely famous. All the male prisoners wore them over their shirts. If they refused, they were placed in solitary confinement.

A car honked behind him—one of the sheriff's deputies. Diego tapped the accelerator and drove ahead to a parking space.

The first thing he noticed when he walked into the building was the gift shop. Copies of Sheriff Don's self-published memoir, *No Coddling*, lined several rows of shelves. Other shelves were filled with bumper stickers that captured his mottos: GO ON HOME. WE WERE HERE FIRST. DON'T TAKE OUR JOBS. PUNISHMENT IS IN TENTS. THIS LAND IS OUR LAND. GOD MADE US GREAT. Pink brassieres hung from hangers in various sizes.

Diego passed the gift shop and walked up to an information desk. "I'd like to talk to Sheriff Don."

The woman behind the desk looked up from a Harlequin novel. Her short hair was dyed black, but the gray showed at the roots. She lifted her glasses off her nose and let them dangle from a chain. "Do you have an appointment?"

"I do not."

"Then why should he meet with you?"

"I'm a priest, and I understand he is a religious man."

"Not a Catholic one."

"Nevertheless."

"Let me see." She set the book down open on her desk and walked down a hall and around the corner. Diego waited. Minutes passed. He walked into the gift shop. A teenage girl worked the counter.

"Does this stuff sell?" he asked.

"Sure," she said. "Mostly online, though."

"Who's buying it?"

The girl looked over to the empty information desk, presumably to make sure it was safe to talk. "We sell a lot to people from Arizona and Alabama. Texas."

Diego nodded. "Do you like working here?"

"No."

"Why do you do it, then?"

"My dad makes me."

"Your dad? He's—"

"Yep." She nodded toward the empty information desk. "And she's my mom."

"It's a real family-owned business here, isn't it?"

She shrugged.

When Mrs. Marigold returned, she was smiling. An officer accompanied her, and he was smiling, too. The tag above his pocket said Deputy Harris. "I'll take you back to see him," he said.

Diego followed Harris down the hallway and around the corner. "Wait in here," the deputy said, waving Diego into an interrogation room. It was empty save for a small table with two chairs on one side and one on the other. He took the lonely chair. Harris left him.

Fifteen minutes passed. They were, it seemed, toying with him. Another ten minutes passed. Diego stood and started to pace. If they weren't going to meet with him, they could just tell him. Five more minutes, and he decided to leave. When he grabbed the doorknob, it wouldn't turn. He was locked in.

Diego banged on the door. "Let me out of here!" After a few minutes of that, Harris unlocked and opened the door.

"Sorry, these things lock automatically. Usually, we've got a suspect in here."

"I am not a suspect," Diego said.

"Of course not," Harris replied. He was carrying a box, which he set on the table. "The sheriff is ready to see you, but I have to register you first. I'll need to make a copy of your driver's license."

"Why?"

"We keep records of all of our visitors."

"I'm sure you do." Diego pulled his wallet from his pocket and handed his license to Harris.

"I'll be right back." Harris left with his license.

Diego sat down and stared at the box on the table. What was it? He started to lift the top, but Harris opened the door. Diego let the box top drop.

"Here's your license," Harris said. "Now, I need to take your prints."

"What?"

"Fingerprints." Harris opened the box and pulled out an inkpad and a card. The card had various boxes labeled *R. Thumb*, *R. Index*, and the like.

"This is absurd. You can't make me give you my fingerprints."

"We're not making you. If you want to talk to the sheriff, give them to us. If you don't want to talk to the sheriff, you can walk right out that door and drive away."

"This is because of my name? Because of my skin?"

"Standard procedure."

"I don't believe that for a second."

"Then walk out that door," Harris said.

Diego weighed his options. To submit would be degrading. To leave would be cowardly. "Fine."

He rolled up his sleeves and gave his prints. Harris smiled. "You can see him now."

The sheriff's office was big and deep. Wood-paneled walls were decorated with deer heads and photographs. One picture showed the sheriff with the governor. Another showed him with a senator, and another with Donald Trump, wearing a *Make America Great Again* hat. A sign on the sheriff's desk read **THE BUCK STOPS HERE**. The sheriff sat behind it.

"Truman fan?" Diego said.

"I like to drop big bombs," the sheriff said, and then he laughed. He was a large man, with thick jowls. His hair was mostly gone; the little that remained was cut close to the scalp. His mustache was bushy and brown. He was dressed in uniform: a light-brown shirt with patches and emblems and a dark-brown tie. "Father Rodriguez, I've heard much about you. It's a pleasure to finally meet you."

"It's Vega. Father Vega." Diego guessed that the slight was intentional. "I've come to you with a matter of grave concern."

"I'm all ears." Sheriff Don leaned back in his chair and locked his hands behind his head.

"A dozen or so immigrants have gone missing in the past week or so. I came here to see if you rounded them up."

The sheriff leaned forward, opened his desk drawer, and grabbed a pen. "This sounds like a very serious matter. Give me their names."

"I can't do that."

The sheriff dropped his pen. "Then I don't see how I can help you."

"None of the people I'm taking about have been posted on your website. My understanding is that everyone you detain is photographed and placed on the website, correct?"

The sheriff said nothing.

"Is that correct? If you detained someone, it would be listed on the web?"

"That is correct."

"And you haven't detained anyone who you haven't listed?"

"That is also correct."

"And you haven't turned anyone over to ICE who you haven't listed?"

"Mr. Vega, if we catch someone, we post it. I'm the most transparent sheriff in the country."

Diego thought for a moment. "Have you found any bodies?"

"Dead bodies?"

"Yes. Have you found any dead bodies in the past week or so?"

"No."

"Do you have any idea where a dozen missing men might be?"

"If these men were from Mexico, I could only hope that they realized the immorality of their occupation of our country and went home."

Diego sighed. "I didn't come here for the show, Sheriff. I came to ask my questions."

"Here's a question for you, Mr. Vega. Where were you born?"

"I was born in America, just like you."

The door to the office slammed open, and a Bilford city police officer stormed in. He was young—late twenties, maybe. "Goddamn it, Sheriff! I will not have any more of your men interfering with city investigations. Next one does, and I'll throw his ass in jail!" He tore off his hat and threw it to the ground.

Sheriff Don smiled. "What's your beef this time?"

"I spent six months working with a CI to convert him, get him prepped, feeling safe. Finally get him wired for a meeting. He's a half hour in, and we're starting to get something, and then twelve armored men with assault rifles break down the door, explode flash grenades, and carry my man away."

The sheriff shrugged. "Illegals are not welcome in my county, officer."

"He's not a goddamn illegal. He's here on a visa."

"If his paperwork checks out, we'll let him go."

"Jesus Christ!" The officer spun around and noticed Diego. He looked chagrined. "Sorry, Father. I'm just so goddamn mad."

"It's okay," Diego said.

The officer turned back to the sheriff. "I'm working a real case. Sexual assault, human trafficking . . . and your bullshit immigration crusade derailed the whole thing."

"My bullshit immigration crusade is a matter of federal law and is certified by ICE."

"I'll certify my fist up your ass if anything like this happens again." The officer stormed out of the room and slammed the door behind him.

Sheriff Don laughed. "Now, there's a guy who knows how to tell a joke."

"Who was that?" Diego asked.

"Officer John Beamer. It's almost cute, isn't it? The way he thinks he can talk to me like that without any repercussions."

Not cute, Diego thought. Admirable.

CHAPTER 5

....

They used to stand in the parking lot of Lowe's. Contractors, movers, and landscapers would swing by before sunrise and scoop them up by the dozen. Those who weren't hired would load supplies into cars and trucks for tips. Sometimes they rode home with customers to assist with installations.

After Sheriff Don was elected, they moved to the lot behind the store, and then, after the raid, to a spot a mile away, under the shade of a large sycamore tree, next to a gravel road that seemed to go nowhere. Today, there were eleven of them, each shuffling back and forth in his boots, hands lodged in the pockets of his blue jeans. Every twenty minutes or so, a car or truck would turn down the road. They squinted and strained to assess whether each represented opportunity or danger. Most were neither. But when a Bilford County van turned onto the street, they dove into the drainage ditch and waited until it passed.

Carlos Nuevas checked his iPhone. His brother was scouting out leads for employment and had promised to text him if anything came up. "Nothing yet," he said to the group. It had been six days of nothing yet. This was bad news for a new husband with a baby on the way. He took the cigarette from his mouth, tossed it on the ground, and twisted it under his heel.

Carlos knew six of the men from other jobs. The four others were new—both to the group and to the country—lured by a promise of work that was gone. All were younger than Carlos, so he'd become their leader for the day. He was twenty-six.

A pickup turned down the road. Carlos jogged up from the embankment and shaded his eyes with his hands. The truck passed by him. He turned to the others and shook his head, then checked his phone again.

The others walked up to join him. One of the new kids asked in Spanish, "This is how it is? Every day?"

"Yes."

"Then why do we stay?"

Carlos asked himself that question all the time. About half of the Mexican population had left Bilford County since Sheriff Don was elected. "If we all leave, he wins," Carlos said.

The kid gestured toward the empty gravel road. "Isn't he winning now?"

Good point, Carlos thought. But if the president would grant everyone amnesty, everything would change. Maybe they were fools for thinking that would happen.

Another pickup turned onto the road. It slowed as it approached and stopped in front of him. A tall, thin man leaped down from the driver's seat and walked around the front of the truck. He pulled a case out of the front pocket of his flannel shirt, withdrew a cigarette, and set it in his mouth. Carlos reached into his pocket and pulled out a lighter. The thin man nodded, and Carlos flicked a flame under the cigarette.

"You speak for the group," the thin man said.

Carlos nodded.

"English?"

"Yes."

"I've got a big job. Pay is fifteen dollars an hour, but it's hard work. Lifting and cleaning. Climbing. Ain't going to smell good. And I'd need every last one of you."

That was good pay. "We can do that. How long?"

"Week, maybe. Don't want it to go longer than that." The thin man tore a University of Kentucky ball cap off his head and wiped his brow. "You all good with heights? Can't use you if you're not."

Carlos looked around. The men nodded. Carlos hated heights, but he hated missing a week of work more. "It's no problem."

The thin man smiled. His teeth were crooked. "All right, then." He pointed his thumb to the pickup. "Get in the back."

Carlos and the men jumped into the back of the truck. The thin man's quick turn back onto the road tossed them into one another. He looked back through the window of the cab, smiled at Carlos, and shrugged.

It was, Carlos thought, a perfect day. Seventy degrees, blue sky, bright sun—the grass still green and lush, the leaves still hanging mostly to the trees. And the air was as clean as it ever was. It was a good day for work. It was a good day for anything.

They passed Federman's bakery and the smell of sourdough bread. They passed the abandoned Dieter engine plant and an empty used-car lot. Max's Bar and Grille, with its **ENGLISH ONLY** sign in the window. Lefty's Garage. The thin man took them a long way, down two-lane highways, then smaller roads and then gravel ones. Carlos did not know these roads. The thin man turned the truck onto a dirt path through some woods, and the bumpy terrain jostled the men.

One of them turned to Carlos and asked, "Where are we going?"

He shrugged. "To work, I guess."

The truck barreled through the woods and into a barren crop field, toward a white-brick farmhouse, a red barn, and a tall silo. "The silo," Carlos said.

"What?" asked another.

"He said we had to be good with heights."

The thin man parked the truck next to the silo and hopped down with a small canvas bag in his hand. One by one, the men jumped down from the back of the pickup.

Carlos studied the silo. Sixty feet tall, at least. A metal ladder ran up its side. There was a dome at the top, and a doorway into the dome. The walls were made of concrete block.

"This here silo is a monster," the thin man said. "A hundred tornadoes couldn't take this down. Two-foot-thick walls, reinforced by steel. Fifteen-foot diameter. They don't make them like this anymore, but it's a mess. Ain't been used in ten years. Water and garbage and who knows what else at the bottom. Stinks like the dickens. I want to get it all cleaned out. Lift the garbage out in bins. Scrub it down real good. Sealant on the floor and sides. Run some lighting in there. This ain't a working farm, but it's going to be, and I need to get this silo ready." He opened the canvas bag and waved it in front of the men. "If you got a phone, drop it in here. I ain't paying you to make calls. You can check it at lunch, and then get it back at the end of the day."

Some of the men pulled out their phones; others looked to Carlos first. No one had ever asked him to surrender his phone on a job before. The thin man stared at him. "If you can't give up Facebook for the day, this job ain't for you."

Carlos set his iPhone in the bag. Everyone else followed. The thin man put the bag in the back of his pickup, and then walked to the ladder. Grabbing the first rung, he said, "You all can follow me up."

"The only entry is from above?" Carlos asked. It didn't make sense to him. How did they get the grain out?

"If there's one at the ground, it's covered up in concrete block. Once we get it cleaned out, we can figure out where the door used to be, and then blast through somehow." He looked down at Carlos, who was hesitating. "Let's go, boys."

They started up the ladder. With each rung, the wind seemed to pick up steam. A hundred tornadoes might not take down the silo, but an autumn breeze could knock a Mexican a long way, Carlos thought. He kept climbing, looking neither down nor up but only at the rungs in front of him. At the top, he pulled himself through the door in the silo's dome. There was a wood-plank floor under the dome and a round hole in the middle of it, five feet across. A rope ladder coiled around a spool wheel attached to the wall. It crossed the floor and dangled down the hole. There was a crank on the side of the spool. Beside the spool was a chair and a small table with a lamp and a notebook. An ax leaned against the wall next to the chair. The place had a stench to it. Something must have died down there, he thought.

The thin man waited for each of the men to enter the dome. Once they assembled, he began. "There are crates down there with lanterns and shovels waiting for you guys. Empty the crates, and then fill them up with junk. They'll cable to the ladder, and I'll crank it up, empty it out the side of the silo, and send it back down again so you can fill it up. We'll do this all day."

Carlos looked down the hole. It was too dark to see anything.

One of the other men got on his knees and dangled his legs down the hole, settled them upon a rung of the rope ladder, and began to climb down. The rest followed, one by one, except for Carlos.

"You're scared of heights, ain't you?" the thin man said.

"Huh?" He was still looking down the dark hole through which the other men had descended.

"Scared?"

"Yes," he said.

"Well, it's a forty-minute hike back to the bus station."

He couldn't afford to give up a day of work. He didn't even have money for the bus ride home.

One of the men screamed from the bottom of the silo. *"¡Hay cuerpos aquí! ¡Hay cadáveres!"* Dead bodies. The other men started to scream, too.

The thin man backed up to the crank and turned it, spooling up the rope ladder. "Looks like you're going to miss that bus," he said.

It took Carlos a moment to unpack the madness that was unfolding before him. "You're the devil," he said to the thin man, charging at him and plowing into his stomach. The thin man let go of the crank, and the rope ladder began to unspool back down the hole.

Grabbing the ax, the thin man charged at Carlos, swinging at his head. Carlos dove under the blade, barreling into the thin man's knees, knocking him down again. The rope ladder twitched next to Carlos, and he realized that the men were climbing up it.

Sitting up, the thin man raised the ax above his head and brought it down on the rope ladder, severing one of the two strands. There was a loud thump, and a scream rose from the hole. One of the men had fallen off the ladder.

The thin man raised the ax over the remaining strand. Carlos reached for the ax as the thin man swung it, and the ax lodged into Carlos's left shoulder. He screamed in pain. Blood poured down his arms. He couldn't move his fingers.

The thin man brought the ax down on the other strand of the ladder, and the rest of the men fell to the bottom of the silo. Carlos heard their screams above his own.

"Heights aren't scary," the thin man said. "I am."

He kicked Carlos in the stomach, and he fell next to the hole. The thin man kicked him again, and Carlos fell in.

CHAPTER 6

The Professor's house was an optical illusion. On the outside, it was a small Tudor bungalow—the most modest home in his tony Arlington neighborhood. Inside, it somehow contained a massive, marvelous study—a thirty-by-thirty room with fifteen-foot ceilings. Screens, blackboards, whiteboards—all descended from the ceiling at a push of a button. Plush dark-blue carpet covered the floors. Two couches faced each other, perpendicular to and in front of the Professor's oversize desk. A glass coffee table between the couches offered a view of the embroidered FBI seal below it, the presence of which had not been authorized. Dark, rich-wood bookshelves lined each wall from floor to ceiling, even continuing above the doorframe. Sliding ladders enabled retrieval of books at the highest levels. Behind one of the bookshelves was a secret staircase; it led to a basement workroom that extended past the outline of the house to the limits of the yard, if not beyond.

The workroom was empty because there was no work to be had. The Professor hobbled about his study, lamenting this fact. "Without a case, we cannot have success, and without success, we lose our momentum. Without momentum, we lose our political capital."

"Three dead bodies in St. Louis," Brent said for the second time. He was sitting next to Dagny on one sofa; Victor sat across from them. "Similar MO. Found within three weeks. That sounds like a case to me."

Dagny had grown up in St. Louis, and her mother still lived there. That was reason enough to be against taking the case. "Unless one of those bodies was found in East St. Louis, we don't have federal jurisdiction," she said.

"Were the victims black? Asian?" Victor asked. "Anything that gets us a civil rights case? Did one of the victims live over the river? Transporting over state lines would get us jurisdiction. Did one of them work for the government? There are ways to find jurisdiction."

"I caught a serial killer in St. Louis thirty years ago," the Professor said. "If that's the best I can do now, I might as well shoot myself. Walton, what do you have?"

"Hundred-billion-dollar fraud—"

"Next!" the Professor barked.

"It's a hundred-billion-dollar fraud," Victor repeated.

"And how many deaths?"

"I don't know. When you add up the families that won't be able to afford medical care, you're talking—"

"Bodies! Is that too much to ask for? A hundred billion dollars is nothing. Congress commits more fraud than that every day." It was a reckless accusation, but the Professor was prone to them.

"If I'm right, it's the biggest financial-fraud case ever. Bigger than Madoff."

"And yet smaller than murder."

"I don't think that's true."

"You know how you can tell if a crime is big? If you can put a man to death for it, it's big. Did we put Madoff to death?"

It was rhetorical, but Victor answered it. "No."

"That's because his fraud was smaller than your standard, everyday first-degree murder. Dagny, what do you have?"

"It's a cold case."

"That's worse than Victor's."

Victor laughed at this.

"It's a murder," Dagny said. "You could put a guy to death for it."

"First of all, I know what case you're talking about, and it's personal to you. We already did one of those. We're not doing it again. Second, do you honestly think we can keep our arrangement going by solving cold cases? What keeps us in business?"

"Imminent harm," Brent said.

"Right."

"Like the imminent harm that's going to happen to the next person murdered in St. Louis. And by the way, you can get the death penalty for that, too," Brent said.

"Nobody cares about St. Louis, Brent. I want something big."

"A hundred billion dollars is enormous," Victor said.

"If you can solve a case without a gun, it's not a real case," the Professor said.

No one said anything for a few minutes. "Fine!" the Professor barked. He turned to Victor. "Tell us more about the fraud case."

Victor smiled at Dagny. She shook her head. Not yet, she thought. You haven't won yet.

He grabbed a remote from the top of the Professor's desk and pushed a button to lower a plasma screen, then turned on his iPad and mirrored its display on the TV. "Abner Jenks came up in Goldman, and then opened his own investment firm in 2002." Jenks's picture flashed up on the screen. "And everything his investment firm did was a fraud." Victor flipped to the next slide. "Here's how it worked—"

"It's a Ponzi scheme," the Professor said.

"Yes. Let me show you—"

"I know how a Ponzi scheme works. Skip ahead. Why are you the only person in the country who knows about this particular Ponzi scheme?"

"Because I'm the only person with the patience to sift through the documents." Victor took them through eighty-three slides of financial jargon and spreadsheets that compared Jenks's representation of the performance of mutual funds in statements provided to investors to the actual market performance of the stocks comprising them. The fraud seemed pretty clear. "It's an easy case," Victor concluded.

"And a boring one. I can't believe this is the best thing we have," the Professor said, sighing. "But it's the best thing we have."

Victor smiled at Dagny again.

"One more week. If we haven't found something better in one week, we'll do Victor's case. Lord help us."

Dagny looked at Victor and shook her head to say, *Not yet.*

"Brent and Victor, you're excused. Dagny, I'd like a moment."

They looked at her, and she shrugged to signal that she didn't know why the Professor wanted to talk to her, even though she had a pretty good idea. After they left, the Professor sat next to her on the sofa.

"When I was a toddler, I didn't eat my vegetables," he said. "It became a point of contention with my mother such that there was much yelling and screaming, tussling and punching. I tossed my plate to the floor on many occasions. Once, in a fit of anger, I kicked a hole through the kitchen wall."

"Strong toddler."

"Poor construction," he said. "Another time, I threw my plate at her head, sending her to the hospital."

"Strong toddler," she repeated.

"Indeed. Two days later, my mother returned home. And do you know what she did?"

"What?"

"She served me a plate filled with nothing but vegetables. So what does that tell you?"

"That she was as stubborn as you are?"

"One way or another, I'm going to make you eat your vegetables."

Even the analogies always came back to eating. "I agreed to try a one-on-one session."

"Not try. Do."

"Okay, Yoda."

"Dr. Childs is excellent. I need you to be serious about this."

"I will."

"This is important. Do you understand why?"

"Because you care about me on a personal level."

"Because our group is going to big places."

"And also because you care."

He shook his head no, which was how he said yes in sentimental moments.

She smiled. "Okay, Professor."

Grabbing her backpack, she started to leave. When she got to the door, he blurted, "Martha and I never had children."

Dagny turned back, surprised by his statement. She struggled for a response. "I lost my father when I was twelve." By stating facts known to both of them, they were acknowledging a relationship they'd never discussed.

"I need you to be healthy, Dagny."

"I understand."

She turned to flee before any more feelings were expressed. As she left, he yelled, "Big things, Dagny!"

CHAPTER 7

Hank Frank was a radio survivor.

As a freshman at Miami University, he had worked the two-to-six overnight shift, spinning The Clash and Zeppelin for, perhaps, a half-dozen drunken frat brothers and an insomniac sociology professor or two. He was terrible, missing station breaks, fumbling with the commercials, launching rambling sentences he couldn't finish. But he got better. He improved his enunciation, and between the songs, he began to talk about things that mattered. Disarmament. Homelessness. Poverty. The disconnect between the campus bubble and the factories closing around it. He said things that upset the school administration, and that's when people started to listen to him. When they finally pulled him off the air, he was the station's most popular DJ.

His first job out of college was selling ad time for WBRP, Dayton's pop-rock station. When the afternoon-drive DJ left for Des Moines, Frank filled in and kept the spot. He was the first DJ in the area to play Michael Jackson's *Thriller*; the first to play Madonna; the first to play his favorite song, Murray Head's "One Night in Bangkok." They moved him to the morning drive, paired him with Jennifer Lovely, and they bantered and joked and flirted between songs. They married after a year, divorced after another, and continued as the morning team for three more.

When Nirvana and Pearl Jam became popular, station management didn't know what to do, so they fired everyone. Jennifer Lovely took a job doing the weather on television. Hank Frank drank. Beer and vodka and Scotch. A few pills here and there. He passed out on a sidewalk, spent the night in jail, and wandered into an AA meeting the next day. His sponsor owned a small AM station in Bilford and gave Hank a job playing oldies after Rush Limbaugh. One day the CD player broke, and he had to fill three hours with talk. He talked about the weather, and then the high school basketball team and the county fair. And then he talked about his failed marriage and his struggles with booze. By the end of the shift, he was crying. So was much of the audience.

They never fixed the CD player.

He couldn't continue to fill three hours on his own each day, so he started taking calls and booking guests. The library director. City Council members. Restaurant owners. The pet shelter. Lawyers with legal advice; doctors with medical advice; stockbrokers with investment advice; therapists with sex advice. (He married one of those therapists, Trudy Day.) When Clear Channel bought the station, it was beating Dayton stations in the ratings. New management boosted the station's signal so it could be heard from Cincinnati to Columbus.

He never intended for the show to become political, but it went that way. The terrorist attacks of September 11, 2001, were part of it. Having a kid was the rest. The world looked different to him as a dad. He saw dangers where he'd previously seen excitement. And so he became another right-wing talk-radio host, although he thought maybe he was a bit more than that.

"My dad worked the line at Deters for twenty-eight years, blowing heat that shaped the pipes that carried the exhaust out of a million cars or more. You probably drove one of them, back when you could feel good about a car.

"Sometimes I'd ride my bike over to the factory after school and watch the line from up in the rafters. The sparks flying, and metal yielding, and the pouring and the lifting—it was a sight to behold. Real men making something. How often did you see that? My father did it every day, along with another hundred and fifty guys just like him. Guys breaking their backs to put food on the table and send their kids to school.

"One time the chain on the crane broke, and a piece of steel fell down on my father's leg. He was in the hospital for a week. Everyone from the plant, from the newest hire to the company president, stopped by to see him. Man, that made an impression on me, to see the president of the company stop by.

"My dad limped the rest of his life after that. 'These things happen,' he said. Went back to work as soon as he could. Did it with a smile. That man always smiled, no matter what was thrown at him.

"All that time, he made a decent wage, and we had a good health plan. The union did all right. We had a house and a car—neither fancy, but I didn't know it. The TV worked. Sometimes we drove down to Riverfront and watched the Reds from the high seats. We were middle class when *middle class* meant getting by. He put me through college, scrimping and saving.

"When my father was fifty-eight, Deters announced they were closing the factory down. Not because their parts weren't selling—they were, more than ever. No, they were shutting it down because they knew they could open a factory in Mexico and pay everyone three dollars an hour, and the company would make a lot more money. So my dad was out of work. Fifty-eight years old. He'd given his life to that factory; it was the only skill he had. And they shut it down.

"What do you do when you're fifty-eight and your résumé has thirty years of factory work on it? Apply to work at Chester, maybe? Oh, that's right, they shut down in 1987. Toolweather? They shut down in 1993. Maybe at OK Steel? They haven't poured since 1982. There used to be jobs for people like my father. We sent them to places like China and Indonesia and Mexico.

"He took a job at Harvey's Auto on McLean. Fifty-eight years old, and he was starting a second career as a mechanic. He knew cars well enough and knew how to fix them. Answered to a boss who was half his age and knew a third as much. Fifty-eight, and he was sliding under engines, getting dirty. Long hours. Was paid a fraction of what he got before. No health benefits.

"Three years later, they let him go. Said business was down, and they had to trim costs. He got a job at Walmart after that. It was a great job for him. Finally, he didn't have to work with his hands. He just had to smile. Welcomed people to the store so that they could buy things we don't make anymore at low, low prices. The company was good to him, too, although he didn't make nearly what he'd made at Deters. When my dad passed away, I counted forty-three coworkers from Walmart at the funeral. There were a hundred from Deters. No one came from Harvey's Auto.

"This morning I picked up the local paper and read that Sheriff Don Marigold raided Harvey's yesterday and picked up two Mexicans. Both here illegally. Fake Social Security numbers, phony paperwork. And all I could think was, thank God for Sheriff Don. These Mexicans aren't bad people, for all I know. But they took two jobs from hard-working Americans. One of those jobs used to be my dad's. Sheriff Don gets it. He looks around and sees that we're all suffering here, and there are hardly any jobs, and it's absolute insanity that we'd give those jobs to people who came here illegally instead of people who were born and raised in this community. The feds don't care about this. The feds don't care about you. That's why Sheriff Don is doing their job. Because they won't.

"The phones are all lit up, and I'm going to get to your calls, but before I do, I want to tell you something my dad used to say. He said a great man doesn't complain for himself, but he'll complain for others. My dad never complained for himself. I'm privileged to do it for him, and for guys like him. We owe them that much."

Hank glanced up at the monitor and held his finger over the first button on the phone. "Let's go to Margaret on line one." He pressed the button. "Hello, Margaret, you're on *The Hank Frank Show*."

"Hank, you had me in tears again." She sounded old.

"That's what I do, Margaret."

"I want to add to what you're saying, because it's not just the jobs. My son goes to Harrison Elementary in Englewood, and did you know that they have Spanish class? Not a class where the kids learn to speak Spanish, mind you. A class where everything is taught in Spanish. Math is taught in Spanish. History is taught in Spanish."

"Yep. Yep."

"English is taught *in Spanish*. My God. They've got these kids who speak Spanish at home, aren't learning English, and we're not even trying to teach them. And we put up with it."

"I hear you, Margaret."

"People used to come here and learn our language. Learn our ways. Learn our values. And now we don't expect them to. I don't even blame them. If we don't expect them to, why should they expect it of themselves?"

"Thank you, Margaret."

"Thank you, honey."

He dumped the call and freed the line. It filled immediately. "You know, everything Margaret says is true. We have lowered our standards, and once you lower them, it's hard to get them back. But even more than that, we've got these kids in our schools, and we're spending extra money to accommodate them, and half of their parents aren't paying taxes into the system to support the schools. And it all just adds up, you know. We lose good jobs to them, and then we lose our bad jobs to them, and then, as we're struggling to get by, we're still paying to educate their kids so they can take our kids' jobs."

He pushed down on the second line and glanced up at his monitor. "John, you're on with Hank Frank."

"Hanks a million."

"Hanks back at you."

"Brother, you are speaking the truth today. You are speaking the word of God."

"I'm just speaking my mind."

"Your mind is on fire." The caller laughed. "Sometimes I feel so alone. And then, to hear your voice, speaking so rationally. Speaking such sanity. These people are taking our jobs. They're taking our money. They are taking our *lives*, Hank."

"Yes, yes."

"They're killing us. They are killing us, Hank. And that's why I'm killing them."

"It's killing us, John."

"Which is why I'm killing them. I'm killing all of them. I'm killing them—"

Hank slammed the button to drop the call. There was a moment of silence as he thought about what to say. When he found the words, he started slowly and softly. "To speak like that, even in metaphor, is abhorrent. To trivialize life like that is abhorrent. To speak of such violence, and to do so with such glee—it's abhorrent. I open these lines so we can all talk frankly to each other. So that we can tell the truth. And some people don't like the truth, and they want to discredit it, so they do what this gentleman did. They call in and pretend to be one of us, and then they say something god-awful. And they do it because they hate us, and they want everyone to hate us. They impersonate us for the sole purpose of trying to make us look bad. You saw it at the Tea Party rallies; there was always someone there holding some racist sign, and it's always some hipster college kid, you know, a plant. He's trying to make us look bad, and it's not working. Mark down his number, Lucy; we're never letting him through again. Let's go to a break."

He glanced through the glass to the control booth, where Lucy shrugged her shoulders. Hank removed his headset and walked from the studio to the control booth. "Did that just happen?"

"It did."

"How did he screen?"

"Totally normal."

"Jesus, you don't think he really . . ."

Lucy shook her head. "Of course not. It's like you said."

"Because if he really did, then we should call the police."

"I think it's just a hoax."

"Yeah." Hank paused a minute. "If he were killing people, we'd be reading about it, right? Jesus. What's wrong with people?"

She shrugged again.

"You get his number?"

"Blocked it."

"Good."

CHAPTER 8

"Focus on that."

"On what?"

"Losing him."

"I can't talk about that."

"That's why you're here. To talk about the things you can't talk about."

"No. I'm here because my boss said I had to attend therapy."

"Well, I don't have a boss. And I'm here to get you to talk about things that matter. For forty minutes, though, we've been talking about nothing."

"You haven't asked me about anything I want to talk about."

"What do you want to talk about?"

"I don't want to talk about anything."

"Have you always been like this?"

"I don't know."

"Have you confided in people in the past?"

"Yes."

"Who?"

"My father." Dagny paused. "Before he was killed."

"When was he killed?"

"I was twelve."

"Can we talk about that?"

"No."

"Who else have you confided in?"

"My friend Julia."

"Tell me about her."

"We went to law school together."

"Are you still friends?"

"Yes. She's my best friend." She paused. "She's my only friend."

"Do you still confide in her?"

"She has a husband and kids. She doesn't need to hear about my petty problems. She's got enough going on."

"Has she told you that?"

"What?"

"Not to confide in her? That she's got too much going on?"

"No. But it's obvious. I barely see her anymore."

"How do you feel about that?"

"There's nothing to feel. It's just the way it is."

"Just because you can't change something doesn't mean you don't feel something about it."

"What do you want me to say? That it bothers me?"

"Does it?"

"I'm happy for her. She's got a great husband and great kids. It's what people want."

"Is it what you want?"

"I don't know what I want."

"Are you a happy person?"

"That's a ridiculous question."

"It's probably the most important question someone can ask herself."

"It's not the most important thing to me."

"What's more important than happiness?"

"Competence. Morality. Ethics. Knowledge."

"You'd rather be knowledgeable than happy?"

"I would turn down the soma in *Brave New World*."

"That's not what I'm asking."

Dagny sighed. "I like my job."

"It makes you happy?"

"It leaves me content."

"Or does it take your mind off other things?"

"Those aren't mutually exclusive."

"Your job is a roller coaster."

"Every job has ups and downs."

"No. I mean, when you get on a roller coaster, it's hard to think about anything besides the ride. Try it sometime. Try thinking about taxes or your relationships or your mother issues—"

"I didn't say I have mother issues."

"Or anything. You can't do it. Not while you're on the ride. Because the ride is all distraction."

"My job is a distraction?"

"Absolutely."

"It's my life. It's who I am."

"Exactly."

Dagny paused. "There's nothing wrong with that."

"A stranger comes up to you and asks what you are. You'd say an FBI agent."

"Yes."

"Not a daughter or a lover, or a woman or—"

"I'm an FBI agent."

"What were you before that?"

"I was a lawyer."

"And that was your life, too, right?"

"I thought therapy was supposed to make me feel better about life, not worse."

"You thought therapy is supposed to make you happy?"

"Yes."

"And that's why you're here?"

"Yes."

"Okay, then." Dr. Childs leaned back in her chair and smiled. "We've established that you'd like to be happy. That's progress." She jotted her first notes on the pad.

Dagny was sad to lose the point. "How did you know I have mother issues?"

"You said you confided in your father. If you didn't confide in your mother, it means you have mother issues. Plus . . ."

"Plus what?"

"Every woman has mother issues." Childs wrote another note. Dagny tried to read it, but the doctor tilted the pad so she couldn't. "Can we go back to the Bubble Gum Thief?"

"It's ridiculous to call him the Bubble Gum Thief, considering what he did. And there's nothing to say. Everyone knows everything. You've read the papers, right?"

"Yes."

"You have a TV?"

"Yes."

"Then you know everything there is to know."

"I'm not interested in the prurient details, Dagny. I'm interested in how you feel about it."

"How would you have felt? If it had been you?"

The question hung in the air for a moment. "I would be burdened by sadness, until I let someone help me."

That statement hung a moment, too.

"Do you know what I hate more than talking about myself?" Dagny asked.

"What?"

"Nothing."

"Why? What's wrong with talking about yourself?"

"People talk about themselves because they're weak."

"That's preposterous."

"When I'm questioning a suspect and he's talking about himself, I know that he'll break. When a colleague goes on and on about his personal life, I know he'll flame out. When—"

"Did you hear about the engineers who were building a bridge?"

"What?"

"They refused to talk about it because they worried it would make it weak."

"That makes no sense."

"Exactly."

Dagny shook her head. "I'm not talking about causation. Talking about oneself doesn't make one weak; it's a sign of an underlying weakness." She paused. "You know what they talked a lot about when they built it? The *Titanic*."

"You want to talk about the *Titanic*? When a ship hits an iceberg and you salvage the ship, you don't just send it back out to sea. You fix the ship. Don't you want to fix the ship before you head out to sea?" Childs looked up at the clock. "Ding, ding, ding. Saved by the bell, Dagny Gray."

"I'm not the *Titanic*."

"You aim at icebergs."

CHAPTER 9

Hattie's Diner was the kind of place that had to be a front for something else. Waitresses outnumbered customers every time Diego had been there. Fresh cakes and pies revolved in a glass box next to the register, and there never was a piece missing. Maybe it had been popular before New Bilford and the chain restaurants came to town, but no one went there now. Diego had picked it because it was a good place to meet someone and not be seen. But Hattie's was crowded today.

"Can I help you?" the hostess asked.

Diego scanned the crowd. "I'm supposed to meet a police officer."

"Around the corner," she said.

Officer John Beamer was sitting in the far booth, nursing a cup of coffee. He stood when he saw Diego. "Father, I must apologize for my behavior the other day. I said all sorts of words I shouldn't say in front of a priest."

"Please, I've heard worse in the rectory. I'm just happy you're meeting with me." A waitress asked him for an order. "Coffee, please. Black."

"I'm a Catholic boy, and it wasn't right. Sometimes I get agitated."

"That's why I wanted to meet you."

Beamer laughed. "Because of my temper?"

"Because you're not afraid of Don Marigold."

"Yeah, well . . ." He shrugged. "My great-great-great-grandparents moved here from Ireland in the 1860s. Marigold can't send me back."

"I wouldn't put it past him to try." The waitress set Diego's coffee before him. He took a sip. It was terrible. Typical Hattie's. "I'm trying to solve a mystery, and I need some help."

"Okay."

"There are at least a dozen men or more who disappeared in the last week and a half. Vanished, without a word to their families. Without a trace."

"Then we should go to the station and make a report. Open an investigation."

"These men are undocumented. And so are their families."

Beamer set down his coffee. "That's a problem."

"I don't want to expose any of them to deportation." Diego grabbed a packet of crackers from a basket at the end of the table. "You strike me as a man who might care more about fighting crime than immigration politics?"

"Yes, but . . ." Beamer hesitated. "If you are asking me to protect folks from deportation—"

"It's not a fair choice for the families. To be forced to leave this country to get justice."

"It's not that simple, Father. First, I may not be a fire-breather like Marigold, but that doesn't mean these people didn't break the law. Like it or not, they did."

"If they did, it's minor compared to what might have happened here."

"We don't know what happened here. They could have gone home. They could have moved to another town looking for work. With the way things are going around here, you couldn't blame them if they did."

"Maybe a man or two might leave without saying anything. But a dozen men, with close friends and families, and none of them says a word? No. Something terrible has happened here."

Beamer sighed. "Would the families talk to us?"

"I don't know. They'd be scared, I'm sure. If they had assurances, credible assurances . . ." Diego noticed Beamer's furrowed brow. "No. Please. Don't do that. You're going to say no."

Beamer grabbed his own cracker packet and tore the cellophane. "If it were up to me, I'd open an investigation. I'd provide every assurance I could. I'd put five men on the job if they had the time. But from a practical perspective, Marigold would find out about it, and he'd start harassing these families. And the reality is, it's not up to me. Any investigation like this would have to be approved by the chief, and in this climate, that's not going to happen." He popped a cracker in his mouth.

"Then he's as bad as Sheriff Don," Diego said.

"No, he's not. He's a man with a wife and four kids, and a job that could disappear if the mayor gets too many calls about him coddling criminals. He doesn't hassle the immigrant population in Bilford, but he's not going to abet them, either."

"They are human beings."

"I'm not telling you how it should be. I'm telling you how it is."

"Isn't the force required to investigate murder, even of a noncitizen?"

"If there were bodies, then we'd have a murder to investigate. You've got, at best, the disappearance of people who were undocumented to begin with."

"These people are real."

"These people don't exist without a body."

"They do."

"In the eyes of God. I'm talking about the eyes of the law."

"Then tell me what to do. I have a dozen families in anguish."

"I'm not used to a man of the cloth looking to me for guidance."

"I'm out of my element. Is there anywhere I could go for help? Somewhere that isn't political. The FBI, maybe?"

"The FBI is as political as anyone else. And, as a matter of policy, they can't promise immunity from deportation. There are cases where they worked with informants for years, folks who put their lives in danger for the Bureau, and when the investigation was over, ICE started removal proceedings, and the Bureau didn't lift a finger."

"Then it's hopeless. You can't help me, and you can't point me to anyone who can." Diego was still holding his packet of crackers; he'd squeezed them to a fine powder.

"You could try a private investigator. I could get you the name of a guy I trust."

"How much would that cost?"

"Eighty bucks an hour, plus expenses. Since you're a priest, maybe less."

"And you think that he might be effective?"

"No. Not really." Beamer ate the second cracker from his packet. "Hmmm . . ."

Diego saw a spark of an idea in the officer's eyes. "What? What, hmmm?"

"I don't know. It's probably a dead end."

"I'll take any end I can get."

"My uncle's with Cincinnati PD, and he worked on a case with an FBI agent. He thought the world of her, and I think she's got a special deal where she works off the grid. Not a rule follower, not a politician. You ought to contact her."

"What's her name?"

"Dagny Gray."

CHAPTER 10

Dagny didn't know her neighbors. She didn't know their jobs or even their names. She didn't know their hobbies unless they did them in their front yards. But she knew their cars and the cars of their friends.

The red Corvette in front of her house did not belong to her neighbors or their friends.

Silencing Aimee Mann, she tugged the earbuds from her ears and coiled them around her iPhone. Using her forearm, she wiped the sweat from her forehead. Even though it was an autumn morning, it was hotter than it had been in weeks. She was dressed in running shorts and a running bra. The man sitting on her steps was covered in black, save for the white tab peeking out of the front of his collar.

He stood. "You run?"

"Every day." She walked toward him.

"How far?"

"Eighteen today. Sometimes less. Sometimes more." He had a small, earnest smile, and she was trying to diagnose it. "Can I help you?"

"My name is Diego Vega."

"And you're a priest?"

"I am."

She'd never spoken to one. "So I call you, what? Father Vega?"

He laughed. "You're not Catholic."

"Jewish. Ish."

"Call me Diego." He extended his hand.

"I'm sweaty."

"I don't mind."

She grabbed his hand and shook it. "I'm Dagny Gray, which I assume you know, since you're sitting on my steps."

"Does it hurt to run with that?"

"With what?" She realized he was looking at the Glock 27 in her jogging holster. "It's like a wedding ring. After a while, you don't notice it. That's what they say, anyway."

"I wouldn't know, obviously."

She wasn't sure if he was talking about marriage or the gun. "I don't know a lot about the Catholic Church, but I've never heard of priests proselytizing door-to-door." There was a lot of handsome being wasted on this priest.

"I'm not here to save your soul. I'm here to ask for help."

Dagny nodded. "Come inside." She unlocked the front door and led him into the house. There was a forged rendition of Jan van Eyck's *Portrait of Giovanni Arnolfini and His Wife* hanging in the entry. He paused in front of it.

"I know this one," he said. "I like it."

She didn't feel like talking about the painting—it only led to sadness. "Can I get you something to drink?"

He followed her into the kitchen. "Water?"

She grabbed a glass from the cupboard, filled it, and handed it to him. "Thank you."

She uncoiled the wires from her iPhone, loaded the web browser, tapped the search bar, and pressed the microphone button. "Who is Father Diego Vega?" she said.

The first link returned a page from the website of the Archdiocese of Cincinnati. A picture showed Diego playing basketball with Dayton teens. The next link gave his church bio. A third went to his Facebook page.

"Okay, you check out."

"So, that's what passes for an FBI background check these days?"

"Google's got a better database than we do," Dagny said. "How can I help you?"

The situation he described over the next half hour was bleak. Immigrants missing in a county that didn't want them. Indifferent law enforcement. Families afraid of deportation. He told her about his conversations with Ty Harborman and Marcia Bell, which only reinforced the conclusion that this world would be hard to crack. His encounter with the sheriff sounded like a half-dozen civil rights violations.

It seemed all kinds of awful and too good to be true. They were desperate to find a case, and this one somehow found her. "Why did you come to me?" she asked.

"I spoke to a city police officer, and he was inclined to help, but without actual bodies, he didn't think he could get an investigation approved. When I asked him about the FBI, he suggested that the Bureau couldn't undertake an investigation without putting the families at risk for deportation. Then he mentioned his uncle was an officer in Cincinnati, and that he'd worked with you on a case."

"Beamer?" She smiled.

"He said you were outside the traditional hierarchy of the Bureau. That your team had a degree of independence, and that this might permit you to make assurances to people."

Dagny wasn't sure what kind of assurances she could make. Each year, the government could give out up to 250 S visas, more commonly called "snitch visas," to people helping with a criminal investigation who would otherwise be deported. It was hard to qualify for a snitch visa. Being a victim of a crime wasn't enough; the applicant had to deliver information critical to a conviction. Only the attorney general had the authority to approve one of these visas.

If they took the case, she couldn't promise any snitch visas. The best she could do was assure the immigrants in Bilford that she wouldn't voluntarily turn their names over to immigration authorities. This might be enough to get them to talk to her. "Do you have a list of the missing? Identifiers? Ages, descriptions, and the like? Have you gathered photographs of them? Listed the places they were last seen, who saw them, and the dates and times of the sightings? A list of people they worked for? Do you have a roster of the families? Addresses and phone numbers? Any of these things?"

He shook his head. "I have a list of the names of the missing. I could get you the rest." He smiled. "So, you're taking the case?"

"It's not my call." A dozen dead, presumably. It was better than a financial fraud case, certainly. The Professor would see that. "Head back to Dayton," she instructed. "Get a sense of whether the families would be willing to talk with me. If I can convince my boss to let me, I'll come out and meet with them." She handed him her phone. "Type in your contact information."

He entered his phone number and e-mail address in her phone and handed it back to her, smiling brightly.

"This isn't *yes* yet," Dagny said.

"But it's not a no. That's enough for me to celebrate."

She walked him to the door. "Dayton is a long way to drive for a half-hour meeting. Why didn't you just call?"

"It's too easy to say no on a phone."

That was true enough. She sent him off, went up to shower, and thought about her pitch to the Professor.

CHAPTER 11

....

"Why didn't you just call?"

"It's too easy to say no on a phone," Dagny said. She was sitting in front of his desk, looking at the reflection of the overhead light on the Professor's bald pate.

"I find it easy to say no every which way." He reached down, grabbed the pneumatic lift of his chair, and rose until the spot of light shifted out of her view.

Her eyes drifted over to the photograph on a bookshelf next to the desk. It showed Director Hoover standing next to a younger, taller, and stronger version of Timothy McDougal. He'd lived a full life even before she'd been born.

She looked back at him. "You wanted a case with bodies," she said. "And you don't have any."

"We have them. We just don't know where they are."

"It's not a murder case without dead bodies." He began to stroke his white beard down to its point. Dagny knew that this meant he was open to argument.

"Plenty of murderers have been convicted without a body."

"Of course, there *could* be a murderer out there. I want to know that there *is* a murderer out there. I want to know that I'm chasing something real."

"These people are real, and they're missing."

"It's weak, Dagny."

"If we don't take this case, no one else will."

"That's not the criteria I use." He opened his right desk drawer, withdrew a bag of Cheetos, and opened it. His fingers dove into the bag and carried orange puffs to his mouth. He tilted the open end of the bag toward Dagny, but she refused. The Professor shrugged. She knew it had been an insincere offer. He wanted the whole bag to himself.

"We'll find the bodies."

"They're probably working in the fields of Mexico right now." *Crunch, crunch.*

"I don't believe that."

"Because of this priest you don't even know." *Crunch, crunch.* It was hard to be taken seriously by a man eating Cheetos.

"I trust him."

"Everyone trusts priests. It's why they were able to molest a million young boys."

"Not fair."

Martha McDougal entered through the door to the study, and the Professor quickly stuffed the bag of Cheetos back in his desk drawer. She set a fruit-and-cheese plate on the desk. "In case you're hungry," she said to Dagny. Although she said it lovingly, she meant: *You need to eat this.* The Professor licked the orange dust off his fingers, but not before his wife noticed and shook her head.

"Thanks, Martha." Dagny took a cube of cheese, and Martha left, assuaged. One point, Dagny figured, and she'd tally it later. "If you need bodies, I'll go to Bilford and find them."

"Suppose you do. A dozen dead Mexicans. What do you think is going to happen to their families when the press descends upon them, and the politicians grandstand, and the local police and this Sheriff Ron see a chance to be part of something bigger than anything they've had before?"

"It's Don. And we can keep it quiet."

"Dead bodies don't keep quiet. You'll end up breaking every promise you make. It will destroy the community."

"If someone is killing folks, he's already destroying the community."

"I don't doubt the problem, but we're not the answer."

"If we're not the answer, there is no answer."

"Exactly," he said. That was the problem with working with an octogenarian, Dagny thought. He'd seen ample evidence that most problems couldn't be solved. But no problem could ever be solved if you didn't try.

Perhaps it would help to remind him of the alternative. "So, you're ready to take Victor's money case, then?"

"Not yet," he grumbled. "We still have two days—"

"Under your arbitrary deadline—"

"To find a better case."

"Then I've got two days to find some bodies in Bilford."

"Dagny—"

"If I find the bodies, this is the case you want. It's important, and anyone else would get caught up in the politics of it. No one else could do it right. That's why you formed this group: to handle the cases that no one else can do. Victor's fraud case, he could hand his files to any field office in the country, and they'd do a competent job at it. But in Bilford, there's no one to help these folks. Only us."

He lifted an empty pipe from his desk, brought it to his mouth, and leaned back in his chair. "In 1958, I was tasked with overseeing a Major Crimes Act investigation concerning the disappearance of three Ute tribal leaders at the Uintah and Ouray Indian Reservation in northeast Utah. Their religion was nature, and they believed that they descended from the bear and not the ape." Dagny could tell that she was in for a long story.

"They were a nomadic tribe, thrust into war with Mormons, of all people, who were a settling tribe. The Utes, you see, are fundamentally different from us to their core, but that isn't what mattered. What mattered was that they *saw* themselves as fundamentally different from us, because, as you know, perception is more important that reality when you're looking for cooperation. I was an agent of a government that was a hundred and fifty years old. The Bureau had been an institution for only fifty. The Utes have lived in the Great Basin area for more than ten thousand years! To them, I wasn't a foreigner; I was a baby alien, and my credentials were less than the feces they used to fertilize. But I thought I was the only one who could help them, and they were terrified enough to let me.

"The warmth shown upon my arrival was like nothing I had seen. I was outfitted with garb and accessories. They feted me with ceremony and ritual and tried to bequeath gifts. Oh, how they showered me with love.

"Two weeks in, I had a working theory. The missing men, I told the tribe, were not murdered or kidnapped—they had fled, along with the small fortune of the community. I was certain I could apprehend them and return the funds, but my overtures were rebuffed. Everyone turned silent. My car was vandalized. My food was poisoned. All because I shattered an illusion they held dear. If I were one of them, would they have shunned me this way? Of course not. But I was an outsider, and they had welcomed only my assistance, not my judgment. To say their own men had stolen from them was to demean and insult their culture. You can only do that from within.

"So, Dagny Gray, you might see yourself as the savior of the immigrant population of Bilford, Ohio, and they might see you the same way, until you get close to the truth."

She shook her head. "First, you made up that entire story."

"Maybe, maybe not."

"Second, I've got someone on the inside: Father Vega. I don't need people to trust me, because they'll trust him."

"You don't know them, and you don't know him, so that's a conclusion without evidentiary support." He paused. "What gave it away?"

"You went too far when you said you were poisoned." She grabbed another cube of cheese—now, there would be two points to enter later. "This isn't an Indian Reservation. It's a small town in Ohio. There are people missing. Their lives matter. Whether my presence is welcome or not, their lives matter." She rose from her chair and started toward the door.

"Two days," the Professor called. "Two days to get me bodies."

CHAPTER 12

When Dagny rolled her suitcase through the automatic sliding doors at Dayton International Airport, Diego was leaning against the red fender of his '69 Corvette convertible, which he'd parked at the curb. He smiled at her.

She pointed up to the dark clouds above and then to his open-topped car. "Pretty optimistic," she said.

"Wildly so." He grabbed her suitcase and placed it in the trunk. "Good flight?"

Between her past life as a lawyer and her increasing years as a special agent, Dagny had spent enough time in planes to qualify for a pilot's license. "Is there such a thing?"

"Every one that lands," he said, still smiling. "I'm so glad you're here."

"They let you park here and wait?"

"Priests get away with a lot."

"Apparently." His giddiness confused her at first, but then she understood. He'd been bearing the weight of the missing by himself, and now there was someone to share it. That's why he was so happy. "Are you sure I can't rent a car?"

"Absolutely not. You'll take mine once we get to town."

"What will you use?"

"I don't have anywhere to be until Sunday morning, and until then, I'll be with you."

Dagny tossed her backpack to the floor of the car and climbed into the passenger seat. "I don't have until Sunday."

Diego sat behind the wheel. "What do you mean?"

"My being here doesn't mean we're taking this case. It means I'm trying to get us to take the case. And I've got two days to find . . ." She didn't want to say *bodies*, in case he still held out hope that they were living.

"Evidence?"

That's cute, she thought. "Yes. Two days to find some evidence."

"And then you'll take the case?" His smile was fading.

"Then I'll make the case that we should take the case."

"And if we don't find anything in two days?"

"I'll be sucked into something else."

His smile was gone. "We need to have a good two days, then."

"Yes, we do."

"Dagny, the list is longer now."

"How long?"

"Twenty-five." He paused, then added, "That I know of."

"Jesus," she said, forgetting for the moment that she was talking to a priest.

He drove fast, or maybe it only seemed like it with the top down. Dagny had been in a convertible only once before, on a date in high school with a boy who later boasted about things that hadn't happened.

She'd harbored a hatred of them ever since. Diego, however, was not that boy—a fact of which she had to remind herself.

"It's an hour to Bilford," he said, but it was hard to hear him over the rush of the wind.

"What?"

"It's an hour to Bilford," he repeated, "but you'll feel years away when you get there."

They drove through the northern suburbs of Dayton, past strip malls and factories, some of each abandoned. Lit by gloomy skies, it all looked like the kind of stock footage politicians used in negative campaign ads. Dagny remembered reading about a surprising study that showed that students were more likely to accept a spot at a college they visited on a cloudy day. No one was sure why this was the case, but the author posited that poor weather made academic activities appear more inviting. It seemed a little crackpot to Dagny, although it had rained on the day she toured Rice University, her alma mater. Nothing about the gloom in North Dayton made anything look inviting now.

A raindrop hit Dagny's arm. "It's starting to rain," she said.

"I think we can beat it," he said, but it was pouring before he could finish the sentence.

Dagny unbuckled her seat belt and stuck her fingers under the hatch that covered the top, but it wouldn't budge. He pulled the car over to the side and turned around. "You have to kind of jiggle it." The hatch opened, and the two of them attached the cover to the frame of the windshield.

"Hold on," he said, jumping out of the car to secure the hatch. When he climbed back into the car, the water from his drenched hair poured down his face.

Dagny laughed.

"This is funny?"

She nodded.

"Maybe a little," he said, smiling back. He pulled onto the road and headed toward Bilford.

When they got to the border, there was a billboard with the chubby, mustached Sheriff Don yanking his thumb over his shoulder. **NO PLACE LIKE HOME**, it read.

"Subtle," Dagny noted. She'd downloaded the sheriff's book to her iPad and had skimmed it on the plane. It was mostly what she'd expected.

"There's one on every major road that comes in and out of Bilford County. He has them at each entrance to Bilford City, too." Diego pulled off the main road onto a smaller one.

"Where are we going?"

"On a camping trip."

The yard was surrounded by an eighteen-foot barbed-wire fence— electrified, according to the various warning signs around it. Inside, the tents were arranged in ten rows of ten. The prisoners wore gray jailhouse garb with bright-pink bras on top of them. Each had a shovel they were using to dig holes in the mud. Diego pulled up next to the fence and stopped the car. "They sleep four to a tent, even though half of the tents are empty. At five a.m., they start shoveling; at nine, they fill the holes; at one, they dig again, and so forth."

"This is supposed to be a holding jail, right? After they're sentenced, they go to a prison."

"Except the prison's full, so the petty criminals are sent back here after sentencing. Thieves and shoplifters, but also guys late on their child support. And if you're undocumented, you're kept here until ICE does something with you. That can take a while."

A bolt of lightning lit the sky. Dagny watched the men continue to dig. Four guards stood watching from under clear umbrellas, holding guns in their hands. One of the prisoners slipped in the mud, and a guard collared his arm and pulled him back up, then motioned for him to keep digging.

"Why do they stay here?"

"The prisoners?"

"The undocumented. Why would they stay in Bilford County?"

"Because it's their home. They have family and friends here. It's a real community. And because moving away means that Sheriff Don wins. We can be stubborn that way. Plus, the president's people keep promising amnesty. It feels like relief is imminent. Of course, they've been promising it for years. But don't misunderstand: A lot of people have left, too—mostly to neighboring counties, although that may not last now that Sheriff Don has been threatening to go after them there."

"He wouldn't have jurisdiction."

"He has an agreement with ICE to provide federal immigration support. Although he hasn't tested it, he claims this gives him power to conduct raids anywhere federal law applies. One of these days, he's going to try it, because being king of Bilford isn't enough for this guy."

"What's his goal?"

"I don't know. Senate, I'd guess. Or a television show. More power or more money, or both. I suspect he'll end up in prison one day for financial shenanigans or something."

"They got Capone for taxes." Dagny looked down at her watch. "This is interesting, but it's not helping me build a case." It was time to move on.

"Right." Diego started the car and drove back onto the road. "They're probably waiting for us now."

He tried to prepare Dagny for meeting the families, offering all manner of advice. *They are afraid. Listen more than ask. Smile. Don't promise anything you can't deliver—their hopes can't take it. Be patient— their English is poor. And smile.* None of this was necessary—her job was to interview people. She knew when to confront and when to comfort. But she understood why he needed to say it.

They followed the winding back roads of Bilford County, driving through Madison and Zakes, to the town of Cleves, which seemed to consist almost entirely of strip malls and fast-food restaurants. Diego pulled into the lot for John Sanders Ford and circled around to the back.

"We're meeting here?"

"Yes." He stopped the car, grabbed an umbrella from the floor, and stepped out. Walking around to her side, he opened the door and held the umbrella above her. Dagny grabbed her backpack and accepted his escort to a large metal garage door. There was an intercom next to the door, and he pushed the button.

"Yes?" a deep voice bellowed.

"Swordfish," Diego said.

The garage door rose. They walked in, and the door closed behind them. By Dagny's quick count, there were about sixty people seated in five rows of folding chairs, arranged in a semicircle. A large man in a suit walked over and extended his hand to her.

"My name is Juan Sanchez," he said. And then he spoke louder to her, but for the group to hear. "On behalf of the families gathered here, I want to thank you for coming. We're a community in despair, as you can imagine. The people here are missing sons and fathers and brothers and friends. We are accustomed to living in darkness, but nothing like this. You are the only light we've seen. Thank you for coming."

The assembled throng applauded. Some of them were crying. An elderly woman rose from her seat and carried a brown paper bag to Dagny. She spoke a few words in Spanish, and Diego translated. "In case you are hungry, she has made you these tamales."

Dagny nodded at the woman. "Thank you. *Gracias.*"

"*Auténticos,*" she said.

"They're authentic," Diego said.

"I got that," Dagny muttered. She walked toward the center of the front row and scanned the faces of the crowd, which ranged in ages from fifteen to eighty, she guessed. All had dressed in their Sunday best. The women wore makeup, and the men wore ties. Hair was brushed and combed and parted in neat, straight lines. Even their posture seemed formal.

"I have a short amount of time—"

A young woman stood up. "I . . ." She paused, unsure of the word she wanted, and then lifted a knitted sweater from her tote and extended it toward Dagny. "For you. Thank you."

She walked toward the woman and took the sweater. "*Gracias.* But this really isn't necessary."

An older gentleman stood. He smiled, then reached down to the floor and came up with a vase full of roses. "To brighten your room, while you stay," he said.

Dagny took the vase and set it and the sweater next to the bag full of tamales. She looked at Diego, but he shrugged. Turning back to the crowd, she began. "When people are missing, time moves fast, so I need information, and as much of it as you can give me, as quickly as possible. So, for each of the missing, I'd like to get the following—"

"Please," Diego said. "You need to slow down so that I can translate."

"*Lo siento,*" Dagny said. She repeated her introduction with appropriate pauses, and he translated each portion. "We need to talk about each of the missing, one at a time, and I don't want to move on to the next person until we've exhausted everything about the last," she said, and then he translated. "Let's start with Emilio Garza. Who can speak about him?"

A middle-aged woman rose. "My name is Rosa Garza," she said in perfect English. "I am Emilio's mother. He is my boy."

Dagny opened her backpack and pulled out her iPad, a tool neither issued nor sanctioned by the Bureau. Diego fetched her a chair and small table, and she sat to type. She opened a notebook program, turned to a blank page, and typed *Emilio Garza* and underlined it, skipped two lines, and typed *Rosa G. —Mom.* "What is his date of birth?"

"June 3, 1998."

Dagny typed it into her iPad. "Did you bring photographs?"

Rosa nodded and handed a small stack to the man in front of her, who passed it through the crowd to Dagny. There were eight photographs in all. Emilio was a handsome young man, with hair that curled and a thin frame that seemed to contort. Dagny placed the photographs on the table in front of her and used the iPad to take pictures of each of them. She dropped the images on Emilio's page in her digital notebook, then looked back to the woman. "Tell me about him, Rosa."

"His father died when he was thirteen, so we moved here to be closer to my brother, who supported us until he was deported. I work part-time jobs where they can be had, but Emilio is the breadwinner. He supported his little sisters and me working for Arden Masonry for a couple of years, and when that dried up, odd jobs here and there. He'll work two or three jobs a day if he has to. He has no time for girls or fun. I tell him he's working too hard, but he says he's young, and that there is time for fun later. He wants to make sure his sisters are cared for.

"When he would work late, I would lie in bed awake until he came home. One night, I heard the lock on the door flip, and Emilio tiptoed inside. 'I love you, Mama,' he said, and then he went to his room to sleep. That was the last I saw of him. The next morning, he left before sunrise to search for more work." She started to cry. "I never saw him again."

It was a moving story, but only Arden Masonry warranted inclusion in Dagny's notes. She needed specifics and asked Rosa for them. The date of his disappearance. Other employers. The names and addresses of his friends. His phone number and the service provider. When Rosa ran out of answers, Dagny turned to the rest of the crowd. A young woman noted that Emilio had been dating her friend—the kind of thing that mothers sometimes don't know. Dagny took the friend's name and contact information. Another noted that Emilio had run up a gambling debt. There was probably more that couldn't be said in front of his mother. Normally, an agent would never conduct interviews in a group setting like this, but there were twenty-five people missing, and she had only two days to do something about it.

After Dagny exhausted all of the information she could get about Emilio, she asked about other missing boys. It took several hours, but she was able to amass a pretty impressive compendium of photographs and data. The oldest missing was twenty-seven; the youngest was sixteen. Nine of them were married. Eleven were fathers. Most of them had graduated from high school. All of them had worked as day laborers. None of them seemed to have a criminal record. All of them had cell phones, but to her dismay, only three of them were iPhones, and that would make things difficult. She understood what to do with iPhones.

She noticed that thirteen of the men had disappeared on the same day, about a week and a half back. Another ten of them had disappeared four days earlier. It seemed likely that they had vanished in groups.

When there was nothing left to be said, Dagny thanked the group for their time and started to pack her things. No one rose from their seats. She looked at Diego, and he stepped forward and said a few words in Spanish too quickly for her to catch any of them. Still no one rose. Diego walked over to her and whispered, "I think they need more."

Dagny set down her backpack and surveyed the crowd. Their eyes studied hers, looking for something. She had misjudged them. It wasn't only sadness and despair that filled them—it was also fear. They were looking for hope.

"The information you've provided will be a significant help," she said. A woman in the front row began to cry. Dagny needed to try harder.

"I've worked many successful cases where we had less to go on than this." Even as she said it, she knew these words were of little comfort. Others began to cry, too. "These boys will be found."

A man rubbed his eyes; another lowered his head into his open hands. The first woman to cry was now sobbing.

"I will find these boys," she said. "I will find them."

It was a terrible thing to say. She couldn't find them in two days. And then she'd be off the case, and no one would find them. She had given them hope, but it was false. So when they swarmed to hug her, it felt like the tightening of a noose.

After the meeting, Dagny and Diego corralled the families of the three men who used iPhones. One of them had no computer. They visited the homes of the other two, and she inspected their laptops but did not find what she had wanted. She dropped Diego at his home and started to drive to her motel. Her iPhone chirped. A text from Victor said: **Met my points.** He sent this text every evening. Though it was disguised as a marker of his own progress, it was really a gentle nudge to ensure that she continued hers.

In 1961, a woman at a grocery admired Jean Nidetch's belly and asked when she was due. She wasn't pregnant. Feeling fat and frustrated, Jean started to diet. Lonely in her struggles, she invited similarly frustrated friends to her house in Queens, and they talked about their problems with weight and their efforts to lose it. The meeting was a hit, and those who attended came back the next week, and the next, with more friends in tow each time. When the crowd outgrew her living room, she rented a room above a movie theater and charged a two-dollar admission. Those brave enough stood on a scale she brought to each meeting, so that progress could be measured and celebrated. Since everyone was watching her weight, she called the group Weight Watchers. After two years of meetings, she partnered with a businessman named Albert Lippert to monetize the concept of communal weight loss. Ten years later, they sold the business to H. J. Heinz Company for $71.2 million. As a result of the program, Jean Nidetch lost seventy pounds and became a multimillionaire.

In the 1990s, Weight Watchers developed its signature points program, which it refined over the years. Every food was assigned a point value, derived by a formula that took into account its fat, carbohydrates, protein, and fiber content. Members were assigned a maximum number of points they might consume each day based upon their age, height, and desired weight. Keeping track of these points was tedious but effective. By logging everything they ate, members ensured that they remained on target for their weight-loss goals.

The Weight Watchers point system was designed to help people *lose* weight. It was not designed to ensure that anorexics *kept* their weight, but that's how Dagny was using it. Victor, who needed to lose a few pounds, was her willing accomplice. While he worked the diet from the top, she worked it from below. They kept each other honest, but mostly, he was doing the keeping.

She wanted to weigh 125 pounds. To maintain this weight, she had to eat twenty-six points of food each day. If she ran, and she usually did, she needed another twenty points. It was a scientific way to monitor her weight. Or, at least as scientific as the program would let her be. Because Weight Watchers didn't consider 125 to be a healthy weight for a woman who was five-nine, she had entered her height into the Weight Watchers website as five-five. This threw everything off a bit.

A Weight Watchers iPhone app helped her look up the point values of foods and keep track of her points on the road. She opened the app on her phone and glanced at the zero on the screen. Surely, she had eaten something that day, right? The bag of peanuts on the plane. She looked up its value: two points. That left her twenty-four points short for the day. A bag of tamales would do it, but she'd left them at the car dealership.

She pulled into the lot of a Shell station, parked Diego's car, and walked into the store. The freezers had three shelves of ice cream. She grabbed Ben and Jerry's Chubby Hubby and looked at the nutritional information on the side. At 330 calories and 20 grams of fat per serving, it would do. She paid for it, grabbed a plastic spoon from a bin, and drove to the Bilford Motor Inn. After checking in, she lugged her suitcase and backpack up the steps to the second floor and found her room. Once inside, she climbed into bed, turned on the television, and ate nearly the entire pint. It was a fitting end to an emotionally draining day.

CHAPTER 13

....

Adelmo Fox sat on a blanket, deep in the woods, waiting for a girl. He pushed the button that lit the face of his watch. Twenty past midnight, which meant that she was twenty minutes late. A breeze blew through the trees, and he shivered, wishing he'd brought his jacket. His mother would have made him bring it, if she had known where he was, and if she had allowed him to be there. Of course, she never would have allowed it—not on a school night, not with this girl, and not when so many people had gone missing over the last few weeks.

At sixteen, Adelmo was sure of a few things. He was sure that Kurt Vonnegut was the best writer in the history of American literature. He was sure that his mother's empanadas were infused with all of the joy of heaven. And he was sure that he was deeply, madly in love with Jessica. He knew this because he called up her Facebook page thirty times a day to see her face, because he replayed her voice mails twelve times in a row, and because he felt a thousand volts of electricity surge through his body each time she grabbed his hand.

As the wind picked up, it whistled through the trees. He opened his thermos, poured a cup of hot chocolate, and took a sip. It kept him warm, but not as warm as a sixteen-year-old girl could. Where was Jessica?

His mother had warned him against American girls, but she didn't understand that he was an American boy. When she'd brought him across the border, he was only two. Every memory he had was of the United States. Only his skin and name were Mexican—everything inside him was all USA. This drove his mother crazy. She tried to force Mexican culture, music, and language on him, but none of it took.

"Why even move here if you still want to live *there*?" Adelmo would ask her.

"Why have a mirror if you won't look at yourself," she'd reply. It made no sense.

He sipped the chocolate again. It was now twelve thirty. She was always late. It was a quirk, like the way she missed the top three buttons of her blouse or how she forgot his birthday, even though he'd been talking about it for a week. He smiled at the thought of these things, but then the smile washed away. Yes, she was always late, but this was later than usual. Maybe her father had caught her sneaking out—the thought of this filled him with panic. He checked his iPhone. No texts. He didn't dare text her—that had been the reason for her grounding to begin with. Tapping the Facebook icon, he loaded her page. No updates since the afternoon.

The sound of footsteps in the distance brightened his mood. He reached into his pocket and found the ring. The half-carat diamond on a gold band had cost him two months' earnings, which was customary according to the woman behind the counter. It was a dozen mowed lawns, thirty painted walls, and two weekends at a moving company.

In the dark dead of the woods, nothing shimmered off the angled side of the diamond, so he ran his fingertips around its smooth edges to make sure it was real. It felt . . . small. Smaller than a pea. Smaller than a tick. It felt like a speck of dust or a microbe. Jessica deserved a bowling ball; he was going to give her an atom. It was the best he could do. His love would have to do the rest.

He kneeled on one knee and called through the dark, "Jessica?"

The footsteps stopped.

"Jessica!"

She began running toward him. Galloping, even—each foot clattering against the leaves faster than seemed possible. Snarling, then growling. Leaping at him with teeth and snout. It smashed into his chest and knocked him to his back. The dog dug its fangs deep into his right upper arm. Adelmo screamed in pain, then threw his left fist into the dog's belly until it released him. The dog darted a few steps away, but then came back at him, clawing at his legs. He gave the dog a swift series of kicks that did little to deter it and screamed the most menacing, crazed cry he could muster, which did the trick. The dog ran away.

Feeling a rush of adrenaline, Adelmo jumped and pumped his fist. This sent a searing pain through his arm. He put his left hand over the wound to try to stem the blood, and when that didn't work, he tore a strip of his blanket and tied it around his arm. Sitting down, he buried his face in his hands and closed his eyes. This was supposed to have been the most magical night of his life, and now he was bleeding, probably had rabies, and Jessica was an hour late.

Then he remembered the ring.

Where was the ring? Adelmo dropped to the ground and lowered his face to try to find it, but it was too dark. He combed his fingers through the grass, frantically at first, and then, after a calm moment of reflection, methodically, like a combine rolling through cornstalks. That didn't help, so he took out his iPhone and turned on the flash, lay on his belly, and held the light low to the grass, looking under each tangled blade for the diamond's shimmer. It took such concentration that he didn't notice Jessica until he heard her voice.

"What are you doing?" she said, standing above him.

He screamed and rolled over. "Jessica?"

"What do you have wrapped around your arm? Is that some kind of gang thing?"

"No." He shook his head. "There was this dog—"

"Adelmo, I can't stay. If I'm not back in a half hour—"

"Your father?"

"I wasn't even going to come, except I wanted to tell you in person."

"Tell me what?" He sat up but kept moving his hands behind his back in the grass, still feeling for the ring.

"Jesus, Adelmo, is whatever you lost more important to you than this conversation?"

"No, of course not." He brought his hands forward and folded them into his lap. "Sit down, Jessica. Please."

She did not sit. "Look, I just wanted to tell you that it's been fun and all, but we both know it's not working, so—"

"No, Jessica, it's working. We're working fine."

"You think my treating you like shit is fine?"

"You don't, Jess. I mean, it's all okay because I love you."

She laughed. It hurt more than the dog bite.

"I let you feel my boobs. And you think that's love? Jesus, Adelmo." She turned and walked away, disappearing into the dark.

"Jessica?" he said meekly, to no one. When the sound of her steps was gone, he spun around and began searching the grass again for the ring.

And there he was—alone in the dark forest with a bloody arm, looking for a ring he'd spent his savings on, so that he could propose to the girl who had just dumped him. He started to cry and laugh at the same time. It was impossible for things to be worse, and there was something funny about that.

He stopped laughing when the shovel hit his head.

When Adelmo woke, he felt dizzy. Slowly, he became conscious of his condition. He was blindfolded, it seemed, and hanging upside down from a rope tied around his ankles. His wrists were bound behind his back. A finger kept tapping him, making him sway away from the man's voice and then back toward it.

"You," the man's voice said, "have had a bad day."

Adelmo tried to talk, but the ball gag in his mouth prevented it.

"That day is about to become worse." The man pushed him now with his palm, and Adelmo swayed higher. "Let me describe the situation. You are at the top of a sixty-foot concrete silo, suspended over a round hole that drops down to a hard floor covered in decaying bodies. Some men in my position would make this a sport and give you a fighting chance. I'm not that kind of man. There is no way that you will escape. You will die."

It seemed to Adelmo that he must be dreaming, because things like this did not really happen. Any second his mother would wake him for school.

The man sighed and shoved Adelmo higher, causing him to flit about in something like a figure eight. "I resent you for the fact that I am doing this." The man pushed him harder and higher. Maybe if he got his hand free, he could punch him when his body swung back. He turned his wrists, but the rope was too tight to slip them free. "If there weren't so many of you, this wouldn't even be an issue. No one would care, except that there's so goddamn many of you." He pushed him again.

"I wasn't even looking for you. I wasn't even looking for anyone, but there you were, waiting for me. A goddamn waste of my time." Adelmo heard something clang—the shovel, he thought. The man swung it such that the metal scoop tore into his back. The pain was instant and real, and none of it was a dream.

The man steadied him, and then took the blindfold away from his head. There was a tall, thin man standing across from him, upside down. The man had a pair of gardening shears in his hands. "I think it will take me three squeezes to cut through the rope."

It only took two. And then Adelmo fell.

CHAPTER 14

In New Bilford, there was a Courtyard by Marriott, a Hampton Inn, a Holiday Inn Express, and a Residence Inn, all within a quarter-mile block. Each of these hotels was less than seven years old and offered clean sheets and hypoallergenic pillows, free hot breakfasts, and Wi-Fi Internet service. Three of the hotels held afternoon cocktail mixers for their business travelers, serving chicken tenders or potato skins. The fourth offered freshly baked cookies with milk every evening in the library. Copies of *USA Today* were free for the taking. If a guest forgot a toothbrush, the front desk could provide one. All of the televisions were plasma and came with HBO or Showtime. On each nightstand was an alarm clock that could dock and charge an iPhone. Each hotel succeeded terrifically at being relatively comfortable. Dagny wasn't staying at any of them.

Dagny was staying at the Bilford Motor Inn, which was the only lodging located in downtown Bilford. At least half of the twenty-nine rooms seemed to have been rented as weekly apartments to disheveled and disruptive men. She guessed that most of them had been kicked out of their homes by their wives for various infractions, all substantial. The two other women who seemed to have rented rooms dressed in tattered clothes and were caked in makeup. She assumed they were drug addicts, prostitutes, or both. Because the walls were thin, she had been jarred from sleep several times by yelling and sobbing and moaning from various surrounding quarters.

The motel did not advertise a hot breakfast; it advertised hot water, and even that was a stretch. There were no newspapers for the taking, and the television was not plasma. The alarm clock next to her bed did not charge her iPhone or even sound at 4:00 a.m., as she had set it to do. Thus, it was a call at five that actually woke her. She reached to the nightstand, grabbed her phone, and pulled it close to her face. It was the Professor. She slid her thumb across the screen to answer it. "Thanks for the wake-up call," she said.

"Time to come home. We're taking Victor's case," he said.

That wasn't acceptable. "On Wednesday, you said that I had two days to get you bodies."

"Yes, and you didn't."

"It's only been one day."

"Wednesday, Thursday. That's two days."

"I didn't get here until yesterday afternoon. Two days is Thursday, Friday. I still have all day today."

"Wednesday was the first day. Yesterday was your second. It's over."

"Absolutely not. That's not how you count days."

"That is, in fact, how I count days."

"Imagine your birthday is tomorrow."

"Why?"

"Imagine that tomorrow is your birthday. Would you say that your birthday is two days away?" When he didn't answer, she did. "No. No, you would not. You would say it's one day away."

"Let's say you have a penny, and I give you one more penny. Would you agree that you have two cents?" the Professor replied.

"Yes, but—"

"Well, I'm not interested in your two cents. We're taking Victor's case."

"Why? This is so much more important. We can wait another day or two."

"No, we can't," he barked. There was a long silence, and then he said softly, "The Director has ordered us to take Victor's case."

"What? How did he even find out about it?"

"Yesterday, I had to brief him on the Benny case, and he demanded to know what we were doing next. I mentioned Victor's case, and he—"

"Seized upon it?"

"Dollars mean more to him than they do to me." He paused. "So I need you back in DC immediately."

After meeting with the families of the missing, she couldn't skip town. "I have to stay. Sorry."

There was a long silence, like the prelude to the whistle of a bubbling teapot. "Goddamn it, Dagny. I am your boss, and you are my subordinate. I may not like the Director's decision, but it has been decided, and I am going to follow his orders, and you are going to follow mine."

"I stood in front of a room of grieving families last night and promised them my help. There is no way I'm abandoning them."

"You had absolutely no authority to make any promises to them, and it was completely reckless and heartless—yes, heartless, Dagny—for you to give them such hope."

"If you had been in the room with them, you'd have done the same."

"There is a two thirty-five flight from Dayton to DCA—"

"Professor, I'm staying."

"Dagny, please—"

"I'm sorry, Professor." She knew she was placing him in a difficult situation. "I won't budge on this, regardless of the consequences."

He sighed. "You leave me no choice, Dagny. You are hereby suspended without pay."

"That's fair," she said.

"While you are under suspension, you are not authorized to take any action on behalf of the Bureau. To be clear, you are not acting under color of law."

"Understood."

"You will remain under suspension until such time that I have been convinced to reinstate you. A notice shall be placed in your file documenting your insubordination."

"I would expect no less."

"And I'm not reimbursing you for any of your receipts."

"You didn't last time, either."

"This is serious, Dagny."

"I know, Professor. But this thing in Bilford . . . it's a lot more serious."

"I'm very angry with you, Dagny."

"I know."

"I'm also proud of you." He hung up.

She roused herself from bed to take as much of a shower as she could stand and thought about what had happened. The Professor had granted her a reprieve in the most Professor way possible. The suspension was real, as was both his anger and admiration. But he was freeing her to continue the investigation. She knew that the job was less important than the work, and so did he.

With respect to the investigation, the suspension was inconvenient but not debilitating. Although verboten, she'd still show her creds as necessary. Getting a warrant or using the crime lab was now out of the question. If she found some bodies, everything would change. With a show of contrition, her suspension would be lifted. The Professor would ignore Victor's investigation and turn his attention to Bilford. Everything would be right again.

As long as she found some bodies.

It was a wonder, actually, that anyone ever found a body. There were 2.3 billion acres of land in the United States. If someone wanted to hide a body, there were plenty of places to hide it. But most murderers were lazy or stupid, or they wanted to get caught—which was why people found bodies all the time.

The water was too cold and too murky to let the shower go any further. She shut off the water, grabbed a towel, and dried off.

It was too late for a morning run. She dressed, grabbed her gun and bag, and locked her motel door behind her. Standing on the second-floor landing, she could see the sun peeking out over the treetops. She jogged down the metal steps to the parking lot, climbed into Diego's car, and started the engine. Back home, her Prius barely hummed when she pushed the "Power" button to start it, but Diego's Corvette roared. A car ought to feel more like a gun than a computer, she thought. She could get used to the Corvette.

Diego was sitting on his front steps when she pulled up. He smiled at her and climbed into the passenger seat. "Were you able to get any sleep?"

"Enough. Where would I find day laborers?"

He shrugged. "I don't know. I've never hired any."

"Who would know?"

His blank stare was not encouraging.

"C'mon, Diego. You've been here for two years."

He pulled out his phone. "Let me try Gabino. I think he does that kind of thing." He dialed the phone and held it to his ear. "*Hola, ¿Gabino?*" A flurry of Spanish passed between them, and then he hung up the phone. "Fowler Road, off 183. By the large sycamore tree."

Dagny punched Fowler Road into her phone's GPS and started on course. "Who's Gabino?" she asked.

"He's one of my favorites. Nineteen years old. Graduated with a 4.2 GPA. Has AP credits in calculus, world history, government, English, and more. Brilliant kid."

"And he's a day laborer?"

"His mom has lupus. She's sick all the time, and they don't have health insurance. He takes care of her and saves what little is left for college."

"He can't get a scholarship?"

"There's only a handful of scholarships available to undocumented kids. And he couldn't leave his mom, even if he got one."

"So now he waits next to a tree by the side of the road every morning, hoping someone will hire him to mow a lawn?"

"Except Sunday mornings, when he comes to church. He never misses it."

"How can he believe in God when this is his life?"

"You don't believe in God, Dagny?"

"I'm an agnostic Jew."

"And I'm an atheist priest," Diego replied. "So we're not too far apart. But Gabino doesn't have the luxury of not believing. That's something only the well-to-do can afford."

"You're not exactly living the high life, Diego." She would have to follow up on his strange confession of atheism later.

"I am completely unburdened, Dagny. There's not a soul who depends upon me. I am less significant than the butterfly's wings. If I were to vanish tomorrow, not one thing would change."

Fowler Road was a gravel road that seemed to stretch between nothing and nothing more. There was, sure enough, a large sycamore tree halfway down the lane, and three young men were standing under it. Each of them scampered down into the ditch along the road when the Corvette came within their view.

Dagny pulled over to the shoulder and turned off the car. "Wait here," Diego said, and he disappeared into the culvert. Three men was a small crew, and that worried her.

After a minute, he jogged up the hill and motioned for her to get out of the car. "I had to explain why you are here," he said. She nodded and followed him down into the ditch.

The three young men stood in a tight triangle, with the two meek ones behind the bravest of them. All of them looked younger than she had expected. Teenagers, surely.

"I'm Special Agent Dagny Gray. I'm investigating the disappearance of a number of young men in this area."

"Father Vega told us," the boy in front said. "My name is Paco." He extended his hand, and she shook it. "These guys," he continued, motioning to his friends, "are Francisco and Romeo." Both of the boys nodded but did not extend their hands.

"This is where you look for work?"

"Everyone used to hang out in the lot behind Lowe's or the U-Haul store. But Sheriff Don cleaned those places out and threatened to arrest the store managers if they let us onto the property again. The spot has changed a few times since then, but it's always next to a public road— we don't want to get nobody in trouble. This spot is good because people looking to hire know to stop by the tree, and because we can hide in the ditch if we have to. Sheriff Don hasn't run us off, so we figure he doesn't know about it yet."

"Can you get work every day?" Dagny asked.

"No, ma'am. These days, you're lucky if you get something three days a week. Used to be able to work all seven if you wanted to." He looked at his watch. "Seven thirty now. We might wait until eight thirty, and if there's nothing by then, there's not going to be."

"How come there are only three of you?"

He shrugged. "A lot of our friends are missing. The rest are scared. About a week ago, I was supposed to be here, but I had to help my mom with an emergency and didn't come. Everyone who showed up that day is missing. My cousin, Carlos Nuevas, was one of them. I would be missing if I had come."

"You think they were picked up here?"

"I think someone picked them up and killed the whole lot of them. Nobody heard from any of them after that morning. I heard someone bragged about killing folks on *The Hank Frank Show*."

Diego piped in. "On the radio?"

"That's what I heard. Someone said they were going to kill all of us."

"When was that?" Dagny asked.

Paco shook his head. "I don't know, ma'am. I didn't hear the show. I just heard it happened." He looked at his friends, but they said nothing.

She made a mental note to visit Hank Frank. "Help me understand, Paco. You believe that a man picked up workers from under this tree and killed them about a week ago. And yet you're waiting under this tree right now, looking for work. Aren't you scared?"

"Shitless, ma'am." He turned to Diego. "Sorry, Father."

Diego smiled.

"So, why are you here?" Dagny asked.

"We need the work. Times are tough, ma'am. And I have this for protection." He opened his coat and showed her a gun.

She looked at his friends. "You guys carrying?"

They shook their heads no.

"Paco, I'm glad you've got that, and if you meet the guy responsible for all of this, I hope you blast his face off. But as a general rule, don't show a federal agent that you're carrying a concealed weapon without a permit."

"Okay, that makes sense," he said.

She reached into her backpack and pulled out her iPad, then ran through the names of those on her list of missing men. Paco offered his best guess as to whom had disappeared with his cousin the week before, and then offered up some additional details about some of the others.

None of the information seemed likely to help the investigation, but she took it all down and thanked the men.

When she and Diego started back to the Corvette, one of the other boys shouted, "Excuse me!"

Dagny turned around. "Yes?"

Romeo ran up to her. "I have this friend at school, and he went out last night to meet a girl. This morning, his mother called me to see where he was. I figured he spent the night with the girl, so I told his mom that he had crashed at my house. But he didn't, and he hasn't answered his phone, and I tried him a bunch of times."

"What kind of phone does he have?" she asked.

He seemed puzzled. "An iPhone. Does that matter?"

It did. Finally, a lead. "What's his name?"

"Adelmo. Adelmo Fox." She took down Adelmo's address and Romeo's cell phone number, and they were off.

Dagny's phone called out directions, but it could barely keep up with her, as fast as she was driving. "I didn't realize my car could do this," Diego said.

"If you're going to own a Corvette, you ought to drive it like one," she said. She knew she had to prepare him for what was coming. "The clock is ticking, so I'm going to be abrupt with Ms. Fox if she's home. You may have to smooth things over while I do my thing." She turned the car left, which flung Diego at his window.

"And if she's not home?" he said.

"Then I'm going to break down the door and find his computer."

"You think he's alive?"

"I doubt it. But I think his phone could have some juice left, and that could be the break we need." She turned a sharp right, causing the tires to squeal. "Do you know Ms. Fox?"

"No."

"In case she doesn't speak English, practice your introduction in your head. You've got about twenty seconds to explain the situation to her."

"I'm not sure I fully understand the situation myself."

"Now you have ten seconds." She parked the car in front of the Fox house, ran to the front door, and pounded on it. Diego sprinted to catch up.

A heavyset Hispanic woman opened the door. "Ms. Fox?" Dagny said. The woman nodded, and Dagny flashed her creds. "Your son is missing. I need to find him."

The woman started to cry. "I knew that boy was lying to me when he—"

"Does he have a computer?"

She nodded. "In his room."

The woman led Dagny upstairs to the boy's bedroom and opened the door. The walls of the small room were covered in music and football posters. Dirty clothes were piled on the floor. The twin bed was unmade. Stacks of papers were piled on the small desk against the wall. Under one of the stacks was a MacBook. Dagny pushed the papers aside and picked up the laptop.

Under different circumstances, she would have cloned the contents of the laptop in a forensically responsible manner before using it. There was no time for that now. She opened the laptop, clicked on the Safari web browser, and navigated to the history folder. It was empty, which meant he probably didn't use Safari. She clicked on the icon for the Chrome browser, opened its history, and hit Control F. Typing *iCloud* returned a number of hits. "Thank God."

She clicked on iCloud and got a log-in screen. The username was AdelmoF19@yahoo.com. The password field was blank. "Ms. Fox, do you know his password?"

She was crying. "I don't," she blustered.

Apple forced iCloud users to adopt complicated passwords—they had to have at least one capital letter and two nonconsecutive numbers. There was no way Dagny was going to stumble upon Adelmo's password by guessing. Fortunately, there was an icon next to the browser's omnibus that looked like a lock. She recognized it as belonging to the program 1Password, which stored usernames and passwords for multiple websites so that a user only had to remember one password. She clicked on it, and an empty password field popped up.

"No idea what his master password could be, Ms. Fox?"

"No," she cried.

Dagny glanced up at the posters on the wall. One showed a picture of Bengals quarterback Andy Dalton. She typed *Dalton* into 1Password, and when that didn't work, she tried *AndyDalton*, *andydalton*, *Bengals*, CincinnatiBengals, and a dozen other permutations. The next poster was for the band Django Django. She typed *Django* into the field, and then *DjangoDjango*. Neither worked. There were eight more posters on the wall, but she held out little hope for any of them.

Romeo had said that Adelmo was supposed to meet a girl at the park. "Ms. Fox, who was Adelmo dating?"

The woman shook her head. "Nobody."

Teenage boys and their secrets. Dagny minimized the browser and opened the Mail program. She scrolled past e-mails from boys until she found one from a girl: Jessica Marigold. She maximized the Chrome browser, hit the 1Password icon, and typed Jessica. A window popped up, showing a series of black dots under the password field for Adelmo's iCloud login. She right-clicked on the black dots and chose "Show Password" from the options. The dots turned into letters: *Jessica16*. She typed *Jessica16* into iCloud and was presented with a screen of icons. One of them read "Find My iPhone."

"This is good, no?" Diego asked.

"This is good," Dagny said. "If his phone is on."

She clicked on the "Find My iPhone" icon. A map appeared, along with an animated compass. The status line under the compass read *Locating*. "Please," she whispered.

A street map flashed onto the screen, along with a green dot. She clicked on the dot, and a bubble read *Adelmo's iPhone*. Under it, the words: *Located less than a minute ago.* She hit the plus sign to zoom in, and then pushed the Hybrid tab so that they could see a satellite image overlay the street map. The green dot was in the middle of a large wooded area next to Hillsborough Park.

She unplugged the laptop. "Ms. Fox, I need to borrow this."

"You found him?" she said, with more hope than was warranted.

"I found his phone."

"You found him?" she said again, begging for affirmation.

"It's a good sign," Dagny said, hoping it would appease her. She carried the laptop down the steps and out to the Corvette. Then she pulled out her iPhone and opened the settings.

"What are you doing?" Diego asked.

"Tethering the laptop to my phone so we'll stay connected while we drive." After turning on her phone's tethering, she clicked on the Wi-Fi icon in the task bar of Adelmo's computer and selected "Dagny Gray's iPhone network" from the list. She handed the laptop to Diego. "You're navigating. Keep refreshing the status of Adelmo's phone."

"In case he moves?"

"In case his phone does."

He called out directions as they drove. "The dot isn't moving."

She had hoped that it would, since dead bodies lay still. "Keep refreshing."

The gardens at Hillsborough Park were gorgeous, filled with blooming flowers of endless variety and color, surrounded by fresh and fragrant mulch. All of this flora formed the periphery around three tennis courts with sagging nets, a basketball court with a busted hoop, and playground with a seesaw surrounded by cones behind a sign that read **UNDER REPAIR**. Some teenage boys were shooting hoops at the good end of the basketball court. A woman was pushing a toddler in one of the swings. The park's gardener was driving his maintenance cart along the path that meandered through the gardens.

Dagny parked the car, pulled out her creds, and held them high as she ran toward the gardener. "Stop!"

The gardener turned his head and stopped.

"I need your cart!" she shouted.

Diego was standing by his car, seemingly unsure of what to do. "Bring the laptop," she shouted to him.

The gardener was a little old man, with patches of white hair dotting his otherwise-bald dome. A retiree, she figured, volunteering his time to make the city's garden beautiful while everything else fell apart. He looked at her creds and said meekly, "Something going down?"

"Perhaps," she replied. He ceded her the cart, and Diego climbed aboard. She grabbed the laptop from him and studied the satellite image on the map showing Adelmo's phone. After getting her bearings, she drove the cart along the path and turned onto a dirt trail that headed into the woods. The iPhone dot was about fifty yards east of the trail. She parked the cart. "We walk from here. Don't walk on the trail; stay on the grass next to it."

"Why?"

"Because the trail may have evidence."

He followed her to a flat, grassy clearing in the woods. "It looks like it's in the center on the map," he said.

"That's not always as precise as you would think." She set down the laptop, walked to the center of the clearing. Dropping to her knees, she ran her fingers through the thick grass, searching for Adelmo's phone. Diego dropped to the ground and did the same.

A flash of light sparkled a few feet in front of her. She fished through the grass and spied a woman's diamond ring. She opened her backpack, grabbed a Ziploc bag, and turned it inside out. Wearing it as a glove, she lifted the ring from the ground, then inverted the bag and zipped it closed.

"That's evidence?" he asked.

"Everything is evidence," she replied, placing it in the pocket of her backpack. "Keep looking."

He worked his way left while she worked her way right.

"Is this something?" he called, pointing out a mound of freshly turned dirt.

It was something. Dagny sprinted back through the woods to the gardener's cart and opened the trunk. There were two long, wood-handled shovels, and she grabbed both. She raced back to the clearing and handed one of the shovels to Diego.

She shoved the blade of the shovel into the dirt and stepped down hard on it to push it in farther. It gave easily. She tossed the dirt to the side and shoved the shovel in again. Diego did the same. Two feet down, the dirt still gave easily.

"Deep hole," he said, and she nodded.

Three feet down, the frayed edge of a rope appeared. "Stop," she said, and he obeyed. She opened her backpack, withdrew two pairs of latex gloves, put on one, and gave the other to Diego. Dagny kneeled down and tugged at the frayed rope with one hand while scooping the dirt around it away with the other. She followed the rope down to a metal ring in a piece of canvas. The rope wove in and out of a series of holes that lined the top of a large bag.

As they uncovered more of the bag, she noticed a tear sliding down Diego's cheek. "We don't know anything yet," she said. Even she didn't believe it. It seemed likely that they'd be pulling Adelmo's body out of the ground in a matter of minutes.

They dug some more, and when the bulk of the large bag was exposed, they pulled at its sides to lift it from the hole. The bag was about four feet deep and three feet wide—large enough for a body that was folded the right way.

Dagny loosened the rope, opened the top of the bag, and looked inside.

Cell phones. A ton of them.

"Oh, my."

Diego leaned over the opening of the bag. "There must be a hundred phones in there."

The magnitude of the crime was larger than she had imagined. She closed her eyes and brought her palms up to her forehead. There was simply too much to do and not enough manpower or time to do it. Although she still hadn't found any bodies, she had a bag of gadgets full of volumes of information, all of which would need to be extracted and analyzed. But first, she had to process a crime scene.

She turned to Diego. "Do you have Beamer's number in your phone?"

"Yes." He handed her his phone.

"Go back to the cart and get a garbage bag from the trunk. Remember to stay off the trails."

"Okay." While he sprinted off, she scrolled through his contacts, found Beamer's number, and touched it.

"Father Vega?" he answered.

"Special Agent Dagny Gray, actually."

"I can't tell if that's good news or bad."

"Another young man disappeared last night. We tracked his cell phone to the woods behind Hillsborough Park. It was buried in a bag with about a hundred or so other cell phones."

"Jesus Christ."

"I figure each phone came from a victim. So, we're dealing with a mass murderer, most likely. I need help."

"Jesus. What can I get you?"

"This is a crime scene. It needs to be processed. Hair, clothing, fingerprints—anything we can find."

"Anything visible?"

"No, but we'll need to comb it. Tape it off."

"Tell me you're taking the lead and that you've got a team for this."

"The team is me and a priest in over his head. I don't have an official investigation. In fact, I'm technically suspended from the Bureau. I'm not even supposed to be looking at this thing."

"Oh, Christ."

"So, I need your help. I also need you to keep it quiet. So you can't tell your chief."

"Christ, Christ. Why?"

"Because he's not going to take direction from an agent gone rogue, and I need to be in charge right now."

"So, you need me to get together a team to comb through Hillsborough Park for evidence of a serial murderer and not tell my boss."

"Yes."

"What else do you need? A unicorn?"

"Do you have a Cellebrite?"

"What's that?"

"A machine that lifts data from cell phones." They were expensive, so it seemed unlikely that Bilford had one.

"No, we don't have anything like that."

Everything was going to be harder without the Bureau's resources. "You have phone chargers?"

"Not a hundred of them."

"I need a safe place to store and process evidence. The Bilford Motor Inn won't cut it."

"You can't use the station and keep the chief from knowing. It's a small force."

"You have a nice house?"

"Holy Christ."

"With a good basement? Door that locks? Something secure?"

"You want to use my basement? To run a secret investigation?"

"Hey, you're the one who sent Diego to me."

"I don't know about this."

"You have a wife? Kids?"

"No."

"Good. Look, John, once we find bodies—even one body—the Bureau is going to make this thing official, I'm going to be reinstated, and you'll have your basement back. We'll brief your chief and work in tandem to find this monster. But until then, I don't want to scare away the people we need to help us, and I don't want politics getting in the way of finding this guy."

"I could lose my job, Agent Gray."

"You do, and I'll get you another job. A better job. You can call me Dagny."

"It sounds like you've barely got a hold on your current job, Dagny, and you're going to get me a new one?"

"Three people. Two, even. Just you if that's all we can get. Some tape. Evidence bags. Plaster, cameras. And your basement for maybe a week. Probably less."

He sighed.

"Please."

"Give me thirty minutes."

"Great." She hung up.

A Cellebrite was too expensive for Bilford, but Cincinnati probably had one, she figured. She texted Beamer's uncle and asked if she could borrow one. He promised to deliver it that night, no questions asked.

Diego returned with the garbage bag. It was large and heavy—designed for volumes of cut grass and leaves, not evidence gathering, but it would hold a canvas bag full of cell phones fine. She grabbed the bag from his hand and held it open. "Lift the canvas bag carefully, and set it down in here."

"Okay." He held the top of the bag closed with his left hand while scooping his right under the bottom, and set the canvas bag into the plastic one. "What now?"

"We're about to descend into a process of enormous tedium," she said. "I'm going to ask you to do as little as possible. Don't take it personally. You're not trained in law enforcement, and some lawyer would point that out down the line if he thought it would get him reasonable doubt. This whole area is a crime scene." She stopped to think. "Burying this bag out here, instead of burning it or throwing it in a river . . . that tells us the unsub wants our attention. If he wants our attention, maybe he isn't being careful with footprints or hair, or clothing or fingerprints. It's a fresh scene, so there's some hope."

"Is there anything I can do?"

Dagny pulled her wallet out of her backpack and handed him a credit card. "We need every phone charger you can find. Hit Walmart, Target, the Verizon store, wherever, and buy them all out. Every make and model. Hit Goodwill to see if they have older ones the stores don't carry."

"Why do we need to charge the phones?"

"Because they're full of information. We'll be able to figure out who owned them, which will give us a list of the missing. The last e-mails and texts they sent will give us a timeline for their disappearance. GPS data, calendars, social networks—put it all together, and you get a narrative."

"And all it takes is a process of enormous tedium."

"While you're at it, pick up fifteen power bricks, ten extension cords, and every whiteboard you can find. We're setting up shop at Beamer's house."

Diego nodded and started toward the parking lot.

"Wait," she called.

He turned around. "Yes?"

She pointed to the pile of dirt they had extracted from the hole. "Give me one nice footprint in this dirt."

He walked over to the pile of dirt and stepped down into it. "To compare?"

"Yes. I don't want anyone to get excited about finding your footprints in the woods. Remember, walk off-trail on the way back to your car."

"Will do." And with that, he left.

Dagny planted her own foot in the dirt next to his. She pulled her Canon DSLR from her backpack, took a picture of the hole in the ground, then backed up and took another picture to give it some context. Circling around the hole, she photographed the scene, moving a bit farther out with each pass. Along the way, she snapped and bagged a cigarette butt, a candy wrapper, an inch-long piece of flannel fabric, a toothpick, a coffee-cup lid, and a Livestrong bracelet. There were a few sets of footprints smaller than hers. She thought about the diamond ring. Maybe it had been intended for Jessica Marigold. She called Romeo's cell phone.

"Hello?"

"It's Special Agent Dagny Gray."

"Oh, hey. Did you find Adelmo?"

"Not yet, but I'm looking. You said he was meeting a girl last night. Was it Jessica Marigold?"

"Yes, that's her name."

"Was she at school today?"

"I don't know. I didn't go."

"Can you call someone who would know and find out?"

"Sure."

"Another question: Is Jessica related to Don Marigold?"

"Yeah. She's the sheriff's daughter."

Adelmo had been playing with fire. "One more thing."

"Yeah."

"Was he going to propose to her?"

"Adelmo? He didn't say anything about it."

"Is it something he might have done?"

"He's stupid enough to do something like that. He's all into her, and she's just fooling around with him. He's whipped, for sure."

As she hung up the phone, three officers emerged from the woods. She had meant to tell them to stay off the trail, but it was too late. The first of them looked to be in his late twenties. His blond hair was trim and neatly parted, and he was short but cute in an Eagle Scout kind of way. He dropped a large duffel bag on the ground and extended his hand. "Nice to meet you, Dagny."

"Nice to meet you, John. How's your uncle?"

"Talking about retirement."

"Hope it's just talk." The other two officers were even younger than Beamer. This was good, because it meant their training was fresh. She told them to tape off the trail to reduce entry, scour the parking lot for evidence, and lift the trash bags from their cans and place them in fresh, marked evidence bags. "Don't walk on the trail on the way out," she said. "We need to minimize the damage we inflict on the scene." Before they left, she had them stamp their feet in the dirt next to Diego's footprint.

As they jogged off, Beamer seemed confused. "We going to pick the trash?"

"At some point, we might have to. We'll keep them in your basement for now."

"Figures."

"We'll be gone in a week. You ever cast prints?"

"I think I did it on a case once."

Maybe it was something she should do herself. "I've been circling outward from the hole. You can take over while I cast?"

"Sure. Plastering equipment is in the bag."

She kneeled down, opened the duffel, and withdrew a six-pound bag of Hydrocal plaster, a two-gallon jug of water, a set of mixing cups, two spatulas, and a roll of plastic bags. There were five distinct tracks she had already spotted. One looked like it belonged to a dog, one probably belonged to Adelmo, one may have been Jessica's, and two were unknown. One could be the unsub's. She carried the materials over to the first set of tracks, loaded some Hydrocal into a mixing cup, added water, and stirred the mixture with a spatula.

"My uncle raves about you," Beamer called over as he scooped up a paper cup and placed it into an evidence bag.

"He was a big help to me a few months ago."

"He says all he did was get out of your way."

"That's my favorite kind of help."

He chuckled. "I wish I could give you that kind of help."

"I wish so, too."

He scooped up a cellophane wrapper and bagged it. "You think there's any chance that the people who had these phones are still alive?"

"If there were ten phones, or twenty phones, maybe there'd be some chance. But you can only hide a hundred people if they're dead."

"That would make this the biggest serial murder case in this state since . . ." He paused. "Maybe ever. And right now, there are four of us working the case, two of whom are traffic cops."

When the mixture had the consistency of pancake batter, Dagny stopped stirring it. She held the spatula a half inch over the print and slowly poured the plaster so that it landed on the spatula before it trickled into the dirt.

"Why do you do that?" he asked.

The kid wanted to learn, which was a good thing. "If you pour it in, the force of the mix hitting the dirt alters the print. You want it to trickle in, so it doesn't mess up the impression."

Once the print was filled, she ran the spatula up and down the top of the plaster, mashing out air bubbles. It would take about fifteen minutes to harden, so she moved to the next print and repeated the process.

While they collected evidence, she filled Beamer in on everything she had learned, recounting her meeting with the families the night before, the interview with the boys in the morning, and their tracking of Adelmo's phone to the woods. She asked if he had heard a rumor that someone bragged about killing immigrants on *The Hank Frank Show*, and he said he had not.

After two hours, she was satisfied that they had the bulk of what they could get. In a perfect world, a team of fifty agents would have shut down the park for days so they could comb the place for evidence. This wasn't a perfect world.

CHAPTER 15

Officer John Beamer lived in a small brick house on a street crowded with them. He pulled into the carport next to the house, and he and Dagny carried sacks filled with evidence to the front door. Sliding the key into the hole, he turned to her and said, "Please excuse the mess. I didn't expect my house to be commandeered today."

"You're single and, what? Twenty-seven?"

"Twenty-eight."

"Then you live like a college student, except you frame your posters instead of taping them to the wall. I'm not expecting you to be tidy."

He pushed the door open, and she stepped into the small foyer. A *Star Wars* poster was framed on the wall. She smiled at him.

"It's an original from 1977. Hung in the glass box outside the Bilford Movie House," he said defensively. "And it's in great condition."

"I didn't say anything."

"It's a work of art." He led her to the kitchen. An empty pizza box lay on the counter. Dishes were stacked in the sink. He caught her eyes inventorying it all. "Look, I told you I didn't clean up."

"John, I haven't said a word."

"You don't have to say anything when you think as loud as you do." He opened the door to the basement and flipped on the light. They carried the bags down the steps.

The basement was small and lightly finished. The floor was carpeted, the walls were plastered, and drop panels and fluorescent lights covered the ceiling. In one corner of the room was a large flat-screen television and a love seat. PlayStation controllers lay on the floor between them. Seven long tables were set up along the walls circling the rest of the room, covered by an elaborate electric train set that wound its way through model towns and countryside. Dagny walked closer to study it. Hand-painted figurines performed the work of the townsfolk. A mailman was sliding a letter into a mailbox. A painter stood on the top of a ladder in mid-brushstroke, touching up the sign on a restaurant. A policewoman was placing a ticket on a car windshield.

"This is incredible," she said.

He smiled with pride. "I've been working on it for years. Look at this." He reached behind the barbershop and flipped a switch. The barber pole on the front of the shop began to spin. "I did that last night."

"You're a complete nerd."

"Well, I don't think, I mean—"

"I mean it in the best possible way, from one nerd to another."

He harrumphed. "A pretty girl isn't a nerd just because she got good grades."

"Well, sincerely, I think this," she said, gesturing to the train set, "is fantastic. Remarkable, really. I love it." She paused for a moment. "It's a shame we need these tables, and it all has to come down."

"Excuse me?"

"We need these tabletops. There's a lot we need to lay out and mark."

"But—"

"Do you have any other folding tables? Another room we could set them in?"

He shook his head. "But—"

"It's a fantastic train display. On the other hand, we've got something like a hundred murders to solve."

"It doesn't just come off—it's all screwed down. The mountains are plaster of paris."

"I promise I'll help you put it all back together when this case is over. We'll be careful with the mountains and rebuild anything that breaks. I'll even fix the barber pole so it spins the right way."

"It spins the right . . ." He paused to study the pole. "You really think it's supposed to go the other way?"

She nodded.

Dagny snapped photographs of the train display so they would have a guide for reassembling it. They spent the next two hours taking down the train set: placing each box in a marked plastic bag, inventorying them, and arranging them carefully in cardboard boxes that stacked under the tables.

Once the tables were cleared, she put on a pair of latex gloves and opened the bag with the phones. Using the tips of her index finger and thumb, she pinched the top phone—a Motorola Razr flip phone—at the bottom corners, which seemed to be the part least likely to have been touched. She carried the phone to the first table and set it down carefully.

"John, I need you to put a Post-it with numbers, starting with one, in front of each phone that I set down. Get a notebook and start keeping a page for each phone, listing its number, make, and model. Leave the rest of the page blank—we'll fill it in more once we're able to extract information from the phone."

"This is going to take us a while," he noted.

"You have some *Clone Wars* episodes you need to watch or something? Or do you only care about canon?"

He shook his head. "*Clone Wars* is canon. *Rebels*, I'd argue, isn't, although many would disagree. Where do you stand?"

"I don't even consider the prequels to be canon. See, I told you I was a nerd."

"You're not a nerd if you only like the original trilogy."

"I liked The Force Awakens."

"Not a nerd."

It took them nearly an hour to unpack and number the phones. Diego arrived with a dozen bags of cables and cords as they were marking the last of them: number eighty-one.

Eighty-one phones. Altogether, they covered almost every square inch of Beamer's train tables. Each one represented a young man who was most likely dead.

"How can this be?" Diego said. "How can this many people disappear before anyone cares?"

No one answered, because there was no good answer. They stood in silent contemplation of the scope of the crime. She wondered where someone could hide eighty-one dead bodies.

If they were going to do something about it, there wasn't time for moping. She turned to Beamer. "How are your printing skills?"

"I have excellent penmanship."

"I mean fingerprinting."

"Good," he replied, with some hesitation.

"We can dust these phones for prints twice as fast if you start from one end and I start from the other."

"I can do it."

Cops were better than special agents at getting people to talk. They knew their communities. They noticed when things were wrong. They were capable of empathy and knew how to employ it in service of their job. But when it came to matters of evidence handling and chain of custody, cops were terrible. Some of them lacked the patience for it. Some of them figured they'd make their case on witness testimony.

Some of them knew that the medical examiner or coroner would cover for them, blessing their shoddy work in court. And some of them didn't know they were doing it wrong every time they did it. Beamer didn't seem like that kind of cop, but Dagny needed to be sure. She dug into her bag for her kit and tossed it to Beamer. "Show me what you can do on number one."

He walked over to the Motorola Razr on the first table and opened the kit. "So, I have to pass a test?"

She nodded.

He looked at the phone, and then at the various powders in the kit. The Razr was silver, and he was trying to decide whether that meant he should use a white or black powder, she figured. After moving his hand back and forth between them, he picked black.

"Wrong."

"I was going to pick white."

"Black is fine. But before you do any dusting, you have to photograph the phone. You might catch some prints that way, especially on the screen."

He nodded and set the kit down. "Hold on." He ran upstairs and came back with a desk lamp and a camera.

"For each one, snap a picture of the Post-it with the number on it first, so we know which prints came from which camera."

"Okay." He followed her instructions and took several photographs of the first phone. Then he opened the canister of black powder and applied it to the phone. A couple of good prints appeared. He lifted them with tape and placed them on a transfer card. Dagny inspected his work. It was fine.

"Print your name, the number, the location, and the date on the card."

He spoke as he wrote it. "John Beamer, Number One, my basement . . ."

"The location *where we found it*," she said.

"I was joking," he said. "The fact that you didn't know tells me how dumb you think I am." He held up the card so she could see it. Under location, he'd listed the coordinates from the park where the bag of phones had been found. "Really dumb, it seems."

"Sorry," she said. "It's a reflex." She turned to Diego. "I need you to set up the power bricks and extension cords, so they'll be easily accessible at each table. Then try to find a cord that will power each phone after we lift prints from it. Touch the phone only with gloves, as little as possible, at only the bottom corners of the phone. As soon as they power on, switch them to airplane mode and power them down. We've got to keep them from being contaminated with new data."

Diego nodded. "You weren't kidding when you said this would be tedious. It's almost like—"

"A Catholic Mass?" she said.

"Like a thousand of them," Beamer replied.

He started with the first and Dagny with the last, and they worked their way toward the middle. Diego followed behind them at each end. By eleven thirty they had finished dusting for prints. About half of them had yielded usable results. They were able to power all but two of the phones, which seemed to be particularly obscure, foreign models.

Before leaving, she took the men through a task list. The most important items were to extract all usable information from each telephone, run the prints through IAFIS, and interview Hank Frank and Jessica Marigold. Pulling the phone data was crucial, and it was likely to take days. Beamer wasn't free to keep shirking work to assist, and Diego could assist in small tasks but couldn't undertake much on his own. If this case were going to be cracked, it was all on Dagny.

Beamer gave her an extra key to his house and walked them to the door. When they walked outside, a car was parking in front of the house. A short, bald man stepped out of the car and walked toward them, carrying a Cellebrite in hand.

She smiled. "Ron Beamer, so good to see you."

He gave her a hug. "You, too, Dagny." Turning to his nephew, he said, "Johnny, Johnny, what have you gotten yourself into?"

"It'll be in all the papers eventually," the young cop replied.

"That bad?"

"Worse than you can imagine."

Ron handed her the Cellebrite. It looked a little like a larger, heavier version of a Nintendo Game Boy. "These things cost fifteen thousand dollars, so—"

"I'll be careful."

"Cheap for Feebs, but expensive for CPD."

She smiled at him. "Thank you, Ron."

While the Beamers caught up with each other, Diego handed her the keys to his Corvette. "Take it," he said.

"I'll give you a ride."

"I'm not far from here. I can walk."

"It's no problem," she said.

"I need to process everything," he said. "It will be good for me." He started down the sidewalk and then turned back. "I can do a lot, Dagny. Use me. It's not all on you."

She nodded. "Get some sleep. We're both useless if we're tired."

He started walking again toward home.

She climbed into the Corvette and started the engine. Her phone buzzed, which meant that Victor had sent his nightly text reminding her to enter her points into the Weight Watchers program. There were no points to enter, of course, since she'd gone the entire day without eating. This, she knew, was a bad habit to start. No matter how frantic the pace of the case, she had to stop for meals. Two a day, at least.

She drove around the streets of downtown Bilford. Boarded-up storefronts were plentiful. So were convenience marts and dollar stores. There was not a drive-through to be found. The entire town seemed to be asleep.

It was a twenty-minute drive to New Bilford and its plethora of parking lots and Applebee's. Box stores, full and empty. Gas stations on every corner. And plenty of fast-food restaurants, all of them bustling.

McDonald's, Burger King, Taco Bell, and Wendy's were all open. She chose the least awful of them and pulled into the Wendy's drive-through lane. Scanning the menu board, she assessed the calories and calculated what she needed for a full day.

"I'll have a Double with everything, large fry, and a medium Frosty."

She drove foreword, paid the tab, and took the bag and cup from the cashier. It was heavier than any bag of dinner should be, she thought. She pulled into a parking space and took out the burger. It was a mess. Ketchup was dripping off the side. The cheese hadn't been centered, so a good part of it was stuck to the inside of the foil wrapper. She scraped the cheese off the foil with her finger and put it in her mouth.

It was after midnight, and she was alone in the parking lot of a Wendy's in New Bilford, Ohio, forcing herself to eat a disgusting bag of meat and grease. This was her life. Constantly battling anorexia. Suspended without pay from her job. Heading back to a filthy motel room. No one knew where she was at this moment because no one cared. She was thirty-five years old and had nothing to show for it, and no one to show it to. And there was no reason to think this would ever change.

She started to cry as she stuffed the edge of the burger into her mouth. Moments like this seemed to come too often these days.

She thought about calling Dr. Childs. Instead, she turned on the radio and listened to classic rock while she ate. First, a Zeppelin tune played, then one from Pink Floyd. The third song was Nirvana. The music Dagny had listened to in high school was now classic rock. She flicked off the radio and finished her meal. On her way out of the parking lot, she drove up to a trash can and pitched her bag and cup.

Driving to the motel, she fretted over the impossibility of the task at hand, because despairing over a case was always easier than despairing over life. Her troubles were trifles compared to the losses suffered in Bilford.

As she pulled into the motel parking lot, she noticed the silhouette of a man sitting in front of her door. She grabbed her gun and walked up the steps.

When she stepped onto the landing, Victor stood and walked toward her.

He was exactly what she needed. She holstered her gun, threw her arms around him, and gave him a hug. "You're supposed to be in New York."

"The Professor still thinks I'm there, so don't say anything to him."

She broke the embrace and smiled at him. "What are you doing here?"

"I finished my case and figured you could use some help."

"You finished it?"

"I've been through all the documents. I told the Professor it would take me a couple of more weeks, but I'm done. Everything labeled and tabbed, even marked as exhibits for a trial. All tied up in a bow."

"And Brent?"

"He's still interviewing witnesses, taking statements. As far as he knows, I'm still at the document warehouse."

"How did you put everything together so fast?"

He shrugged. "Sifting through and making sense of massive amounts of information is my idea of fun, Dagny."

She smiled. "Well, then, I've got the job for you."

CHAPTER 16

....

The thin man sat in his parked Ford F-150 pickup, taking swigs from his flask, trying to make sense of the scene playing out on that second-floor landing. The woman had hugged the man waiting at her door and then invited him in. What was their relationship? A lover? There was no kiss. Family, perhaps. A brother, maybe. Or her partner.

None of it made much sense to him. He had killed eighty-five Mexicans. He'd confessed to the crimes on Hank Frank's talk show. He'd planted the cell phones in the park. Cops should have been combing the streets. It should have been the biggest news story in the country. Instead, four people spent a few hours picking up trash in the park. When they finished, they didn't go to the police station—they went to the young officer's house. Who was this woman? She wasn't local. Possibly ICE, possibly FBI. Probably FBI, he decided. But why were they working out of the officer's house?

The door to her motel room opened, and the man stepped out. Red hair, young. Some meat on his bones—fleshy, not muscular. The guy walked down the landing and opened another door. So, he had his own room. Clearly, they were not lovers. And now she was alone.

The thin man opened the glove box and pulled out a box of Camels, slid one from the package, and lit it. He rolled down his window and blew out a cloud of smoke. She was pretty, wasn't she? And she was up in that room, all alone, thinking about him. That made him smile.

He imagined opening his car door, walking up those steps, and opening her door. Her eyes would be closed; her chest would be heaving with every breath. A quick gag to the mouth would stop her from screaming; he could detain her with ropes around her wrists and ankles, tied to the bedposts. Reaching down below his seat, he pulled out his bowie knife, unsheathed it, and turned it in his hand. He imagined plunging it into her chest as she lay tied on the bed. Eighty-five dead Mexicans wasn't enough to get some attention, but a knife in the heart of an FBI agent would do it.

She could have stayed anywhere in the county, but she chose the Bilford Motor Inn. It was almost as if fate demanded he do it.

If he was going to do this, she'd need some time to fall asleep, and he'd need some time to get supplies. He turned the key, started his engine, and drove home, thinking about the FBI agent. She was thin, like him. There was virtue in that. There was too much fat in the world, too much gluttony and greed.

He lived in a two-story house on a large, rural lot, surrounded by trees. Parking his truck on his gravel drive, he ran inside and down the steps to the basement, where he gathered sheets, rope, and a tennis ball, and stuffed them into a bag. Cardboard boxes were stacked against a wall, and he picked through them until he found a Ziploc bag full of keys. Reaching into the bag, he found a gold key with an oversize handle that read in engraved letters BILFORD MOTOR INN, MASTER. He'd swiped it during his short tenure as the motel janitor a few years back.

The thin man ran up the steps with the key and the bag and darted into the kitchen. There was a black case on top of the refrigerator, and he pulled it down and set it on the counter. Opening it, he pulled out the gun, loaded a cartridge, and tucked it into his waistband. She'd have a gun, he figured, so he'd need one, too.

It was nearly 3:00 a.m. when he parked across the street from the Bilford Motor Inn. He tossed his knife into the bag with the ropes and sheets and pressed the gold key in his hand. Steeling himself, he lit a cigarette and took some puffs. All the room lights at the motel were off. He rolled down his window to listen. Bilford was quiet, except for the breeze. He stepped out of the car and carried the bag across the street and through the inn's parking lot. Grabbing the rail, he started up the metal steps to the second-floor landing, his fingers wrapped so tightly around the teeth of the master key that they pierced his skin. He lessened his grip and walked toward the woman's door, tossed his cigarette to the floor, and stepped on it. Setting his bag down, he grabbed the gun from his waistband with his left hand and inserted the key into her doorknob with his right.

He tried to turn the key, but it wouldn't turn.

He smiled. The bastards were too cheap to give him a raise, but somehow they'd found enough money to upgrade the locks.

It was time to come up with another way to get some attention.

CHAPTER 17

After World War I, the military sent its return vehicles and tanks on a cross-country tour from New York City to San Francisco. Lieutenant Colonel Dwight Eisenhower traveled with the convoy over broken, confusing, and meandering roads, many of which weren't paved. Some vehicles slipped into ditches, while others got stuck in mud and sand. Twenty years later, General Eisenhower advanced his troops into Germany on the Autobahn, the beautiful and durable four-lane super-highways that permitted rapid, uninterrupted movement from city to city. Smitten with the soaring overpasses and wide lanes, Eisenhower made a nationwide highway system a centerpiece of his political agenda. As president, he signed the Federal Aid Highway Act of 1956, allocating $25 billion to the construction of a massive interstate highway system.

Detroit, unions, planners, and the oil and construction industries did well under the Federal Aid Highway Act. So, too, did the big cities that were connected by the national highways and the small towns lucky enough to be included on the routes between them. But these highways couldn't connect every town. Once planners decided the high-way wouldn't pass through downtown Bilford, there wasn't any reason to build anything new there.

The Bilford Motor Inn was the last significant construction in downtown Bilford. It opened in 1953, with a ceremony involving the mayor, a ribbon, and a comically oversized pair of scissors. Folks were proud of the addition to their town. Families spent their post-war sur-plus on vacations, and they didn't fly—they drove. Bilford might not have been a destination, but it was a place they'd stop along the way, and maybe they'd spend a buck or two while they did. The motel was clean and new and modern; it had a television in every room, like a Hilton. For its first three years, the motel's neon **VACANCY** sign was never lit. But once the highways went in, no one passed through Bilford anymore, and the vacancy light was always on until it burned out.

When her phone beeped at four forty-five, Dagny was already tying her sneakers. Getting by on three hours of sleep was about as smart as feasting on midnight combo meals, but running was the only thing that calmed her. She holstered her gun under a *Late Night With David Letterman* zip-up sweatshirt and grabbed the earbuds for her iPhone. Fiona Apple's "Extraordinary Machine" carried her out the door, down the stairs, and over the sidewalks of Bilford.

Dagny had a sense of New York and Austin and Cleveland. She understood Portland and Decatur, Macon and Orlando. When she was chasing Martin Benny, she knew Chicago, and that kind of thing mat-tered. She had no sense of Bilford. She didn't know, for example, if the downtown streets were dangerous or just desolate. The money in New Bilford was coming from somewhere, but she had no idea what it could be. Agriculture? Pharmaceuticals? Was there a factory making things? Was there old money there? What was the average income? What was the median income? What kind of music did the local bands play? Were there any local bands? What percentage of townsfolk had high school diplomas or college degrees? When kids left Bilford to go to college, did they ever come back? She knew Sheriff Don held an elected office, but was there a sizable opposition to the man? A vocal one?

As she sprinted past homes, she noticed that many of the smallest of them had American flags and window boxes of flowers. Although there were some Toyotas and Hondas in their driveways, there were more Fords and Chryslers. These details told her that she was in a small town but little else. There were bumper stickers on the back of some of the cars, and they tended to favor politicians and policies rarely featured on bumper stickers back in her hometown of Alexandria. She noticed that the sidewalks were cracked and uneven, upended by tree roots at irregular intervals. It was not a runner's paradise, but Bilford probably wasn't a runner's town.

Track four—a driving, bouncy song called "Better Version of Me"—propelled Dagny to the downtown business district. There wasn't a lot of business in it. The half-lit marquee above the theater read 12 Angry Men: The Musical. The Bilford Art Gallery appeared, by her quick glance, to be more of a craft show, though a well-stocked one. Half the storefronts were empty. The remainder seemed makeshift antique stores and restaurants, all decorated lightly enough to suggest their owners weren't counting on anything.

Everything about downtown Bilford was charming, and all that charm was being wasted. She tried to imagine a circumstance that could bring it back to life but couldn't. People who like cities move to bigger ones. Nobody was going to move to Bilford.

But that wasn't true, Dagny realized. Immigrants had been coming here, and a hundred small towns like it. The rent was low. Farms were close and needed labor. So did dairies and meatpacking facilities. There was a lot of construction in New Bilford. Someone had to put the roof on an Applebee's. Someone had to clean the Hampton Inn. She wondered what would happen to downtown Bilford if the immigrants were free to live conspicuously. Maybe it would thrive.

She sprinted through the city square and around a statute of a soldier on a horse. There must be some law that said every small town had to have a statue of a soldier on a horse, she figured. Each step woke her senses and jolted her with a burst of life. She hurdled a park bench, just to prove she could, and then hurdled another.

Bolting across the street, she raced up the thirty-seven steps that led to the entrance of the Bilford courthouse. It was enormous—a relic from a time when every town required an imposing edifice fronted by marble columns. She paused at the top of the steps to take in the view of the city, or what she could see of it in the predawn light. Somewhere out there were anguished families, praying that the missing were still alive. Somewhere, in the dark of the night, was a madman bent on more devastation.

Dagny bounded down the steps of the courthouse and ran for another hour and a half—up the hillside, across one-lane bridges, beyond the city limits, past Sheriff Don's tents, through cornfields and woods. As she circled back, the sun began to peek over the horizon. It gave a glowing aura to the silhouette of a man kneeling on top of a small house, pounding a mallet against the roof. She stopped in the front lawn of the house and looked up. The man was shirtless, trim and muscular. He wiped his forehead with his arm and then pounded some more.

"Good morning, Diego."

He stopped and looked down at her. "Up early, I see."

"You, too."

He walked to the edge of the roof and climbed down a ladder. A scorpion tattoo covered a good third of his back.

"Didn't know a priest could have a tattoo."

"Rabbis can't?"

"Jews can't."

"That's funny," he said. "I've known plenty of Jews who had them."

He grabbed the T-shirt that was lying on his front porch and put it on.

"You really don't believe in God?" she asked.

"Huh?"

"Yesterday, you said you didn't believe in him." She'd let the statement pass at the time, but it lingered in her mind.

"Yeah, I don't know."

"How can you be a priest if you don't believe in God?"

He shrugged a little and smiled. "I like the idea of God. And at the end of the day, it's more important to like the idea of him than it is to actually believe in him."

That made some sense, and she decided not to question it further, lest it fall apart. She wondered what inspired the scorpion tattoo but decided not to ask. "A colleague of mine—Special Agent Victor Walton Jr.—is going to tackle the phones today."

"You've brought in reinforcements?"

"Only one, and he's here on the sly. But there's no one better for this kind of thing. I want you to spend the day with him. He'll need help translating texts and e-mails."

"Sure. What are you going to do?"

Hank Frank was leaning on the hood of a Ford Escape in the parking lot of WKBL studios. As soon as Dagny pulled into the lot, he was off the car and coming toward her. Middle-aged and slightly worn, Frank had an earnest look about him. He seemed to be a man who had lived a few lives and was grateful for the one he had now.

"I thought it was a prank," he said, leaning over her car. She grabbed her backpack and slung it over her shoulder. "We get those sometimes in radio."

He was, it seemed, looking for absolution—for her to tell him that it wouldn't have made a difference if he had gone to the cops about the phone call. He'd have to work for absolution; she didn't give it out for free.

She climbed out of the car and shook his hand. "Good to meet you, Mr. Frank."

"I'm so sorry if this guy was real. But there was nothing in the papers. No one was talking about missing people. So, it seemed like a hoax."

"Why don't we go inside?"

There wasn't much to WKBL studios. Two glass booths, a control room, and a handful of small offices, one of which had a **HANK FRANK** nameplate on the door. Frank took a seat behind his desk, and she sat across from him. He grabbed a disc from the shelf behind his desk, put it into a CD player, and hit "Play."

"Brother, you are speaking the truth today. You are speaking the word of God."

It was, in all likelihood, the voice of a mass murderer. Their voices were always chilling, she thought. It wasn't because they spoke with a different cadence than everyone else; it was because they spoke with the *same* cadence as everyone else. A serial killer sounded like the neighbor you'd spoken to only twice. That's why their voices were terrifying.

"Sometimes I feel so alone. And then, to hear your voice, speaking so rationally. Speaking such sanity. These people are taking our jobs. They're taking our money. They're taking our lives, Hank."

She reached over to the player and hit "Pause." Frank started to say something, but she stopped him with a wave of her hand. Something struck her about the caller's tone. She hit the back arrow and listened to the start of the call again, playing it through to the end.

"They're killing us. They are killing us, Hank. And that's why I'm killing them."

And then Hank Frank's voice: "It's killing us, John."

And the murderer: "Which is why I'm killing them. I'm killing all of them. I'm killing them—"

Click.

She played the message a few more times. The sentences built upon each other in a very natural way—too natural for extemporaneous speech. *Taking our lives* flowed into *killing us*, which served as the predicate for the declaration that he was *killing them*. It wasn't merely a declaration; it was an argument, stated in its simplest form. It was a performance, in fact. The unsub wanted to declare his crimes in a dramatic way. To heighten the drama, he wanted his reveal to be a surprise. And so he used the vernacular of the average caller to build to that reveal.

There were two main reasons a murderer would kill illegal immigrants, she figured. First, he might despise them for all the reasons they were sometimes despised: misguided patriotism, bigotry, fear, or delusion. Second, he simply might like killing, and it was easy to kill illegal immigrants. There's no documentation of their existence. Families feared working with the authorities. People assumed the missing had moved back home or to another town. It seemed to Dagny that the killer here was wearing the guise of the first kind but was more likely to be the second.

In a way, Hank Frank was right: The call was a prank—of sorts. He wanted the police to look for someone full of political malice and hatred, because he didn't have any.

Or maybe that was all wrong. Listening to the recording one more time made her less confident of her conclusions. She wished she had the Professor's opinion of the call. He was a genius at deciphering the psychological makeup of an unsub.

"Do you have the number of the caller?"

He slid a piece of paper across his desk. It was a printout from the station's log, and it listed the number, date, time, and duration of the call. In a proper investigation, she would subpoena telecommunication companies for any information regarding the ownership of the account associated with the number. Better yet, she would query the FBI's own database. Although Bureau spokespeople had publicly denied it, the FBI kept a database of information on millions of cell phones—things like device identification numbers, phone numbers, owner names, and addresses. The NSA had even more data like this. She lamented the fact that her antisocial disposition within the Bureau left her with no friendly contacts with those who had access to this kind of data. This was the price of surliness and introversion.

She pulled out her iPhone.

"You're calling him?"

"No." If the unsub were still using the phone, calling the number would cause him to ditch it, and they wouldn't be able to use it to track his movements. She used her phone to Google the number, and when nothing came up, texted the number to Victor to see if he might have some luck with it.

Dagny punched the "Eject" button and put the disc back into its sleeve, placed it and the printout in her backpack, and stood up to leave.

Frank rose, too. "That's it?"

"That's it, Mr. Frank."

He walked her to the door, continuing his quest for forgiveness. "I assure you, ma'am, if I thought he was really killing anyone, I would have reported it immediately."

"How many listeners do you have for an average show, Mr. Frank?"

"Twenty thousand or so."

"Well, twenty thousand people heard the same thing you did, and none of them called the police, either. So I wouldn't feel so bad."

He nodded, but it was slight enough to show that he appreciated the effort more than he actually bought it.

Bilford High School was fifty years old and looked every bit of it. Worn brick, cracked windows, peeling paint—the only thing that looked new was the football stadium scoreboard, half of which served as a billboard for John Weeney Chevrolet. A security guard stood inside the door. When Dagny flashed her creds, he didn't know what to do.

"Tell me where the principal's office is," she said, and he did.

As she walked toward the office, the bell rang and students poured out of the classrooms, headed toward their next classes. About a tenth of them seemed to be Hispanic. She tried to gauge whether there were more girls than boys, but it was hard to keep track as the sea of students kept shifting.

High schools made her uncomfortable. She'd struggled during her high school years—not academically, but in every other way. The institution was cruel by design. It's the last time in life that people don't get to choose their environment and their acquaintances. Everyone is stuck being with everyone. It's like being at the DMV for four years, except that someone is elected prom queen.

The principal's office had a waiting room with eight seats along the wall facing the receptionist. Half the seats were filled with surly teens; one, with a nervous parent.

"I need to talk to the principal," Dagny said, setting her creds on the counter.

The woman picked up the credentials and inspected them. She seemed worried. "Is there a bomb?" she whispered.

"No."

The receptionist eyed her for a moment, then led her to the back office, where a middle-aged woman sat at a desk, sifting through one of many stacks of papers on her desk. "Can I help you?" A sign on her desk read **PRINCIPAL GEATHERS**.

She handed the woman her creds. "I'm Special Agent Dagny Gray."

The principal glanced at the credentials and handed them back to her. "I'm Deborah Geathers. What can I do for you?"

"One of your students is missing. Adelmo Fox."

"Dear Lord. Adelmo?" She frowned.

"I need two things. First, I'd like to see his file. Second, we need to talk to Jessica Marigold. A private room would be best. She may have been the last to see him."

"Of course." The principal buzzed her secretary. "Sandra, I need the file on Adelmo Fox, please." She turned back to Dagny. "Jessica has Spanish now. I'll go get her." She pointed to the door at the back of her office. "You can use my conference room."

Any principal who knew when a student had Spanish class was doing her job, Dagny thought. And the fact that she was fetching Jessica Marigold suggested that she cared more about her missing student than she was afraid of Sheriff Don.

Dagny went to the conference room and took a seat at its small round table. Sandra brought her Adelmo's file, and she paged through it. Mostly A grades. Never in trouble. Played on the soccer team. Adelmo was a good kid.

There was a knock at the door. "Come in."

A gangly girl with long, straight hair and a crooked smile walked in. Dagny didn't like her immediately.

"So, like, what's the deal here?" Jessica asked.

"Please, sit down."

The girl obeyed.

Dagny opened her credentials. "I'm Special Agent Dagny Gray."

"Do I need a lawyer or something?"

"No. Adelmo Fox is missing, and I'm talking to everyone who saw him over the past few days." This was stretching the truth, but it would make Jessica feel more comfortable and, hopefully, more candid. No one wanted to be the only person questioned about anything. Little lies like this were the fuel that powered all investigations. "I know you saw him two nights ago?"

"Yes."

Dagny pulled out her iPad and started taking notes. "You were his girlfriend?"

"We dated," she said, which was less than *yes*.

"For how long?"

"A couple of months."

"You saw him two nights ago?"

"Yes."

"Where?"

"In the woods behind Hillsborough Park."

"What time?"

"It was, like, midnight."

"Can you do better than that?"

"Maybe close to one."

"Why were you meeting in the woods?"

"We couldn't meet at his house, and we couldn't meet at mine. He didn't want to be seen in public, because of my dad, I guess." She shrugged.

Dagny stared at her; sometimes that worked better than asking questions.

"I don't know," Jessica said. "He was weird sometimes. I think he thought it was romantic to be in the woods at one in the morning in the freezing dark."

"So, it was his idea to meet?"

"Yeah."

"Why did he want to meet then?"

"To make out, probably. He always wanted to meet after his mom went to bed. I'd sneak out, too."

"You don't seem to care much about him."

"I like Adelmo, but he's way too much into me. It's a little creepy."

"Explain."

"He always wanted to talk to me about his feelings. Insisted on carrying my books in the hall. Holding doors. Stuff like that."

"So, he was really nice to you and wanted to talk a lot?" Dagny had tried to suppress the judgment, but this slipped through.

"We're sixteen," Jessica said, which was a fair enough retort.

"Who got to the woods first?"

"He did."

"What was he doing when you got there?"

"Like, kneeling on a blanket. Looking for something in the grass."

Dagny reached into her backpack and pulled out a clear Ziploc bag with the ring in it. She held it up for the girl to see. "This, maybe?"

Jessica stared at the ring for a few moments. A tear started down her cheek. "You found that in the woods?"

"Yes." Dagny put the bag back in her backpack.

"I didn't know . . ." She didn't finish the thought.

"Did he propose to you?"

"No. I mean, I went there to break up with him. I wanted to do it in person. That seemed like the right thing to do."

"Tell me what happened."

"I told him that I cared about him, but that something wasn't right in our relationship, and if we continued further, we'd both end up getting hurt. I told him I wanted him to find the girl he deserves, but right now, that wasn't me."

"You said that?" Dagny was pretty sure she hadn't.

"Yeah."

"And how did he take it?"

"I don't know. The whole thing was very emotional—very hard for me. So I left."

"And he was still in the woods?"

"Yes."

"On your way out, did you notice anything unusual? Anyone?"

"No."

"What time did you leave?"

"Like, five minutes after I got there. So a little after one, maybe."

"Did you drive to the park?"

"Yes."

"Parked in the lot?"

"Uh-huh."

"Anyone else in that lot?"

"No."

The answer had come much too quickly. "Think harder."

She sighed. "Well, maybe there was a truck."

"What kind of truck?"

"A pickup truck."

"What make?"

"I don't know. It was night. If I saw it, it was out of the corner of my eye."

"Color?"

Jessica drew a heavy breath. "Dark, I guess. Not white, I think. Something dark."

"Big, little, medium in size?"

"Big, I guess. Not little."

"Did you see a driver?"

"No."

Dagny opened a sketch program on the iPad and drew a version of the parking lot. "Show me where you parked and where the pickup was."

"I was here," the girl said, touching a space to the far left on the map. "And the pickup was here," she said, touching a space on the far right.

"License plates?"

"I don't know." She sighed.

"Anything in the back of the truck?"

"I don't think so."

"Bumper stickers?"

She sighed again. "I mean, I told you I don't know."

Dagny leaned back and stared coldly at the girl. "Whoever drove that truck probably killed Adelmo that night, right after you left. You may not care about that, but I do, so I'm going to keep asking you questions until I can't think of any more."

This was enough to summon some tears. "You said he was missing," the girl said. "I thought you meant he'd run away or something." She wiped away the tears, but they kept coming. "You didn't say he was dead."

Dagny was relieved to see actual emotion from the girl. "This is important."

The girl nodded. "I don't remember bumper stickers or anything."

"Did your father know that you were seeing Adelmo?"

"No." The girl studied her. "You don't believe my dad did something, do you?"

"No." If Adelmo had been the only young man to disappear, the xenophobic father of his girlfriend would be high on the list of suspects, but there were others who'd gone missing as well. "I find it interesting that you would date a young Hispanic man in light of your father's public stance on immigration."

"Yeah, well, that's just him, you know. It's not me."

"Why were you seeing Adelmo?"

She shrugged. "I don't know. I guess I was curious."

"Curious about?"

"What they're like."

"You mean Hispanics?"

"Yeah. I mean, everyone is making such a big deal about them."

"And what did you learn?"

"Nothing. I mean, he's the same as any other guy."

Dagny smiled. If you're going to learn nothing, this was a good thing to learn. "You have any Hispanic friends?"

"No."

"Do you know whether any other kids have gone missing?"

"No. Why? What happened here?"

"If I knew, I wouldn't be asking you questions." The girl wasn't as bad as she had first thought. Being the daughter of Sheriff Don was enough to mess anyone up, and she was doing pretty well, all things considered. "What's the atmosphere here at school with respect to immigration?"

"Less crazy than outside school, I guess. Nobody cares, really. I mean, don't get me wrong, there's not a lot of hanging out between groups."

"Any tension?"

"They're just another clique. I don't hang out with skateboarders, either."

"Anyone date across lines—apart from you and Adelmo?"

"Not really."

She wanted certainty and specificity. "Anyone at all?"

"Not that I can think of."

"Why not?"

Jessica shrugged. "I mean, it's not just here, right? Black people marry black people. White people marry white people. Asians marry Asians. Yeah, sometimes people cross those lines, but you notice when they do because it's so unusual. It's not like this is the only fucked-up place in the world. My dad may be an asshole, but he didn't ruin everything." The girl seemed to register Dagny's disapproval. "Whatever. I'm sorry I cursed."

Dagny looked down at the girl's shoes—pink canvas sneakers. "Those the shoes you wore to the park to meet with Adelmo?"

She looked down at her feet. "Yeah."

"Hand me one of them."

"Seriously?"

Dagny nodded.

Jessica took off a shoe and handed it to Dagny, who photographed the bottom and top of the shoe to capture the pattern of the sole and the shoe size. She gave the shoe back to the girl. "We're done."

"Can I see the ring?"

Dagny reached back into her backpack and pulled out the Ziploc. "It has to stay in the bag." She handed it to the girl.

Jessica pinched the ring through the bag and held it against her ring finger. She started to cry again. "I was mean to him. I was terrible. And all he did was love me." She handed the bag back to Dagny, stood, and started to leave.

"Jessica."

She turned back. "Yes?"

"You're sixteen."

"Yeah."

"You'll be nice the next time."

When the girl left, Principal Geathers was waiting at the door. She placed a stack of folders down. "I've got four more kids who disappeared over the last month. It didn't seem like anything because kids come and go, their families move around. But if you think something happened to Adelmo, you ought to look at these, too."

Dagny flipped through the stack. All boys. Average and above in grades. "Have you tried their families?"

"Yes, but there was no response."

"That's strange."

"You'd think so, but it's not. A lot of Hispanic families won't take our calls."

"Why?"

"They see us as the government. We make them nervous."

"How many Hispanic kids are in the school?"

"Sixty, maybe."

"How well do you know them?"

"Some well, some not very."

"Could you pick out a few to talk to me? The ones most plugged into their community, and most likely to talk to me. My Spanish is bad, so fluent in English would be helpful, too."

Geathers hesitated. "That makes me a little nervous."

"I understand," Dagny said.

"I've tried very hard to make them feel this is a safe place. Some families still won't send their kids here. I don't want to lose the ones we have. If they go home and tell their parents that I had them talk to an FBI agent—"

"I will make them feel comfortable. I promise you, I will. But this is important."

Geathers took a moment to decide. "Okay."

Standing in the front of the classroom, Dagny imagined the life of a teacher: going to the same room every day to talk to the same kids every day, moving page by page through the same book every year. The room started to feel like a prison cell. She looked out to the eighteen students Principal Geathers had gathered and figured they were eager to be paroled.

"My name is Special Agent Dagny Gray," she said. "I'm with the Federal Bureau of Investigation." She could feel them pulling away from her, leaning back, crossing their arms. "I'm not concerned with immigration or your status, or the status of your families. I don't care about that at all." She sat on the front of the teacher's desk. "I'm here because Adelmo Fox is missing, and I believe that some harm may have come to him. From what I've learned, others may have disappeared, too—men older than Adelmo, but some his age as well. And I need your help. Will you help me?"

No one said anything.

"I need to know the names of anyone who is missing. How long they've been missing. I need to know the last place you saw them."

Again, there was silence.

"I need this information because they may still be alive."

She scanned the crowd, looking each student directly in the eyes. About two-thirds of them were girls, young and pretty. Some dressed in trendy clothes; some, in hand-me-downs. The boys were a varied bunch—some nerdy, some rough. Two had wispy mustaches. All of these students returned her stare with skepticism but indifference.

"Again, I don't care about whether you or your family are undocumented. I don't work immigration cases, and I don't assist ICE. I mostly stop serial killers, and I think there's one in Bilford."

A boy started to talk, but the crowd shushed him. Never interview people in groups, Dagny thought. The students' eyes darted to the ceiling, the floors, the walls, and at anything that wasn't her. She remembered a time when she was young and a law-enforcement officer asked her questions she didn't want to answer.

Maybe that was something worth sharing.

"When I was a girl, I loved my father as much as any girl could," she said, drawing their interest. "He was a smart and gentle man who took me to Cardinals games, taught me how to ride a bike, read me books every night, and stood up for me when I was picked on." She paused. "When I was twelve, someone shot and killed him." She slid off the desk and started to pace across the front of the room, each step a metered punctuation to her story. Her voice shook as she spoke. "I cannot express to you the extent to which this completely and utterly devastated me. It broke me—because I lost his love, of course, but also because I felt helpless."

They were all looking at her now. "The cops mishandled the investigation—I'm almost sure of it. They didn't talk to everyone they should have. They came to conclusions too quickly. I wasn't impressed with them. I thought cops should be better. At twelve years old, I decided that I was going to be a cop, and I was going to do things right."

These were things she didn't talk about with anyone, and she was sharing them with a class full of teenage strangers. "Sometimes life takes you off track. I grew up and went to college, and then law school. Took a job at a big firm in Manhattan and made a lot of money. Being a lawyer was comfortable and miserable. I sank into the kind of deep, dark depression you don't even know you're in. Every day, I found myself going through the motions, and entire years slipped by and I had nothing to show for them except my bank statements."

Dagny sat back down on the front of the desk. "And then one day a friend of mine was killed by a bomb in the London Underground. My friend and fifty-one others were killed as part of a coordinated attack by al-Qaeda. Their families felt a mixture of loss and helplessness—the kind I knew well. The big-city law firm seemed like the most useless and pointless thing in the world. And I remembered what the twelve-year-old me had understood so clearly.

"I quit my job and applied to the FBI. I was tired of a life without meaning and purpose. I wanted to help people who suffer like I have.

"I've been in Bilford for only a couple of days, but I've seen a helplessness and suffering that feels all too familiar. I can help this community, but only to the extent it will let me. It makes me enormously sad to say that, right now, I'm the best hope you have. So, you need to tell me everything you know. Who is missing? When did they disappear? Where were they last? If you don't tell me these things, more people will disappear. You'll never know whether talking to me could have saved them, but that worry will haunt you for the rest of your lives."

She reached down into her backpack, pulled out her iPad, opened the Notes program, and waited. After ten seconds, a boy said, "Alex Trevino. He's been gone for two weeks. He graduated last year. Last time I saw him, he was trying to get me to help him on a lawn-service job that he'd lined up. He didn't sound like someone who was planning to leave Bilford."

"Thank you," Dagny said, jotting down notes.

A girl raised her hand, and Dagny gestured to her. "Manny Oscar. He's my cousin. Twenty-one. We haven't heard from him in over a week, and we're scared."

Dagny nodded. "Anyone else?"

All of the kids put their hands in the air.

CHAPTER 18

Victor attacked the phones like Vladimir Horowitz at the piano or Bobby Fischer at a chessboard. The sequence was rote, but he performed it like a ballet, connecting the Cellebrite to the phone, sucking its information to an SD card, popping the card into the laptop, downloading the information to a folder, and then moving on to the next phone. Throughout it all, the redheaded boy wonder's hands flitted effortlessly about buttons and ports and keystrokes.

"You're good at this," Diego said.

He laughed. "That's funny, Father."

"No, I'm serious. And please, call me Diego."

"Of course, Father."

Some people wouldn't call a priest by his first name. "Are you Catholic, Victor?"

"Protestant."

"And do you believe?"

Victor stopped for a moment and seemed to give the question some genuine contemplation. "I think so." He returned his attention to the Cellebrite.

While the Cellebrite sucked data from each phone, Diego used the laptop to open the file folder from the previous one, identifying the owners' names and phone numbers, and recording them in the notebook they'd started the previous night. Some of the names, he knew; most, he didn't. He wasn't even sure updating the notebook was helpful, but he had to do something besides sit there.

Victor's phone buzzed. He glanced at the screen and said, "Hmmm."

"What is it?"

"Dagny texted the phone number the unsub used to call *The Hank Frank Show.*"

"That seems promising," Diego said. "I feel dumb asking, but what's an unsub?"

"Unknown subject. Don't feel dumb. I didn't know what it meant until a few months ago."

"So, you only recently became an agent?"

"Graduated from training at the beginning of the year."

"And before that?"

"I worked for an accounting firm for three years out of school."

"How did you end up working with Dagny?"

"Her boss told her she needed a partner. We were in the same counterterrorism class at the academy, and she picked me."

"High praise."

"No, the opposite," Victor said. "She chose me because she thought I was incompetent."

"That doesn't make sense."

"Well, she knew what she was doing," he replied.

"It seems like she always does. She's kind of . . ." Diego searched for the right word.

"She's amazing," he said.

It was close enough. "Yes."

By noon, they'd made their way through half of the phones. Diego jogged to the downtown Quiznos and picked up three sandwiches—the third at Victor's request, just in case Dagny should arrive in time for lunch. She didn't. By two, Victor was hungry again, so he raided Beamer's pantry for some Fig Newtons, despite Diego's efforts to prevent the foraging. Dagny's sandwich, he noted, was still in its wrapper, but Victor refused to touch it.

At three, they were done, having downloaded the information contained on all but two incompatible phones of unusual make and vintage. Victor turned one of them on and dialed a number. His own phone rang. "Now we know the number." Diego recorded the number in the notebook.

Victor picked up the last phone, turned it on, and dialed. When his phone buzzed, he started to hand it to Diego, but stopped when he saw the number on the screen. "Darn it!"

"What?"

"It's the number Dagny texted me. The one the unsub used to call Hank Frank."

Diego wrote the number in the notebook. "If the unsub had used his own phone, we could have tracked it, I guess, and maybe found him. But we can't, because he used a victim's phone."

"Now you're sounding like one of us. But what I really need is for you to sound like a priest."

"What do you mean?

Victor picked up one of the unidentified phones and navigated through the menu screens until he found a call history. "If we call the most-dialed number, the person on the other end will be able to tell us whose phone it is."

"Yes." That made sense.

"But when they see what number is calling them, they're going to be excited, thinking that their loved one is alive and calling them."

Diego saw where this was going.

"So, when they realize you aren't their loved one, they're going to be devastated. Personally, I could never handle trying to help them through that. But a priest could." He handed over the phone.

Diego scrolled through the calls and found a number that had been dialed several times a day. With some trepidation, he pressed the number.

The woman who answered said only one word—"Raul?"—but it was tinged with all kinds of anxious hope, love, and elation. She sounded young—a girlfriend or a wife, not a mother, Diego decided.

"This is Father Diego Vega," he said in Spanish. "I'm helping with the investigation into the disappearance of a number of young men, and we found this phone and others. We're hoping to get information about the owners of these phones. I take it that this one belongs to someone named Raul?"

There was silence at the end of the line, and then the kind of sobbing that suggested the woman hadn't heard anything other than the sound of his voice and the fact that he wasn't Raul.

"We are doing our best to find these young men, but to do this, we'll need all the information we can get. What can you tell me about Raul?"

"What can *you* tell *me*, Father?"

"I can tell you that the only thing I care about is finding these boys. But I need your help."

The sobbing slowed. "His name is Raul Nieto. He is twenty-three. We are engaged. My name is Anita Gordillo. I haven't seen or heard from Raul in twelve days. He went to look for work and never came back. I've called his phone a thousand times, and there was never any answer."

He placed his hand over the mouthpiece and turned to Victor. "What else do I need to ask?"

"Physical description. Address. Friends and family. Where he went to look for work."

He asked for each of these and more, taking down detailed notes. When he finished, he thanked her for her time.

A sense of relief poured over him when he hung up the phone. "You did great," Victor said.

"I survived."

Diego picked up the second phone and called the number most dialed. A man answered the phone, again with excitement and joy, only to descend into tears as Diego explained the situation. "Antonio Perez," the man said, identifying his son. Diego wrote it in the notebook.

They had names for all of the phones. They had downloaded data from almost all of them.

"What now?" Diego said.

"We need a way to put it all together."

CHAPTER 19

Twenty-eight years ago, the thin man smoked what he thought was his last cigarette on the front steps of the Bilford County Hospital, while his father lay dying inside of lung cancer. The old man had been terrible to him, beating him for small infractions, leaving for months at a time without notice or explanation. But after the doctor had given him the prognosis, he'd been a different man. Warm and affectionate. Patient and understanding. Seeking forgiveness. Maybe he was trying to make himself right with the Lord.

There was no Lord, but the thin man gave his father forgiveness, anyway. The old man had won $120,000 from a scratch-off lottery ticket the week before his diagnosis. It was easy to forgive the dying rich. Forgiving the living poor—that was hard.

Standing on the hospital steps, the thin man smoked the cigarette down to a stub, dropped it to the concrete, and headed back to the old man's room. His father's eyes opened when he walked through the door. The old man looked terrible—tubes running to his nose and into his arms. He was thinner than the thin man for the first time in his adult life. Motioning with his hand, he drew his son to the side of the bed.

The thin man pulled up a chair and put his hand on his father's. The father smiled, and a tear rolled down his cheek. "Promise me two things, son."

"What, Dad?"

"Promise to be a good man, because I wasn't. And promise me you'll never smoke again."

He nodded.

"I need you to say it."

"I promise, Dad." He said it because you gave the dying what they wanted, so long as it didn't cost anything. Promises were free.

They sat together in silence for the rest of the day, and the thin man watched the life drain from his father. By dusk, the doctors pronounced the old man dead. The thin man asked them for one last moment with his father, and when they left, he used the phone in the room to call his father's lawyer to find out about the will. It had only taken a couple of hours to break his first promise.

He kept the second promise for twenty-eight years—not to honor his father, but because he didn't want to die weak and weepy like his dad. Once he started killing the Mexicans, though, he knew he'd never make it to lung cancer, so a pack of Camels seemed like a good idea. One pack led to two, which led to two a day.

Climbing into his pickup, he pulled a new pack from his pocket. Grabbing the ribbon, he tore the cellophane, withdrew a cigarette, and set it in his mouth. He lit a match and brought a flame to the cig. Drawing a deep breath, he leaned back and smiled. It felt like he was young again.

Anderson Demolition was six hours and two states away from Bilford, Ohio, but the thin man liked it that way. The demolition company had gone bankrupt because people only destroyed buildings if they wanted to build new ones, and no one was building much of anything these days. While a trustee sorted through Anderson's debts, the company's inventory of supplies sat there, ready for the taking by anyone who could jump a fence and pry a window. The thin man could do both, and he did.

He was never one to keep a job, and that served him well; he learned to do a lot of different things. Over the years, he had learned to fix motel toilets, recruit laborers, maintain foreclosed properties, and bring down a building or two. He wandered among the shelves of materials, scrutinizing them with an educated eye. Putty, wire, powder, and a handful of digital timers, triggers, and remotes—he took more than he would need, just in case he ever needed to do it again, and slipped out the window. Climbing into his pickup, he dropped the materials into the passenger seat, lit another cigarette, and started back for Ohio.

There was an elegant way to take something down—an artistry, actually. A careful and choreographed implosion would leave the least scatter of debris and the smallest cloud of dust. That wasn't what he wanted. He wanted nothing less than a volcanic eruption. There would be nothing elegant about this explosion. It would be all fireworks, no ballet.

Material on hand, now he needed the fuel. Outside of Dayton, he spied a place called Canter's Gas, right off the highway, all by itself. He pulled up to a pump, swiped Guillermo Bespa's credit card through the machine, and popped the diesel dispenser into the first of the six metal barrels in the back of his pickup.

When the barrel was half filled, the pump shut off—he had reached the credit card transaction limit. The thin man swiped another card. He had at least fifty of them, pilfered from various victims of his spree. Each barrel took two dead men's cards.

By the time he was filling the fifth barrel, the gas station clerk was watching through the window. The thin man nodded toward him, the way someone would nod if he were up to nothing. The clerk did not nod back.

He switched pumps for the last barrel—gasoline this time, because it was a better explosive and would help get the show started. As he stuck the pump into the barrel, the clerk came out of the store and walked toward him. He was a small guy with some stubble around his chin that he probably called a goatee. "How you doing today?" the clerk asked, studying the barrels in the back of the thin man's truck.

The thin man grinned. "I ain't never been better in my whole life."

"Looks like you need a lot of gas today. Mind if I ask what for?"

"Fleet of tractors at the farm. Like to keep a supply on hand."

"I hear you." The clerk circled around the back of the truck, looking at the barrels. "Not sure these meet the regulations for transport. That's an awful lot of fuel to be hauling around back here."

"Ain't never had trouble with them before."

The clerk nodded, then circled back around the truck. On the way, he glanced down at the license plate, pausing long enough, it seemed, to remember it. It was an unfortunate glance. Now the thin man would have to do something about it.

He looked at the name tag on the clerk's shirt. "You worried about regulations, Tim?" He lifted a cigarette from the pack in his shirt pocket and popped it into his mouth.

"You can't smoke here."

He lit a match and brought it to his cigarette. He inhaled, then blew out a puff of smoke. "Looks like I can, Tim."

"You can't smoke by the gas pumps, sir! I need you to put it out."

"Okay," he said. He pulled the pump out of the barrel and turned the spout toward the clerk, squeezed the handle, and sprayed gasoline all over him.

"Jesus! Are you—"

The thin man flicked his cigarette onto the clerk and waited for him to ignite. Nothing happened.

"Are you crazy!" the clerk shouted.

Nothing was easy. The thin man reached into his truck, pulled out his gun, and shot the clerk. He doused the body with more fuel and replaced the pump. With a flick of his wrist, he lit a match and dropped it onto the body. The flame extinguished before it landed.

"Oh, for Christ's sake." The thin man lit another match, shielded it with his hands, and touched it to the clerk's wet pants. The flame took.

It seemed like a good time to leave, so he climbed into his truck and drove. He was a couple hundred yards away when he saw a flash of light in his rearview mirror, followed quickly by a loud boom. The entire station had exploded. This was a good thing, he decided. All his fingerprints at the pump would be gone. If there were any security cameras, the tape would be destroyed. Maybe they'd chalk the whole thing up to an accident—a clerk who had smoked too close to the pumps or something. Maybe they wouldn't even find the bullet.

He stopped at the first McDonald's, bought himself a celebratory Big Mac, and savored it on the ride back. It was a big moment for him. He'd killed an American citizen—his first.

Not, he expected, his last.

CHAPTER 20

Dagny hadn't yet stepped down to the basement floor when Victor shoved a Quiznos Honey Bourbon Chicken sandwich into her hand. Six hundred calories and fifteen points on the Weight Watchers scale. She opened one end of the wrapper and took a bite. It was cold, which was fine. The taste didn't matter; she needed the numbers.

"Tell me good news," she said.

"We were able to download all the phones but two, and we've used the call history of those to identify their owners," Victor replied.

"You dialed them?"

"Diego did."

It was a breach of any number of protocols, but they'd already broken so many rules, it hardly seemed to matter. She looked over at the priest, who slouched in a chair, lost in thought. She worried about the toll the case was taking on him.

"You okay?"

He nodded, but it wasn't reassuring.

"We've got a ton of data for the phones," Victor said, "but it hasn't been synthesized. We need to put it all together, see how it all relates."

She took another bite of her sandwich. Even with all these calories, she'd need to eat another entire meal before the end of the day. The thought depressed her. "The Bureau has software that will take all the information from the phones and plot it on a chronological map," she said. "Each phone will be an icon, and we can watch them move on the map over time."

"Yes, but it's not very reliable, and to get the software, I'd have to reach out to the Computer Analysis Response Team, or the Regional Computer Forensics Laboratory for the Miami Valley. But we can't do that, right? Because neither of us is supposed to be working this case."

He was right, of course. Being off the reservation made things difficult. It was a catch-22. They needed to find the bodies in order to get the resources necessary to find the bodies.

"What about commercial software?"

"There isn't a program out there that can do what we want," he said. "So, we're going to make one."

Dagny smiled. "How?"

"A contest."

She had worked with a lot of agents who were good at articulating reasons why they couldn't do what needed to be done. Victor was the rare partner who solved problems. "Let me guess. Colleges?"

"MIT and Caltech. Twenty-four hours to deliver the best product."

"Starting when?"

"About an hour ago."

She looked at her watch. It was six o'clock. In twenty-three long hours, they would be able to replay the movements of eighty missing men. "Winner gets?"

"Bragging rights and a shout-out in the press release when the case is closed."

"If we solve this case, you and I won't even get a shout-out in the press release."

Victor laughed at this, but Diego remained quiet and numb. She sat down next to him and searched for some words of uplift.

"The worst part of this job is notifying a family member that something has happened to a loved one," she said.

He shook his head. "It's not that, Dagny. I can console people. It's one of my few skills."

"Then what is it?"

He turned to her. "It's the enormity of it all. And the helplessness I feel. This all happened on my watch."

She shook her head. "Your job is to save souls, not lives. To inspire, not protect. A lot of people ought to feel shame for the fact that this has happened. You're not one of them."

He nodded in a way that conveyed appreciation but not agreement.

"Actually, there's only one person who should feel shame," she said. "And we'll catch him."

"Things like this aren't caused by one man," he said. "They're caused by a rot in the community. I have all the confidence in the world that you'll catch the murderer because I know you're good at your job. But I know that I won't heal the community, because I'm bad at mine."

This mix of depression and self-loathing was completely familiar to her. Over the next twenty-three hours, it was likely to get worse. Once the information from the phones was synthesized, everything was likely to unfold at a breakneck pace. The best thing to do would be to relax, because it would be their last chance to do so.

"We're all going out tonight," she declared.

"Where?" Victor asked.

"To the theater."

The lights dimmed between the acts, and stagehands rolled the judge's bench away and replaced it with a large conference table and a dozen chairs. When the lights came on again, eleven men were seated around the table while one man stood on top of it. He started to sing in a slow, deep baritone:

> Guilty, he's guilty, he's guilty—it's clear.
> Let's vote this man guilty and get out of here.
> Murder and manslaughter, it's all the same.
> If we make it quick, I can still make . . . the . . . game.

And then he began to tap dance.

It was as earnest and sincere as any performance she had seen— and terrible in the best of ways. More important, it was working on the three of them. Victor was stifling laughter, and Diego was smiling broadly. For Dagny, the show gave her a few moments of sheer joy that punctured through the cascade of questions circling inside her mind.

Why did he call the radio show? Was he playing a game? Did he want attention? Did he need to feel like he mattered? All of these, perhaps. Why did he bury the cell phones? Was he sloppy? Was he teasing them? Did he want them to have the information on the phones? Did he want them to find the bodies?

It was easy to dispose of one body. How did someone dispose of eighty-one of them? You can't bury that many. You can't dump them in a river.

You burn them, she thought. You burn them until they are ashes and dust.

If they didn't find bodies, they couldn't open a real investigation.
If they didn't find the bodies, they would never catch the killer.
If they didn't find bodies, she was out of a job.

CHAPTER 21

The thin man woke with vigor and excitement. This was the day that his work would become famous. This was the day the world would start coming for him.

He dressed and brushed, put on a shirt and overalls, tucked a gun into his pocket, and grabbed his keys. Bounding outside, he paused at the top of his porch steps, spread his arms wide, and took a deep breath. The predawn air was crisp and clean—enough to make a man feel like he was twenty again.

But he wasn't twenty, and to rig the explosion, he'd need some help. Mexicans weren't itching for work in Bilford, so he took the truck for a long drive. When he flipped on the radio, Springsteen's "Born in the USA" was playing. He lit a match while driving, admired his own dexterity, and took a long drag from a cigarette. Freedom was smoking a cigarette, driving down the road, and listening to the Boss.

Forty miles later, he pulled into a Lowe's in Springfield. Two young men were standing in the parking lot, looking sad and desperate, accosting every customer who exited the store. These boys will do fine, he thought. He rolled down the window, made his case, and they hopped into the back of the truck, right next to the barrels he'd filled the day before. The thin man didn't even have to get out of the cab to rope these boys in. Lowe's was a drive-through employment agency.

When they got to the silo, he took their phones with his standard spiel, then had them pile each of the diesel tanks onto a scissor lift he'd stolen from a construction site. Once the barrels were loaded onto the lift, they all hopped aboard, and he pressed the lever to lift them toward the sky. As they rose to the top, the thin man scanned the horizon. Would they see the magnificent fireball in Springfield? Wilmington? Dayton?

They rolled the barrels into the top of the silo and set them on the raised floor while he explained the task. Four of the barrels would remain at the top of the silo; two would be lowered to the bottom. The men would go down to the bottom of the silo and wait for him to lower the two barrels, so they could set them in place. They listened closely—interrupting only to ask about the smell. Dead animals, he explained.

The thin man pulled a new rope ladder from a spool on the silo wall, draped it into the hole in the floor, and cranked out enough slack to send it to the bottom of the silo. The first boy started down the ladder, followed soon by the second. As they dangled, the thin man cut the rope with shears and let them fall.

Both were hurt by the impact—their screams confirmed that much. They screamed again when they realized they had fallen onto a mound of rotting bodies.

It wasn't easy to concentrate with the noise, but he lined up the six barrels and attached putty, explosive, wires, and a timer to the one that held the gasoline. At the appropriate time, the timer would send a pulse through the wires, which would trigger the explosives, shattering the barrel and creating a giant fireball. One by one, each of the barrels would explode, and one of them would pop the top of the silo. That was his theory, anyway.

The only thing left to do was set the timer. To light up the sky, he'd have to wait for night. Not too late, though. He didn't want everyone to be asleep—he wanted families to gather in their yards, admiring the glow of the sky. These fireworks were for everyone. Nine p.m., he decided. Dark enough for a show, and early enough for an audience.

CHAPTER 22

....

Dagny bounded through the streets of Bilford in a predawn drizzling rain, wishing that Victor had given the schools twelve hours instead of twenty-four to develop the software to collate the phone data. Sure, she'd spend the day interviewing more families, taking down more notes, but none of that would matter. The phones were the key. Clicking through her iPhone, she found Track One from Tom Petty's *Hard Promises* album, clicked the repeat icon, and let it cycle while she ran. A flash of lightning lit the sky, followed by a big boom of thunder. Everything about this day felt ominous.

Her mind drifted from the case to the dream that had ruined another night of sleep. It was the cafeteria dream again. When she was in her twenties, she figured that she'd grow out of her issues with food. At thirty-five, she knew they were something she'd be saddled with for the rest of her life.

A man driving an old, rusted Ford Escort tossed a McDonald's bag out his window and onto the sidewalk. Dagny picked it up and tossed it into the trash, then felt compelled to clean up the rest of the copious litter she encountered on her run. Plastic bottles and pop cans. Food wrappers. A copy of the *Dayton Daily News*. She paused on the image of the burning gas station on the front page of the paper. According to the article, local authorities blamed the explosion on a smoking attendant, the sole victim of the fire. The newsprint began to drip under the weight of the rain. She tossed the paper into the trash and continued her run.

She returned to her motel and showered. As she dressed, her phone rang. Expecting a call from Diego, she answered without looking at the screen.

"You missed your appointment yesterday."

It was Dr. Childs. "I'm sorry about that. I forgot to cancel."

"Again, my understanding is that attendance is a condition of your employment."

"I've been suspended from the Bureau, so I suppose it doesn't really matter."

It took a moment for that to register. "Why were you suspended?"

"Insubordination."

There was silence for a moment. "Dagny, I really think you should come in for a session."

"I can't. I'm in Ohio, working on a case."

"I thought you were suspended."

"I'm working pro bono."

"I don't know how the FBI works, but that sounds . . . preposterous."

"I can understand that. Here's the deal: I was suspended because I wanted to pursue a murder case where there are no bodies. But as soon as I find some bodies, I'll be reinstated." She heard the words as she said them. "I know I probably sound like a crazy person, but I think I'll have some bodies within a day."

"It does sound strange. How long will you be in Ohio?"

"I don't know. As long as it takes to catch the guy."

"The guy who has killed the bodies you can't find?"

"Yes. Exactly."

"Dagny, I really think you should come back home."

"This only sounds crazy because there's a lot I'm not telling you. People are missing by the dozens. I'm going to find them. I can't say any more about it."

"If you're not coming back, I think we should consider doing regular sessions by phone."

It was easier to leave the Church of Scientology than it was to get out of therapy with Dr. Childs. "I can't commit to anything. Once we find the bodies, everything's going to get crazy."

"Then maybe we should talk now. Before things get crazy."

Dagny looked at her watch. She had a few minutes before she had to leave.

"How are you feeling?" Childs asked.

"Just . . ." She stopped to consider the question. "Impatient, mostly."

"Are you upset about the suspension?"

"No, it's going to be fine."

"Are you eating?"

"I am. I've got a good support network for that." It sounded more effective to refer to Victor as a network.

"Any trouble sleeping?"

"No, just . . ."

"Just what?"

"I have weird dreams."

"Hmmm."

"What?"

"Well, Freud said that dreams are the royal road to the unconscious."

"Yeah, but he also came up with penis envy," Dagny said.

"Touché. Tell me about one of your dreams."

It seemed harmless enough. "I'm back in college. I'm wearing pajamas in the cafeteria, and I'm surveying the options. There's the salad bar—very sensible. There's pizza and the waffle station and the sand-wich bar. And I can't decide what to get, so I keep circling, looking at each station again and again. Meanwhile, everyone else is picking up their food, taking it to tables, eating, and leaving. But I keep circling, and the food keeps disappearing. Eventually, everyone's finished eating, and I'm still trying to decide what to get, except the only thing left is the picked-over garbage that no one wanted. And it drives me crazy, because I can't even get away from my food issues when I'm sleeping."

"Hmmm."

"So, what do you think?"

"I don't think the dream is about food at all."

"Then what's it about?"

"It's about men."

"No, it's . . ." But thinking about it, she realized that Dr. Childs was right.

"Let's talk about men, Dagny. Let's talk about Mike."

"I can't. I've got to run."

CHAPTER 23

....

Google led Diego to the website for The Clergy Project, a group dedicated to helping clergy leave the priesthood after they had lost their faith. The group seemed to have some affiliation with the scientist and secularist Richard Dawkins, who noted in a welcome letter that a departing clergyman "risk[s] losing all his friends, being cast out by his family, being ostracized by his whole community." Diego didn't stand to lose any of these things. He had no friendships of merit. He had drifted from his family when he was a teen. He hadn't felt like part of a community in years.

And then Diego understood. He had already left the clergy.

He closed his eyes and rubbed his temples. All his boyhood friends were married to people who loved and adored them. They had careers that let them build or make or manage things, and that earned them money and bought them homes. Their children greeted them with smiles and hugs when they walked through the door. On weekends, they had cookouts with the neighbors. In the winter, they vacationed in places that were warm and sunny.

He had only a 1969 cherry-red Corvette convertible. It was a teen-ager's version of adulthood. It was pathetic.

He closed the browser, showered, and dressed. Dagny wasn't coming until nine fifteen, so he had an hour to kill. He picked up his phone and did something he'd thought about doing for two years. He called Katrina.

"Diego?" She said it with befuddlement.

"Hi."

"You said you never wanted to talk to me again."

"No, no. I said we never should talk again."

"That's the same thing."

"It's very different. There are lots of things I want to do that I shouldn't."

"Why are you calling me?"

"I-I—" He stammered a bit. "I guess I wanted to hear your voice. To see how you're doing."

"You know how I'm doing. I hear you call around to check up on me."

"Just to see that you're okay," he said.

"Why now? All this time, and now you call?"

"I don't know. I guess I miss you."

"That ship has sailed."

"I know, Katrina. I just miss talking to you."

"You don't have anyone to talk to in Bilford?" She said *Bilford* as if it were the name of a mistress.

"No. No, I don't."

"Then get a shrink."

"I know you're still angry, but—"

"No, I'm not angry," she said. "I'm . . . confused. I don't know how you can be so close to someone and then shut it off like that."

"Katrina, if I didn't—"

"What?"

"I would—"

"What would have happened, Diego?"

"I would have led you on a path that wasn't good for you."

"That's sexist, Diego. I could make my own decision—"

"But you did make your own decision, Katrina. Because I left, and you still—"

"You made the choice for me."

"No. I didn't. And you still went ahead." He searched for a truer answer. "And, honestly, I—"

"Didn't want to feel responsible?"

"Yes."

"Because, heaven forbid, you take responsibility—"

"Because I wasn't worth it."

There was a long silence. He knew she was still on the line; he could hear her short, exasperated breaths. And then she said, "It's taken me two years to see it, but you're right. You weren't worth it."

This was why he'd called. Not for forgiveness, which he would never get or deserve, but for absolution. She was better without him, and she understood it, and that meant he'd done the right thing. "Thank you," he said, not realizing that this might confuse her.

"Is that all you wanted? For me to be mean to you?"

Maybe it was. Or maybe he wanted to relive memories from the last time he felt happy. "Do you remember that night we drove to Chicago?"

"Of course I remember."

"And we went on that architectural tour—"

"It was ten degrees, with winds like a hurricane."

"And we went into the atrium of the Rookery building—"

"And stayed there while the rest of the tour left—"

"And talked for six hours, sitting on those steps."

"I remember," she said.

"Losing all track of time. Looking up through the clear glass roof and seeing that it was night, and not knowing how that happened."

"Yes."

"What did we talk about that day?"

She laughed. "You really don't remember?"

"No."

"We talked about baseball. And the Marx Brothers. We talked about Joni Mitchell. About politics and obligations and family. Childhoods. Fear. Death. We gossiped about people in the church. And you talked about that stupid red Corvette, which I hope you don't still have, but I'm sure that you do."

"I do."

"Of course. And we talked about love. What it felt like, and what it meant."

"And we talked about time," Diego said.

"Because we were sitting in a masterpiece—"

"That Burnham and Root and Wright had designed a hundred years ago."

"And it held up."

"Enough that they would use it in *Home Alone 2*."

"And I didn't know why a thirty-year-old man—"

"Thirty-two, then."

"Would know that."

"I read it somewhere."

"That's what you said, but you seemed really familiar with the movie."

"No, no," he protested, the same way he had three years earlier. "I just like reading about architecture."

"That's probably why you became a priest. For the architecture."

"That's how they get you. With the architecture."

She laughed again. "You think you miss talking to me, Diego, but you don't. You just miss talking to someone."

"You were a great someone to talk to."

"Yeah, well . . . that's nice of you to say."

"I mean it, Katrina."

"It was more than talking with the two of us."

"I know."

"But I miss it, too. That's why we can't do it anymore."

"I know."

"Good-bye, Diego."

"Good-bye, Katrina."

As he hung up, pain swelled in the pit of his stomach. He had called seeking closure, and now, having gotten it, he felt worse than ever.

CHAPTER 24

....

They spent the day talking to more families of the missing. Most of the families greeted them with cautious smiles and guarded optimism, drilling Dagny with questions aimed to elicit good news and drifting into a somber, quiet despair when she failed to deliver any. Diego facilitated the conversations and made the families feel comfortable. Victor sat in general silence. She had invited him to come because he had earned it; she'd also admonished him to say nothing, lest the number of inquisitors overwhelm the families.

None of the visits provided any useful information, but Dagny hadn't expected any. They were talking to these families because they needed to feel as if they were working the case while they waited on the phone data.

At 4:00 p.m., they returned to Beamer's basement, ordered pizza, and waited for the schools to deliver the promised software. The pizza came first. She ate three slices, which brought her all the points she needed for the day. John Beamer arrived next; he had knocked off early to see what her eminent domain of his basement had yielded. At 4:59, two e-mails popped up on Victor's laptop, each with a link to download software.

They huddled behind him and watched him download MIT's software first. When it opened, Victor clicked File in the menu bar and selected Import Data. A pop-up showed a progress bar that grew from 1 percent to 73 percent, and then stopped. The arrow on the screen turned into a spinning rainbow-colored ball, and then the application crashed.

"Darn it," he said. He opened the application again and tried to import the data. Once again, it crashed at 73 percent.

"C'mon, Caltech," Beamer said in the hushed tone of a prayer.

Victor clicked on the link from the Caltech team and downloaded the software. A button on the top bar read Import Data, and he selected it. The progress bar moved slowly from 1 percent to 73 percent, where it froze. The four of them stared in silent dejection.

"Please, please," Victor muttered. It must have worked, because the progress bar moved again, all the way to 100 percent. "Caltech wins."

A street map showed greater Bilford. Toggle buttons on the side of the screen let him choose between satellite, street, and hybrid views as well as flip between Google and Bing maps. He clicked on the "Filter" button on the top of the screen, and a drop-down list of the eighty-one names appeared. A slider above the map was labeled "Timeline." A button to the right of this read "Settings," and he clicked on it. A text-entry box let him set the duration of the timeline; he selected six months.

"Just to be safe," he said.

Another box said "Extinguish Red," and an explanatory note beneath it said, "Turn dots red when data ends due to loss of power." He clicked to turn on this option.

After closing the settings, he grabbed the button on the slider with the arrow and started to drag it along the timeline. They watched the dots move about the geography of the screen. At times some of them would converge, move together, and separate at the end of the day. "This is what their lives looked like," Victor said.

Something seemed wrong. "I don't think there are eighty dots on the screen," Dagny said. "It's more like thirty."

"Well, we won't see dots for all the phones all of the time," Victor said. "Some of the phones only store seven days of GPS data, and some store even less than that."

"That's terrible."

"It's not as bad as it sounds, because most of the phones have apps that can log GPS, too," he explained. "If they made phone calls, we'll have an approximation of their location from cell towers. And most people had location services turned on, so their location might be logged within Twitter, Facebook, Yelp, whatever other app they might be using. This will pull those locations."

"Then it still seems like there should be more dots," she said. "Can you zoom out?"

Victor hit the minus sign to zoom out, and more dots started to appear. He stopped when the entire state of Ohio was visible. The dots were concentrated in the southwest quadrant of the state. The biggest pocket of dots was around Bilford, but some appeared in the outskirts of Cincinnati, Dayton, and Columbus, too.

He continued to tug the slider along the timeline. When he hit the three-month mark, a cluster of dots converged and turned red in Bilford County.

"Go back and slow it down."

He backed up the slider, hit a button that said "1/2 speed," and pushed the "Play" button on the bottom of the screen. They watched as a cluster of eight free dots formed next to Fowler Road. "That's where they gathered to look for work," Dagny explained.

The dots left together, packed so closely they looked like a single, pulsating dot. They traveled down a few roads, and then veered off the street. "Hit satellite," she said, and Victor obeyed.

The dots moved through deep woods and across a dirt road that bisected a clearing on a farm. They stopped at a giant silo, and then, one by one, flipped to red. He right-clicked and put a pin on the silo.

"Keep it going," she said.

Another week passed on the timeline, and then a cluster of dots outside of Dayton traveled on the highway to Bilford County and the same farm. Again, the dots stopped at the silo, then turned red as they extinguished.

"John, do you know where that farm is?" she asked.

"That's the old Hoover farm. It was foreclosed. Been abandoned for years," Beamer replied.

"Perhaps not entirely abandoned," she said.

The timeline continued to play, and dots continued to move about their lives. Another cluster gathered along Fowler Road and made its way to the farm.

"Eleven more," Victor said as they turned red.

A week later, twelve more dots from north of Cincinnati filtered across the screen to the silo. Then eight more from south of Columbus. Another thirteen from Fowler Road. Twelve more from Dayton.

"My goodness," Diego said. "We're watching people die."

Clusters kept aggregating, floating to the silo, and extinguishing. As more of the green dots disappeared, the remaining traveled in smaller and smaller groups to their end. Occasionally, a dot would travel there all by itself.

When there were three green dots left, two of them traveled to the silo, where they stayed for two days. Then they made their way to Hillsborough Park, where they met with the last remaining dot. Victor clicked on that dot, and a data box appeared with Adelmo Fox's name and address, along with buttons that revealed other metadata from his phone.

"That's when the unsub went off to bury the bag of phones. It looks like Adelmo happened to be at the wrong place at the wrong time," Dagny said.

The two other phones expired, and only Adelmo's dot burned green. The dot worked its way to Beamer's house, where all the other dots flashed green again. "Because we plugged them in," Victor explained unnecessarily.

Dagny turned to John. "Can you drive us to the farm?"

"I can drive," Diego said before John had the chance to respond.

"We can't all squeeze into your hot rod," she said. "And besides, you're not coming."

Diego grimaced. "Dagny, I have to come. This is all on me."

"Too dangerous. You're a civilian."

"I'll drive," John said.

As Victor and John headed up the stairs, Diego grabbed her arm and stopped her. "I don't have kids or a wife or a family. I have literally nothing to lose. Do you understand that?"

"Yes." She understood it well.

"I have nothing except the notion of purpose. All I have is the belief that I might be useful. And I would be useful. I'm strong and fit—more than Victor, more than John."

"You've never done anything like this."

"Neither has Victor, right?"

"It's dangerous, Diego."

"I can handle a gun."

"You've fired a gun?"

"Yes," he said.

There was a lot she didn't know about the priest. She yelled up to Beamer. "John!"

"Yes?" he called from upstairs.

"We're going to need to borrow an extra gun."

CHAPTER 25

Dagny, Victor, and Diego waited in Beamer's car behind the police station while the officer covertly absconded with four Kevlar vests and a police-issued gun. Dagny claimed the extra gun and gave hers to Diego, since Beamer might be excused for lending a gun to an FBI agent—albeit a suspended one—but it would be impossible to explain giving a gun to a priest. Only a fool would give this priest a gun, she thought.

At her direction, Beamer drove them to the T.J.Maxx in New Bilford, where they purchased black shirts, pants, and shoes, so they could move freely as dusk turned to night. The store had a limited range of sizes, so Victor's clothes were snug. "I look like a fat ballerina," he muttered.

"It'll do, Black Swan."

On the way to the farm, they stopped at the Bilford Motor Inn, where she fished through her suitcase for the Radar Scope she'd once borrowed from a military friend and had never returned. Beamer eyed the green device when she slipped back into the front passenger seat of his Civic. "What does that do?"

"You hold it against the wall of a house, and it tells you if anyone is inside."

"Never heard of such a thing."

"They used them in Iraq."

Victor leaned forward between the front seats. "So, we're going to war?"

Perhaps they were. They had assumed that a single culprit was behind the mass abductions, but it could have been a group or a cult. If there were a gaggle of armed Koreshians waiting in the farmhouse, they needed to know.

It took twenty minutes to navigate the maze of back roads to the Hoover farm. They parked two properties away and walked through the woods toward the farm on foot. Five minutes in, they could see the crest of the massive silo. It took another ten minutes to make it to the clearing that brought the rest of the farm into view. A gravel drive bisected fields of high grass and led to a two-story, nineteenth-century farmhouse, then curved left to a large barn and the silo. Beyond the barn were fenced fields, seemingly empty of the livestock they'd once fed.

Although it was dusk, the windows of the farmhouse were dark. That did not mean that the house was empty. Dagny ordered the others to stay low and still until she gave them the signal to proceed. She crept through the grass to the right side of the farmhouse and pulled the Radar Scope from her backpack. The scope sent out a stepped-frequency radar and looked for changes in the Doppler pattern of the returned signal. If someone were inside the room on the other side of the wall, it would blink. She held the scope against the wall and pressed the button. No blink. Crawling along the perimeter of the house, she tested the scope at even intervals. The first floor appeared to be empty. She rose and peeked through a window, staring into an empty living room. No furniture, no rug, not even a picture on the wall. The lock on the window was unlatched. She placed both hands flat on the glass, pushed the window up, and climbed into the house.

The place was dusty and smelled like cigarette smoke. She grabbed a flashlight from her backpack and surveyed the room. A flattened cigarette stub lay in the middle of the floor. She noticed that the wood floor was lighter at the perimeter than the middle, which meant that there used to be a rug in the room. The cigarette stub had been dropped after that rug had been removed. She took some tweezers and a Ziploc bag from her backpack, picked up the stub, and dropped it into the bag. A small find, but cases had been solved with less. Grabbing a marker from the front pocket of her backpack, she scribbled the date and location on the white part of the bag.

She continued to search the first floor of the house, but no matter how softly she tiptoed, the floors squeaked. Gun drawn, she flitted through the kitchen and dining room.

Thump.

The noise came from upstairs.

Thump.

Dagny ran to the foyer and stood at the bottom of the staircase, holding her gun steady with both hands. She started up the steps, arms straight, gun leading. Her heart was pounding.

Thump.

There were three bedrooms at the top of the stairs. She went into the first of them, crouched low, gun ready. The room was spare; the opened closet was empty. She ducked into the second bedroom. Empty. She peeked into the bathroom on the way to the last bedroom. There was a pedestal sink under an open and empty medicine cabinet. The shower was clean; no curtain hung from the rod.

Thump.

It came from the last bedroom. She crouched in the hallway and peeked through the open door. There was a folded metal cot next to the window on the left wall, and a small closet in the far one.

Thump.

It came from the closet.

Dagny took a deep breath and charged into the room, gun first. She kicked open the closet door.

A bat flew into her head. It chirped and hissed. She swatted it away and ducked down. It flew into the wall, and then charged back at her. She dropped to the floor, rolled to the wall, and opened the window. The bat flew out.

She peered out the window and watched the bat fly into the dark sky. When it disappeared, she headed down the stairs and stifled a laugh.

Downstairs, she climbed out the open window. Scampering through the grass, she approached the barn and withdrew the Radar Scope once again. A trip around the barn perimeter indicated it was empty. She pushed open the barn door and walked through with her flashlight. A black tarp covered something. She tore it away and found a scissor lift. There was a keyhole on the control panel, but it was empty. The rest of the barn was littered with dirty junk—a broken wheelbarrow, paint cans, distressed lumber. Anything of use or value had been removed, save for the scissor lift, which was pristine. A recent addition to the barn, she decided.

She stepped out of the barn and pulsed the flashlight. The three men came running. They should have been creeping close to the ground, but they weren't. Dagny had forgotten to tell them. This group needed close instruction. Although she had confirmed that the house and barn were empty, there were plenty of other hiding spots around the farm. The boys didn't appreciate the potential for danger.

"Stay down," she barked in a screamed whisper. They ducked low to the ground and made their way to her.

"What about the silo?" Beamer said, crouching beside her.

"That's where we're going. Guns out, gentlemen."

"Even me?" Victor asked. Most of his prior firearm experience involved the word *mishap.*

"Even you." She paused, and then added, "Maybe keep the finger off the trigger."

Dagny led them along the ground to the silo. She placed her hand on the side of the towering cylinder and felt the cold, rough concrete. Somewhere there had to be a door. Circling the edifice, she found a large rectangular opening that had been filled in with concrete. The unsub had turned the silo into a tomb.

A metal ladder ran up the side of the silo, held six inches from the concrete by bolted metal arms every ten feet or so. She counted the intervals and concluded that the silo was about seventy feet tall. A difficult climb for anyone. Even more so with a body.

Victor must have been thinking the same thing. "Tough climb."

"He used a scissor lift," she said. "It's in the barn."

The silo's concrete wall was probably too thick to allow for sonar, but faulty assumptions had killed many investigations. She took the Radar Scope from her backpack anyway and held it to the wall.

The scope blinked.

"Does that mean someone's alive in there?" Diego asked.

Dagny banged against the side of the silo. "Hello!" she screamed. The others joined in.

A faint voice emanated from behind the concrete. It sounded like: "Help."

"Someone's alive!" Beamer said.

"We need the lift," Diego added.

"The key's missing," she replied. "It won't work."

Diego turned to the ladder and stuffed his gun in the waistband of his jeans. "Then it's this," he said, grabbing the bottom rung and pulling himself up.

"No, Diego, stop!" But he ignored her and kept climbing. She grabbed the bottom rail and pulled herself up.

Victor looked up at her. "Maybe we should stay down here. For cover."

"Yes," Dagny called down to him. "For cover." She looked up at Diego, who was half a dozen rungs above her. "Diego, you don't know what's at the top."

"I know what's inside. That's enough." He continued up the side of the silo.

She increased her pace, spearing the rungs and pulling herself higher. Halfway up, she looked down at Beamer and Victor and felt a little dizzy.

"You don't mind heights?" she called up to Diego.

"Hate them, actually," he replied.

The wind seemed to swirl more the higher they climbed. "What do you plan to do at the top?" she said. "You don't have rope. I doubt there's a staircase inside."

"I don't know what I'm doing," he said. "But I have to do something."

"We've lost wars with that kind of thinking." Then again, if he hadn't started up the ladder first, she would have. Sometimes you had to do something.

She looked down again. Fifty feet to the ground. Victor and Beamer looked blurry to her. She had to stop looking down, so she looked up at Diego. He glanced at her.

"You okay?" he asked.

"I wish my job were a little less vertical."

"Just fifteen more feet and then—"

She felt the explosion first—a violent shaking of the ladder that nearly threw her down. The sound followed—a thunderous blast that rang in her ears after the noise itself had dissipated. Then there was the flash of the fireball that blew out the top of the silo, blinding her, while the sparks of the explosion rained down and singed the skin on her arms and scalp.

"Diego, are you—"

A second explosion shook the silo with such force that the top half of the ladder detached from the silo and, with their combined weight pulling on it, folded down and smashed into the lower half of the ladder. Dagny now hung above Diego. The right rail of the ladder broke where it had folded in half, so only the pinched left rail was holding them. This caused the ladder to swing to the left, and she lost her grip. He caught her as she fell.

"I've got you," he said.

"You've got me," she replied. "Who's got you?"

The pinched joint in the left rail started to give. They grabbed rungs on the attached part of the ladder as the dangling half fell to the ground. He started down first, and she followed.

"Run!" she yelled at Victor and Beamer, who were watching slack-jawed beneath them. They obeyed.

They were ten feet above the ground when the third blast shook them from the ladder. Diego landed flat on his back. She landed on his chest. He put his arms around her and rolled them to the side, just in time to avoid a falling chunk of concrete. She felt his heavy breath against her cheek.

"We need to run," she said, pushing off him and joining Beamer and Victor in a sprint toward the barn.

"Agreed," he said, chasing after them.

A fourth blast lit the sky and shook the ground. She turned back and watched the fireball shoot from the top of the silo. "Call every fire department in the region," she yelled to Beamer.

"Already on it," he said, cell phone in hand.

"And we'll need the biggest construction crane we can get. With a spotlight."

He seemed confused by the request, but he didn't question it.

While he worked the phone, the rest of them sat in the grass, watching the silo erupt like a giant volcano. Someone was dying inside that silo, and there was nothing they could do about it.

CHAPTER 26

Eighteen trucks came of various sizes and shapes—engines, pumpers, ladders, and platforms, converging from three counties in the middle of the night. They bathed the scene in flashing red light, the ambience of tragedy. The largest ladder extended seventy-five feet, which was just enough to aim hoses down into the silo. Dagny watched the effort at the side of Max Conroy, Bilford's fire chief, a gray-haired shrivel of a man who had the experience and sense to provide her with his expertise but defer to her judgment. It was their fire, but it was her crime scene.

By 3:00 a.m., the fire had been reduced to embers, and steam, not smoke, billowed from the top of the silo. She turned to Conroy. "How hot is it in the silo right now?"

"About four hundred degrees, I suspect."

"Still?"

"That's down from more than two thousand."

"How long before it cools down more?"

"It will be hot all day," he said. "Those concrete walls are more than a foot thick. Whole thing is like a stone pot at a Korean restaurant."

She wondered when he'd been to a Korean restaurant, and then chastised herself for thinking everyone in Bilford was an unworldly simpleton. It was a bad East Coast prejudice, particularly for a woman from St. Louis.

"I'll need to borrow a fire suit," she said.

He studied her for a moment, sizing her up physically and mentally, it seemed. Putting his bullhorn to his mouth, he turned to the gaggle of firefighters. "Mayer!" A firefighter jogged over to them. "I need your suit," he said.

The firefighter took off the goggles, then the helmet and the protective hood beneath it. She looked at Dagny. "For you?"

Dagny nodded and extended her hand. "Dagny Gray."

"Nicole Mayer."

She was in her twenties. Slender but fit. Face full of freckles. The lone woman in the bunch. Dagny knew what that was like. "How's it going to feel in there?" she asked, nodding toward the silo.

"Like hell." Nicole removed her glasses and set them on the ground. "How are you going in?" she asked.

"That's what the crane is for."

Nicole nodded, taking off her outer coat and pants, tossing each to the ground with a thud. Dagny picked up the coat—it weighed a ton—but the firefighter shook her head. "Do the hood first, so it will be tucked under the coat."

She picked up the hood. It was made of thick white material that had a square cutout for the face. She slipped it over her head. "Okay. Next?"

Nicole held up the pants so Dagny could step into them. The firefighter looped suspenders over her shoulders and held up her coat so Dagny could slide into it. The whole thing was heavy enough to make her stumble. "You get used to it," Nicole said. "After a year or two." She smiled and handed over her boots.

Dagny put them on and took a few labored steps. "Your job is harder than mine."

Nicole looked over at the silo. "If that thing is full of bodies, I don't think so."

Dagny walked over to Diego, Victor, and Beamer, who were sitting in the grass, staring numbly at the scene. "John, who's in charge of the crane?"

"Steve Johnson. Local 925. Good guy."

"Let's go," she said.

The crane was parked fifty feet from the silo. Its hundred-foot arm was swung away from it. Johnson sat in the cab, smoking a cigarette. He hopped down when he saw them coming. "Hey, John!"

"Steve, thanks for coming out."

"Of course, man. This is something else, ain't it?"

Dagny extended her gloved hand. "Dagny Gray."

"Jesus, there's a woman under all of that?"

"Yes."

"FBI agent," Beamer explained.

"What can I do for you?" Steve asked.

"You're good with this thing?" she asked, motioning to the crane.

"Yep."

"I need you to lower me down the center of it. Carefully. So I don't bang against the walls."

"You want to go in there? Right now?"

"Yeah. To dangle and get a look."

He smiled, shaking his head in a *well, this beats all* kind of way. "All right."

"Can we attach the spotlight to the arm, so it will shine down into the silo and illuminate the inside?"

"This can't wait until dawn?"

"No." Every minute counted when a killer was loose.

He bit down on his lip. "We can do it. Getting the line rigged will take a few men."

Dagny looked over at the sea of firefighters milling about the scene. "That shouldn't be a problem."

The fire truck's ladder made it easy to lift the spotlight to the top of the crane. The firefighters attached it, threading the cables down the jib to a generator behind the cab. When the light came on, it was blinding enough that everyone shielded their eyes. It would do.

She walked over to the cable that dangled from the arm of the crane and studied the foot-wide steel hook at the bottom of the hook block. If she planted her foot into the cradle of the hook, she would have to hold the cable, which would move up and down as it flittered through the pulley system that raised and lowered her. There had to be a better way. Victor walked up as she was pondering a solution.

"It's not safe, Dagny."

It was a sensible observation, but not enough to deter her. "Then help me make it safer."

He sighed. "Well, the firefighters probably have a harness."

They did. They placed it on her like a backpack, clipped the front at her chest, and pulled the straps to make it tight. Removing the hook, they tethered her to the crane's hook block. She signaled to Steve Johnson, who pulled on the lever that lifted her. The suddenness of the jolt caught her with such surprise that she laughed a little, and the inappropriateness of this shot her back to sullen despair.

As she flew toward the sky, the scene below receded like a young director's Scorsese shot. Spinning wildly, she grabbed onto the hook block to steady herself. Johnson lifted her ten feet higher than the charred, steaming top of the silo and swung the arm of the crane directly above it. The heat burrowed its way through her suit, and within seconds, she was drenched in sweat. Steam from the silo glowed white under the intense light shone from above. As the cable lowered her into the cloud, she thought of David Foster Wallace's commencement address, "This Is Water," and how he referred to dinner as supper. She never used the word *supper*—it was always dinner, even though the words were interchangeable. Perhaps a robust vocabulary would make use of both, she thought. Was it a regional quirk that lodged dinner as her default, or was it familial or cultural—a Jewish linguistic quirk or prejudice, perhaps? As she debated the issue, she wondered whether the fumes from the explosion were clouding her mind. She felt sick and wet and heavy.

She emerged from the steam cloud in the belly of the silo, lit by the spotlight above as brightly as an operating room. It was with crystal clarity that she observed the lines and colors of each piece of charred wood and blistered concrete, all of which dissolved into background once she spotted the dead and damaged and often detached pieces of human body among them.

There was no way to signal to Steve to raise the hoist, so they'd agreed she would dangle for five minutes of inspection before he would lift her. This was, she realized, a terrible overestimation of the time that was desired. It took only seconds to ascertain the gravity of the scene; every moment beyond this was torture. Between the heat, the weight of the uniform, and the extent of the atrocity before her, she *was* dangling in hell.

Some of the faces in the debris were burned beyond recognition; others were ashen but intact, even retaining expression, although Dagny wondered whether she was simply projecting emotion into the lifeless. There were twelve human heads visible in the wreckage: some attached to entire bodies, some torn from their owners. Countless other bodies lay under them, certainly. Whoever did this, she decided, had no soul. They were dealing not with a man but a monster.

She closed her eyes and bowed her head, and the sweat poured from her hair against the face of her mask. These were the longest five minutes of her life.

When she felt the tug upward, it was as if she were ascending from hell to heaven through the steamy white cloud into the cool embrace of the crisp night air.

Johnson slung the jib and lowered her to the ground. Firefighters swarmed her, unclipping her harness and removing it. She lifted her helmet, tossed it to the ground, and removed her mask. Victor helped her with the coat.

"It was awful in there," he said.

"Yes. How did you—"

"The look on your face."

She pulled off the boots, removed the fire-suit pants, and pulled out her iPhone. After wiping the sweat from her hands, she opened the phone app and hit the first entry on her favorites. The old man answered, grumpier than usual.

"Chrissake, it's four thirty in the morning," he barked.

"I found your goddamn bodies."

CHAPTER 27

"Wonderful," he said. "You're reinstated. Which is good, because I never got around to filling out the onerous paperwork required to suspend you."

"This is huge, Professor. This isn't something we can do ourselves," Dagny said. "I've got a silo full of bodies here. We need agents, technicians by the dozens. For fingerprints, we need the Disaster Squad." It sounded like a team of comic-book superheroes, but it was the actual name for the FBI's team of mass-disaster forensic specialists.

"That bad?" There was an unseemly relish in his tone.

"At least eighty-one bodies. Probably more."

"I will take the first flight to Dayton from National, and shall instruct Brent and Victor to catch the same from New York."

When she hung up, she sent Diego off to get some sleep and dispatched Victor to the Dayton airport, so that he could fly back to LaGuardia in order to join Brent Davis on a flight back to Dayton. It was madness, but they saw no way around it. He was supposed to be in New York per the Professor's orders, and although she could get away with insubordination, his leash was shorter. If they had trusted Brent, they could have explained the circumstances and asked him to cover for Victor. But they didn't.

After bidding Victor good-bye, Dagny basked for a moment in the turn of the tide. Now she had a case—a real, live case—and that meant she could open a file, subpoena documents, search databases, and amass teams of skilled experts. Glancing at Beamer, she caught his smile. He felt it, too—a pocket of joy in the shadow of tragedy.

"John."

"Yes?"

"I need you to call your chief and introduce me."

He glanced at his watch.

"It's worth the waking," she said.

He nodded and dialed his phone. "Officer Beamer here. Sorry to wake you. The FBI is in Bilford investigating the murder of more than eighty individuals. Special Agent Dagny Gray is the lead agent on the case, and she has . . . More than eighty, sir. . . . At the Hoover farm. She's right here. Let me put her on."

She took the phone but covered the microphone with her hand. "What your chief's name?"

"Wiggum."

"Seriously?"

"Yes. He's sensitive about it, so don't joke."

She nodded and put the phone to her ear. "Chief Wiggum, this is Special Agent Dagny Gray. As you heard, we believe that eighty-some young men have been killed here. Bureau personnel will be descending by the dozens over the next couple of days, but I'll still need substantial assistance from your force. I would like Officer Beamer to be appointed as the full-time liaison to my investigation to help coordinate efforts and—"

"I'm concerned—"

"—keep you informed. Yes, sir?"

"Perhaps it is the haze of sleep, but I believe I must have misheard. How many bodies?"

"Eighty-one, at least."

"Jesus. In Bilford County?"

"We have a silo full of bodies here. Some of them came from other parts of southwest Ohio."

"A silo?"

"We just put out the fire."

"That's the sound I heard last night?"

"Yes, sir."

"Okay. I'm coming over, if that's all right."

"Of course. But in the meantime, I need John to start making calls for me."

"That's fine. Whatever you need, we will provide."

"Thank you, Chief."

When the Professor arrived, he would be in charge, but until then, it was Dagny's show, and she intended to make the most of it. Over the next three hours, she instructed area police departments to set up roadside checkpoints in case the unsub was making his way out of town; obtained a pledge of assistance from the medical examiners of Bilford and its surrounding counties; arranged for the assignment of the Bureau's best mass-disaster specialists and forensic examiners; ordered additional construction equipment to the site for the careful excavation of the silo; briefed Chief Wiggum in person and enlisted his men to guard the perimeter of the Hoover farm in order to preserve the scene; isolated a sample of residual fuel from the silo explosion for analysis; scanned and sent the fingerprint data collected from the cell phones for matching through the Bureau's IAFIS system; drafted a case summary with all known material information for circulation to selected team members; rented factory-strength air-conditioning units, stainless-steel tables, body bags, and blankets; hired three refrigerator trucks for transport; procured a promise of assistance from Principal Geathers; and reserved two more rooms at the Bilford Motor Inn.

Dagny was on the phone, finishing the last of these talks, when Beamer tapped her shoulder and pointed to the glow of the sunrise, which was painting lines across the horizon behind the silo. The bottom line hugged the earth in a deep, bright orange. Above it were darker orange lines, then blue ones, then the black of night. The scene was so beautiful that she pulled her Canon from her backpack and snapped a photo. The image on the camera's display failed to capture the spectacular definition of the lines of color. Beamer looked over her shoulder at the screen. "Some things you can only see in person, I guess."

"What kind of camera equipment does your department have?"

"The sun will be up all the way before we could get it."

She shook her head. "C'mon, John."

"Oh, you mean to document the scene."

"Yes."

"Some HD video cameras and several DSLR cameras."

"Can you have someone bring them?"

Twenty minutes later, a young officer handed her a box full of various cameras and equipment. Dagny picked a Canon HX camcorder from the bunch. Sifting through the box, she found three HDV cassettes and popped one of them into the camcorder.

She handed her own DSLR camera to Beamer. "Follow me and take pictures. I'll film." She led him back to the farmhouse, turned on the camcorder, and panned from the front of the farmhouse to the crop fields, barn, and silo. After stating the date, location, and her name, she yanked the microphone cable from the XLR input on the side of the camera.

"Why'd you do that?" he asked.

"Any additional audio would be hearsay, and besides, I want us to be able to speak freely. Step only where I step." Dagny led him

around the outside of the farmhouse, filming its exterior and the
landscape around it. She recorded the track from the house to the
barn, looking for signs of egress. Although she found some trampled
grass, there were no usable footprints. From the barn, she filed the
walk to the silo, where there were so many footprints from the previous night that none were distinguishable. Along the way, she found a
few scraps of paper trash that Beamer photographed and she collected
and documented. None of it seemed promising. There was a lot of silo
debris scattered about the explosion, and a few pieces of rusted metal
that she guessed came from barrels that fueled the explosion. Beamer
photographed all of them before she bagged them. They worked their
way back to the farmhouse, where she made one more pass around
its perimeter.

"Can't we go in?" he asked.

"We need a warrant."

"But the house is abandoned."

"Doesn't matter," she said. "It belongs to someone."

"I thought the courts said you could search abandoned property
without a warrant."

"The Supreme Court said you could search abandoned trash at
the curbside. They never said anything about entering an actual house
without a warrant."

"But you went in last night?"

"Those were exigent circumstances—that's an exception to the
Fourth Amendment." This was her story, anyway. Whether the circumstances were actually exigent wasn't clear. Although they later heard
a voice calling for help from the silo, this was after she had already
searched the home. If it became an issue, it could bar the admission of
any evidence concerning the cigarette stub she had collected during her
search. Up until now, she'd been breaking all the rules. From this point
on, they'd need to do things by the book.

"John, you've got to swear out an affidavit for a search warrant. I would do it, but I have to stay here and greet the troops when they arrive."

"Troops?"

Her phone buzzed. "Looks like they're here. I'll walk you out on my way to meet them. See if you can get the warrant within the hour."

"The judges won't be at the courthouse for another two hours."

She knew he'd never worked on anything with such high stakes, and that it would take some time for him to realize the measures the stakes demanded. "Catch a judge at home."

"Okay."

When they got to the edge of the farm, twelve Bureau technicians and crime-scene specialists were waiting—the first batch of what she hoped was much more. She gave them an overview of the circumstances that awaited them and e-mailed each a copy of the case summary she had drafted. Every inch of the property had to be inspected, and every piece of evidence documented and bagged before any bodies could be removed. Extraction of the bodies would likely require some demolition of the silo, which would be performed by construction crews acting under Bureau supervision. Once removed, the bodies would be loaded into bags and placed in the refrigerated trucks for transport to a team of medical examiners and forensic technicians who would attempt to identify each body and capture any evidence associated with them. To the extent that bodies had been torn apart, efforts would be made to reunite the parts. Fingerprints would be identified, where possible, and matched to prints on phones, which would allow them to associate names with the bodies. Fingernails would be scraped in case a scuffle had captured the unsub's skin fragments.

The group dispersed to begin collecting evidence. Dagny watched them for a while to assess their technique and offered suggestions where necessary. Her meddling seemed to irritate only a couple of men in the bunch, to her relief. Once she had confidence in their competence, she called Diego.

"Hello?" he answered in the haze of sleep.

"I need your help."

"For what?"

"Driving in daylight."

"I don't understand, but I'll be there in twenty."

"Great."

The driving was to get some orientation. What surrounded the Hoover farm? They would have to interview any neighbors. Were there cameras in the vicinity? If so, there would be footage to review. The Caltech software program had identified the location of each abduction, and each of those areas would have to be investigated for eyewitnesses or security feed. The amount of work that awaited them seemed overwhelming. She pulled out her phone and dictated a list of items that had to be accomplished. There were ninety-seven entries on the list when Diego arrived, and she wasn't close to done.

"You look terrible," he said, hopping out of the car.

"Thanks," she said, grabbing the keys.

"I'm serious. You're banged up, and your clothes are ripped and wet, and your eyes—"

"I get it."

"—are bloodshot, Dagny."

"It's been a busy night." She slid into the driver's seat.

"You need some sleep. A shower. Some bandages," he said, pointing to the scrapes on her arm.

"No time."

He climbed into the passenger seat. "Breakfast, at least?"

"If we see a drive-through." She turned the key, hit the gas, and they were off.

She drove loops, turning right at each intersection, increasing the radius of the circle each time around. It was obvious why the unsub had picked the farm—the silo was in the center of a hundred acres of land, and each edge of the property was abutted by farms of similar size, which were each in turn abutted by more farms of similar size.

As they drifted farther away from the Hoover farm, a television news van sped by so quickly that Dagny barely caught the Channel 7 News Dayton logo on the side. Someone had already contacted the press. She dialed the police chief and instructed him to block off all streets within two miles of the Hoover farm.

After she hung up, Diego asked, "Is that legal? With the First Amendment and all."

"Everything's legal until a court says otherwise." Another news van sped past. "We can't have them trampling on evidence and recording everything we're doing. Press coverage is exactly what the unsub wants. It will make him feel like he matters, and it will give him a window into our investigation." She looked at her watch. "It's not even nine thirty in the morning, and the circus has begun. Reporters are going to start talking to neighbors, pushing cameras in their faces, before we've even had a chance to talk to them. They'll start all-day coverage, repeating the same two or three supposed facts they think they know." Her phone chirped with a text message from Victor: **Landed Dayton, in car, on our way.**

They needed to meet somewhere away from the chaos. She texted back: **Meet at Beamer's.**

And then she texted Beamer: **Still need your basement for a little while. Meet there in one hour. Bring the warrant.**

He sent back a frowny face and the word *okay*.

CHAPTER 28

Dagny had arranged six chairs in a circle in Beamer's basement, but no one dared to select one until the Professor chose his. The slight, bald man stroked his pointed white beard while he pondered the selection. After too much deliberation, he chose the one that sat the highest. Victor slumped into a seat to the right of the Professor, who studied his droopy gaze and shook his head. "No reason for you to be so tired, Walton. Wake up. You've got a lot to learn in a little time."

Victor bore this better than anyone in his place should have. "Of course."

Dagny began the introductions. "John and Diego, this is Timothy McDougal, but we affectionately call him the Professor." The Professor grimaced at the word *affectionately*. "He's been with the Bureau since the days of Hoover in various capacities, infiltrating domestic terrorist cells, overseeing investigations of multistate serial killers, profiling and lecturing at the Behavioral Science Unit in Quantico. He is widely regarded as the leading intellectual thinker in the FBI." It was a bold proclamation, and one that he himself had drafted, insisting that the Bureau feature it in all of his biographical summaries. "He's the head of our little group, which operates largely outside of the organizational chart of the FBI. The Professor reports directly to the Director, who has issued a blanket order that the resources of the Bureau's other divisions accede to any of our requests.

"Brent Davis," she continued, "is the consummate special agent. He's spent time working in California, Colorado, and Texas, and is very good with working with people. I am not."

Beamer and Diego already knew Victor, but the Professor didn't know that, so she introduced him. "Victor Walton Jr. was previously an accountant for Deloitte & Touche. He joined the Bureau when he realized that he was an accountant for Deloitte & Touche. His capacity for tedium is his biggest strength."

"Hi," Victor said. "Nice to meet you guys."

Beamer and Diego looked confused as to why he was introducing himself as though they'd never met, but thankfully didn't say anything about it.

"John Beamer is our host," Dagny continued. "He's graciously given us his basement until we find new quarters, and—"

"I like it here," the Professor said. "It's discreet."

Beamer spoke. "Our station has a room three times this size—"

"Too much traffic and attention. Let's keep this," the Professor replied.

Dagny continued. "John is Ron Beamer's nephew. He's an officer with the Bilford Police Department. Unlike most police officers, he's competent."

He bristled at that. "I think—"

"It's a compliment, John." Dagny turned to the Professor. "John's been instrumental in assisting our efforts."

"A big help," Victor added.

"How would *you* know?" the Professor said.

Victor opened his mouth, but it took a few seconds for words to come out. "Because they found the bodies, right? So, I can only assume he was a big help."

The Professor shook his head.

"And this," Dagny said, gesturing to Diego, "is Father Diego Vega. His congregation came to him when members of their families went missing. He conducted his own investigation, and then came to me—"

"Enough of this, really," the Professor said, waving his hands. "Father Vega, Officer Beamer, we appreciate your assistance on the effort. We can take it from here. You're free to go."

Diego and Beamer looked at Dagny and started to stand. She held up her hand to stop them. "Professor, I highly recommend keeping both of them as part of our team. I trust them completely. John has been designated as our liaison to the Bilford Police Department, which is currently supporting the investigation by protecting the crime scene and can serve additional functions throughout the investigation. And Diego, apart from his own deep investment in the case, is our ambassador to the local immigrant populace. They trust him, and they don't necessarily trust us. He gives our investigation legitimacy in their eyes."

The Professor studied them for a few seconds. "Very well. But this is it. Just the six of us."

She nodded and began an overview of everything that had occurred, summarizing her interviews of the families and the discovery of the phones, demonstrating the database generated by their metadata and the chronological mapping of their movements, and describing the discovery of the bodies and the ongoing efforts to document and analyze evidence from the Hoover farm. She reviewed the ninety-seven entries on her to-do list, and the Professor added another twenty of his own.

He asked about the billboards at the entrance to the county, and Beamer and Diego explained about Sheriff Don and the politics of the region. "Has there been a record of violence against the immigrant population?" the Professor asked.

"No," Diego said. "Not until this."

The Professor stroked his beard. "A man or men? One or a gang?"

Brent said, "Eighty-one people is a lot for one man to kill."

"No," the Professor replied. "Not over time. Not with an immigrant population afraid to go to the police. Not with the way this labor market works. You show up with a truck and leave with a dozen of them. Take them to the farm. Maybe even have them climb into the silo itself under the pretext of work, and then you never let them out. Easy. One man keeps a secret better than any group can. Cults recruit. They splinter. They fight internally and, therefore, accomplish less. A cult might kill a dozen. Only one man can kill upward of a hundred."

Dagny immediately thought of counterexamples, like 9/11 or the Holocaust, but stayed silent.

"Now, as for motive," the Professor continued, leaning forward and putting his head in his hands. "Three possibilities, at least. One, he hates immigrants. Two, he loves immigrants, and he wants the world to sympathize with them. Three, he doesn't care about immigrants. He's killing them because they are easy people to kill, since their families won't contact authorities and their employment is undocumented and irregular."

"Perhaps the bigger issue is his mental state?" Dagny asked. "You don't kill this many people unless there's something severely wrong with you."

"He's insane," Victor said.

"*Borderline* insane," the Professor barked. "Never use the word *insane*, and if it tumbles out, it better have the word *borderline* with it."

Victor seemed confused, so she explained. "When an investigation starts to use the word *insane,* it seeps into documents and reports, and a defense lawyer can use that to build an insanity defense."

"And they get the Hinckley treatment instead of the death penalty they deserve," the Professor said. "In any event, the unsub here is not insane. To kill for this long without being noticed requires meticulous and careful planning, extraordinary patience, and focus and dedication. The truly insane are not capable of any of those things. He's disturbed but not insane."

Brent joined in. "In terms of a profile, I think it's safe to say we're looking for a white man once again."

Victor whispered to Diego, "It's always a white male."

"But as for age . . ." Brent shrugged.

"You can guess, or I can just tell you," the Professor said. "Middle-aged."

"Because?"

"Because that's who can hire these men," Diego answered, surprising everyone. "They would trust him enough to hop in his truck. A younger man wouldn't have the responsibility for a job big enough to warrant hiring them."

"Very good, Father," the Professor said. "You've jumped ahead of Victor on the organizational chart. Now, let's talk assignments. Brent, I want you talking to any- and everyone who lives or works near the Hoover farm."

"Yes, sir."

"Dagny, oversee the evidence collection at the farm and the transport of the bodies. Frankly, I don't like that there is work proceeding without our supervision this very moment. Victor, I want you to oversee the makeshift morgue. Link up the phone data to as many bodies as you can. Work with the Disaster Squad to set up systems to process the information. I want seamless flow. When a fingerprint analysis comes back, I want it to be automatically incorporated into our master database. We're building something from scratch here, and you need to make sure they do it right."

"No problem," Victor said.

"What can I do?" Beamer asked.

"Assist Dagny with the forensic inspection of the farmhouse, if you're competent enough for her to trust you."

"He is."

"After that, get everything related to the Hoover farm you can. We need the story of the property. Deeds, clients, permits, mortgages, foreclosure documents. Subpoena every document from every bank that ever had an interest in the place."

"Sure."

The Professor looked at Father Vega. "We have a long list of names. Meet with your congregation and go through them. See how many of these families are known. Keep track of anyone who can help us with them. Explain that we'll need their cooperation. Tell them God wants them to cooperate, if that will help."

Diego nodded. "I will."

With all of the others dispatched to their tasks, Dagny stayed back to talk to the Professor. "Nice meeting. But what are *you* going to do?" she asked.

"I'm going to play." He walked over to the computer setup, sat down, and opened the cell phone database. "What a wonderful toy. It's the key to everything. The data shows where he abducted his victims. You see the importance of this, right? The NSA has GPS data for nearly every cell phone in the country. If we could find a cell phone that traveled with these dots to the silos, we'd have the unsub."

"So, if our data shows twelve phones at Fowler Road—"

"The NSA data might show a thirteenth phone joining them, which would belong to the unsub."

"To get NSA data, you're going to need approval from the FISA court," she said.

"It won't be a problem."

"The *F* in FISA stands for *foreign*. The court is only supposed to permit data mining when there is a suspected foreign terrorist threat."

"A man has killed close to a hundred illegal immigrants. Sounds like terrorism to me."

"But most likely domestic."

"That hasn't been proven. Don't be naive, Dagny. Do you know how many data-mining requests the FISA court has ever rejected?"

"No."

"The answer is point zero three percent. They will approve the request."

He was probably right. "NSA said they stopped collecting domestic location data in 2011."

"And since then, there has been only incidental bulk collection of bulk data. Which means they have almost everything."

"How do you know that?"

"Because there's no oversight of NSA. Their decisions are scrutinized by a secret court that is subject to no judicial review or public scrutiny. They have dirt on every politician who might be inclined to check their power. They do whatever they want." He sighed wistfully. "They're like we used to be."

Dagny didn't pine as hard for the days of Hoover. "What if he doesn't carry a cell phone? When he called the radio station, he used a victim's phone." She reached into her backpack and pulled out the disc from *The Hank Frank Show*.

He inserted it into the computer and waited. The drive spun, and the disc popped back out.

"The words need to face up," she said.

He flipped it over. As audio of the killer's phone call played, he smiled.

"Why are you smiling?"

He looked up at her with wide eyes and a grin. "Because he's real, and we're going to catch him."

CHAPTER 29

When Dagny parked Diego's Corvette at the edge of the Hoover farm, Sheriff Don was standing at the border of the property with a dozen deputies and a tank. The tank had track wheels, an armored skirt, a large main gun, and the words SHERIFF DON'S SWAT TANK painted sloppily on the side. The fat, balding sheriff was screaming at John Beamer, and a television crew was filming the confrontation.

"This is goddamn unincorporated land, and that means I have jurisdiction over this site!"

Beamer shook his head. "This is Bilford City, and it's the Bureau's case, anyway." He turned to Dagny as she approached. "He brought the press past the checkpoint."

"Like hell I'm going to let incompetent Feebs run this show," Marigold sneered. Saliva was hanging from his overgrown mustache, and the tantrum had left him drenched in sweat. "I will roll over you and this crime scene with my tank if I have to."

Dagny walked up to the news crew and flashed her creds. "This is a crime scene. I need you to leave right now. Everyone who is here is impeding forensic work."

A young man in a suit extended his hand, but she didn't take it. "Jack McDaniel," he announced. "Field producer for Channel Two News. Sheriff Don said he was bringing us onto the property."

"Full transparency," the sheriff barked. "I am a champion of the free press."

She ignored the sheriff. "You and your crew have three minutes to pack up and leave, or you'll all be arrested for obstructing this investigation."

"Like hell, young lady!" Marigold shouted. "This is my county and my people, and I'm not going to sit back and let you botch it all up."

McDaniel looked at Dagny for a moment, seemingly uncertain of what to do. "Now you have two minutes, Jack," she said.

The cameraman lowered his camera, but the young brunette reporter next to him yanked it back up, pointed it at Dagny, and slid into the frame next to her. "This is Allison Jenkins for Channel Two News. What can you tell us about the silo?" She shoved a microphone toward Dagny's face.

Dagny turned to Jack and said, "One minute." Jack made a slashing gesture across his throat, and the cameraman turned off his camera. Jenkins pouted as they packed up their gear.

Sheriff Don glared at the crew. "What are you doing? You cowards! Turn that camera on. I'm going in there with a tank, and you're going to film it."

The television crew ignored him. Marigold turned back to Dagny. "What's your name, girl? I'm going to need it for the lawsuit I file. The Constitution guarantees me freedom of the press."

"Too bad it didn't guarantee you an education. Or manners. Or hygiene."

The sheriff charged forward and stuck his face in front of hers. "This is unincorporated property in Bilford County, over which I have jurisdiction. Murder, if there was any, is a state crime. And the FBI can't take over a case without the consent of the proper local authority, which is me."

It was true—the FBI couldn't stop local law enforcement from investigating a crime within its jurisdiction. The thought of investigating the scene in tandem with Marigold was horrifying. She turned to Beamer. "Is this unincorporated?"

"I think it's in the city of Bilford. Near the line, but still the city."

"Dog shit, it is!" Marigold said.

Dagny turned to Beamer. "What's the county auditor like?"

"Completely honest and reasonable. Nothing like the sheriff," he said.

One of Marigold's deputies laughed, and the sheriff spun to search for the offender. "Who was that?" No one gave him up.

"Call the auditor," Dagny said to Beamer. "Get him out here with deeds and papers and survey equipment if he needs it."

He made the call, and then they waited. Forty minutes later, a man arrived with rolled papers and a sack filled with equipment. They explained the urgency of the situation, and he got to work. Over the course of an hour, they watched over his shoulder as he consulted documents and moved his tripod and viewfinder to various locations on the farm.

The auditor pushed his glasses higher on his nose and announced, "Part of the farm is within the city limits, and part is unincorporated."

Sheriff Don started to march onto the property, but Dagny stopped him with a stiff arm. "Where is the silo?" she asked.

The auditor looked back down at his papers and spun around to face the silo. Shielding his eyes with his hands, he announced, "The silo is in the city."

"What about the farmhouse?" the sheriff barked.

"All the buildings are in the city. The fields over there," he said, pointing to the right of the farmhouse, "are unincorporated."

"What about where we're standing right now?" Dagny asked.

"City."

She turned to Sheriff Don. "Leave. Now."

His men started to leave, but Marigold walked closer to her. "I've got friends in high places and an electorate that loves me. I'm not going to let some silo full of illegals tear apart everything I've worked for. This is a murder case, not some liberal-agenda, amnesty-now talking point. Whoever did this thing was trying to make this county look bad because we believe in America. I'm not giving up the fight. We may be leaving, darling, but the war ain't over. If you think I'm going to lose to some dyke Feeb, you are sorely mistaken."

As he started to walk away, Dagny said, "I feel sorry for you."

He turned back. "What did you say?"

"I said I feel sorry for you."

He narrowed his eyes and clenched his fist. "You're lucky you're a woman." Shaking his head, he stormed away.

All too often, deeply flawed and preposterous people found great success in politics. Wealthy scions who drove girlfriends off bridges. Movie-star action heroes. Hockey moms. Real-estate billionaires. Appalachian-trail hikers. Serial adulterers and their enabling spouses. Normal people don't succeed in politics because they don't crave stardom or power. Only the crazy want the spotlight, so only the crazy get it.

This all made for entertaining newscasts, but not for very good government. The desire for power over others is the character defect that makes one unsuitable for the role. Bilford needed a good and decent candidate to run against Sheriff Don. But what good and decent person would put up with the fight?

Dagny turned to Beamer. "You should run against him."

He laughed. "You don't know anything about this place, do you?"

"I know that he has to go."

He laughed again.

"I'm serious. I'm not joking."

"Dagny, people around here aren't going to elect someone like me."

"Why not? You've got law-enforcement experience. You're a likable guy."

"Not going to happen." He shook his head and started to walk away.

She grabbed his forearm. "Why not? I'm serious."

He shrugged. "I'm too young, first of all. And I have no political experience or connections. You need to work within a party. And, I . . ." He stopped without finishing the thought.

"You what?"

"Nothing."

"No, you were going to say something."

He sighed. "Let's go check out the farmhouse, okay?"

CHAPTER 30

As Diego walked from Beamer's house to his own, he worked his way down the contacts list on his cell phone, placing calls to members of his congregation. When the first call went unanswered, he didn't think anything of it. But after more calls went to voice mail, it was obvious that the community was avoiding him. In the end, only one man answered—Juan Sanchez, the car dealer.

"Why won't anyone else talk with me?" Diego asked.

"Father Vega, we came to you because we thought you'd be discreet. Now there's a national investigation and news crews roaming the streets. People are scared and angry with you. No one signed up for this."

"I didn't sign up for this, either. But what did people think would happen?"

"People thought you'd find these boys and bring them back home."

"I wish it had been that easy. But this was a mass murder—"

"Which people found out from the news this morning. That's a rough way to hear about a son or husband."

Diego knew that was true. "I had no control over that."

"These families have been through so much loss and pain, and now they all think they're going to be deported because of you. They've been holding out for amnesty, and now they're going to be kicked out before a bill passes."

"Juan, again, I don't have control over these things."

"You brought that woman here and made everyone trust her."

"She didn't do anything wrong."

"Used to be only the boys were afraid to leave their houses—now everyone's in hiding."

"She has nothing to do with that. It's news because the unsub blew up a silo, not because of anything she did."

"What's an unsub?"

"The guy who did this."

"Is that an FBI term or something?"

"Yes."

"That's exactly what I'm talking about. You're supposed to be a priest, Father Vega. Not a federal agent."

Diego wanted to argue. He wanted to tell him that he was only acting like an agent because the community had drafted him into an investigation. But he needed Sanchez's help, not approval. "I need to get everyone together. We have to talk as a community."

"Not going to happen. People are panicked."

"All the more reason we need to meet. If we're going to catch this murderer, we need to work together. We need to share information. People need to help identify bodies."

"Where do you think this all leads? A trial? Where the nationality of every victim's family becomes a public record? If they put this man away, even if they put this man to death, do you think the story ends?

What will Sheriff Don do? What will ICE do? All of our people settled in Bilford because they wanted to be invisible. Instead, we've got news vans setting up camp all over downtown. This is going to be a media circus, probably for months."

And then there was silence. Juan Sanchez had hung up on him.

CHAPTER 31

In July 1877, the *American Journal of Microscopy and Popular Science* published a lecture by Thomas Taylor titled "Hand Marks Under the Microscope," which suggested that hand and fingerprint identification could solve crimes. To the layman, the idea that a criminal could be caught merely because he touched something sounded like alchemy or witchcraft. If people had read Taylor's article, they might have been convinced otherwise. But nobody read it.

People did read Mark Twain and his 1894 novel *Pudd'nhead Wilson*, the story of a young lawyer who solved a small-town murder using fingerprints. Shortly after the story was published, prisons began cataloguing the fingerprints of their prisoners in order to create a resource for crime detection. In 1911, a jury found a former prisoner, Thomas Jennings, guilty of murder based upon fingerprints he left in wet paint on a porch rail at the scene of the crime. It was the first successful use of fingerprints in a courtroom. Hours before Jennings's scheduled execution, the Illinois Supreme Court halted the proceedings in order to consider whether fingerprints were reliable. After consideration of expert testimony, the court ruled that fingerprints were scientifically trustworthy and could support a jury's verdict. Other courts followed suit.

The value of fingerprints is generally expressed in terms of their uniqueness, but their resiliency is almost as important. A good set of prints on the right material can last forty years. So in a space as large as the Hoover farmhouse, there should have been hundreds of residual fingerprints on the walls, doors, and windows, but Dagny found none.

Although there was dust in the air, there was none on the windowsills. She remembered the cigarette stub she'd bagged the night before. The house had smelled like smoke then, but less so now. "He wiped the place clean right before we got here," she said. "We need all of the property records. Can you get them?"

"Sure," Beamer replied. She stared at him for a moment. "Oh, you mean now?"

"Yes."

After Beamer left, Dagny opened her backpack and pulled out the clear bag containing the cigarette stub she'd found. Sitting on the floor, she peeled the cigarette paper from the butt and set it flat on top of the bag. Reaching into her backpack, she withdrew her fingerprint kit and opened it. She dabbed her brush in the black carbon powder and held the brush over the cigarette paper but didn't lower it. Powder didn't pick up fingerprints as well as luminescence and chemical agents, and infrared spectroscopic imaging was even better. Everything was a calculus—was it better to get instant results with a mediocre process or to wait for a better process but lose time? She put the brush back with the kit. Even if they couldn't get a good fingerprint off the cigarette, it was possible that it contained saliva residue, which would give them a DNA sample. She would let the lab do it.

Dagny started to put the butt back into its bag but stopped. She had collected it without a warrant. If it yielded usable prints or DNA, there was always the chance that a judge could decide to exclude it from evidence. She grabbed another clear plastic bag, wrote the current date and location on it, and dropped the paper and filter from the butt into it. Now it was the product of a warrant and unquestionably admissible. Investigations were built on small cheats like this.

She packed up her things and walked out of the house, toward the silos. Construction workers waited idly by their equipment while Bureau technicians gathered evidence. Dagny talked to each of them, reviewing the evidence they had collected. Most of it was inconsequential. One had found a piece of a digital timer, which suggested that the unsub had left the scene prior to the detonation. She had wondered whether the unsub had placed a trigger on the ladder or if he had been watching from a distance and remotely detonated the silo when he saw them climbing up it. Apparently, the fact that they had been climbing up the silo when it exploded was only a coincidence.

Another technician found a piece of a rusted barrel with a good amount of liquid cupped in its fold. Dagny waved her hand over the piece to catch its fragrance. It didn't smell quite like gasoline, which meant it could be diesel. Diesel wasn't a very good explosive. Either the unsub didn't know what he was doing or he didn't want to destroy too much of the silo's contents.

She remembered the explosion from the newspaper, pulled out her phone, and added another item to her to-do list: investigate whether there was video from the gas station.

When the technicians finished the bulk of their work, Dagny had the crane lower her inside the silo once again so she could take video and pictures. This time, the silo was cool enough that no fire suit was required.

Under the light of day, the bodies in the debris were more distinct than before. One young man's lips were cracked, and his face was coated in dust. The top of his skull had burned to a black char, but the fire had left one good eye staring up at her. All of the bodies on the top of the stack were like this—half cinder, half man. She assumed that the bodies farther down in the pile had been there longer. They may have escaped the fire but were more likely to have decomposed. Removing them from the silo was not going to be easy.

Dagny called the crane operator with her phone and had him lift her out of the silo. She gathered the technicians and construction workers and explained the task at hand. Calls were placed to augment to the team and procure additional equipment. Experts debated and disagreed, and she had to play referee as to methodology.

At first, they attempted to chisel away at the top of the silo, but hours of this yielded little progress. Eventually, they employed a wrecking ball, which was not used to smash down the silo but simply grazed it to cause fissures in the walls without having them collapse inward. Once the silo walls were weakened, the crew attached chains drawn by trucks to the silo's top edges, which tore apart the walls. It took several hours, but eventually the top half of the silo was entirely removed, leaving an eight-foot lip above the content they would have to extract.

A makeshift platform was constructed with lumber and placed across half of the top of the remaining silo. Technicians dropped down from this platform into the debris, gathering pieces and placing them into sacks, which were carried by crane to stations for cataloging. Bodies and body parts were loaded into refrigerated trucks. By midnight, the team had excavated a third of the silo's contents. A new team of technicians and agents tagged in, and Dagny stayed to direct them. By morning, another third of the silo had been emptied, and she rode in the truck that carried them to the makeshift morgue. She hoped Victor had it up and running. On the way, she dialed John Beamer.

"I've got the property records," he said.

It had taken a long time. "Great. Get them to the Professor. Who's the county coroner?"

"Beatrice Minor."

"Is she good?"

"She's a strange one. But good at her job, and you can trust her."

"That's all I need to know."

CHAPTER 32

When she got to the high school, Dagny went to Principal Geathers's office to thank her for her assistance. Before she could finish, a man threw open the door with such force that the principal's diploma frames rattled against the wall. He was spewing words in such an animated frenzy that they tumbled all over one another.

"This is unacceptable. Not in the least, for crying out loud. Absolutely can't take it," he said. He was wearing shorts and a golf shirt, and carrying a basketball under his arm as if for emphasis. "It's completely wrong. Everyone needs to get out of here. It's . . . unbelievable. We've got a game against Madison tonight—"

Principal Geathers shook her head. "I rescheduled it. You'll play at their place tomorrow."

"But this is a home game!"

"The whole season will be away this year," Dagny said.

He turned to her and threw up his hands. "That's not fair! This is the last year we have Jackson and Collins. This is a big season. We've got a shot at a state championship."

The principal shook her head. "Larry, this is bigger than a state championship."

"It's just not fair. This year, of all years. You know . . ." He howled, then sighed, and then, seemingly sapped of his anger, asked meekly, "Can I at least get my things out of my office?"

"I'll go with him," Dagny said.

As they passed through the halls of the school, the mass of students parted to each side. No one spoke or made much noise at all. Even the lockers seemed to open gingerly; footsteps barely patted the floor. Whispers were too hushed to discern. Dagny felt the eyes of the students fix upon her. Maybe they were looking for answers or assurance or relief. The best she could do for them was project competence. She noticed that there were no Hispanic kids in the hallways, and she couldn't blame them for staying home.

"Everything is weird today," the coach muttered.

"Get used to it," she replied.

When they got to the gymnasium, two tall men with closely cropped hair guarded the door. If they hadn't been special agents, they would have played them in the movies. Dagny flashed her creds. It wasn't necessary—they knew who she was—but a protocol had been established, and it would be followed. One of the agents opened the door, and a chill escaped. That was good—it meant the refrigeration units were doing their job. She led the coach into the gymnasium.

A hundred rectangular folding tables were arranged in neat rows across the gymnasium's two basketball courts. Each table was numbered, as indicated by hanging, laminated cards. Nearly half of the tables were covered in bodies in various stages of decomposition, ranging from funeral-ready to near-zombie to half-skeletal. A dozen Bureau technicians were tending to the bodies—documenting conditions, lifting skin cells, and the like. Members of the Disaster Squad were lifting prints. Others were taking delivery of the latest arrivals from the silo at a sorting station near the rear door. Victor was with them, giving instructions and taking an inventory. Dagny caught his gaze, and he smiled at her. She held up a finger to let him know she'd catch up with him in a minute.

Next to the sorting station were eight tables pushed together and covered with loose body parts and appendages that could not yet be assigned to a body. When the coach saw this, his entire body heaved, and he threw up into his right hand. Dagny grabbed a plastic bin from a stack of them and handed it to him. "Try not to drip. We've got a lot of people working here."

He let the vomit fall into the bin. "I'm sorry," he said.

She escorted him into the locker room, and he washed his hands. "You understand now that this is bigger than a championship?"

"Yes."

They went to his office, where he filled a box with papers and artifacts, and then she escorted him, his box, and his puke-filled bin out of the gym. She wandered the halls until she found a vending machine. It was filled with assorted multigrain chips and hand fruits—not a candy bar or Doritos bag in the bunch. Thank you, Mrs. President, she thought. She put a dollar bill into the feeder and traded it for an apple.

To preserve the sterility and cleanliness of the makeshift morgue, Dagny ate the apple in the hallway and pitched the core before returning to the gym. As she stepped back into the cold, she pulled out her phone and opened her Weight Watchers app. Searching the point database, she found that an apple was worth zero points. She had forgotten that certain fruits and vegetables were deemed so healthy as to merit no points at all. There were at least one hundred calories in the apple, so earning zero points for it wasn't fair. She manually entered two points into the app, which seemed like the right thing to do. Victor walked toward her.

"I'm entering my points," she said in an effort to preempt his hectoring.

"I wasn't even going to ask."

"You were, too."

He looked ridiculous, as he often did. All of his suits had been inherited from his father, a taller and fitter man, so they were too long in some places and too tight in others. This was part of the reason he still looked like a child at twenty-five. Sometime, she would have to take him shopping—a task she hated doing for herself, but one she could stomach for him.

"So, what do we have here?" she asked.

"We're separating and numbering the bodies, documenting all we can. Then we'll try to merge all of that information with the information from the phones."

"Do we have the families lined up to identify the bodies?"

"No luck with that yet, but Diego is trying. Some of the guys had wallets in their pockets. Most of them didn't burn too badly, so we've been able to tie some names to bodies. Hopefully, with witness identification, we'll have a lot more. Combined with the phone data, we'll have a comprehensive picture of each of their lives. Everything they did, every place they went, every item they bought. Everything they said. The life story of every victim."

"That's pretty amazing." And it was truly amazing. But she wondered where it all led. "How will any of this stuff help us catch the unsub?"

"Well, once we get the info together, we can . . ." Victor paused, took a deep breath, and closed his eyes. "I don't know." He surveyed the hyperkinetic activity around them. "Is this all a waste?"

"If we catch the guy, all of this stuff will be evidence the US Attorney can use to tell the story of the crime. But unless we find his DNA on a body, I'm not sure it gets us any closer to catching him."

"Well, Sherlock, if we don't find his DNA, how do we catch him?"

"We do what we usually do."

"What's that?"

"Hope he makes a mistake." Her phone buzzed with a text. She glanced at the screen. "She's parking."

"Who?"

"Beatrice Minor. She's the county coroner. I called her on the way here."

"Okay." He reached up and tugged at his red hair. "He will, right?"

"She. The coroner is a she."

"No, the unsub."

"Will what?"

"Make a mistake. If he were a genius, he wouldn't be killing people, right? He'd be investing in something that made him rich."

That was the thing that always saved them. People who were smart enough to get away with murder generally had better things to do.

They walked to the door, where Minor waited. She was a round, squat, middle-aged woman with short arms and a long face. Her skin was pale, her eyes drooped, and she wore about a dozen dour expressions on her face at the same time. Dagny shook her hand. "I'm Dagny Gray," she said.

"Bea Minor." She turned to Victor. "And you?"

"F Sharp," he said.

She grimaced. "I don't care for humor under normal circumstances. Do you think it's appropriate under these?"

He sunk back in his stance. "So sorry. Victor Walton, ma'am."

The coroner scanned the room for a moment, then nodded. "Okay, I get it. Staging. Isolation. Sampling. Yep. You've got refrigeration. Not ideal, but adequate."

"Let's sit down and talk." Dagny led the two of them to the gym coach's office. Sliding into the chair behind the desk, she motioned for them to take the chairs on the other side. "I don't know what you heard about—" Something smelled terrible. She followed the scent to the bottom-right drawer of the desk. Opening it, she found a rotten orange. She closed it. "We found a large number of bodies in the silo—"

"It's on the news. I heard about it. You're concerned that there might be bodies he didn't put in the silo. Unsolved cases involving Hispanic bodies."

"Yes," Dagny said. "I'd like it if you could—"

"Pull any files concerning Hispanic bodies—male, certainly, but female, too. Segregate all of them that are unsolved, but you'll want the others, too, in case someone has been wrongly convicted. You'll want any samples we associated with these cases. Now, I won't have the actual investigation files—that's Sheriff Don for the county stuff, and it's not too hard to guess why you aren't going to him for it. If you need his files, you'll have to get a warrant, because he won't turn them over otherwise. If you get a warrant, you'll probably need a SWAT team to enforce it. But that's not worth the trouble unless you think you have something that might be a lead, and everybody who turns up in Bilford goes through my office, so I'm a good place to start. That about right?"

"Yes, that's about right." Dagny smiled. "Now, I also need—"

"Me to coordinate with surrounding county coroner offices to do the same? There's no reason to think this guy would limit his activity to Bilford alone—"

She nodded. "I'd start with—"

"Hamilton in the south, Franklin in the north, and everywhere else in that circle."

"Yes."

Victor leaned forward. "The sooner the better, of course."

"Tomorrow morning work for you?"

"That will do," Dagny said.

"I'll have all the coroners from the neighboring counties come with responsive materials first thing tomorrow morning, at my office. Mind you, we start early."

"We love early."

"Five a.m. work?" Minor asked.

"I'm sorry," Victor said. "That's not morning; that's still night."

"We can make it," Dagny said.

"We can make it," he repeated. "We might need a couple of gallons of your strongest coffee, but we'll make it."

"Five a.m. at 109 Brightward Road. I'll bring the coffee; you bring yourselves. We set?"

"One more thing," Dagny said. "That gas-station explosion was Franklin County, right?"

"It was."

"Can you have the Franklin County coroner bring the autopsy file for the gas-station clerk?"

"I will."

She loved this woman. "Thank you for your—"

"Efficiency is the reason I get reelected coroner. No politics in me. I just get the job done."

"Well, thank you."

They led her back through the gymnasium to the exit. After she left, Dagny turned to Victor.

"I like her."

"She's a character. Wouldn't let you talk."

"Didn't need to. She knew what we needed."

"Speaking of things we need, we need to sleep. Five a.m.? Really? I took a two-hour nap, but I know you've been up for two nights now."

"That's how these things go."

"It's not sustainable, Dagny."

"Keep things going here. Get shipments out to the labs every four hours. Fibers, hair, fingerprints . . . we don't have time to save it all up and submit at the end of the day. Chain of custody is everything. Spot-check the labeling and documentation. Assess competence. Pick the three best people you find, and give them reporting authority to you. And most of all . . ."

"Yes?"

"Don't let them know you're winging this. Act like you know what you're doing. You're twenty-five years old, and you look like you're sixteen, so the only way people are going to follow you is if you don't give them a chance to realize how silly that sounds. Right?"

"Right."

She was distracted by his suit sleeves, which hung nearly to his knuckles. "Seriously, Victor, when this is over, I'm taking you to buy some new suits. Tell me you at least got a fitted tux for your wedding?"

"Not yet."

"It's less than two months away."

"Well, I might have to postpone it if we're still working this case."

"Good Lord, we'd better be done by then." She glanced at her watch and then patted him on the arm. "I've got to run."

As she darted out of the gymnasium, she heard him yell, "What's wrong with my suits?"

CHAPTER 33

The thin man's thumb flitted among the buttons on the remote as he cycled through the channels once more. The local stations and cable-news networks had suspended their regular programing for around-the-clock coverage of his crimes. Famous people were talking about him. Anderson Cooper, who made $11 million a year, was talking about him.

He watched Anderson Cooper from a worn, plaid La-Z-Boy recliner, surrounded by a filth and squalor that began with Yanna's death and had overtaken the 1,100-square-foot house when his murders began. Piles of papers from court proceedings. Empty bottles from both pills and drink. Pizza boxes. Discarded wrappers. Crumbs. The rats—they were new. There were two of them at least, hiding somewhere in the mess. He'd seen them a couple of times but heard them all the time, the patter of their feet scurrying along the floorboards.

Flip.

And then Lester Holt was talking about him—another national news anchor. Amazing. A famous, rich man in a suit in New York was talking about something he did. The thin man had never mattered before, and now no one mattered more.

The station threw the feed to Allison Jenkins, a Channel 2 reporter who was standing in front of Bilford City Hall. The building had nothing to do with his crimes, but they needed a backdrop, and the FBI wasn't letting reporters go anywhere near the Hoover farm. Ridiculous, he thought. Even worse, Jenkins had no information, apart from the fact that "dozens" of Mexicans had been left to die in a silo. Dozens? Dozens could be twenty-four or thirty-six. He had killed eighty-six people. She should have known this.

Flip.

Channel 7 had an aerial shot of the Hoover farm, thanks to the station's news chopper. A crane lifted a body bag from the silo and lowered it to a team of federal agents. The agents placed it on a gurney and then loaded it into a large truck. Using diesel for the bulk of the combustion had worked well—it gave a nice, explosive show for the community but still preserved the bodies enough that maybe they could be counted. Then they would understand the superlative nature of his accomplishment.

Flipping through the channels some more, he marveled at the ubiquity of the coverage of his crime. What was going to happen? It both delighted and scared him that he didn't know. Would he get caught? He assumed he would. Almost every mass criminal was. Even the Unabomber, alone in that shack in the middle of Montana, was caught.

Or he could flee. To where, though? To Mexico? Now, that would be ironic. To move to their country after he'd killed so many who had moved here. It seemed poetic and also sensible. He didn't need much. A roof, a small plot of land. He could work as day labor, if necessary.

He flipped back to Channel 2. Now Allison Jenkins was referring to him as the "Monster of Bilford." This was outrageous. He wasn't a monster. He was a victim.

Jenkins was telling the wrong story. It was time to make her tell the right one.

CHAPTER 34

Although Bilford's motels and restaurants were booming from the media influx, most of the other businesses were closed. Nearly all of the locals were staying home to watch television or to avoid it. The few who ventured outside walked the sidewalks with obvious trepidation, their necks craning nervously back and forth, searching for signs of trouble. Children sprinted from their buses back to their houses and locked the doors behind them. It didn't feel like a man had carried out a mass murder—it felt like there was a virus polluting the air. Everything in Bilford was cloaked in gray, rusted and worn, dulled and muted. Even the sun seemed to have dimmed three notches.

And then there was Diego's bright-red Corvette, looking like a clown at a funeral as it barreled down Bilford's weary streets. The pride he had for his car had never felt this sinful, so much so that his body began to shake and quiver, and he had to pull over. As anger welled up within him, he pounded his fists against the steering wheel until they started to bleed. He wasn't mad at the car—the ludicrous red carriage didn't know any better. He was mad at himself for spending so many hours to make it pretty while the world around it became uglier and uglier. The car was everything he hated about himself—vanity, selfishness, isolation. He felt trapped inside it.

When his calls to the congregation had gone unanswered, he'd borrowed his Corvette back from Dagny so he could bang on some doors and beg for people to answer. No one did. The community had shut him out, which proved conclusively that he was never part of it to begin with.

Staring at the blood on his hands, he recalled a verse from the Bible and spoke it aloud.

"'It is your crimes that separate you from your God. It is your sins that make him hide his face so that he does not hear you. For your hands are defiled with blood, and your fingers with crime; Your lips speak falsehood, and your tongue utters deceit. No one brings suit justly, no one pleads truthfully. They trust an empty plea and tell lies; they conceive mischief and bring forth malice.'" Diego paused, trying to think of the rest. Something about adders' eggs. Shaking his head, he continued. "'The Lord saw this, and was aggrieved that there was no justice.' So what did God do? Did he give up? Did he go home and shut the doors and cry?" He welled up. "No! 'He put justice on his breastplate, victory as a helmet on his head; he clothed himself in with garments of vengeance, and wrapped himself in the mantle of zeal.' That's what God did. That's what we all can do. That's what we all *must* do. That's what we learn from Isaiah 59. We don't fear evil; we confront it. Together."

There was a rousing sermon in there, and if there were a way to force his congregation to hear it, it might change a mind or two. But people who were avoiding his calls weren't going to come to an impromptu session of church.

Unless he found a way to bring church to them.

Diego pushed his car back onto the road and sped home. Sitting at his kitchen table, he jotted down notes on the back of an envelope, scratching and replacing everything that rang false.

When it was finished, he opened his laptop, stared into the web-cam, and started recording. "My name is Father Diego Vega, and I have failed you," he said in Spanish. "My job is not to carry you through the best, but to prepare you for the worst. Right now, this is the worst. It is too late for me to guide you. Only the Lord can carry us through these times. So let's talk about what the Lord says." He recited Isaiah 59, waving his bloody hands before the camera, his voice nearly cracking, rising in volume with each lyric, swelling to crescendos more common to a Baptist preacher than a Catholic priest. His eyes stared deep into the camera throughout, determined to pop through the screen into the homes on the other side. Determined to shame people into action.

After the fire and brimstone, it was time for his plea. "I am asking only that you visit and identify the bodies at the high school, and that you sit with the agents working the case and give detailed and thorough statements. I will make sure you have safe transport. I can, if you'll let me, work to arrange for security near your homes. This is not a time to burrow and hide and cower in fear. This is a time to stand with God. It is easy to stand with him in good times. Virtue is standing with him when times are bad.

"If you'll stand with God and help with the investigation, please reply to this e-mail so that I can make the necessary arrangements. Thank you."

CHAPTER 35

The Professor was still sitting in front of the computer in Beamer's basement when Dagny walked down the steps. Before she could speak, he held up his hand, silencing her. She followed his eyes, darting about the map on the screen, following each dot as it moved toward its murder. He paused the action and closed his eyes, seemingly searching for deep insights and revelations.

She set her backpack on the floor and sat next to him. When she opened her mouth, he again silenced her—an impressive trick, since his eyes were still closed. After a few minutes, he shook his head. "I can't decide."

"Can't decide what?"

He ignored it. "How is the morgue?"

"Operating. Organized."

"They're still emptying the silo?"

"Yes. It's my next stop."

"You talked to the coroner?"

"I did." She enjoyed it when the Professor was dialed in to a case. There was no small talk.

"What else is on your immediate agenda?"

"I want to check to see if there is video of the gas-station explosion."

He shook his head. "I talked to the local police. The only camera was inside the station, and that melted down."

"Some neighboring business had to have a camera."

"It's a rural gas station, they say. But you should confirm it."

"What can't you decide?"

"The president wants me to fly back to DC to brief him on the case."

"The president of the United States?"

"No, Turkmenistan." Sarcasm was the only form of humor the Professor ever displayed.

"That's unusual."

"So is finding eighty-one illegal immigrants in a small-town silo in Ohio."

"You can't do it by phone? Video?"

"One should never pass up the chance to meet with the president in person, Dagny."

"Isn't this something the Director is supposed to do?"

He smiled. "I have a better handle on the facts."

"And the Director is okay with it?"

"The Director doesn't know."

Dagny shook her head. "That seems unwise."

"To the contrary. The president has lost confidence in the Director."

She had met the Director once, and he had been reasonable enough under the circumstances. He had also permitted their little group to operate without supervision. Alienating him seemed risky. "Are you sure about this?"

He smiled. "Come with me to DC."

She shook her head. "I have too much to do."

"Mistake on your part. I'm going to take credit for everything good in your absence."

"And everything bad?"

"All yours."

"Tell me you've got a profile for the unsub."

"I have some preliminary ideas. I think he's a local. Mechanically minded. A handyman of sorts."

"Why?"

"He modified a silo and then rigged it to explode."

"Fair enough."

"I suspect he has been unable to keep a job for very long, maybe uninterested in doing so. Prefers to be left to his own devices. Not dumb, but not cultured. Something traumatic happened to him, I'm guessing. Likely former military."

"Why former military?"

"Because our military attracts the aimless. It teaches them discipline, authority, and confidence."

"And where do you see that here?"

"He loaded up a truck with migrants, took them to the silo, ordered them to surrender their phones, and convinced them to climb up and then down to their deaths. You can only pull that off with an air of authority and a great deal of confidence. Plus, the canvas bag that held the phones."

"So, canvas is a military thing?"

"Of course," he said.

"Anything else?"

"Not much family," he continued. "Not around him, anyway. Maybe estranged."

"Physically?"

"Generally fit. Something like this takes energy. Taller rather than short. Thinner rather than fat. When are you getting the files from the various coroners?" Most people paused when changing topics, but the Professor never did.

"Tomorrow morning."

"Get some sleep tonight."

"We'll see."

"It's an order, not a suggestion. You look terrible. As for the coroners, I'm guessing they'll have some unsolved murders of Hispanic men, but I doubt our guy is the one who did it. Although he was likely a cruel man, I don't think he was a criminal one until something set him off."

"What?"

"I don't know. But the grandeur of his enterprise isn't something that festers within a man throughout his life. With your average, run-of-the-mill serial killer, that evil was always inside him. But something like this was sparked. Our unsub was always a bad man. But not bad like this."

As profiles went, it was fine. But in the end, profiles were just guesses, and she preferred evidence. She didn't dare say this to the Professor, who had made a career out of such behavioral analysis. "What can't you decide?" she asked again.

He pushed a key on the computer, staring at the flow of dots on the computer screen. When the dots came together, he paused it. "That's the point of abduction. The NSA may very well know whether another phone was in the vicinity at that time. But my contact at the NSA won't do a search for me because of new safeguards and such. Thank you, Edward Snowden," he sneered.

"I seem to remember someone suggesting it might be difficult to get this data from NSA without a terrorist connection," Dagny said.

"Yes, a very annoying person suggested that. Even a broken clock, you know the rest. In any event, I can't decide if I should ask the president to make the NSA cooperate."

Of course he should, she thought. "What's the downside?"

"Apparently, the use of this data to solve crimes is now a political issue, what with all the civil-liberty nonsense going around."

Dagny believed in more of that civil-liberty nonsense than the Professor. "If you don't ask the president, what's the alternative?"

"I have a friend who works for an NSA contractor."

"That sounds far-fetched."

"That he can access the data?"

"That you have a friend."

"You're delightful when you haven't slept in two days. If my friend is caught, he'll be fired. Perhaps prosecuted. They'll trace it to us unless I find a way to contact him without leaving a record. That's harder than you'd think these days."

"Buy a burner."

"A what?"

"You've obviously never worked a drug case."

"They're beneath me. What's a burner?"

"You buy a cell phone with prepaid minutes from Walgreens, and you throw it away when you're done."

He shook his head. "They'd find some way to trace it. Tie it back to the store and watch video footage to see who made the purchase."

"Then wear a hood and pay in cash."

"I miss the old days, when you could get away with anything," the Professor said. He stroked his beard for a moment. "I have the answer. I'll casually float the idea to the president, and let him decide whether he wants to order NSA to cooperate or, alternatively, if he will agree to stymie any investigation into a breach of NSA security associated with my friend's inquiry into the data. That option would give him the opportunity to maintain plausible deniability."

"The mark of any true leader."

"You don't become president by being a *true* leader, Dagny." He glanced at his watch. "My cab should be here any minute. A private jet is waiting for me at the Bilford County Airport. I'll be in the Oval

Office three hours from now. There's a possibility that we'll have an answer from NSA one way or the other tonight. We're close, Dagny."

She hoped he was right, but she wasn't optimistic. In his profile, the Professor had described a man with no job, no friends, and no family. Someone who lived a life of isolation.

It didn't seem like someone like that would carry a cell phone.

CHAPTER 36

Hank Frank sipped ice water from an insulated, oversize travel mug and moved the mic closer. He spoke at a near whisper. "I was going to talk about the sales tax today." He paused. "Not even the whole tax. I was going to talk about point five percent. That was today's topic. I had notes. I had spreadsheets. I had guests lined up to talk about a half a percent increase in the sales tax.

"It was all going to be about another penny on two dollars." He took another sip of water, and then looked up to Lucy in the control room, who seemed to be watching him—really watching him—for the very first time. "That's what we do, right? We argue about small things with righteous passion and relentless indignation, certain in our infallibility. Certain that those on the other side of the issue are stupid or dishonest or ignorant." He sighed.

"I don't really care about the sales tax, or having to wait five days to buy a gun, or what they read in a high school English class. I mean,

I care about them enough to have an opinion about them. And when I tell you that opinion, it's sincere. Right or wrong, everything I've said, I really meant.

"But . . ." He took another sip of water. "What really matters to me? What really matters is my life with my wife and son. Dinners together. Baseball games. Christmas mornings. School plays. The kiss my wife gives me when I leave the house. The smile my son gives me when I pick him up from school. Family vacations. All of those things, and thousands of those things. The thousands of those things still to come.

"No matter what your politics, those are the things that matter. We share that, regardless of party or politics, religion or skin color. Or even place of birth."

Tears started to well in his eyes. "We're hearing now that several dozen young men may have been killed. That means there are dozens of families that have lost sons and brothers and fathers, and many dozens more that lost friends or lovers. The greatest tragedy and loss one can imagine, and it's being felt in hundreds of homes, here, in and around our small town." He stopped a moment in the enormity of the tragedy he had described, and then he continued.

"And I feel great personal shame because it happened here, in our town, with our eyes closed. We talk about Bilford pride, but there is no Bilford. There's no sense of community. Only pockets of people who look like one another, so they hang out together and ignore everyone else. We surround ourselves with mirrors, not windows, and there's so much we don't see as a result.

"And the real shame I feel? That in two years, I'll be ranting on here about the sales tax or abortion or even immigration, because I will move on just like so many of you who were lucky enough that a madman in our midst didn't hate the color of our skin or the place we were born. We all have the luxury of forgetting. There are a thousand folks in Bilford who don't. I urge you all—every one of you—to reach out to that community with all the love and help you can. At the end of the day, we're not Republican or Democrat, young or old, white or black or brown, citizen or noncitizen. At the end of the day, we're all human. We feel the same emotions and grieve the same losses. There's no 'them' today in Bilford. There is only us."

CHAPTER 37

When Dagny arrived at the farm, technicians and crew were still working on the last of the silo's bottom remnants, mostly small, charred pieces of bodies and clothing mixed among animal carcasses and feces, all of which was difficult to segregate. The lead technician on duty gave her an overview of the excavation. Everything had been done with commendable efficiency and expertise, but there was no surprise find or smoking gun. Things would be sampled and dusted and scanned, and it was likely to tell them nothing at all.

Brent's booming voice lifted her from the gloom. "Dagny!"

She turned and saw him walking toward her. Tall, fit, handsome. Impeccably attired in a well-tailored and pressed suit. Hoover would have cloned him back in the day, if he had the technology and hadn't been racist.

"Tell me good news," she said.

He spun around, pretending to leave. "I'll try to get you some."

"Just tell me what you've found."

He turned back, smiling. He was always smiling with her. As far as she knew, he was always smiling with everyone. It was an inclination she couldn't understand. Pretending to be happy was exhausting. To do it all the time would kill her. She supposed he might have been smiling because he was genuinely happy, although this seemed impossible to her. Happiness was something Dagny understood in theory, like a black hole. She knew black holes existed, but they were several thousand light years away.

"Why do you always look at me like you're an anthropologist?" he said.

"The neighbors?"

"I've interviewed everyone contiguous and three properties out. Was waking people all night long." He pulled out a notepad. "Fifty-nine interviews at thirty-one properties. Four interviews were fruitful."

"How so?"

He flipped through his notes. "Susan Marks, twenty-eight, house-wife, lives in a farmhouse three properties south. Was taking her kids to school and passed a pickup truck with a bunch of Hispanic men in the back. It was headed this way. Couldn't remember the color of the pickup. Thinks there were about eight men in back. Didn't notice the driver. That's all she had."

"Second?"

He flipped the page again. "Douglas Stills, lives next door. Mid-fifties, white. Said the Hoover farm has been vacant three years. Foreclosed by the bank. Hoovers moved to Georgetown, Kentucky. Thinks Terry Hoover got a job at the Toyota plant. Hasn't seen them since. Farm was in disrepair; property was uncared for. Stills was happy a few months ago when he saw a pickup truck pull into the property with a, quote, 'bunch of Mexicans in the back.' Figured the bank was finally getting the property ready for sale. Guessed that the truck was black. Didn't notice who was driving. Said the truck didn't use the driveway, but figured that maybe the men were clearing some of the woods. That's it for him."

"I hope you're saving the best for last. Third?"

"Maxwell Hammond. White, forties. Leases part of the Baker farm for growing soybeans. Saw a pickup drive by twice with Hispanic men in the back. Hammond was working down by the road. Says it was a blue pickup. About a dozen men in the back each time. Says he thinks the driver was black but can't remember anything else."

"Black?" That didn't meet the Professor's profile for their serial killer. It didn't meet the profile for any serial killer. "How far was he from the road when he saw him?"

"Twenty feet."

Dagny nodded. "Fourth?"

"Harrison Baker has a farm two lots to the west. Eighty-one years old, lives alone with his dog. Spends most of his time sitting on his front porch with binoculars, watching birds and anything else that happens by. Says he saw a pickup truck headed here with men in the back three times; he saw the same truck headed back the other way, empty, a couple of other times. Couldn't remember the color of the truck. White, he thinks, but he says that's just a guess, and he can't picture it in his head. Never really looked at the men in the back; he didn't know if they were Hispanic or not. His sightings were scattered over the last three months or so; last one was maybe two weeks ago. That's the best he could do on dates. His porch sits about a hundred yards from the road, and he spotted them through a small gap in the trees, so it's all a bit shaky. As for the driver, he said the guy was definitely white and definitely thin."

"White, not black?"

"Yes."

"And thin? He was sitting in the cab of a pickup. How could Baker tell if the guy was thin?"

"That's what I asked him. He said you could see it in the guy's face."

"So an eighty-year-old catches a one-second glance at a man driving a pickup as it passed between some trees, and he could tell the man was thin in the face?"

Brent shrugged. "I'm just telling you what he said."

"So we have one guy who says he's black and another who says he's white." Eyewitness testimony was always terrible.

"Could be two guys working together. Ebony and Ivory. Side by side on the—"

"Assuming it's one guy, who was more credible?"

He smiled. "You know I'm going with the guy who said the unsub is white."

Dagny laughed. "Besides general policy, any reason?"

"Hammond had a Confederate flag decal on his truck. He's had some run-ins with the law. Looked at me the way a Klansman might. Whereas Baker is a quality guy. Keeps a meticulous journal of all the birds he sees, with details on the dates and times. Even sketches them in the margins. When people see me coming up to talk to them, I can tell some are thinking 'scary black guy,' even though I'm wearing a suit. Baker wasn't like that. Hammond was. So if I had to bet, I'd say the unsub is white and thin."

That seemed to be the consensus. "The Professor has him white and thin, too."

"A fat guy would be too tired to carry out something like this, right?"

If Harrison Baker could peg the guy as thin with a limited view for one second, he must be *really* thin. "Meet up with Beamer and find out what's happening with the property and the bank. Why has it been sitting so long? Did anyone from the bank ever come here to check on it?"

"Sure." He started to walk away but stopped. "Can I ask you something?"

"Yes."

He took a few steps back toward her. "I know you have issues with me."

"I don't have any issues with you, Brent."

"Yes, you do," he said. "But I'm asking for a clean slate."

She studied him for a moment, trying to figure out his angle. That was her issue with him. He always seemed to have an angle.

"What?" he said.

"Why are you a special agent, Brent?"

"Why?"

"Yes."

"Because . . ."

She waited. "You're just searching for a palatable way to say it."

"Okay, why do you think I became an agent?"

"As a path to something else. Assistant director. Deputy director. Or maybe running for Congress. Right?"

He smiled. "If you think that's worthy of disdain, tell me, Dagny Gray, why did you become a special agent?"

"To be a special agent."

"And that's more noble, I guess? Ambition is a bad thing?"

"You can't trust the ambitious, because honesty isn't rewarded."

"So, you think I'm a liar?"

"I didn't say that."

"You don't trust me?" He shook his head. "How dare you. I'm the only one who's honest with you. The Professor is happy to have a huge case. That's all he cares about. He doesn't care about you. You think I'm ambitious? The Professor is ambitious. He's auditioning for Director."

The idea seemed ludicrous. "C'mon."

"What?"

"He doesn't want to be Director."

"Yes, he does."

"Why do you say that?"

"Because he told me."

"You've talked about this with him?"

"Yes."

The Professor had never discussed this with her. "He's too old. He'd never be confirmed." It hurt that he hadn't discussed it with her.

"He was supposed to retire when he was sixty-five, and he didn't, and nobody stopped him. Everything about him is ambition, Dagny. Are you so blind you don't see that? And you think you can trust Victor, with his puppy-dog crush on you. He likes you too much to be honest with you. He's never going to lay it out for you. Me? I can lay it on the line."

"So lay it out, Brent."

"Who's running this investigation? Because I was under the impression that the Professor had taken it over."

"Does it matter?"

"Yes, actually. You're giving me orders, and I don't want to be taking orders from you if he wants me doing something else."

This was about his place on the totem pole. He didn't want to be third; he wanted to be number two. "We wouldn't even be here if I worried about what the Professor wants me to do. Sometimes you have to work a case and not worry about how it's all perceived."

"You think I only care about politics, but there's a reason for chain of command. Sometimes it's actually good to run a case in an orderly manner, rather than just jumping on whatever fire is in front of you. You've got a million balls in the air right now and a righteous air about your juggling skills. But you've been up two nights straight, and when you collapse, who's going to catch those balls? This case is too big for you, Dagny. You're trying to manage it and investigate it at the same time. Those are two jobs."

It would have been easier to respond if it weren't true.

CHAPTER 38

....

Over the course of three hours, Allison Jenkins never once let go of her clipboard. She held it on the steps of Bilford City Hall as she smiled at the camera that transmitted her reports to the Greater Dayton metropolitan area. She held it while she ordered a large coffee at Quiznos. She carried that clipboard with her into the restroom and still had it in her hands when she came out. There was a moment when she set it down on the hood of the Channel 2 News van, but it never actually left her grip, and when the cameraman pulled her away for another setup, the clipboard went with her.

Jenkins had long black hair that she twisted into a bun each time she went on the air. The white blouse under the navy-blue suit plunged enough to keep a viewer watching but not enough to be judged unprofessional. She was about five seven, he guessed, and maybe 110 pounds. At twenty-eight years old, she was younger than Dagny. Young enough to dream of anchor desks and big-city affiliates, maybe even a network job. But old enough to know there were a thousand women like her, working in Butte or Bangor or Birmingham. There was probably a little sadness in her, he thought. The sadness that comes when dreams start to close.

The thin man shook his head. She was too pretty to be working for a station in Dayton. The world was not just.

Every once in a while, Allison Jenkins would answer her phone and scribble another note on her notepad. Another tidbit about what he'd done, he assumed. And that was the amazing thing about his relationship with her. She was thinking about him just as he was thinking about her.

The thin man rolled down his window, plucked a pack of cigarettes from his front shirt pocket, and pulled one to his lips. A flick of a match brought flame to it. He scanned the crowd. Every Dayton, Cincinnati, and Columbus station had a van in town. And then there were trucks labeled CNN, NBC, ABC, FOX, and CBS. He even saw ones from Telemundo and Al Jazeera. Some of the crews chose City Hall for their backdrop; some chose the courthouse; some set up right on Main Street. He was pretty sure that his pickup truck was inside the shot that FOX was using, and that thrilled him. He smiled for the camera.

While the rest of the city was quiet, the downtown streets teemed with folks who had come from around the country to see the spectacle, snapping photographs of the national reporters, tweeting their latest sightings. No Mexicans were downtown, though. He hadn't seen any Mexicans since the story broke. It was silly, he thought. They were safer now than they had been in months. He wasn't even interested in killing them anymore. Now that he had the attention of the world, his mind had gone to an entirely different place.

Allison Jenkins wrapped another report and then unfastened her bun, shaking her head so that her hair cascaded down past her shoulders. Her cameraman—a middle-aged, heavyset man with an unruly ponytail and an unkempt beard—said something that made her laugh. Someone like Jenkins would never have talked to someone like that if it weren't for the forced proximity of their employment, he decided. But here she was, chuckling at something he'd said. That was the real miracle of the labor market.

A younger man approached Allison and pointed to something on her notepad. This man wore a tie and cuffed dress pants. His hair was neatly cropped, and he was relatively fit. The thin man guessed he was in his early thirties. Probably had a crush on Allison, just like the cameraman. Maybe had a chance with her, unlike the cameraman.

The thin man watched Allison and her male cohorts load up their van. It was only seven thirty, but they'd wrapped for the day, content to let their clips replay for the rest of the night because there was nothing new to report.

He'd give them something new to report.

When the news van pulled from its spot, the thin man eased his truck into the traffic. The van turned left, then right, and the thin man followed a few cars behind. The news crew made its way to the Applebee's in New Bilford, and the thin man parked at the Kroger across the street and watched them enter the restaurant.

Three cigarettes and one hour later, Allison and the two men walked out of the restaurant, hopped in the van, and drove three blocks to the Hampton Inn. The thin man followed them, parking on the other side of the motel's lot. His forehead throbbed, and he rubbed it with both palms. When the pain subsided, he grabbed a Cincinnati Reds cap from the floor of his truck and placed it on his head. Pushing his door open, he hopped down from his truck and walked to the front of the motel. The automatic doors slid open, and he stepped inside.

The kid behind the counter greeted him warmly. "Checking in?"

"Waiting for a friend," the thin man replied. He grabbed a newspaper from the check-in counter and settled into a seat in the lobby. The front page of the paper had a picture of the silo, and the accompanying headline read, "Massacre in Bilford." He smiled—that seemed about right—and then skimmed through the article. Dozens dead, it said. *Dozens.*

It enraged him. He'd killed more than eighty people. They still didn't understand the scope of what he'd done, which meant they couldn't understand the extent of the pain they'd caused him.

He would make them understand, even if it meant killing a few more.

CHAPTER 39

Dagny found Diego Vega in the back booth of Applebee's, wearing his Catholic vestments, face buried in the menu. She realized she had never seen a priest in a restaurant before. He lowered the menu and looked up at her. "What do you know about the Green Bean Crispers?" he asked. "Because I feel like the Grilled Chicken Wonton Tacos would be a betrayal of my people."

"Your mom didn't make you wonton tacos?" She slid into the seat across from him.

"We have places with more charm in Bilford, you know."

She hadn't picked Applebee's for its charm; she'd picked it because it had Weight Watchers point totals for some of the items on the menu. "How come I never see priests at restaurants? Why is that? They have to eat."

He smiled. "I think you'd be surprised at how little money we make."

"But you guys have all that property."

"Stained glass doesn't clean itself."

As a lapsed Jew, she knew embarrassingly little about Catholicism and the church. "How little do priests make?" Gauche, for sure, but he had invited it.

He set his menu down and leaned back in his chair. "I make twenty-four thousand dollars a year. Plus a housing stipend and a car allowance that helps defray some of the expense of both."

She imagined trying to live on so little. "I'll pick up the check."

"How much does an FBI agent make?" he asked.

"Looking for a new career?"

"Depends upon your answer."

"I make a hundred and twenty-five thousand dollars, but that's because I'm in DC and have a law degree. Most make less than that."

"That's a good living."

"It's enough to pay for cable channels I never watch and insure a house I rarely see."

"How much would you make if you were practicing law?"

"I made a hundred and eighty-five thousand dollars a year when I quit. If I'd kept at it, I'd be a partner now, making at least seven hundred thousand dollars."

"So, thirty years of priesthood is equal to one year of lawyering."

"Yes, but at least *you* can live with yourself."

He shook his head. "Less than you'd think."

The waitress came, and Diego ordered the Green Bean Crispers. Dagny chose the lemon-Parmesan shrimp, which was thirteen points— half of what she needed for the day. She could make up the rest with a dessert.

Once the waitress left, it was time to talk business. "How are we on cooperation?"

"I've got a hundred forty-two people on board to help identify bodies and give statements," Diego said.

The number shocked her. "That can't be all from Bilford."

"I asked people to pass the message along to friends and family throughout southwestern Ohio. I think we're going to be able to get information about almost everyone who was killed."

"I can't believe so many responded," she said.

"I guess I had a little help from God."

"The one you don't believe in?"

"How else can you explain it?" He leaned toward her. "Everyone is still scared. I need transportation and security. People to keep them safe, patrol their neighborhoods. People they can trust."

Dagny pulled out her iPhone and texted Principal Geathers: **Need five buses tomorrow.**

Seconds later, she received the reply: **No problem.**

She turned back to Diego. "I've got you buses, and I'll get you agents to provide security."

"Thank you," he said. "So, what's next?"

"We keep chasing the evidence, wherever it goes."

"I mean, what should *I* do next?"

There was desperation in the way he said it, and Dagny understood it completely. She didn't want to give up control of the case because she thought of it as hers; Diego couldn't sit back because he thought of it as his. "Help with the translation during statements tomorrow. Make people feel comfortable."

"Okay."

"And if you want to think like an investigator, think about this. All of the victims are young, undocumented, Hispanic men—that's the obvious thing they have in common. Is there something they have in common that isn't obvious? Were they all from the same town in Mexico? Did they all work the same job at one time? Maybe the same coyote brought them here. Or maybe—" Her phone buzzed. She glanced at the screen. Restricted. She let it go to voice mail. "We've got all kinds of data about these men from their phones, but no sense of who they are. What brought them together." Her phone buzzed again. Still Restricted. She sent it to voice mail again.

"Who is it?" he asked.

"Unidentified caller."

Her phone chirped with a text from the Professor: **PICK UP THE DAMN PHONE!**

It buzzed again, and she answered the call. "Hello?"

"Special Agent Gray, glad to catch you. It sounds as though we are making progress on the investigation. Any new developments in the past few hours?" It took her a second to recognize the voice, which she knew only from television, and even then, she wasn't sure.

"Mr. President?" Diego's eyes widened when she said it.

"I've been briefed by Timothy on the case. Anything new since he departed?"

She hadn't expected to be briefing the president from the back booth at an Applebee's, and she struggled to find her voice. "We've finished emptying the silo. Sorting and documentation is underway. We're gathering information from the counties in the region to assess whether previous murders might be attributable to the unsub. Members of the local Hispanic population will be giving statements tomorrow and helping to identify the bodies. The database with information from the deceased is growing."

There was silence on the other end of the call. "So, we've got nothing," the president finally said.

That was one way to put it. "Not yet, sir."

"No suspects at all?"

"Soon, we hope."

The Professor jumped in on the call. "We have a good profile of the man, Mr. President. I believe we will capture him within the week."

That was unhelpful. "Or soon, anyway," she said, trying to manage expectations.

"But certainly within a week," the Professor said, with a sternness in his tone that warded her away from further clarification.

"Well, I should hope so," the president said. "Albert, tell Dagny the plan for tomorrow."

She assumed that Albert was Albert Douglass, the president's chief of staff. He spoke with a deep, authoritative drawl—a kind of Southern cadence that calmed and soothed. Dagny imagined that this was half of the reason the president had picked him. No one wants bad news with a New York accent. "At nine thirty a.m. tomorrow, you will appear on the front steps of the Bilford Police Department, where you will hold a press conference for local and national media. The conference shall not last longer than twenty minutes. We will send you a brief statement to read at the beginning of the conference. Please do not deviate from the text, Agent Gray."

"I'm sorry. You want me to do a press conference?"

"Yes. At nine thirty a.m."

She would have preferred a root canal. "I really don't think I'm the right person for the job. The Professor is great with the press."

"I'm staying in DC tonight," the Professor said. "They need someone in Bilford, and you're the logical choice."

She thought she'd try again. "Maybe someone from the Office of Public Affairs would be better suited—"

Douglass's deep voice interrupted. "You're a bit of a celebrity, Agent Gray, as well as attractive and, from all reports, competent. We want you to be the face of the investigation."

"I think—"

"Look," the president's famous voice interrupted. "I'm the president, and that makes me the decider, and you're doing it, yada yada, stuff like that."

She hadn't pegged him for a *Seinfeld* fan. "Yes, Mr. President." That was probably what she should have said from the start. "After I read the statement, do I take questions?"

"Yes, you should take questions," Douglass replied, "but be careful not to answer them."

"How do I do that?"

"Just be reassuring," he said. "We are proceeding with the proper protocols. We are confident in the progress we are making. We are taking all appropriate steps. Yada yada, stuff like that." Apparently, they were all *Seinfeld* fans.

"Where do we stand with the NSA data?" Dagny asked. This was more important than a press conference.

"The Professor requested access," the president explained, "and I had to turn him down. The data is only for investigations of terrorism from foreign sources, so it would be inappropriate to access it here. I'm sure you understand."

"I do." She sighed inside.

"Dagny, one last thing," the president said.

"Yes."

"I appreciate your work on this case."

"It's my pleasure and honor, sir. To serve this nation, and under you." And then she added, "Yada yada, stuff like that."

The president's laughter was the last thing she heard before the click. When she looked down, their food was on the table. Her lemon-Parmesan shrimp looked like a huge mistake. "We should trade," she said.

"Don't even," he said.

"Well, those green beans aren't going to fill you up."

"You're going to pretend that it's normal that you just talked to the president? Like that was a normal call?"

It was a big deal, but she really wanted the green beans. "We could do a half-and-half thing."

"You can have all of them if you admit that a weird thing just happened."

"It was weird." Dagny slid her plate to Diego and took his. "Presidents are like everyone else, except with fewer scruples."

"You talking to him is like me talking to the Pope."

"Exactly," she said.

It was easier to be dismissive of the experience after it happened; while it was happening, she had been completely starstruck. That embarrassed her. As a matter of principle, she held politicians in low regard.

Her phone buzzed. It was the Professor. She answered.

"We're getting the NSA data," he said. "He has to be on record opposing it, but he gave us the okay."

"So, he's pretending we can't access it?"

"Correct. But we can."

"How is that being conveyed to NSA?"

"There is a series of winks involved."

"I'm proud to be an American," Dagny said. "How fast do you think we'll have it?"

"For all of the winks to fall in place? Maybe tomorrow morning."

Probably while she was spouting nonsense to reporters, she figured. "Why do I have to do this stupid press conference tomorrow?"

"Because there are bigger things at issue than this case, Dagny."

"Bigger than a silo full of bodies?"

"We are laying the groundwork for something huge."

He hung up before she could ask him to explain. Perhaps Brent was right, and the Professor really was maneuvering to become Director. She grabbed a green bean and took a bite. It wasn't great.

"Did you really 'yada yada' the president?" Diego asked.

"Yep," she said. And it felt pretty good.

CHAPTER 40

The only things in the exercise room at the Hampton Inn were one elliptical machine, one exercise bike, and two dumbbells. After the dumbbells left, Allison Jenkins wiped down the elliptical with a towel, and then rode the machine at its highest incline and against its highest resistance as fast as she could for thirty minutes. When she was finished, her gym clothes were drenched in sweat, and she felt great.

She drew a few stares in the hallway on the way back to her room, perhaps because of her celebrity, or maybe because not many women looked like her in Bilford. Fitness didn't seem to be a priority in the town. Neither did hair or skincare, as far as Allison could tell.

When she slid the key card into her door, the light flashed red. She tried it again, to no avail. This happened to her every time, at every hotel. She marched to the front desk and waited behind a white-haired woman who argued with the clerk over a lost reservation, ignoring Allison's throat-clearing suggestions that she wrap it up. When the woman finally stormed off, Allison stepped forward.

"My key doesn't work anymore."

The boy smiled. "A cell phone will do that."

"Do what?"

"Demagnetize it. You probably had your cell phone in your pocket. You're Allison Jenkins, right?" His voice cracked when he said it. The skin on his face was pimply and red. He was slight, with poor posture. It was possible that it would all work out for him in a few years, but right now, he was an adolescent mess. She guessed he was about nineteen and that he was saving up for college.

"Yes."

"Two on your side?"

"Excuse me?"

"The slogan for Channel Two."

"Working for You."

"What is?"

"Our slogan is 'Working for You.'"

"Yeah, I guess it works for me. I mean, I like the idea that you're on my side."

She smiled. "My key?"

"Of course." He grabbed it from her hand. "What room are you in?"

"114."

"Oh, yes. That's a good room."

"Aren't they all the same?"

He blushed. She was used to it. Men stammered and stumbled into silly statements when they were around her. "The rooms are all the same, but first floor is close to breakfast, so that's something."

"Starts at six?"

"Six thirty," he said, sliding her card into a machine and pressing some buttons. "Six thirty," he repeated, handing her key back. "How is the reporting going?"

It was cute that he was trying to draw her into further conversation, but their dealings were done. She turned to leave and bumped into her producer, Jack McDaniel.

"Sorry," he said, waving his key card in his hand. "Demagnetized." He handed his card to the boy behind the desk, gave the boy his room number, and then turned to her. "ABC got an order forcing the FBI to let crews film along the edge of the Hoover property."

"That's fantastic," she said. Finally, they would have a decent backdrop for the reports.

"I'm going to get up at four tomorrow to stake out a spot with Phil."

"Want me to come?" It was the polite thing to say, and she knew he'd refuse it.

"You're the one on air, Ally. You need your sleep. Just cab it."

"Thanks, Jack."

The boy handed Jack his key card. He started to walk away. "Night, Ally," he said, walking toward the elevator bank.

"Hey, Jack!" she called.

He turned around. "Yes?" he asked, smiling.

"The networks are going to stake their spots and hold them overnight. So maybe you and Phil want to head there now? Because at four a.m., it's nothing but leftovers." She watched the smile dissolve from his face. "We want the silo in the shot. Otherwise, we could be standing anywhere. You understand?"

"Yes."

"So, take the pillows from your bed and sleep in the back of the van."

"Maybe I'll send Phil."

"You need to pick the spot, Jack. Because if Phil gets it wrong, it will be on you."

"Okay."

"Don't sound glum. We could go places from this." She could, anyway.

"You're right. We'll head out now."

"Thanks, Jack. That's why you're the best." Of course, if he were really the best, she wouldn't have to keep telling him how to do his job.

When he stepped into the elevator, she turned back to the boy behind the counter. "Can you arrange for a cab to pick me up tomorrow at five thirty a.m.?"

It was a tall order for a Hampton Inn concierge. "I don't know," he stammered.

She smiled. "You can. Use the phone book. I'll be forever grateful."

"Okay," he said.

She gave him a friendly wave good-bye and returned to her room. The light turned green when she inserted the key card. She pushed the door open, turned on the lights, and plugged her phone into the charger. Picking up the remote, she flipped on the television and cycled through the channels. The network affiliates were back to showing prime-time shows, but MSNBC had one of her reports playing. She climbed onto the bed, leaned back against the pillows, and let herself enjoy the segment. The Bilford Massacre was giving her a national audition. This was her chance—if it didn't happen now, it wasn't going to happen.

CHAPTER 41

....

The thin man lowered the brim of his cap, folded up his newspaper, and walked up to the counter. He studied the boy for a second. The boy didn't notice him—his mind, it seemed, was still on Allison Jenkins. Who could blame him? The boy pulled the yellow pages from a shelf, set it on the counter, and stared at it a bit. He seemed daunted by the challenge it presented.

"Look," said the thin man, "I couldn't help but overhear the young lady. She needs a cab. I work for Red Top Cab and can have one of ours come, if you'd like."

"You could?" The boy seemed relieved.

"Sure. Five thirty a.m., right?"

"Yes, sir."

"It will be here on the dot."

The boy smiled. "Thanks, man."

"It's my pleasure," the thin man said. And it was. Sometimes problems solve themselves. This time, it was almost too easy.

CHAPTER 42

Dagny should have stayed at the Hampton Inn. That's what she was thinking, anyway, as she shook her pillow over the second-floor railing at the Bilford Motor Inn, dropping roaches onto a FOX 19 news van in the parking lot below. All of the other news crews had landed better rooms in New Bilford, but FOX 19 had arrived late, and it was paying the price. Dagny had been there from the start, so she had no excuse.

Most of the roaches fell easily, but one clung for his life. She beat the pillow against the rail until he finally popped off, then went back to her room, locked the door, and drew its chain. Had she gone one night or two without sleep? Two, she realized. Not good.

She went to the bathroom, started the shower, undressed, and waited an eternity for the water to warm before stepping in. The spray washed away the soot from the silo, but it did little to dispel concerns she had about the investigation. The Professor didn't have his head in the game—or rather, he had his head in a different game altogether. If he was making a play for the Director's job, it was a mistake. Right now, their team had complete independence with little accountability. Oversight of the entire Bureau, by contrast, would invite constant scrutiny. The Professor would spend most of his time answering to congressional committees or fielding press inquiries while performing little of the crime fighting he loved. Ambition for its own sake always delivers disappointment. She was surprised that he couldn't see this.

The only good that could come out of the Professor's sojourn in DC was access to NSA data. The calls, texts, e-mails, photographs, and locations of an entire nation sat on massive servers, and there was scarcely a crime that couldn't be cracked with them. Dagny recognized the importance of privacy and opposed the mass collection of this information. But she wasn't above making an unprincipled exception for this case. After all, she opposed mass murder, too.

Of course, the NSA data only mattered if the unsub carried a cell phone.

If the water had stayed warm, Dagny would have showered for an hour or more, but it turned cold fast, so she shut it off. She hated the down moments of an investigation. During the chase, the constant stimulation of new information kept her mind racing ahead. Stopping for showers or sleep gave her mind the opportunity to reflect and feel, two things that got her every time.

Standing naked in a dank bathroom at a cheap motel in Bilford, Ohio, was a good way to experience loneliness.

She grabbed a towel, dried off, dressed in sweats, and climbed into bed. Scrolling through her iPhone, she caught up on missed calls and e-mails. Her best friend, Julia Bremmer, had sent an Evite to her daughter's birthday party. This roused Dagny to tears. Once, they had been on the same track, first at Harvard Law School and then working at big firms for good money. Dagny joined the Bureau around the same time Julia got married, and now they had nothing in common except a bunch of old stories. She tried to picture what it would be like to plan a little girl's birthday party but didn't know where to start. Thirty-five was a terrible age for a woman. You stand in front of the great edifice of motherhood and watch the cracks spread until the whole thing crumbles.

She had two voice mails: one from her mother and the other from Dr. Childs. She played the one from Dr. Childs first. "I've seen the news, so I know you're busy, but I want to remind you that I'm available by phone if you need to talk to someone. Call me anytime. I mean it." Then she listened to her mother's message: "Dagny, I'm watching the news, and I hope you don't have anything to do with this awful thing in Ohio. Please call me and tell me that you're working on something safe instead. Or since you won't call me, send me a text letting me know that you're all right."

Dagny started to type a text—**Safe at my desk in DC**—but deleted it when she remembered that she was committed to a press conference the next morning that would have exposed the lie. **I'm all right**, she typed, and then hit "Send."

Thinking about the press conference sent her into a foul mood. Every minute of an investigation has an opportunity cost. Some minutes have to be sacrificed to food and sleep, both of which refresh the investigator and provide net gains for the investigation. But a press conference was the opposite of those things—all it would do was sap her energy while stealing her time.

It was easy for two old men to assign her to press conference duties, since they had no understanding of the logistics it would involve. Hair, makeup, attire—men never thought about any of these things, unless they were judging a woman for them. Dagny wasn't normally vain, but she also wasn't normally on national television.

If she was going to talk to the press, she figured she should know what she was in for. Since the hotel television was inoperable, she turned on her iPad, opened her Slingbox app, and watched her Comcast feed from back home.

All of it was grim. The cable stations had entered twenty-four-hour mode, which called for the recitation of the same few facts over and over again, augmented by wild speculations and crass political commentary. Although the Bureau had yet to make its first official comment, Sheriff Don seemed to have held four press conferences during the day, each with a different backdrop. The sheriff maintained that pro-immigrant forces had most likely committed the mass murder in order to engender sympathy for their cause. When pressed for evidence to support his hypothesis, the round demagogue rolled his eyes and accused the inquiring reporter of having an agenda.

The sheriff wasn't the only person injecting politics into the massacre. Hacks from both political parties busily spun events to the benefit of their associated interests. The whole mess proved that we needed gun control, although there was no evidence that the unsub had used a gun. No, the crimes demonstrated that taxes were too high because of the flow of capital overseas.

While talking heads did their thing, the networks played video of the silo taken from a helicopter, followed by an exterior shot of Bilford High School, which, according to the text banner below it, was *Operations Headquarters for the Bilford Massacre*. That's what everyone was calling it: the Bilford Massacre. At least they had given it a serious name—nothing silly like The Bubble Gum Thief.

Once she felt confident that she had seen everything they had to show, she turned off the light, placed her head upon the roach-free pillow, and pulled the covers to her chin.

As she lay in bed, every sound in Bilford crept into her ears. Two men shouting in the parking lot about betrayal. The beep of a car horn. The slamming of a door. Something scampering, possibly across her floor. Footsteps on the landing. Laughter. A baby crying. The successive plops of a suitcase tumbling down a staircase. A man and a woman fighting, and another door slam. After twenty minutes of this, Dagny grabbed her phone, opened a white-noise app, and increased its volume to the highest level.

With the sound of Bilford blanched by static, her mind began to clear, and she fell into the great, big empty of a silent black. Her breathing slowed. Her muscles relaxed. She drifted into the embrace of sleep, and then she was spinning in a dream.

Black faded to gray, then pockmarked white. Spinning and swaying, she pushed her legs against the concrete walls to stop the motion. Looking up, she saw the spotlight beaming down from the neck of the crane. Looking down, she saw the bodies—a mosaic of bone and flesh and ash and cloth. The cable pulled her away from the bodies, higher and higher, until she dangled way above the mouth of the silo. And then the cable broke, and she fell, back into the chamber of the silo and into the cushion of body and bone. The decapitated face next to hers seemed familiar. When it came into focus, it was Diego's severed head.

Dagny bolted upright, heart racing, drenched in sweat. The clock on the nightstand said it was 3:40 a.m.

CHAPTER 43

····································

At 3:40 a.m., the thin man parked his pickup in an empty Kroger lot. "Kashmir" was playing on the radio, and he let it play. It reminded him of being fifteen, back when anything was possible, and trouble was Judy Gelson and a six-pack of Hudepohl under the bleachers at a football game.

His father had been a welder at the Dakota plant, which used to be the kind of job that let you provide for a family even if you had a prison record. One night, the old man came home with a brand-new olive-green Buick Skylark and a smile he'd never shown before. It was the only nice thing the old man ever bought for himself, and the old lady let him have it for it. Their voices carried up the stairs to his room, where the thin boy lay in bed thinking about Judy Gelson and a six-pack of Hudy.

His parents were still fighting the next morning—the silent kind of fighting that makes you shovel down your eggs and toast and leave for school earlier than the half-hour walk required. Thirty minutes every day, he walked through the cesspool of Bilford, passing the dumb and dull in their run-down homes and their driveways full of rusted and dented cars. People in secondhand clothes. Women caked in too much makeup. Everyone doused in cheap perfume and colognes, trying to get the stink of Bilford off them. The figurative stink, but the literal one, too. It came from the sulfur factory, and the Hayes Cooperative rendering plant, and a landfill they built too close to the center of town. Even on sunny days, Bilford was overcast from the industrial smoke and soot that kept everyone even on the mortgages of their tiny homes.

He wanted out of Bilford.

That night, after his parents went to bed, he slipped down the steps and grabbed the keys to his father's new Skylark. He started it up and backed out of the driveway, edged it forward quietly for a block and a half, and then gunned it, tearing his way out of town. Merging onto the highway, he watched the speedometer bend toward one hundred, and then past it. He turned on the radio and cranked up the volume because the station was playing the entirety of Led Zeppelin's *Physical Graffiti* album. Track Six was "Kashmir," and the pulsing beat shook the car so much that he felt the song in his hands as he gripped the wheel. In that moment, with the music blasting and the car shaking, he felt more free and more alive than he ever had before, so much so that he didn't notice the police car behind him or its flashing lights and blaring siren.

He was in trouble, the way kids used to get in trouble. No arrest, no record, no real repercussions. The cops left it all to his dad, who beat him silly, but then it was done. Life went on as it had before. He finished high school, joined the navy, started a family, and somehow ended up back in the stench of Bilford.

Now, he was in a different kind of trouble. Now, there would be repercussions. Life would not go on as it had before.

Bilford was teeming with cops and agents, reporters and photographers, gawkers and scandal junkies. That's why he'd driven to the Kroger in Cleves. Things were quiet here. The streets were empty. No one would be suspicious of a pickup truck in the Kroger parking lot.

He pulled an empty suitcase from the back of the truck and pulled it through the lot, across the street, down sidewalks east and north, until he got to 739 Harrison St., a house he knew to be empty and secluded. Sitting on the front step, he waited twenty minutes until a pair of headlights turned onto the road. The thin man walked to the base of the driveway, and the taxi pulled up, right on time.

The cabbie was an old man, with an old man's sense of manners and propriety, so he hopped out of the cab and walked toward the thin man. "Early morning for you?" he said with uncommon cheer.

"And for you," the thin man replied.

"Actually, a late night. You're my last job, and then I'm on vacation." Another fortunate turn of events. "For how long?"

"Two weeks."

Then it would be two weeks before anyone realized the old man was missing. "Anyplace special?"

"I've got a cabin in Michigan. Like to go up there and hunt."

"I like a good hunt, too."

"Big game?"

"The biggest. Would you mind popping the trunk?"

"Of course." The cabbie slipped his key into the trunk and opened it. "Here you go, sir."

"And here you go, sir," the thin man replied, lifting a gun from his coat pocket. He pulled the trigger and shot the cabbie three times.

The thin man opened his suitcase and laid it on the ground, lifted the cabbie's body under his arms, and dumped him into the cavity of the suitcase. The corpse's legs dangled over the edge of the suitcase, and the thin man tried to bend them up against the cabbie's chest so that he would fit inside it. No matter how hard he pushed, he couldn't get the old man to fit.

He lifted the old man out of the suitcase and tossed him in the trunk. Because there was no good place to stash a bloody suitcase, he tossed that in the trunk, too.

It was time to pick up Ms. Jenkins.

CHAPTER 44

....

At 4:55 a.m., there were already eleven cars in the Bilford County Morgue parking lot. Dagny pulled into the only empty space.

"Bunch of morning people," Victor muttered.

As they exited the car, Dagny was startled by the anguished call of a wounded animal, but it was just Victor yawning. "I'm not a morning person," he explained.

"No, you're not."

Bea Minor bounded out of the front door. "Right on time," she said. "Like to see that."

"Even early," Victor replied.

"Early is on time," she shot back. "On time is late in my world. Now follow me. You're going to help me with this."

They followed her to the rear of a Ford compact. She shoved a key into the rear lock and opened the trunk.

Dagny peered in at a boxed coffeemaker, an unopened package of four ceramic mugs, a bulk-size thirty-pound bag of ground coffee, a box of filters, and a brown box marked *Cream and Sugar*. "You said you needed coffee," Bea said to Victor. "Well, here it is."

Bea Minor had gone to Sam's Club.

"You bought all this stuff last night?" he asked.

"We don't drink coffee here."

"And you did this just for us?"

"Not us. You. I didn't ask for coffee," Dagny noted.

"You said you needed coffee if we were going to meet in the morning," Bea said to Victor.

Dagny wasn't sure what was more unbelievable—that the coroner's office didn't have a coffee machine or that Minor didn't understand that Victor was joking when he demanded coffee for their early meeting. She decided to enjoy his discomfort rather than think about the bewildering circumstances that had created it.

"I'm sorry," he said. "I didn't know you would—"

"We take hospitality seriously in Bilford, Special Agent Walton." She shoved the coffeemaker into his hand. Dagny picked upon the enormous bag of Folgers, while Bea lugged the rest.

They followed the coroner into the building and down a hallway to her office. There were ten men and women of various ages and races standing there, waiting with somber visages. Each had a stack of folders, some several deep, in their hands. Dagny noticed that the papers in Minor's office were all neatly stacked; there were jars filled with various tissues and organs, presumably human, and all of them were expertly labeled. A whiteboard on the wall was filled with drawings of various body parts and annotated with impressive and opaque scientific terminology.

Bea gestured for Victor to set up the coffee machine at the empty end of the table under the whiteboard, in the gap between neatly stacked piles of documents. He set his box down on the table and turned back to the assembled coroners, all of who were staring at him. "We can start," he said.

"Get your coffee first," Bea ordered.

"It's really okay." No one replied, but they all kept staring at him. Dagny signaled that he should make the coffee, lest Minor be offended that her troubles to procure the materials had been a waste. He set the box on the floor, opened the top, and lifted the Styrofoam casing from it. Pulling apart the Styrofoam, he removed the coffeemaker and set it on the table.

"There's a sink over there," Minor said, motioning to the back wall of her office. He took the carafe from the maker to the sink, filled it, and started back toward the machine.

"You really ought to rinse it out a few times," one of the men offered.

Victor nodded and headed back to the sink, where he rinsed the carafe three times before filling it again. "Who else wants a cup?" he asked the crowd. No one answered. "So only me, then." He turned to Dagny, looking for a lifeline. "You want one?" His face stayed frozen in a hopeful smile.

She let him suffer for a moment, and then said, "Yes, please."

He mouthed, *Thank you*, and she nodded.

The crowd watched silently as he poured water in the coffeemaker, placed a filter in the machine, and dumped three scoops of coffee into it. Flicking the switch started the machine. He turned back to the crowd. "Okay, let's start."

Beatrice Minor stepped forward. "Between us all, we've got every unusual death of a Hispanic person for the last eight years in a two-hundred-and-fifty-mile radius. When I say unusual, it means that I have excluded deaths from obvious illness, clear accident, or a well-documented drug overdose. In sum, we're talking about thirty-four people. Thirty-five once you count the death of the gas station attendant you asked about—we have that one, too."

"Thank you," Dagny said. "Who has that one?"

"I do." A young woman in a white lab coat stepped forward and handed her a stack of three folders. "It's on the top."

Dagny opened it and skimmed through the file. Color photographs showed a charred body. The head had suffered the worst of it—only a sliver of the back of the blackened skull bone remained. "My goodness."

"Yes," the woman replied. "It was a bad one."

She thought for a moment. "If he were standing back from the fireball, he'd have turned away before it hit him. If he were standing over it, it would burn him from the bottom up. I can't imagine a way this wasn't something unexpectedly inflicted upon him by another."

"That's what I found," the woman said, flipping through the report and pointing to its conclusion.

Victor called out, "So, no one else wants coffee? You sure?" He had a mug in his left hand, and he lifted the carafe with his right. "Just Dagny, then?" He set two mugs on the table and began pouring. Tilting the pitcher too high, he poured coffee over the rim of the mug and onto the table, soaking some of Minor's papers. He rushed to the sink and tore off a stream of paper towels, then wiped at the mess, all under the dour gaze of the coroner set. "So sorry."

"When you pour, you should tilt it less," one of the women suggested.

"Yes," Victor said, dabbing at the spillage. "I think you've nailed the problem." He looked up at Minor. "Really sorry about this."

"It's okay," she said. "I'm sure I will be able to read through the stains on those death papers." For a moment, Dagny thought there might have been some humor in Minor's deadpan delivery; there seemed to be a slight uptick at the corners of her mouth as she said it.

Turning to Dagny, Minor was all business again. "I've got samples for each of the cases in these files in the evidence room. Given the volume, I figured you wouldn't want to take those with you, but they're here if you need them."

"Yes, that's right." Dagny turned to face the group. "In terms of prioritizing our review, it would help to note if anyone thinks they have something that might be linked to the unsub in our case."

No one spoke.

"That's what I figured," Dagny said. "Thank you all for collecting these files—we truly appreciate it."

They spent the next twenty minutes filling out the paperwork necessary for the transfer of the files into her custody. Each county had its own forms, and Dagny had hers. Photocopies were made, stapled, and clipped. Victor, perhaps out of obligation, drank three cups of coffee during the process.

As the coroners started to leave, Dagny pulled aside the woman who had examined the gas station attendant. "By any chance, did you get a sample of the fuel from the station?"

"Which one?" the woman replied. "All of the tanks blew—unleaded, supreme, diesel."

"Which one started the fire?"

"We don't know."

"Did the investigators discover which fuel had been pumped last?"

"Not that I know of. My understanding is that the computers in the store were destroyed in the fire and that no data could be extracted from them."

"Presumably a credit card would have been used to start the pump. Do you know if they checked to see which pump had been triggered last?"

"The transmission doesn't have pump information attached to it, only the credit card number and amount of the charge."

Dagny knew the charged amount wouldn't identify the fuel type. Maybe there was another way. "Did any of the clerk's clothes survive the fire?"

"The soles of his shoes. Parts of his pants. A piece of his collar."

That might do it. "His collar?"

"It's in Bea's evidence room. I can get it."

"Please do."

The woman left and then returned with a small jar containing the collar fragment. Maybe it would help. Every gas company's product had a different fingerprint. If the victim's face had been doused in fuel, the collar might retain some of it. The FBI lab could try to extract it from the collar to see if it matched the fuel that had been collected at the silo. But then what? They were amassing good evidence of where the unsub had been, but none of it was helping discover who the unsub was or where he was now.

Dagny and Victor grabbed the stacks of files the coroners had given them and thanked Minor for her efforts. On their way out, Dagny handed Victor the keys. "You're driving." That way, she could start looking at the files in the car.

He opened the driver's door. "By the way, thanks for helping me out with the coffee thing," he said.

"Thanks for providing some comic relief."

"Where are we going?"

"To the Bilford police station. I've got to get ready for a press conference."

CHAPTER 45

When Allison Jenkins pulled her bag out the doors of the Hampton Inn at 5:32 a.m., the taxi was waiting. Its driver, a tall, thin man, leaned against the front passenger door.

"I know you," the thin man said. "You're the woman on the news. Abigail something?"

"Allison Jenkins." This happened a lot—people insisted that they knew her but never remembered her name. It never failed to annoy her.

"That's right," he said.

"Can you pop your trunk?"

He looked at her suitcase somewhat wearily. "You going on a trip?"

"No." The bag was filled with cosmetics, notes, papers, pens, her laptop, and a change of clothes—her standard haul for a remote shoot.

"Why don't you climb into the backseat, and I'll put this in the trunk for you," he said.

"I'm capable," she replied.

He grabbed the bag from her hand. "I'm an old-school driver, ma'am. My passengers don't handle their own bags. They just ride in comfort to their destination." He opened the rear door and gestured for her to slide inside. Rather than fight him on this, she obliged. He popped the trunk and shoved her bag inside, then climbed into the driver's seat.

"Allison Jenkins. Oh, my. A celebrity in our midst. What brings you to Bilford?"

Was this man an idiot? "I'm here for the massacre."

"Of course you are," he said. "It would take a massacre to bring a fine lady like yourself to our hillbilly town. Where should I take you this morning?"

"Do you know where the silo is?"

"I do."

"Take me there," she said.

He turned the key and pressed the accelerator with such force that the car jolted forward. Allison grabbed the seat belt from above her shoulder and secured it to the seat.

The driver looked back at her. "Hard to believe something this big is happening in Bilford, don't you think?"

Just her luck, she had a chatty cabbie. She pulled out her phone and scrolled through e-mails and texts. He didn't take the hint.

"Have to imagine this is a pretty good deal for you?" he said.

That was a crass thing to say. "Excuse me?"

"Biggest story in the country. Have to think you're getting some screen time on the network news. That's got to be good for you."

Of course it was good for her, but talking about it was unseemly. She ignored him and looked back at her phone. A text from her producer said they'd staked out a great location.

"I saw you on television yesterday," he continued. "Looked pretty good to me. If I were a bigwig at NBC or something, you'd bet I'd hire you. Put you smack-dab on *Good Morning America* or something. You're every bit as good-looking as any of them."

She'd had enough of it. "I'm sorry, but I've got to concentrate on some e-mails I'm getting for work—"

"New developments in the case?" he asked.

"No."

"Like a lead on the guy who did all of this?"

She sighed. "No. I'm sorry, but I need you to be quiet so I can concentrate."

"Of course," he said. "I'm the same way. Hard for me to read if someone's talking. Don't worry, Ally. I will keep myself quiet."

The forced familiarity of his use of *Ally* startled her. It was something only friends and family called her. There was something menacing about a man who went straight to a nickname.

She clicked into her Twitter account, trying to find the latest reports on the case. Instead, she found a lot of commentary but no new information. She clicked the "Compose" button and typed: *Pretty sure my taxi driver is a maniac. Shades of De Niro.* She clicked the "Tweet" button, but the tweet wouldn't post. Her phone couldn't connect to a network because she was a million miles from civilization.

"Now, me, I ditched my cell phone," he said. "Don't like what they do. We got along fine without them, so why do we need them now? You might need them for your job, I guess. I don't need them for mine."

"How does the dispatcher send you on a job if you don't have a phone?" He'd tricked her into conversation. In her heart, she was always a journalist. No matter how little she cared about someone, she still couldn't help but ask them questions.

"I've been driving for thirty-five years. All the cell phone did was make it easier for folks to get a ride from someone who doesn't drive a cab."

The car locks clicked. She looked up at the rearview mirror and caught his eyes looking back at her. "Forgot to lock them before," he said. "Seems prudent, with a maniac out there."

Or a maniac in here, she thought.

He laughed for no apparent reason. "Maniac, or whatever he is. Or she, I suppose. Could be a she, or even a them, I guess. What do you think?"

"I think I need to read through my texts," she said, with little hope that he'd take the hint.

"Maybe it's a them," he said. "Probably a lot of people out there feeling what he feels. Feeling . . . a frustration." He turned onto a small road. "Shortcut," he explained.

It was an hour before sunrise, and the side windows showed solid black. Sixty miles from Dayton might as well have been on the other side of the earth. He turned the car again. Allison looked out the front windshield, where the headlights shined upon a single-lane road that twisted through the woods.

"You do know where the silo is, right?" she asked.

"Better than anybody." He stopped the car and bent down, reaching under the seat. When he came up, there was a gun in his hand. "Give me your phone," he said.

She froze. A cascade of thoughts flashed through her head. The certainty of death. The fact that he was Bilford's murderer. The notion that surviving this encounter gave her the story of a lifetime.

"Give me your phone, or I'll kill you right now," he said, slipping a white glove over his hand.

The phone was her only connection to the rest of the world. When she surrendered it, it felt like she was letting go of a rope as she dangled above a canyon. He took the keys from the ignition and put them in his pocket, opened his door, and stepped out of the car. Lifting the phone high above his head, he threw it down against the pavement. She heard it shatter into pieces.

She grabbed the passenger-door handle and gave it a yank, then threw her weight into the door. It wouldn't give. The thin man climbed back into the driver's seat. "It's not going to open. I turned on the child-safety locks." He started the car, backed up, and turned around. "We're going back to my house. While I'm driving, you may be tempted to try something bold. Maybe it will work, and you'll manage to overtake me. Maybe I'll reach back with my gun in time to stop you. Maybe we'll both career off the road to our mutual deaths. I'm fine with any of that. But right now, you're the only person in the world who knows who I am, and you're about to be the only person who will know why I did it. If you want to be the next Katie Couric, maybe you ought to sit back, relax, and enjoy the ride. Because as scared as you are right now, you need to understand that I'm giving you a gift."

As scared as she was, she decided to take it.

CHAPTER 46

A man with a gambling problem notices the lottery tickets at every checkout counter. An alcoholic knows the names of every bar he passes on the way to work. Sex addicts find temptation in every subway train, on every office floor. But anorexia is harder. Breakfast, lunch, and dinner—anorexics confront their disorder three times every day. How well would AA work if the body needed three drinks a day to stay healthy? It wouldn't work at all.

Dagny was eating an Egg McMuffin because junk food was convenient, and because it tasted good, but mostly because it was packed with Weight Watchers points. Accumulating these points now would free up time she'd have to search for them later. She needed fewer points than normal because she wasn't running. This was a problem, because her legs needed about ten miles in the morning for her to feel spry, and her brain needed them, too. Her morning run let her focus her thoughts, process her emotions about them, and feel invincible. Now she'd missed the run for several days. How many exactly? She wasn't even sure. That's how addled her mind was without the run.

Victor was also eating an Egg McMuffin. They were sitting in an empty office at the Bilford police station, waiting by a computer for an e-mail with the official FBI statement Dagny was to read at the press conference.

"The genius of the Egg McMuffin is the Canadian bacon," he said. "Perfectly round, so it reaches every edge of the sandwich, and yet thin enough that it's not a calorie buster. You put sausage on this, and it overpowers the sandwich. The grease permeates it. You want meat in every bite, but you want to taste the egg and cheese, too. That's why this is the quintessential breakfast sandwich."

She was half listening to him. Most of her mental energy was trying to think of ways to obfuscate when she was asked questions at the press conference.

"If you were on *The $25,000 Pyramid*," he continued, "and Fran Drescher says 'Breakfast sandwich,' ninety-nine out of a hundred people are going to say Egg McMuffin. That's how powerful it is. If Fran says 'Facial tissues,' most people will say Kleenex, but some will say Puffs. Egg McMuffins are more dominant than Kleenex."

"Bacon, egg, and cheese," Dagny said.

"What?"

"A lot of people are going to say, 'Bacon, egg, and cheese.'"

"W-well," he stammered. "Not that many."

Her e-mail chimed. She opened the Word file and hit "Print." "Let's go," she said, grabbing the papers. On the way to the station's front door, she caught her reflection in a window. She looked like a woman who hadn't slept more than four hours in three days. It wasn't a good look for the Bureau to convey on every television and newspaper in the country. Dagny turned back and wound her way through the station, sizing up the five women who worked there.

"What are you doing?" Victor asked, chasing her.

"Sizing up my options," she said. The first woman she saw was caked in makeup. Dagny ruled her out immediately. The next two seemed to be completely indifferent to their appearance. She related to them, but they were of no use to her now. The fourth woman seemed to be in her sixties; she was well groomed and attractive, but her red lipstick suggested a less-than-natural approach to presentation. The fifth woman, a uniformed officer, had her hair tied back in a ponytail. Her cheeks seemed naturally red; her lips, naturally pink. There were no bags under her eyes even though there were pictures of small children on her desk. Dagny pulled a chair next to hers.

"Forgive me for asking this, but are you wearing makeup?"

"Can you tell?" she said, seemingly mortified.

"No, I can't. So if you're wearing some, it's perfect."

The woman smiled. "You need some?"

"I need you to do it. I don't know how. Not like you do, anyway."

"Sure." The woman opened her desk drawer and pulled out supplies.

"Also, I need it done in four minutes. I have to give a press conference at nine thirty."

"That's not a problem. I'm lucky if I have two minutes in the morning between the first diaper change and breakfast."

Dagny closed her eyes as the woman applied the makeup. It felt like she was a thousand miles away, sitting in a Sephora in South Beach, listening to the gentle hum of ocean waves. When she opened her eyes, Beamer was fiddling with the static on a radio.

"You're on in two," he said.

The woman handed Dagny a makeup mirror, and she admired the results, thanked the woman, and grabbed her papers. Marching through the station, she studied the statement she was to give. It was filled with lots of words and little content, which was fine with her. She hated giving any facts about the investigation to the public. If it were up to her, she'd deny there was any investigation, or even a city called Bilford.

Victor opened the front door of the police station for her. "You ready?"

"Ready to get it over with."

A podium sat at the top of the steps in front of the station, facing out. She walked up to it. Seated behind her was a row of white men of municipal importance, like the police chief, whom Dagny knew, and many others she didn't. The mayor, certainly, various councilmen and other civil leaders, she assumed. Not a Hispanic among them. Typical Bureau optics.

On the other side of the podium was a sea of lights and cameras, along with faces that poured down the steps, into the street, and across it. As she stepped to the microphone, the assembled mass leaned forward in such perfect unison that Dagny had to suppress a smile, lest it be misperceived. She set her papers on the angled top of the podium and smoothed them with her fingers, even though they weren't the least bit wrinkled. And then she began.

"Our entire nation mourns the loss of life that has devastated so many families in Bilford and its neighboring counties. As of this morning, we have confirmed more than eighty deaths in what can be described as nothing less than a mass atrocity. All of the victims appear to be Hispanic men, ranging in age from mid-teens to forty."

There was little of substance in the rest of her remarks. She expressed condolences to the families and assured the public that the president had directed the FBI to use all means available to it in service of this investigation. To her dismay, she also had to announce that a hotline had been established, and that a $100,000 reward was being offered for any tip that led to the capture of the perpetrator. Now, every crackpot had the power to divert precious Bureau resources on a wild goose chase.

Reporters shouted inquires at her. Altogether, they formed a cacophony of noise. Dagny thought about asking the reporters to raise their hands and take turns but realized it was better if she didn't. As long as the questions were unintelligible, she could supply any answer she chose. She leaned forward into the mic. "In answer to the question, the president is fully committed to the apprehension of the murderer. He has been briefed and is monitoring developments accordingly. Next."

More shouted inquiries. "Yes, the chief of police for the city of Bilford has been supporting the investigation in the fullest manner possible, and we are extremely grateful for his support. All of the officers under his command have been tremendous in their assistance. In particular, Officer John Beamer, as liaison to our investigation, has proved to be invaluable." She hoped that compliment might pay dividends in the future.

More questions were shouted, and she couldn't understand any of them. "Too soon to say," she said in response to a question that hadn't been asked.

More noise. "Not at this time," she said in response.

"Thank you for your questions," Dagny said. "I'm afraid we're out of time." With that, she was done. She walked over to Victor, who was standing by the station door.

"Nice trick," he whispered.

"Thanks."

He handed her his phone. "The Professor."

She walked back into the station and ducked into an empty interrogation room. "NSA?" she asked.

"They have nothing. Our unsub doesn't seem to have been carrying a phone."

Just as she'd feared. "We can't catch a break."

"I'll be back to Bilford this evening," he said. "In the meantime, don't ruin my investigation."

"*Your* investigation?"

"You can have it back when something goes wrong."

She smiled. "See you tonight."

"One more thing. Nice job with the press conference."

"You watched?"

"No. But if you had done a bad job, I would have heard about it by now."

Dagny hung up the phone and told Victor the bad news about the NSA data. "Maybe their search is too narrow," he said.

"What do you mean?"

"They looked for metadata showing phones that were in the vicinity of each of the abductions, right? But if the guy is smart enough to leave his phone at home, they should look for a phone that didn't move at all in the time before and after an abduction."

"That's probably a hundred thousand phones."

"Sure. But the phone they want would have to be still for each of the abductions. So that will cancel out most of them."

"Then maybe we're down to thousands of phones."

"Maybe. Maybe less."

"Call the Professor and have them try." It was worth a shot.

"What else should I do?"

"Head back to the high school. Make sure everything is moving forward." She dug into her backpack and pulled out the collar fragment from the coroner's office. She also found the cigarette butt she'd collected at the farmhouse, which she'd forgotten. "Have them run the DNA on the butt and try to compare this fuel to the diesel from the silo."

He took them. "Okay. What else?"

"Diego is bringing families to the high school to give statements and identify bodies. Make sure it goes okay."

"Will do."

"I want to start thinking about the things the victims have in common. Can you e-mail me the database as it currently stands?"

"Sure. Where are you going?"

"To see about a gas station."

CHAPTER 47

Chloroform has a sweet smell, and that's the last thing Allison Jenkins noticed before her arms went numb and she went blind. She woke hours later in a bedroom, bound to a chair next to a twin bed. At the other end of the room was a desk, pushed against the wall. Newspaper clippings, photographs, and maps were tacked to corkboard above the desk. Allison tried to read them, but they were too far away. The door at the far end of the room was closed. She assumed it was also locked from the other side. On the left was a window. The shade was drawn shut. Two shelves hung next to the window. They were filled with small trophies, ribbons, and a few framed photographs. One of the photographs looked like a high school graduation picture; the boy in it was wearing a cap and gown.

She was in a teenage boy's bedroom.

Her hands were tied with rope behind the back of the chair, and her ankles were crossed and tied with rope to the chair legs. A steel chain wove in and out of the ropes, between her legs, under her arms, and around her neck. The lock connecting the ends of the chain hung beneath her chin like a necklace.

Her mouth was dry, and she felt dizzy. There was a glass of water on the desk. Condensation was dripping down its side, glistening in the sliver of sunlight that slipped past the side of the shade. She threw her weight forward, trying to scoot her chair toward the glass of water, but the chair wouldn't budge.

She heard his footsteps walking toward the door to the room, and then it swung open.

He had a small head with a little chin and thin, greasy hair slicked back on his scalp. His eyes were narrow. There was a slight arch in his back, and his arms hung long on his torso. He smiled in a pronounced, menacing way, flashing crooked yellow teeth. A red-and-black plaid shirt hung loosely on his torso, tucked neatly in blue jeans, which were tucked neatly into a pair of worn leather boots.

Taken together, the man was tall and ugly and stained and bent. He was all of these things, but mostly he was thin. Not emaciated or malnourished or weak. But he was put together with narrow bones and small organs. A tight rib cage and small lungs, and beneath that, a small heart.

"Who are you?" she asked.

He shook his head and laughed. Pulling the chair from the desk, he spun it around and straddled it backward, three feet in front of her. "You know what you get for your first murder?" he asked.

She shook her head.

"You get the death penalty. Know what you get for your second murder?"

She shook her head again.

"Nothing." He took a big breath and stared at her. "You're a pretty girl, Ally. I could do anything I want to you, and there would be no consequence at all. Now, if I were you, I'd be scared. But I'm not you—I'm me. And do you know how I feel?" He locked his hands together and cracked his knuckles. "I feel free."

Allison Jenkins was not free. She was physically incapacitated three feet from a mass murderer with some kind of crush on her and nothing to lose. All she had was her voice. She'd interviewed enough men to know when people like to talk, and this guy was a talker. It might be enough to keep her alive. "What do you want?" she said.

"I wanted the world to make sense, but we're long past that now."

"Why did you kill all of these men?"

He shook his head. "Try again."

"Where are we?"

"At my house."

"Whose room is this?"

He didn't answer.

"Do you have a son?" she prodded.

His eyes drifted over at the photos of the boy on the wall. "No," he said. "I do not have a son." Still scanning the pictures, he added, "I never did."

There was wistfulness in his voice. She wondered who the boy was and what he had meant to her captor. Somewhere underneath the monster's skin lurked a human heart. "What's your name?"

He looked back at her, and his eyes hardened. "Tell me what I should do with you, Allison."

She sensed that the right answer could save her life, so she phrased it carefully. "I'm a journalist. I tell stories for a living. I can tell your story, any way you want it told. People are forming their own picture of who you are. Don't lose control of your narrative. When history records what happened in Bilford, it can be fair to you or it can be unfair. I can make sure it's fair." She pitched it like a story to a news director.

For a minute or two, he stared at her, his mind seeming to cycle through thoughts and permutations. It felt as though a coin had been

CHAPTER 48

Canter's Gas was a big pit now. The explosion had burned everything above the ground, and the EPA had required them to dig up everything below it. A chain-link fence surrounded the lot and bore signs of various warnings.

Dagny scaled the fence and jumped down to the other side. There was no real reason to do this; there were no clues to be found *on* the lot. But the unsub had been there, and being inside the fence made her feel closer to him.

On her way to the site, Victor had passed along two pieces of information that were hard to reconcile. First, credit cards tied to at least three of the deceased showed large purchases at Canter's Gas on the day of the explosion. Second, the gasoline on the attendant's shirt collar didn't match the diesel fuel that blew up the silo. Maybe the unsub had filled up most of his tanks with diesel, but then used gasoline for the last one, since it was a better accelerant. Maybe the attendant had come out to question him about the large purchases, and the unsub sprayed him with gasoline, tossed a match on him, and the whole place blew. Maybe, but unlikely, she figured. That kind of thing only happened in the movies. *MythBusters* even debunked it.

Peering into the pit, Dagny spied a mess of beer bottles and sandwich wrappers, remnants from a night of teen mischief. When you live in rural Ohio, drinking beer and eating junk food in a giant hole in the ground ranks among your better social options, she figured.

There was nothing around Canter's except the highway entrance ramp. No witnesses. No traffic. No bank with a camera at the ATM; no rival gas station with its own security feed. Just bare lots owned by speculators, who were waiting for the suburbs to grow to them. That's why the unsub had picked Canter's.

You can't be a serial killer in the city anymore. You have to go to the countryside if you don't want to be caught.

She climbed back over the fence, got into the car, and drove past the highway entrance on the off chance that the unsub had taken back roads back to Bilford. Ten minutes later, she saw her first signs of life: an actual stoplight, with a McDonald's on one corner and a Wendy's on another. Dagny pulled into the Wendy's and walked inside. She studied the calorie counts on the menu and ordered a grilled-chicken sandwich. Along with the Egg McMuffin from breakfast, it would get her most of the points she needed for the day.

A video camera hung above the kitchen, pointing at ordering customers. Dagny turned around and looked at the passing traffic outside the front window. If the unsub had taken the back road, he'd be on the security feed. The clerk placed her sandwich in a bag and handed it to her. She, in turn, flashed her creds and asked to speak with the manager.

The manager—no older than twenty-two, she guessed—was camped in an office between the drive-through windows, hunched over paper schedules and employee rosters, scratching and erasing indecipherable marks on them. When Dagny asked to see the video archives, he froze for longer than a moment, seeming to reach deep into his reserves for some nugget of advice from managerial training. Finally, he asked if he could talk to his regional manager. She told him he didn't need to, and he relented.

The surveillance feed was backed up on a remote server, but it was accessible from a computer in the back of the restaurant. He led Dagny to the terminal and logged her in. She sat in front of the monitor while the manager stood behind her. The interface was intuitive. A column on the left listed dates, and clicking on a triangle in front of each of them dropped a submenu of clips by the hour.

"You have two weeks of film?" Dagny said, surprised.

"It used to be one week," he said. "But they keep adding capacity, and the price keeps dropping."

One day, everything would be recorded and saved, and there would be no need for history books.

She opened the submenu for the day of the gas-station explosion, scrolled down to the hour after the blast, and hit "Play." Three people stood in line at the counter. Traffic passed in the window behind them. A customer hesitated in her order, rubbing her forehead as she seemed to vacillate between various options.

She hit a button to double the playback speed, but passing cars moved too quickly for her to identify any of them, so she slowed it down to real time again.

"What are we looking for?" the manager asked.

She gave it her best guess. "A pickup carrying barrels of fuel."

As she said it, one passed across the screen.

She stopped the video and backed it up, playing it again at half speed. It was a black pickup truck with at least five barrels in the back. The license plate was not visible. The driver was a thin blob. In all, the truck was on screen for less than two seconds. Dagny stopped it and played the sequence again, but it didn't help. After a third play, she let it run. The pickup left the frame, and then came back into the frame when it turned into the McDonald's lot across the street and pulled into the drive-through lane.

The truck was too far from the Wendy's camera for it to provide any useful detail. But the McDonald's would have cameras, and one in the drive-through window would be pointed right at the unsub's face. It was the lucky break she'd been waiting for.

She called Victor and had him arrange for a Bureau video forensic team to come to the Wendy's. Before leaving, she used her own iPhone to record the Wendy's footage of the unsub's pickup.

She downed her sandwich on the walk across the street to the McDonald's. Walking through the door, she flipped open her creds and asked the woman behind the register to get her manager. The clerk returned with a thin, middle-aged woman in a blue business suit. She introduced herself as Margorie Davies, the owner of the franchise. Davies gave Dagny a tour of the restaurant, pointing out each of the security cameras. Two of them were pointed directly out the drive-through windows, capturing the faces of customers as they paid for their orders, and again as they picked them up.

"How long is the footage archived?"

"I don't know. We've never had to use it," Davies replied.

Like the Wendy's feed, the McDonald's footage was sorted remotely and accessed via an Internet portal. Dagny followed Davies back to her office, where she sat at her computer, opened the login screen for the service, and stared at it for a few seconds. "I don't remember the password," she said. "We've never had to log in."

It took a half hour to navigate the security site's phone tree, verify the necessary credentials, and obtain a new password. Dagny logged into the program, navigated to the date of the gas-station explosion, and found the folder empty. Scrolling through the calendar dates on the left side of the screen, she saw only three days of saved footage.

A young man in India answered her call to the security company's customer-service line. "I see only three days of footage," she said. "Does that mean there are only three days of stored footage or that this account only gets access to the last three days?"

"I don't understand the difference, but I would very much like to help you."

The difference was the world. "Was the footage overwritten or is it simply blocked from view by the account holder?"

"It's not available," he said. "But I would very much like to help you."

Dagny was very much ready to do something else to him, but instead she asked for his supervisor. The representative obliged, and then dropped the call during the transfer. She called back, pressed all sorts of buttons at various prompts, connected with another agent, and was successfully transferred to a manager who assured her that he would very much like to help her.

"I can confirm that the footage has been deleted," the man said.

"But has it been overwritten?"

"That I can't tell you."

There was a possibility that forensic experts could resurrect the deleted footage from the security company's servers. Every new second of footage recorded, however, threatened to overwrite that which was previously deleted. "Whatever server or drive you're storing this account's feed to—you have to pull it off the system immediately," she said.

"I can't do that without jeopardizing the storage of today's feed. There would be a gap as we swap out the systems, and we could be liable for that."

"I can get consent from the customer."

"Not good enough. Other customers are on that server, too, and their footage could be compromised."

"I guarantee you that whatever the cameras fail to record isn't as important as what we're trying to save."

"I can't do it without a court order."

"Where are the servers located?"

"Albany, New York."

Dagny got the address. "You'll have a court order within the hour."

Dagny grabbed a piece of paper from Davies's desk, scribbled a sworn declaration, and signed it. She photographed the paper with her phone and e-mailed it to Bureau counsel with instructions to enlist an AUSA in Albany to serve an ex-parte emergency order at the storage center.

Her phone buzzed with news that the video-forensics team had arrived at the Wendy's. She jogged back across the street and knocked on the sliding rear-passenger door of an unmarked black van with tinted windows and numerous antennae. The door slid open, and five technicians jumped out. After introductions, Dagny instructed the team to download and analyze the video from Wendy's while they awaited a court order for the McDonald's feed.

A half hour later, they had the order in hand. An agent in Albany served it on the security firm while the FBI forensic team logged into the servers remotely from the back of the van, culling through deleted files, searching for the surveillance feed from the day of the gas-station explosion. Because the metadata of the deleted files had been corrupted, review required a tedious process of playing back the beginning portion of every deleted clip in order to ascertain the time stamp of the recording. They divided the task, each member of the team taking a chunk of the files. The lead technician logged Dagny into a terminal so that she could contribute, too.

It took three hours to make their way through all of the deleted clips, which went back only to the day *after* the gas-station explosion.

This was a punch in the gut. If she had investigated the explosion at Canter's one day earlier, they would have had a photograph of the murderer.

Dagny gave herself a moment to mourn, then gave the troops their orders. The road to Bilford was littered with fast-food restaurants, drugstores, and gas stations, and they needed to check surveillance footage from each of them, even though it was unlikely that any captured more than the passing blur of the black pickup.

After the troops left, Dagny climbed back into her car and checked her phone for messages. Victor had sent her an updated victim spreadsheet, and she pulled her iPad from her backpack so she could study it on a larger screen. The information—culled from phones, witness statements, and physical evidence—was voluminous. Columns logged calls, contacts, addresses, birth dates, family members, texts, estimated dates of abduction and death, relationship status, social media accounts, medical health, condition of the corpses, biological evidence gathered, hair color, eye color, weight, height, car, computer, phone, employment history, relationship history, and even the coyote who had brought the person to America, where it was known.

The variables in combination were overwhelming. The database listed 387 addresses, 813 family members, 419 employers, and 1,543 contacts. It contained 250,345 text messages and 597,452 e-mails. By right-clicking on the header, Dagny could see how many different entries there were for each column. Thirty-seven cities of origin; seven variants on hair color; five kinds of relationship status (including "it's complicated," lifted from Facebook). Under coyote, there were three entries.

Three entries. Three was a lot more workable than hundreds or thousands. Three was the kind of variable that could lead somewhere.

She scrolled down the coyote column. About two-thirds of the boxes were blank—either they had made their way across the border without paid assistance or the courier was unknown. The rest were divided, more or less equally, among three names.

Delgado. Erickson. Sanchez.

She called Victor. "Where did we get the coyote information?"

"Witness interviews. How's the gas station?"

"A day too late. How about the cigarette stub?"

"No print. Lifted DNA, but no match in CODIS. You think the coyote is important?"

"Maybe. Where's Diego?"

"Right here."

"Put him on."

A moment later, Diego was on the phone.

"Before you got me involved, you talked to an employment coordinator for undocumented workers, right?"

"Ty Harborman."

"Tell him we need to talk. I'll be back at the high school in an hour."

CHAPTER 49

There was nothing new on television that afternoon, just the same chatter from the same mannequins repeated on the same endless loop. No one answered the questions that mattered. Were they close to finding him? Had any witnesses come forward? Did he leave behind any fingerprints or DNA? How much longer would this go on? These were the questions that left him anxious and jittery.

The thin man clicked off the television and put on his jacket. It was time to see the epicenter of the investigation in person. Since the police were likely looking for a black pickup and missing taxi, he decided to walk. He used the hour it took to come up with a plan.

A plan. It was about time for one. He'd killed the first batch of Mexicans on a whim, with no understanding of why he'd done it except that he was angry and confused and that he felt betrayed. Now, he understood that the murders were an attempt to atone for his own sins. Having helped to bring Mexicans to Bilford, it was his duty to remove some.

With those bodies in hand, he'd remembered the silo at the Hoover farm. Terry Hoover had plugged up the door to the silo when the bank served its papers, so now it was just a big concrete tomb. The thin man had stolen a scissor lift to do general maintenance on the property, and he used the lift to take the bodies up to the top of the silo, where he dumped them sixty feet to the bottom. He should have felt bad about the whole thing, but he felt good.

If he had stopped then, perhaps nothing would have come from it. Over time, he might have erased the murders from his memory. Life would have continued as it had before.

But he didn't want life to continue as it had before.

He killed the second group to recapture the feeling of release that came from the first. The boiling rage inside him receded as they died, and he felt vibrant and alive in ways he never had.

When he killed the third time, he expected the sensation to dull, but it didn't. If anything, the swelling count of his victims made him feel powerful, and he needed to feel powerful.

The fourth time, he put the Mexicans to work first—repairing the ladder that ran up the silo and building the platform floor inside the top of it. After they carved a hole in the middle of the platform, he sent them down it under the pretense that they would clean out the floor below. He listened to their cries and pleas for several hours before leaving them to die. It wasn't enough to just kill them anymore; he had to hear the terror in their voices echo up through the cylinder of their concrete tomb.

Within weeks, there were more than eighty bodies in the silo, and no one had noticed they were gone. It was enough to make the thin man question his sanity. Was it all a dream or hallucination?

The fireball made it real, which was what he wanted. It also made him famous, but only in the most generic sense. Nobody knew who he was. Nobody understood what had happened to him.

As the thin man took a seat on the rocky hillside overlooking Bilford High School, he thought about the story Allison would help him tell. A story about fatherhood and victimhood, and how he rose above it. People would understand. History would be kind to him. Long after he was dead, people would talk about him, his struggles, and his signature achievement.

And if Allison couldn't see the beauty in what he'd done—if she couldn't see the poetry of it all—he could kill her and find another reporter who could.

He removed his binoculars from their case and surveyed the scene at the high school. Two dozen unmarked trucks were parked parallel near the gymnasium doors. He wondered what they were. Mobile laboratories for analyzing hair, fibers, fingerprints, and DNA, perhaps. Had they found any tangible evidence of him? Even though he was a lifelong scoundrel, he'd managed to avoid arrests, so his fingerprints wouldn't be found in any government databases unless the military had digitized old files, which he doubted. A lab had his DNA from the paternity test, but it had never made its way into a case file as far as he knew. The people in the vans were working hard for naught, he figured. More taxpayer dollars being wasted.

A red Corvette pulled into the lot and drove up to a checkpoint, where a hand extended a badge out the window to a guard. The guard handed the badge back and let it through. The thin man followed the car with binoculars, watching it park. When the door opened, Dagny Gray stepped out. He'd watched her press conference that morning and had been captivated by her lithe beauty. The thin woman had delivered her remarks with eloquence and poise. He was glad he had not killed her. A man in a black suit and clerical collar walked out of the school and approached Dagny. A priest. His hair was cropped close and clean, and there was stubble on his face. Hispanic. He looked familiar to the thin man. He'd just seen him somewhere recently, maybe just a couple of days ago, but not dressed like a priest.

The priest and Dagny stood by the Corvette. It was a real-American car, and that made the thin man smile. The priest leaned against the back fender, talking, while Dagny nodded along. She said something, and then he did. She shook her head, and the priest laughed. He said something, and she nodded.

The priest walked her to the passenger side of the car, placing his arm behind her body, with his hand dangling ever so lightly upon her waist for a moment, before he jerked it away abruptly. And then again, when the priest opened the door for her, his hand curled around her sleeve, just above her elbow, as she slid into the car. Twice the priest had touched her, with an ease and a comfort that was wholly inappropriate for a man of the cloth. Twice this priest had disrespected God.

The thin man smashed his binoculars against the rocky hillside and bolted from his seat. As he walked home, he thought about the ungodly priest, and remembered where he had seen him before.

CHAPTER 50

As they drove to Dayton, she could still feel Diego's touch on her arm and waist. Her friend Julia once confided that she'd stopped noticing her husband's touch after two years of marriage. Dagny had never carried a relationship long enough to grow used to the sensation of the man's hand, no matter how short or incidental the contact. She rubbed her arm to shake Diego's trace.

They were driving to Dayton because Harborman wouldn't talk with Dagny, but he'd agreed to talk with Diego again through the protected filter of confession. This meant that Diego would have to do all the talking. "We need to run through scenarios," she said. "How good is your memory?"

"I forget," he replied. Then, after waiting for a laugh she wouldn't give, he added, "Good enough, I think."

Good enough wasn't good enough. Anyone can ask a question; the art of interrogation is knowing what to ask next. She had attended numerous lectures about interrogation at Quantico. Sometimes a seasoned agent imparted his or her lifetime of knowledge through the recounting of an anecdote. Sometimes a psychologist summarized vaguely scientific studies. Sometimes a professor showed video of his students answering questions in exchange for money. Treatises had been written about the art of questioning, and Dagny had read many of them. They were good, mostly, for inducing slumber. In the end, the only way to learn about interrogation was to do it several hundred times. After that, you started to get the hang of it.

But Dagny couldn't give Diego this experience. After an hour of instruction, she tried to boil it down for him. "There are two things to remember to chase in an interview. First, you have to chase the things they are trying to say. Second, you have to chase the things they are trying not to. This means asking the follow-up questions the subject is begging for while remembering to go back to the questions they are dodging."

"Dagny, I do this for a living. It's confession."

"No, Diego. Confession is where people bare their sins. Interrogation is where people hide them."

"What's Harborman trying to hide? Do you think he's involved in the killings?"

"Probably not. But his career is placing undocumented workers into illegal employment. In my experience, that's not a background conducive to candor. Everyone has secrets, Diego. You probably haven't heard a completely honest confession in your life."

When they parked in the lot behind Saint Paul's parish, Dagny noticed his grip tighten on the wheel. "You nervous about Harborman?" she asked.

"No, I'm good." His eyes drifted to the back door of the church, and she realized that it was the place, not the person, that was making him anxious. His exile in Bilford wasn't just about community outreach. Something had driven him away.

He led her through the back door and then shuttled her down a hallway. There were offices on each side, and every face in them looked up as they flew past. "Diego?" someone shouted, but he ignored the call. They pushed through a series of doors, the last of which opened into the cathedral. The majesty of it overwhelmed Dagny. As a girl, she had attended a reform temple in the suburbs of St. Louis. It had drop-panel ceilings and wall segments on tracks, which let them expand the sanctuary to accommodate the part-time Jews that only came to temple in September and October.

Diego tugged at her arm. "After a while, it just becomes another place."

"That's hard to believe," she said. "Show me where you're going to talk to him."

He led her to a confession booth on the other side of the sanctuary. "This seems pretty old school. What happened to Vatican Two?"

"People can confess face to face if they wish, but a lot of them prefer it this way."

"Why?"

He shrugged. "I guess so they don't have to look me in the eyes. Want to try it?"

Diego slid open the curtain on one side of the booth, and Dagny slid in. He took his place on the other side.

"What do you think?"

She saw the appeal of being walled away from her confidant and wondered if Dr. Childs would go for a similar arrangement. "So, this is confession," she said.

"Anything you'd like to confess?" he said from the other side.

"That I find this ridiculous."

"Congratulations," he said. "You've confessed your first sin."

"Would it be a sin if you called me so I could listen in while Harborman is talking to you?"

"Very much so, I would think."

"Will you do it anyway?"

He paused long enough to draw out the suspense. Unable to see his face, she couldn't tell which way he was leaning.

"Okay," he said.

This surprised her. "You will?"

"Sometimes the wrong thing is the right thing to do. Let me find a place to hide you."

Dagny followed him to an empty office at the back of the church. "It used to be mine," he said. "For a while, they kept my name on the door. Then, one day, they decided to take it down. Now, it's a visiting office."

She sat at the desk, pulled her phone from her pocket, and checked the time. Harborman would be there any minute. "Good luck."

"Thanks." He left to wait in the confessional.

She looked around the office. Bare shelves, empty drawers, blank walls. What had it looked like when Diego had been there? Did pictures hang on the walls? Of whom? Family? Did he have any? What books lined the shelves? All theology? Maybe books on car restoration? What else? She knew so little about him that she couldn't even imagine any details to fill the office. And yet she was trusting him to interrogate an important witness in the biggest case in the country.

Her phone rang. She answered it, put her end of the call on mute, and held it to her ear.

"Father Vega?" a man said.

"Yes. Is that you, Ty?"

"When I talked to you before, I had no idea that anything like this was going on."

"I assure you I didn't, either."

"We were already dealing with the sheriff, and now we have five million federal agents swarming around. I don't want my business to be swept up into all of this, Father."

"I don't think it will be, Ty."

"I have no work now. I've got no income. You understand that? I am stressed out."

"If we can catch whoever did this, then the investigation ends, and everything goes away."

"Nothing is ever going to be the same again," Harborman said. "Something like this doesn't wash away."

"I need your help, Ty."

"You're going to share everything I say with the investigators, aren't you?"

"No."

"You will. You will."

"No. I'm going to protect you. I'm going to give them your information without identifying you as a source."

The lie sounded convincing to Dagny, but Harborman stayed silent.

"Please," Diego implored.

Harborman sighed. "What do you want?"

"I need you to look over another list."

Dagny heard the rustling of paper as Diego passed it to the other side of the booth.

After a minute, she heard Harborman say, "Christ, they've got a lot of information."

"And yet no way to make sense of it," Diego replied. "I know you work with coyotes. Maybe some on the list?"

"Where is that?"

"Last column."

"Got it."

A minute passed. Dagny heard him flip through the pages.

"Christ."

"What is it?"

"This is bad."

"What, Ty?"

"The guys you have listed are all guys I've worked for. Delgado, Sanchez, and Erickson—I've placed folks for all of them. I mean, there are a couple of names you've missed. Like, right here, Alberto Sanchez. He came in with Erickson. And Roberto Rico, he was Delgado. Then you've got some folks who came in with a group called Mario that I recognize, but none of that matters because—"

"Would you mind writing in their names?" Diego asked.

"I'm not putting my handwriting on anything. Look, there's one group that's brought in more people than all the other outfits combined, and they aren't on your list. All of their customers, as far as I can tell, have somehow managed to avoid this massacre. I don't think that's by chance."

"Who?" Diego asked.

"Diablo Rico."

"Diablo Rico? Have you done any work with them?"

"Absolutely not."

"Why?"

"They're like the mafia. There's no honest dealing with them."

"And they send people near Bilford?"

"They send people everywhere. Even to Bilford."

"But none of the folks on the list came from them?"

"I couldn't tell you for sure. I just know they've brought a lot of people, because I've had employers tell me they didn't need anyone from me because they were dealing with a guy from Diablo Rico."

"What employers?"

There was a long pause. "I'm not going to tell you that. If someone starts asking them questions and it comes back to me, I'm a dead man."

"Diablo Rico is that dangerous?"

"They aren't just evil. They are insane."

"Who is Diablo Rico? Who runs it? Do they have a headquarters?"

"No idea. It's a name to me and nothing more."

"How do you know they are insane if you don't know who they are?"

There was a long silence.

"Ty, I'm not giving you up. I'm not giving investigators your name. I believe in the sanctity of this confession. I believe in the judgment of God. Please help me."

Harborman sighed.

"A few years ago, a big client told me they didn't want my services anymore. Said I'd been underbid. I drove out to meet with the guy, to see if I could offer better terms and entice him back. It was a good meeting, and he agreed to come back to me. When I got home from the meeting, my dog was lying on the kitchen table, hacked to pieces. A note on the counter said, 'You lost the contract. Leave it alone.' Signed, 'Diablo Rico.' You consider that evil?"

"Speaking as a priest, I would say so," Diego said. "Who was the client?"

"Nope."

"But they could lead me to Diablo Rico."

"And then we'd both be dead men. If you want them, you've got to find them on your own."

There was a long pause. "Okay," Diego said. "How can I find them?"

"You can't. You're a priest."

"Then the FBI. How could the FBI find them?"

Harborman sighed again. "I guess I'd send a Mexican agent across the border and have him pose as a migrant headed for the USA."

"Where in Mexico?"

"Any border town would do."

"And do what, exactly? How would I get to them?"

"I don't know. Find a café full of old men and discreetly ask where you could find a coyote."

"Would I mention Diablo Rico by name?"

"*You*, Father?"

"I mean, the agent."

"If you mention Diablo Rico by name, they'll figure you know too much. Just make it known you need the best protection you can get, and that money is no object. Be hazy on the details. They will assume you are running from the law."

"And then, what would I do?"

"Father, you keep talking like it's you that's going to do this."

"Humor me. Suppose I did." It was possible that Diego was simply asking a hypothetical question that would be helpful in case the Bureau sent an agent down to Mexico to pose as a coyote customer. But Dagny inferred from his tone that his question was not abstract, and he was, in fact, thinking of going to Mexico himself.

"With all due respect, Father, you can't pass for a Mexican. They'd smell too much America on you and be suspicious."

"What would I do to be less suspicious?"

Harborman groaned. "You'd need to look naive."

"That won't be hard. I am naive."

"No, you'll look scared. And that means to them that you know enough to look scared. Which means you aren't naive. And then they'll know you aren't who you say."

"And if they think that?"

"They'll butcher you like they butchered my dog."

"Well, then." Diego paused. "I guess it would be best to appear naive. What should I say about money?"

"Tell them you need to go to America and that you'll pay anything. They'll give you a number that won't sound like that much to an American, but it would be impossible for someone like you. You need to seem shocked at the amount. You'll have to ask if that's the lowest they can do. You need to do it in a plaintive, submissive way. They may lower the number a bit; they may not. You will need to say that you don't know if you can do it, but that you'll try. You'll need a week to try to get the money together. If they buy your performance, they'll give it to you."

"And then?"

"And then you leave."

"But I haven't learned anything."

"I was telling you how to survive the meeting. I don't know how you get the information you want."

"I understand."

Dagny had another hundred questions for Harborman, but Diego let him go. A minute later, he joined her in the office. Sitting across from her, he opened his palms to her and said, "Hear me out."

She shook her head. "The answer is no."

"Just hear me out," he repeated.

The drive back to Bilford was one big argument. Pleading was met with exasperation; passion battled logic.

"We don't even know that Diablo Rico has anything to do with this," Dagny said.

"They're the biggest supplier of Mexicans to the region, and not one of them ended up in the silo. Harborman's right: either they're involved in the killings or they know the killer, and the killer is afraid of them."

"Or Harborman has no idea what he's talking about."

"I think he does."

"Or Harborman himself is involved." She pulled the car onto the shoulder of the highway. "Give me your phone."

Diego obliged. She called up Harborman's contact information and texted his phone number to the Professor. **See where this guy was during the abductions,** she wrote. She handed the phone back to Diego.

"I'm going to do it, Dagny."

"There are more than nine hundred Hispanic special agents in the FBI, and every one of them is better trained and better suited for this than you. Why in the world would I ever let you do this?"

"Because the FBI can't investigate in Mexico without the consent of the Mexican authorities, right? I'm betting that takes time and diplomacy and negotiations, and then, even if they let you conduct the operation in Mexico, someone in their bureaucratic channels is probably on the payroll of Diablo Rico, and they're going to tip them off. Right? This whole gambit only works if it's off the grid."

He was right. If the Bureau were going to investigate in Mexico, it would have to get the approval of Mexico's Federal Ministerial Police, and there was a good chance someone there would pass news of the operation to Diablo Rico. A rogue operation in Mexico stood a better chance of success than an official one.

That didn't mean that Diego should do it. "They will kill you, Diego."

"Maybe."

"Why would you risk that?"

"What else do I have to live for?" He said it plainly, but it was the bleakest thing she had ever heard.

"For every moment of life you have yet to live," she replied.

"Those moments will be filled with nothing but regret and shame if I don't do this." Diego's phone chirped. "The Professor texted back."

"What does it say?" Dagny asked.

"'Nowhere near the abductions. Don't use Diego's phone for Bureau business.' See? Harborman's good."

"The fact that his phone wasn't near human abductions doesn't mean he's good or that he had nothing to do with the abductions. It just means his cell phone wasn't there."

"I'm going to Mexico, Dagny."

"You wouldn't have the slightest idea of how to navigate it, Diego. You'd have no chance of surviving."

"Then come with me. You could navigate me through it."

"I can't do that."

"Why not?"

"Well, first, I would need to explain why I'm leaving Bilford for two days during the height of the investigation."

"You don't have to say you're going to Mexico. Say you're going to Texas border towns to ask around about channels of migration."

"We already have agents down there who could do that."

"Then say you're going down to brief them on the case and give them instructions."

"You're asking me to lie to the Professor?"

"Yes."

Lying to the Professor was wrong. Leaving Bilford on a wild-goose chase at the height of the investigation was wrong. Helping a priest try to outwit a murderous crime organization was wrong. Everything about it was wrong.

Sometimes the wrong thing is the right thing to do.

CHAPTER 51

The Professor sat on top of the gym teacher's desk, with his legs dangling, his fingers pointing, his bald pate sweating, and his veins pulsing. Dagny, Victor, and Brent stood in front of him, dodging errant saliva. For fifteen minutes, the Professor cataloged their failings, listing all of the things they did not know and assessing their limitations, both physical and cognitive. Normally, Dagny would have interrupted him to stipulate to their shortcomings in order to move things along, but she had a con to pull, and deepening his foul mood was not going to help it succeed.

"We live in an age of ubiquitous surveillance, geopositional tracking, and DNA forensics. It is inconceivable that this man is eluding us!" he shouted with the stilted cadence of a German dictator. "Performance to date is simply unacceptable. If we don't catch the man within the week, my credibility is shot, and this entire enterprise will collapse upon itself. Resting upon our success is not merely the lives of those lost but the very future of the Bureau! We will either make history or we will be it!"

It was a lot of hyperbole, but meeting with the president had raised the stakes. For good or bad, the president would judge him on the resolution of this case. If Brent was right and he wanted to be Director, he needed to catch the unsub, and he needed to do it soon.

Victor was the first to breach a pause in the tirade. "They are still processing evidence from the silo. So there's still hope that—"

"Hope is for horses," the Professor sputtered. Dagny didn't know if the phrase was archaic or if it was just something he had made up on the spot. She turned to Brent. He shook his head, shorthand for: *You're crazy if you think I'm going to speak now.*

If she didn't speak now, the Professor would start up again, and they'd lose the rest of the hour. "I want to chase another lead," she said.

"What lead?" he barked.

"Diablo Rico is one of the major coyote outfits that service this region. None of the dead seem to have been escorted by them. I want to go to Texas and see what I can find out about them."

"Fine," he said, surprising Dagny, who had expected an argument. "Take Brent."

She couldn't take him, of course, because she was taking Diego. It was time to lie some more. "Not necessary. I've already lined up a team of agents from several Texas field offices—"

Brent interrupted. "I spent some time in Texas and am probably familiar with a lot of those guys. I'd be glad to come and help—"

"Again, not necessary," Dagny said. "Victor's overseeing the collection of physical evidence. We need Brent to do the same with witness interviews."

"Agreed," the Professor said. "I don't want too much of the team to be gone. Dagny, this can't take more than a day or two."

"Understood," she said. It might take three days with the travel, but this wasn't the time to press the point.

The meeting lasted another thirty minutes, which allowed the Professor to continue to lead by reprimand and still digress on unrelated topics like the designated hitter, the Hays Code, and Jung's Theory of Temperaments. He was in the middle of a sentence about Alexander the Great when he stormed out of the room.

They waited in silence.

"I don't think he's coming back," Victor said.

Brent turned to Dagny. "Why'd you box me out of Texas? I could help you down there—I have a ton of contacts."

Flattery seemed to be the best bet to defuse the situation. "The heart of the investigation is in Bilford, and I don't like leaving the Professor alone with it. I need you here to make sure he doesn't do anything crazy."

"Yeah, well . . . I guess that makes sense."

"Texas is dotting the *i*'s and crossing the *t*'s. But it probably won't lead to anything."

He nodded. "I get it. Just wanted to make sure we're okay," he said, gesturing between the two of them.

"We're great, Brent."

"All right." He gathered his things.

Victor waited for Brent to leave, then asked her, "So, what's the real reason you didn't want him to come to Texas?"

"I'm taking Diego to Mexico to find out more about Diablo Rico."

"That sounds really unwise. What's the plan?"

"He's going to pose as a Mexican seeking transport to the States."

"And you?"

"I'll be listening through an earpiece in a van, maybe."

"And if things go wrong? Do you need a team for this, preferably of the tactical variety?"

"We would need the approval of Mexican law enforcement, which would be hard to get and would require a visibility within the Bureau that would preclude Diego's participation."

"Well, he shouldn't be participating," Victor said. "I'm not qualified to do what you're asking him to do, and I'm a special agent."

"We'd never pull it off as an official part of the investigation," she said. "Too many sign-offs required, too much chance for tipping off Diablo Rico. Diego's set on doing it with or without me, anyway. His chances are better if I'm involved."

"Diego has a death wish."

"Diego wants to give meaning to his life."

"That's the brave-sounding way to describe a death wish," he said. "Why don't you at least let me come? Three is better than two."

"No, you're too important to come. I need you here."

"That's the same line you used on Brent."

"But I mean it with you." This wasn't flattery. Victor's oversight of the collection and analysis of physical evidence was the best thing they had going. He had cracked the phone code that got them to the bodies, and he might just crack whatever code would get them to the unsub. Dagny grabbed her bag and slung it over her shoulder. "See you soon, Victor."

"You better, Dagny. You better."

CHAPTER 52

The thin man sat at his kitchen table, staring at the blank front page of a legal pad. His right hand's fingers wrapped around the shaft of a blue Uniball pen and squeezed harder with each additional minute the page stayed bare. After forty-eight minutes, he dropped the pen and shoved the pad from the table.

The clock on the oven said it was 12:37. He opened his refrigerator and pulled out a package of Kraft American Cheese. It would do. He tore the tab to open the wrapper, peeled the plastic from three slices, and slapped them between two pieces of Wonder Bread Classic White. For a moment, he lost track of what he was doing. It was hard to concentrate on the task at hand with the Catholic priest still rattling around inside his head. The imposter priest, that is. The man wasn't holy—he was just another migrant from Mexico.

Making a sandwich for the girl—that's what he was doing. He thought about grilling it. There was little more disappointing than a cold cheese sandwich. But how much kindness did he owe her? None—he owed her nothing. She was a parasite, trying to become famous on his accomplishments.

A piercing pain shot through his head, and he fell to the kitchen floor. The seizures had started after he'd learned the truth about the boy and had grown worse with time. Pressing the palms of his hands against his temples, he writhed on his back. His eyes closed, and he could not open them. His teeth locked down on his tongue, and he screamed.

The pain receded slowly in the back recesses of his mind until it disappeared. Wiping away tears, he stood back up and looked at the cold cheese sandwich. The girl was going to be the vessel through which he told his story, if he could ever find a way to write it. She needed to see the kindness in him, even as he struggled to.

He grabbed the butter from the fridge, dropped a tablespoon of it in a pan, and turned on the burner.

CHAPTER 53

If they'd been traveling on official FBI business, they could have flown direct to Brownsville on one of the Bureau's planes, but the covert and unsanctioned nature of their mission required them to fly on American, with a layover in Dallas. They didn't get to Brownsville until 11:00 p.m., and it was after midnight when they checked into the Comfort Suites. Diego retired to his room, Dagny to hers. Late and low on Weight Watchers points, she ventured out to the vending machine at the end of the hall and traded two singles for a package of Hostess Twinkies. They left her feeling sad and sick. This wasn't any way to live.

The bed was warm and soft, and it pulled her quickly into slumber. She dreamed that Victor was her son and Brent was her husband. They were in marriage counseling with Dr. Childs, who tried to get them to talk about their trust issues, but Dagny kept ignoring her in order to play Angry Birds on her phone. The Professor barged into Childs's office, walked to the bookcase, and started throwing books at them, screaming that it was time for them to get back to work. When he ran out of books, he glared at Dagny, screamed that lying was beneath her, and accused her of betrayal.

She woke at five the next morning, feeling groggy and gross. It had been too long since her last run, so she laced her Nikes, grabbed her iPhone, and hit the streets of Brownsville. Texas was nothing but highways and access roads, and she hugged the latter, running parallel to US 77, headed south toward the border. She passed a discount tire shop and then a Chili's. The side streets were empty, but the highway hummed with traffic. Dagny clicked through the albums on her phone and settled upon the soundtrack to *Magnolia*. Aimee Mann carried her past the Dillard's at the Sunrise Mall, a chiropractic clinic, and a Whataburger, which took her back to her college days at Rice University in Houston. Whataburgers were everywhere in Texas.

It felt good to run—to spring forward and bounce along to the pulsing beat of music. Each slap of foot against pavement was something that could be counted and accumulated until tens became hundreds and hundreds became thousands. Sometimes she used a run to think about a case. This time, she was using it to escape one. There were no silos, no cell phones, no media vans, and no evidence. There was nothing but music, the pounding of her steps, and the gentle hum of traffic on a warm Brownsville morning. It was glorious.

Dagny Gray was thirty-five years old and as fast as she ever was. That was something. She had that at least.

By seven thirty, she was back at the hotel, changed, and ready for the morning's farce. At eight, two dozen field agents from various Texas offices met with her in the hotel conference room. She showed them a PowerPoint presenting the basic facts of the case and briefed them on the potential importance of Diablo Rico. None of them had heard of the outfit, which said a lot about Diablo Rico's competence and the Bureau's lack of it. At eleven, she sent them off to scatter throughout South Texas, looking for information about the coyote organization.

The rest of the day was spent in preparation for the next one. This meant fitting Diego with the Bureau's smallest wire and transmitter, testing it from several distances, playacting the encounter with him, and talking through various scenarios and options. It also meant providing for some security.

Dagny knew that private security firms that had previously patrolled Iraq and Afghanistan had increasingly accepted work in Mexico. She called a former agent who had worked with Halliburton, and he gave her the contact information for Vance McGilligan at Blackspotted Security. Googling the company's name led her to a *Washington Post* story about the company's soaring income from its Mexican division. The article noted that noncitizens in Mexico were not permitted to carry a gun as part of a security detail, so the company had to team with Mexican nationals. She called McGilligan and explained the nature of the operation, sussing out information concerning Blackspotted's capacity to support a rescue operation. He quoted her a price of $60,000 for a team of two Blackspotted officers, five armed Mexicans, and an armored truck. Dagny told him she needed a few minutes to consider it and that she would call him back.

Since it wasn't a sanctioned FBI expenditure, she would have to finance it with her own funds. That would require her to liquidate some assets—something she didn't have time to do. Even if she had the time, funding a rogue paramilitary exercise in a foreign country was the kind of thing that could set off a diplomatic crisis if things went wrong. It could also land her in jail.

She decided not to personally fund an illegal SWAT team for a dangerous raid against a criminal organization in a foreign country and called McGilligan to explain her decision. He helped her devise a plan for a solo operation and offered to lend her a gun and armored van for free, which she accepted.

Later, she ate dinner with Diego at Chili's, where she discreetly entered the points from her Santa Fe Chicken Salad into her Weight

Watchers app. He ordered the Chipotle Chicken Flatbread, which he nibbled at with the glum look of a man sentenced to death.

"You don't have to do this," she reminded him.

"Believe me," he said. "I don't want to do this. But I *have* to."

After dinner, they returned to his room, where they rehearsed some more. At ten, she instructed him to get some sleep, and she returned to her room. Climbing into bed, she grabbed the remote and flipped on the television. Talking heads on CNN were hypothesizing about the abduction or murder of Allison Jenkins. When Jenkins's picture flashed on the screen, Dagny realized that she was the reporter who had tried to get onto the Hoover farm with Sheriff Don. She called Victor, who told her that the investigation had expanded to include Jenkins's disappearance, although there was no evidence tying it to the prior murders. She hated that she was in Brownsville while things were happening in Ohio.

After the chat, she turned off the lights and slipped under the covers. Her mind drifted, not to sleep but to nightmarish visions of the next day's operation. It was a bad sign that she couldn't conjure images of success to combat them.

She flipped on the lights and fired up her laptop, seeking distraction in the Dear Prudence advice column on *Slate*, and then a few Funny Or Die videos. At midnight, there was a knock on her door.

Peering through the peephole, she found Diego on the other side. She opened the door.

"I saw the light under your door," he said.

"You can't sleep?"

"No. You?"

"No," she said. "Come in."

He sat on the edge of the bed. "You ever been in a dangerous situation?"

She laughed.

"I know. Dumb question." He looked at her with searching eyes. "What was it like?"

She sat down next to him. "Which time? When I was kidnapped by a serial killer? Or shot at by the mafia? Once, I was stabbed during an arrest gone bad. Another time, I was trapped inside a burning house."

He laughed. "Okay, I get it. You're used to it."

"No," she said. "You never get used to it. But if you do it enough, you realize you're stronger than you think. One time, I was even climbing up the side of a giant concrete silo when it exploded, and somehow, I survived. And you did, too."

Diego smiled. "That seems like a long time ago." There was a creak in his voice she'd never heard before. "So, what's the key? How do you not get scared?"

"Honestly?"

"Yes."

"I have a generally low regard for my own life, so I'm not in fear of losing it," Dagny said. "I have no meaningful connections to anyone, so I don't worry about how they'd take it. And my self-esteem is largely pegged to solving cases, so my mind is usually trained on the objective."

"So, the answer is self-loathing and loneliness?"

She nodded.

"Well, I have good reserves of both," he said.

Something had broken him. "What happened to you?" she asked.

"Life," he said, waving his hand.

They sat in silence for a moment, and then she said, "Tell me about it."

He lifted his head and looked into her eyes. Her normal inclination was to turn away from such a gaze, but she stared back at him. They were going to have a real conversation—the kind that usually sent Dagny running.

"I grew up two hours north of here, in Corpus Christi," he began. "My dad was an electrician. My mother stayed at home and later worked as a waitress. They were both wonderful, but I never really understood them, and they never quite got me. Some kids seem to have a telepathy with their parents. We had trouble communicating with words.

"My parents were devoted to the church," he continued. "And so I spent much of my life there. It had such a sense of community. These days, the city's mostly Hispanic, but back then, it was evenly split. Outside the church, there were two Corpus Christis. But inside the church, we were all Catholics. There was something powerful about that.

"When my mom started working, I'd head to the church after school. Eventually, they asked me to become an altar boy. Got to carry candles and ring the altar bell during Mass. I felt like a rock star. Every day, I got to go to the most important place in town and be part of the most important things it did.

"One of the priests—Father Tisch—told me I was special. Said he wanted to become my mentor. I was eleven years old. That this man saw something in me . . . I can't tell you how much I needed that. At school, I never fit in. I was picked on. Didn't have any close friends. At home, my parents provided for me. Treated me fine. But never showed me any affection. No one had ever said I was special before. And now, this man I admired wanted to spend time with me. Just me.

"You know enough about the church to know what happened."

Dagny nodded.

"At fifteen, I ran away to Houston. Lived on the streets. Did things to get by that I'm still trying to forget. I was in a gang for a while, although it's not as exciting as it sounds. Mostly, I stood on the corner and shouted if I saw a cop."

"The scorpion tattoo on your back?"

He smiled. "Yeah, that's when I got it."

"How long were you in Houston?"

"Six months. One day I got caught in the middle of some crossfire with a rival gang. I darted down an alley, over two streets, and right onto a bus that took me back to Corpus Christi."

"Back to your parents?" Dagny asked.

He nodded. "They were relieved enough to see me that they forgot to be angry for a little while."

"Did they know you'd been molested?"

"No. I couldn't do that to them."

"Do what exactly?"

"Destroy their God." He paused. "They needed the church. And so did I, actually."

"You went back to the church?" It seemed inconceivable to her.

"Yes. Got my high school diploma, applied to the Saint Charles Seminary in El Paso, and was accepted."

"What happened with Father Tisch?"

"Both of us acted like nothing had happened. He recommended me for the seminary."

"The seminary—that's how long?"

"Eight years. Finished at twenty-five and became a deacon. Six months later, I was ordained. I requested placement back in Corpus Christi and got it. For a year, I did everything a priest should, but the whole time, I was waiting."

"Waiting for what?"

"Courage and opportunity. And then I was given the honor of leading Easter Mass. When we got to the homily, I said what I'd been planning to say for nine and a half years."

"What did you say?"

"After reading the Scripture, I looked out to the packed house. I was nervous, so it took me a while to start, and I could feel them become restless and uncomfortable. I cleared my throat, and I told them plainly that our church had become corrupt, and that there was a rottenness that needed to be purged. I told them about how Father Tisch had molested me five times a week in his office. I said I suspected that I was not the only boy who had been molested in the church, and I called upon others who had been molested to seek me out."

It wasn't hard to imagine Diego's voice carrying across a packed cathedral, saying these things. She couldn't, however, imagine the reaction. "How was it received?"

"They call it the year I ruined Easter. But twelve boys came to talk to me the following week. Over the next two years, I built an organization in Texas that helped boys in similar situations. We exposed and removed thirty-eight priests."

"That's great."

"It earned me a transfer to Dayton, Ohio."

"You were punished for your troubles."

"They told me there was a growing Hispanic population in Ohio, and that my talents were needed there. But yes."

It was an extraordinary and sad story. "The speech you gave on Easter . . . was that the reason you went back to the church and entered the priesthood? To be able to give that speech?"

"It was part of it, but not all of it. The church can be a wonderful institution, providing community and support, but it had become rotten at its core. The only way to fix it, I figured, was from the inside. I wish someone at church had been there for me when I was being molested. I thought maybe I could be there for the next kid."

The sacrifice seemed enormous. "You gave up a lot to go back to the church."

"Not really. I was in a bad place. Caught up with the wrong people, alone in a big city. No assets, no home. When I came back to the church, I was giving up only misery."

"And a chance for love."

Diego shook his head. "I wouldn't have been very good at that, anyway."

"I don't think that's true."

He blushed at this. "I didn't go to Bilford because I wanted to help the immigrant community. I went because I was running from a problem."

"What problem?"

He sighed. "Her name was Katrina."

"Not the hurricane?"

He laughed. "She might as well have been."

"You loved her?"

"I did."

"That's a problem for a priest."

"An even bigger one for a nun."

"Katrina was a nun?"

"She was a novice then." Dagny didn't know what that meant, and he clarified before she could ask. "A nun in training. She left the convent when we fell in love."

"Did she want you to leave the church?"

"I would have in an instant, to be with her. But she didn't want me to leave the church. The church was too important to her. And that's why I had to leave her."

"I don't understand."

"I realized it gave her a joy and a purpose that I couldn't. So I broke it off and moved to Bilford. I told the elders that I was doing it to help the community there. My departure was abrupt, and I broke many commitments. The congregation was upset. But my hope was that Katrina would return to the convent and that it would be worth it."

"Did she return?"

"She did."

"But you loved her?"

"Yes."

"Do you still?"

He paused. "I do."

It was a lot of sacrifice for a man who didn't fully believe in God, Dagny thought. "That's a sad story, Diego."

"I'm a sad man."

The statement hung in the air. Tomorrow, he'd be trusting her with his life. Today, he was trusting her with his life story. When someone shares secrets like this, it's only fair to share back.

"When I was in high school, I developed issues with food," Dagny said. "No, that's the cowardly way of saying it. I became anorexic. It's a difficult word for me to say. *Anorexia*. It's so difficult, I don't even think the word in my head. That's how messed up I am. Anyway, in high school, I began to starve myself. It got worse in college, and I had to go to a treatment facility. Again, that's a coward's way of saying it. I went to a mental hospital. And I got better, and I thought I was done with it. But it started up again at law school. I got better, and then relapsed when I was a lawyer in New York. I've relapsed a couple of more times at the Bureau. Now I'm thirty-five, and I realize that this is who I will always be. There's no cure. I won't grow out of it. All I can do is cope with it."

He leaned toward her and touched her arm. Some people knew how to touch a person in a way that signals compassion. Dagny didn't, but he did.

"I didn't realize," he said. "How are you coping?"

"I'm in therapy for it, against my will. As a condition of my employment. I hate it."

"Why?"

"Because I know I can't be fixed, so all it does is remind me that I'm broken." She was being as emotionally honest and open as she had ever been.

"But now you're eating, right? I mean, I've seen you—"

"I've trained myself to think of food as fuel. But I have no ability to judge whether my tank is full, so I rely on, of all things, Weight Watchers. It tells me I need a certain number of points each day to maintain my weight, and I tally up my points to make sure I get them."

"And it works?"

"It works okay. I eat a lot of junk food late in the day to make my target."

His hand left her arm. He probably wasn't even aware of it, but Dagny was. "How do you feel when you're eating?" he asked.

"If I think about it, I feel shame and disgust, mostly. So I try hard not to think about it. If you see me eating a cheeseburger, my mind is trying its hardest to imagine it's at a gas pump."

"Are you ever happy?" It was the kind of question most people wouldn't understand to ask.

"Sometimes," she said. "When I'm running, sometimes I feel joy. Sometimes when I sail. Always when we crack a case."

"And the rest of the time?"

"The rest of the time, I'm trying to ignore how sad I feel." She was telling a priest she barely knew things she couldn't say in therapy or to her closest friend. "I'm at that age where, if you want to have kids, time is running out. Especially if you have no prospects. I don't know that I even want kids, Diego. I guess I'm mostly sad that I don't know what I want, because I was supposed to know by now. Men have it easy—they can have kids in their fifties, without having to wade through statistics about the odds of birth defects. After thirty-five years, I'm as lost as I've ever been. The only thing I understand is my job, and it's not enough to make me happy." As she heard the words come out, she realized how silly they seemed in comparison to his story and laughed. "I feel ridiculous, Diego. You went through actual hardship, and I'm complaining that I haven't grown out of teen angst."

He took her hand with his left and cupped it with his right. "Listen, I've heard enough confession to know that everyone carries around their own kind of pain, and that none of it is loftier than anyone else's." He released her hand. "We're all lost, looking for purpose. That's why tomorrow is so important to me. When I went to Bilford, I said I was going to help people. I didn't give the people of Bilford what I had promised, and now I have to make up for that. I have to make things right."

He stood and walked to the door. "We should try to sleep now," he said.

Diego might waver in his faith, she thought, but he was unquestionably the most priestly man she had ever met. She walked over to the door and opened it for him. He turned toward her and looked at her. The intensity of his gaze almost drove her away, but she stayed focused on him.

"I feel a lot better, Dagny. Thank you," he said. He cupped the back of her neck with his hand and pulled her slowly toward him.

The kiss was gentle and deep and long. When he released her, she studied his face, trying to find some explanation of what had just happened.

He shrugged. "I don't know," he said. "It felt right. Good night."

Dagny closed the door behind him, turned out the light, and lay in bed thinking about what had just happened.

CHAPTER 54

The Rio Grande wiggled and zigzagged such that there were parts of Mexico directly north of parts of Texas. Only the random path of the river determined where taxes were paid, whose law applied, and what lives were had. The land was the same kind of land, and the weather was the same kind of weather, but everything else was different.

In Brownsville, for example, there were lines on the roads that designated lanes, cars stayed within those lanes, and drivers signaled when they wished to switch between them. In Matamoros, Mexico, the lines had all faded, and no one tried to abide by them. Drivers plodded and pushed along wherever they liked, without much regard for order. And while there were lots of reasons for this, Dagny thought, the biggest was that the Rio Grande bent a certain way.

She plodded and pushed with the best of them, and Diego grimaced and yelped with each jerk and screech. The GPS called out directions and took them to the Mini Super El Rey, a bright-yellow food mart that advertised Corona Extra and Tecate Light. Dagny turned the corner, pulled into a grassy, brick-walled lot behind the store, and parked next to the unmarked white van McGilligan had left for them. Diego hopped out of the car and pulled the solid gate closed. Feeling under the rear right-tire well of the van, Dagny found a magnetic key holder. She withdrew the key and used it to open the rear doors of the van. Diego popped the trunk of their rented Chevy Impala, pulled out a large duffel bag, and tossed it in the back of McGilligan's vehicle. They climbed inside, closed the doors, and turned on the overhead light.

There was a hard-shell black briefcase on the floor, locked by combination. She rolled the numbers to 7-8-3, opened the case, and pulled out a monitor (which she placed on the passenger seat), a watch (which she gave to Diego), and a Glock 23 and shoulder holster (which she fastened to herself).

"That's a big gun," he said.

"I like big guns," she said. "And I cannot lie."

When he smiled at the joke, she figured it might be the only smile of the day.

Diego opened the duffel, pulled out grubbier attire—moderately tattered and dirty clothes that he could have plausibly worn on a trek through Mexico to the border—and changed into them. It gave her another glimpse at his scorpion tattoo on his back, and she tried to imagine a fifteen-year-old version of the man before her.

She wired him up and gave him $2,215 in varied, wrinkled bills. It was likely—perhaps certain—that Diablo Rico would take this money from him while sending him out to gather more. If this were the Bureau's money, this wouldn't have hurt, but it was hers, so it did. On a government salary, $2,215 was a lot of money. Then again, if all they lost was the money, they'd be lucky.

Diego closed his eyes and took a deep breath. "Okay. Let's do this." He opened the van doors, hopped down, and opened the gate. She backed out of the lot, and he jumped back in the van. McGilligan had programmed the GPS with recommended directions, and she followed them.

The plan was to park on an abandoned, gated lot on the other side of town. Most lots in Matamoros were gated, it seemed. Diego would leave the van and meander along a predetermined path until he came to a bar called El Gallo Rojo. Upon entering, he would engage the bartender, who was known to refer clients to Diablo Rico.

They drove in silence under the weight of the prior night's revelations and the subsequent confusing kiss. A mission conceived by acquaintances was now being executed by close friends, or something more. She wanted him to back out of the mission but couldn't ask this of him. He had to pull out of his own accord, and she knew he wouldn't.

When they parked, Dagny grabbed a cane from the duffel and handed it to Diego. "Right foot," she said, reminding him where his limp would be. He nodded. "I'll be watching your location on the monitor. Swing your wrist every once in a while to make sure the signal is strong." The watch, provided by McGilligan, was outfitted with a secret GPS transmitter that let her keep tabs on Diego's whereabouts. "Remember, I haven't spoken any Spanish since high school, so I'm not going to be able to follow much of what you say. I'll record it, so we can decode it later, but that's not going to help you in a jam. If you need me, the safe word is—"

"Cincinnati."

"And not just once, but a few times, in case there is a transmission problem. The mic is in your belt buckle, so try not to obstruct it."

"Okay."

Diego grabbed a worn backpack from the duffel, slung it over his shoulder, and opened the back door of the van. She grabbed his arm and pulled him back for a hug. "You'll be fine," she said, thankful that the embrace had placed her tears out of his vision.

CHAPTER 55

As Diego limped away from the van, he felt like an astronaut drifting from the space station. "What have I gotten myself into?" he muttered, and then, remembering that Dagny could hear him, added, "Just kidding, just kidding," to calm nerves. He wasn't kidding, though. He was scared.

Despite his Mexican lineage, this was his first time in Mexico. There was no excuse for this. When he lived in Corpus Christi, it would have been easy to take a day trip to the border. He never did, not even when others from the church invited him to join them on their own excursions. He didn't know why he always turned them down. Maybe he was afraid of Mexico. Not afraid of crime or danger or anything like Diablo Rico. He was afraid, perhaps, of knowledge. Knowledge of conditions. Knowledge of the arbitrariness of circumstance. Knowledge of how lucky he was, no matter how difficult his life had been.

He took a deep breath and plunged forward, walking a predetermined path past the dilapidated homes and businesses he'd seen on

Google Street View earlier that morning. A small, pink one-story building with a flat roof had vinyl sideboard tacked to the front wall that read Iglesia Cristo Evangelica Biblical Del Esp. Santo. It was a church, every bit as holy as the grand cathedrals he knew well, and perhaps more so. There was a window air-conditioning unit that jutted out from the front of the church; like everything else of value in Matamoros, it was encased in steel bars to prevent its theft.

A mother was walking her young son on the sidewalk toward Diego. She was carrying two canvas sacks filled with groceries, and the kid was untethered. He was maybe six and had a mop of hair down to his eyes. In his hand, he held a small rubber ball, which he bounced and caught off the sidewalk in metered time. As they passed, the ball hit a crack and careened into the street as a delivery truck turned onto the road. Diego dropped his cane and grabbed the boy's arm, preventing him from darting into the street. The truck screeched to a halt, and Diego let the boy go. The boy grabbed the ball and continued walking with his mother. Neither said a word about the encounter. Diego picked up his cane and continued limping along his trek.

"A boy darted into the street, and a truck hit the brakes," he said for Dagny's benefit. "Everyone is all right." He wished she had the ability to talk back.

El Gallo Rojo had a five-foot-tall, painted-wood rooster on its flat roof. The rooster was missing its head, and Diego wondered how long it had been missing. He took a deep breath and pulled open the dented, metal front door.

It was dark inside the bar—so much so that Diego waited for his eyes to adjust in order to make sense of the place. Once it came into focus, the bar was bigger than he expected. There were a dozen folding tables, each surrounded by four or six chairs, and almost all of them were filled by rough men who paused midconversation to stare at him. He nodded to them in return but did not smile as he hobbled past them on his way to the bar.

The bartender looked him up and down and said in gruff Spanish, "I don't know you."

"Let me buy a drink, and you will. I'll have a Mahou." It was a popular Spanish beer that he had no intention of actually drinking.

"Twenty pesos."

Diego reached into his pocket and slid a Mexican bill across the bar. The bartender took the money, pulled a bottle from a cooler, and popped the top. "Why are you here?"

Diego scanned the faces of the patrons of the bar, who had all gone back to conversation, and then whispered, "I heard that you can help make connections."

"You heard that?"

"Yes," he said softly.

The bartender placed both palms on the bar and leaned forward. "Who do you want to know?"

"I want to travel north, and I need the best escort I can get. I only want to make the trip one time."

The bartender looked him up and down. "You don't look like you could afford the best."

"I have been saving for this," Diego said. "I heard there is a group called Diablo Rico."

The bartender laughed, which drew some looks from the crowd. "Now I know you can't afford it," he said.

Diego waited for the patrons to turn away their attention, grabbed a hundred-dollar bill from his pocket, and tucked it discreetly into the bartender's hand. "Perhaps you underestimate how much my travels mean to me."

The bartender peeked at the American bill and nodded. "Okay, you're serious. Give me another one of these, and I'll help you."

He knew he had to provide the right amount of nervous protest to sell his role. "Another? This should be more than enough."

"The first one got my attention. Now, you want a meeting or not?"

Diego dug his hand back into his pocket and pulled out another hundred dollars. He opened his hand so the bartender could see it, then closed his fingers around it. "I'll give it to you when you arrange my meeting."

The bartender smiled, then stuck two fingers in his mouth and whistled. A couple of large men rose from one of the tables and started toward them. "Take this guy to your bosses," the bartender said, digging the bill out of Diego's hand.

Both of the men were taller than Diego. They were wider and stronger, too. One of them wrapped his hand around Diego's arm and pulled him toward the door. This, he realized, was the point of no return.

Once outside the bar, the second man became impatient with his limping and grabbed his other arm to hurry him along. The two trotted him through a maze of back alleys. If their intention was to confuse him about his whereabouts, it was working.

They stopped in front of a long, narrow building made of unpainted cinderblocks. There were no windows on the building and no words or numbers on its walls—just a steel door and a small metal box hanging to the right of it. One of the oafs pushed a button on the box and said the word *calico*. The door buzzed, and the other oaf pushed it open.

A third oaf patted him down on the other side of the door. The microphone in his belt buckle escaped detection. This was a relief.

They pushed him through a long, narrow hallway that wound left and right. Along the way, they passed a number of rooms, each filled with bunk beds and oafs, all with various armaments strapped to parts of their bodies. They craned their necks as Diego was shoved past them. He was in a heavily armed, dangerous concrete fortress. If he screamed "Cincinnati," there was nothing Dagny could do. "A lot of people here," he muttered.

There was a red door at the end of the hall. The first oaf knocked on it and pushed it open. A small man sat behind a metal desk, sifting through paper. He had a black mustache and a cigarette dangling from his mouth. It took more than a minute before he looked up, and when he did, he nodded toward the chair across from him. Oaf Two planted Diego in this chair.

The man set his cigarette in the ashtray and studied Diego. *"Es esta una especie de broma."* An oaf closed the door and locked it, and then both oafs stood behind Diego with their arms crossed.

It wasn't a good start. "I'm sorry?"

"Is this some kind of joke?" he repeated. "And now, you are crippled?"

"I can hobble," Diego said, confused. "But I can't hobble across the desert. I heard that you can assist my travel."

The man scrutinized him. "It's been, what? A month? We fulfilled our obligation. You were delivered to the States without incident. What happens after that is out of our control."

"I think there has been a misunderstanding," Diego said. "I have never been here before. Perhaps you have confused me with someone else."

The man studied him some more, and then picked up his cigarette. "My apologies. I have made a mistake. Tell me what you want."

"I have family in Ohio. You've seen the news? Things are dangerous for them now, and I need to be there for them."

"You want to go to Ohio?"

"Yes."

The man studied him some more. "He went to Ohio, too."

"Who?"

"Why do you want to go to a place where people like you are killed?"

"Because I have family there. They need me."

"Then they should move, don't you think?"

"I can pay you for safe transport. Can you guarantee me safety in Ohio?"

"For you?"

"And for my family."

The man smiled. "What is your name?"

"Paco."

"Paco, are you a wealthy man?"

"I have money."

"How much?"

"I have two thousand dollars."

"Let me see it."

Diego dug into his pocket and pulled out his stack of bills. He held it up for the man to see.

"Very good, Paco." The man gestured toward an oaf, who reached down and ripped the money from his hand.

"Does that mean you will take me?"

The man leaned back in his chair, grabbed his cigarette, and took a drag. "Six thousand dollars. Consider this your deposit."

"Six?" He tried to strike the right tone: believable outrage, expressed cautiously. "Six thousand?"

"That is the price, Paco. If you got two, you can get another four, can't you?"

This was an opportunity to leave the building alive, but he hadn't come to survive a rite of passage—he had come for information. "What do I get for six?"

"You get to Ohio safely."

"And once there? Will my family be protected?"

"There are no guarantees."

Diego sat back in his chair and studied the man. "I heard that the people you've delivered to the States have been spared from the massacre. I thought maybe you had some kind of connection that protected your clients."

The man smiled. "And this you believed?"

"I hoped it was true."

The man narrowed his eyes. "I don't think I can help you, Paco. I'm afraid it's time for my men to show you the door." He deposited the money in a drawer, and one of the oafs pulled Diego up from his chair.

He knew he needed to stay in the room if he was going to get any more information. "I can get you ten thousand dollars, if you can guarantee protection. If you can keep my family safe."

The man pointed back to the chair, and the oaf shoved Diego down into it.

"You can't get ten thousand dollars."

"It will take a few days, but if you can guarantee safety, I will get it."

"I'll tell you what, Paco. If you get us fifty thousand dollars, I will guarantee safety."

"That's too much," Diego said, feigning anguish. "I can't get that much."

"Your family wants to be safe. I'm sure their friends do, too. If they can gather fifty thousand dollars, I will guarantee their safety."

"How?"

"By killing the man behind the massacre." He said it with the cadence and manner of a man capable of doing it.

"You can do that?"

"Of course I can."

"Who is he?" Since the morning of his goats-and-sheep sermon, Diego had been looking for someone who could answer that question.

The man shook his head.

"I might be able to get fifty thousand from the community in Ohio," Diego said. "A lot of people will give some, and a few people will give a lot, to make this monster go away. But if I'm going to convince people to send me their money, I'm going to need to persuade them that it will work." He hoped it was convincing.

The man sat silent for a moment. "The man killing people in Ohio used to place our clients in employment. He no longer works for us but has enough sense to know that he should not cross us. That is why our customers have been safe."

"Do you know where he lives?"

"Of course."

Diego decided to push him a little further. "Can you tell me where he lives?"

"Paco, you are looking for safety, correct?"

"Yes."

"Then perhaps you should stop asking questions."

"Can you give me a description of him? So that I can pass it along to my family, so they can keep clear? Is he Mexican?"

"Do not try my patience."

Diego had to keep trying; they needed more information. "Isn't my two thousand dollars worth at least that?"

The man reached into his bottom desk drawer. Diego hoped it was to retrieve his money, but instead the man pulled out a gun. He cocked it and pointed it at Diego. If there were any way for Dagny to rescue him, this was the moment he would have screamed "Cincinnati."

"I use this gun to clean up problems, Paco. Don't become a problem. Come back in a week with fifty thousand dollars. Don't disappoint me." He gestured to the oafs, who pulled Diego up from his chair. One of them flicked the locks on the door.

Diego looked back at the man. He took another drag on his cigarette and blew a puff of smoke. "Tell them to watch out for a thin man." He laughed as the oafs dragged Diego from the office.

CHAPTER 56

Her high school Spanish was good enough for her to follow highly enunciated, slowly articulated sentences, but most of what Dagny heard came so fast it sounded like gibberish. There was, she knew, lots of talk about dollars. And then, at the end, there was the word *pistola*—spoken plain and clear—and she knew that meant *gun*. Her heart, already racing, was pounding after that, and it continued to pound until a couple of minutes later, when she heard Diego's voice in her earpiece. "I'm out of there, Dagny. Everything is okay."

Studying the GPS monitor, Dagny logged the coordinates of Diablo Rico's headquarters, and then watched Diego's dot traverse the map. It took twenty-two minutes for that dot to return to the lot where she was parked, but it felt like hours. She climbed to the back of the van and threw open the doors as Diego was opening the gate.

He hopped into the back of the truck and smiled at her. "I'm glad that's over," he said, hugging her.

Behind him, a white pickup truck stopped in front of the open gate, blocking any exit. Four large men stood in the back of the truck. "You were followed," Dagny said.

The men in the back of the truck drew guns. She pushed Diego down and pulled the van door closed as they started to fire. "I didn't know!" he yelled over the sound of the bullets pounding the back of the van.

Dagny climbed into the driver's seat. "Hold on!" she yelled back, turning on the van and shifting to reverse. "We're going to crash."

With her eyes fixed on the rear-camera display on the dashboard screen, she floored the accelerator, hurtling the van toward the pickup. "Oh, please, dear Lord," Diego muttered, crouched to the floor.

The van smashed into the pickup, spinning it ninety degrees and knocking the men down. She turned the steering wheel, threw the car into drive, and accelerated away.

Glancing at the side-view mirror, Dagny watched them back into a driveway and turn around to give chase. She pushed the button to roll down her window, grabbed her gun from its holster, and slammed on the brakes. Leaning out the window, she fired at the pickup's tires. A shot hit the front-left wheel, and the pickup careened into an iron fence by the side of the road.

Dagny hit the accelerator, turned onto a six-lane roadway, and forced her way through the traffic by charging among cars and forcing them to cede the road. Diego climbed into the front passenger seat. "You're scaring me," he said.

"I'd rather dodge traffic than bullets."

She saw a Matamoros police car ahead of her and pulled off onto a residential street, squeezing between the cars parked on each side. When she got to the end of the block, she saw the white pickup pull onto the street in her rearview mirror.

"Nothing is easy." She turned left at an intersection, then right at the next one, barreling down a narrow street that ran between the gray-concrete walls of two abandoned factories.

"I'm sorry, Dagny. I really thought I was convincing."

They passed an alley on the left side of the road. She slammed on her brakes, put the car into reverse, and backed into the alley.

"What are we doing?" he asked.

"Going on offense again." She heard the screeching of the tires. With buildings on both sides of the alley, she couldn't see who was coming, but she guessed it was Diablo Rico in the white pickup. She put the car in drive, slammed her foot against the accelerator, and propelled the van toward the street. Her timing was right—the pickup was crossing in front of them, and the van shoved it against the concrete wall on the other side of the street. Dagny backed up, straightened the van, and took off. As she turned the corner, she watched the stationary pickup disappear from their view.

She looked at Diego, who was shaking. It seemed like a reasonable response to what had happened.

They took the most meandering path they could back to the lot where they had deposited their rental car, and she permitted Diego to open the gate only after she was certain they had lost their tail. After driving in the lot and closing the gate, he changed back to his regular attire. They cleaned up the inside of the van. There was nothing they could do to clean up the outside. Smashed headlights, folded hood. Broken rear bumper, dented doors. About fifty indentations, some with compacted bullets still inside them. Dagny wrote a note and left it on the driver's seat:

> Sorry about the damage; it was worse for the other guys. Will try to make you whole.

She had no idea how to make McGilligan whole.

They hopped into their rental and backed out of the lot. As they drove toward Brownsville, she scanned the streets, searching for any sign of Diablo Rico.

"You're still nervous," Diego said.

"It's easier to shake a tattoo than these guys," she said. They'd been in Mexico for less than eight hours, but it felt like a month.

The backup at the border looked like it might take another month. She eased the Impala into the line, craning her neck to find the front. There were at least fifty cars ahead of them. She turned on the radio and scanned her way through the stations until she found an NPR newscast.

Bilford was still the top story, except now it wasn't about eighty-some Mexican boys—it was about the disappearance of Allison Jenkins, the beautiful up-and-coming newscaster from Dayton, Ohio. "They finally have a white girl to carry on about," Diego said.

Twenty minutes of talk about Jenkins revealed only two facts. First, she was missing. Second, her cell phone had been found, smashed in the middle of a road. The rest was backstory, speculation, and a meta-examination about why her disappearance was overshadowing the deaths of the undocumented young men found in the silo.

Slowly, they inched forward in line. Dagny kept looking in the rear mirror for a banged-up white pickup, holding her breath until the man at the Mexican checkpoint waved them along.

Diego sighed relief. "It feels good to be home."

They weren't home yet. Although they had passed through the Mexican checkpoint, the US checkpoint was still six cars ahead. A young border agent approached their car. She wore a black vest embla-zoned with the letters *CBP* and a gold badge pinned to the front. A gun and other tools of the trade hung on her belt. She bent down next to Dagny's window and motioned for her to unroll it. Dagny obliged.

"Headed to the United States?"

Where else would she be heading? "Yes," Dagny said, reaching for her wallet.

The border agent held up her hand. "No need yet. You'll do that when you get to the station." She looked at Diego. "Visiting our country?"

"My country," he said.

She smiled. "Of course. Anyway, just wanted to let you guys know that you've been selected for a random canine examination. I'll be bringing Cassandra over to your car to sniff around it." She left and came back with a leashed German shepherd that she led around the car. Dagny watched the dog as it sniffed the car's exterior, poking her nose in the wheel wells, the undercarriage, and along all the car's openings. When the dog was done, the agent handed the leash to a colleague and motioned for Dagny to roll down the window again.

"Okay, just to let you know, the dog signaled that there are drugs present in your car, so we have probable cause to search the vehicle. I'm going to have you two come with me to a holding area while we execute the search."

"The dog didn't alert for any drugs," Dagny said. "I watched her." She was well acquainted with the training of canines by law enforcement.

"She passively alerted to the presence of narcotics in your vehicle, ma'am. At this time, I'm going to need the two of you to step outside this car."

A male border agent walked over to Diego's side of the car. His hand was resting on the grip of his holstered gun.

Passive alerts were only used for bomb detection; canines were trained to bark aggressively if they detected drugs. "You're lying," Dagny said. "Presumably because my friend is Hispanic, and you're profiling him."

"Ma'am, if you're not willing to cooperate, we will pull you from this vehicle. Any further obstruction will lead to criminal charges."

Dagny pulled her FBI creds from her pocket and flashed them for the agent. "We've had a long day. Please let us through."

The woman shook her head. "Again, ma'am, for the last time, I'm going to ask you to get out of the car."

Dagny looked at Diego, and then opened her door and stepped out of the car. He followed suit.

"Please follow Agent Jasper to the border station, where you can wait during the search of your vehicle."

"I'm going to stand right here and witness the search of my vehicle."

"Again, I'm going to have to ask you—"

"I'm going to stay right here," Dagny said firmly, "unless you want to be charged with impeding my investigation of a crime."

"What crime is that?" the woman said.

"Illegal searches and seizures on the border. Profiling of citizens based upon skin color. Planting of evidence."

"There's no planting of evidence," the woman protested.

"That's what I need to witness. If you obstruct me in this investigation, I'll arrest you right now," Dagny said.

"Fine," the woman grunted. She reached into the car and pushed the buttons to pop the trunk and hood of the car. Along with her male colleague, she rifled through the car, lifting up upholstery and permitting Cassandra to sniff throughout. While they searched, the other cars drove into the country without canine examination.

After two passes through the car, the border agent gave up. "There appear to be no drugs at this time," she said. "It must have been some marijuana shake from past usage that Cassandra noticed. Not uncommon for rental cars."

"You should be ashamed. This is all a charade," Dagny said, gesturing to the entirety of the checkpoint.

"This 'charade' is what keeps our country safe," the woman sneered.

"You have no idea what keeps our country safe. You can't even imagine." Dagny climbed back into the car and motioned for Diego to do the same. They drove up to the checkpoint stand and were waved through the border crossing.

As they passed into downtown Brownsville, Diego started to laugh.

"What's so funny?"

"All of that, and they never once asked to see my ID."

She shook her head. They were back in America, indeed.

CHAPTER 57

Dragging her suitcase through the parking lot of Dayton International Airport, Dagny noticed Diego wasn't at her side. She stopped and turned around. He was standing still, twenty feet back.

"What's wrong?" she asked.

He walked closer and tossed her his keys. "I need to wrap up some things before I head back to Bilford."

"Diego, I can't take your car."

"I'll rent something. See you in a day or two." He turned and headed toward baggage claim. She watched him until he was gone. He never looked back.

It was a strange end to their trip, and she ruminated over it on her drive back to Bilford. After their mutual confessions, the hotel kiss, and repeated brushes with death, there was a lot for a priest to process, she supposed. The kiss had surprised her. It reminded her of being in love, even if it wasn't love. It had sprung, she supposed, out of the intimacy of the evening and the stress of their endeavor, but maybe there was something more to it. Diego was handsome, smart, kind, and, it turned out, brave. By any measure, he was a catch.

Bilford was as she had left it—teeming with news vans, crime junkies, and law enforcement, and despite this, or maybe because of it, everything felt depleted and soulless. With luck, the interlopers and investigators would be gone in a matter of weeks, but Bilford would never be the same. Its name would forever be synonymous with an atrocity. Municipal rebranding was hard. She remembered reading that Hamilton, Ohio, had added an exclamation point to its name in the eighties, but the US Board on Geographic Names—an actual federal organization since 1890—declined to acknowledge it, and Rand McNally wouldn't put it on its maps. Eventually, the city dropped the exclamation point. Hamilton would always be Hamilton, and Bilford would always be the place with the massacre.

Dagny flashed her creds at the guard station behind the high school and parked. Three days had passed since she'd been there, and she worried about what had transpired while she was gone. It was something like what parents must feel when they go away for the weekend and leave their children with their grandparents.

Grandpa McDougal was sitting at the desk in the gym teacher's office, fingering, alternatively, papers from a large stack and Fritos from a large bag. She stood in the doorway a full minute before he looked up at her. "I'm glad to see you're alive," he said. "Going after Diablo Rico in Matamoros is serious business."

She was shocked that he knew. "Victor told you?"

The Professor frowned. "No, but now I'm angry that he didn't."

"Then how did you know?"

"I follow your movements on your phone's GPS."

"You had the NSA watching me?"

"I don't need the NSA for that. Exercising my management discretion, I had a patch put on your phone so I can trace you at all times."

"Just me?"

"And Victor and Brent, of course."

She was outraged. "That's an invasion of privacy."

"Privacy is something that existed only as an intellectual abstraction between 1965 and 2001. And you're changing the subject. Tell me about Diablo Rico."

There was too much to do to waste time arguing about civil liberties. "Diego posed as a potential migrant." She reached into her backpack and pulled out her mp3 recorder. "I taped the encounter."

"Play it for me."

"It's in Spanish."

"Just play it."

She hit "Play." At various points of the recording, the Professor nodded and smiled. When it was done, he said, "Diego did rather well."

"You missed the part where they followed him back to me, and we had a shootout in the streets of Matamoros."

"Oh, to be young," he said wistfully. "Well, in light of the shootout, I guess we can't pay them the fifty thousand and be done with it."

"Diablo Rico claims that the unsub used to place its clients in employment. If the NSA has phone numbers used by Diablo Rico, they can search for calls to Ohio. If there are a number of calls to a single number, it's probably the unsub. I can swear out an affidavit for the warrant."

"Section 702 of the FISA Amendments Act permits the NSA to target foreign communications *without* a warrant. Diablo Rico's calls are almost certainly contained in NSA records." He grimaced. "However, I've spoken with several people at the NSA, and they have no idea who Diablo Rico is, so they can't isolate their calls."

"I've got geographic coordinates for their headquarters. The NSA could simply look for calls originating from that vicinity."

The Professor smiled. "So, the trip was worthwhile after all. Finally, something the NSA can use."

"I think we should get a warrant from the FISA court, just to be safe."

"As a matter of principle, we won't. There's enough judicial interference with investigations today."

"You're surprisingly neocon on this surveillance stuff for a guy who was demoted thirty years ago for objecting to illegal searches during the Weathermen investigation."

"This isn't remotely similar. The NSA does not break into people's homes. It does not trespass property. People do not own the phone lines that transmit their calls. They don't own the Internet that sends their e-mails. When you put your communications through the property of others, you are surrendering those communications and any privacy associated with them. If you want to talk privately with someone, invite them to your house."

"What about when you and I are talking on the phone about a case?"

"That is completely different," he said.

"How so?"

"I'm not above hypocrisy, Dagny. I'll call NSA immediately about Diablo Rico."

"I missed this Allison Jenkins thing while I was gone."

"Attractive girl. Looks like a much-younger version of you."

"I'm only thirty-five, you know."

He held up his bag of Fritos and pointed the open end toward her. "Help yourself."

She reached in and grabbed about two Weight Watchers points. "Doesn't make up for the age crack."

"Jenkins was supposed to meet her news crew at the edge of the Hoover farm early in the morning but never showed up. Smashed cell phone suggests abduction. Brent is heading the search. No physical evidence found yet."

"They seem to think it's the same unsub on the news."

"Could be. Or it could be a nut with a crush."

"You're the profiler. What do you think?"

He leaned back in his chair, as if to announce he was falling into pensive reflection. "I think they are related."

"Why take her? It doesn't fit his MO," she said. "To go after an American girl. Maybe she was onto him?"

He shook his head vigorously. "Are you suggesting that a tele-prompter reader was on the tail of a guy who has eluded us? Impossible. My guess is infatuation, which is good for us. It means he's caught up in watching the story unfold on the news. Makes him feel important."

"Why is that good for us?"

"If he's enjoying the high from the notoriety, then that's a weakness. Perhaps we can exploit it."

She stood and grabbed her backpack.

"Where are you going?" he asked.

"To find Allison Jenkins."

"Good."

She started toward the door, then paused. Something felt wrong. It seemed like she was getting off too easy. "So, you're not upset that I lied to you about why I was heading to Texas?"

"Of course not. I was hoping that you were lying and that you intended to venture into Matamoros. Lying gave me plausible deni-ability in the event that things went wrong. Lying was polite—the most loyal thing you could do. When Victor lied about being in New York while he was helping you find the bodies, I was overjoyed. I lied to the president and told him that I wouldn't use NSA data to look for the unsub, and that's exactly what he wanted me to do. Lying is the grease that keeps our engines moving. Lying is one of my favorite things in the world. I lie to you all the time."

Dagny wasn't sure what to make of that confession. "About what?"

He ignored the question. "Go help Brent find Allison Jenkins. Lie all you want if it helps."

"Thanks, Professor. This has been a great chat."

She was lying already.

CHAPTER 58

The funny thing was that Jake Finney had actually driven a tank for years. Every day, sixty tons of steel and metal had rumbled over Iraqi roads, dirt and paved, controlled by his hands. Now, these hands were folded in his lap, because only Sheriff Don drove the Bilford County tank. Ever the loyal solider, Finney sat quietly next to Sheriff Don, who was a great man doing great things, so of course, he deserved to drive the tank.

Behind the tank was an armored truck. Like the tank, it was a gift from Homeland Security. Behind that truck was the Channel 6 news van. Channel 6 was the sheriff's favorite. It provided the most balanced news coverage of Sheriff Don's accomplishments. Other stations occasionally gave voice to fringe elements critical of the good sheriff's love for America.

It took an hour and a half to drive eight miles, partly because the tank was slow and partly because the sheriff had trouble turning corners. When they landed at 1230 Homestead Drive, Finney checked the address on the warrant four times to make sure they had it right. They'd botched their last operation, raiding the wrong house because someone misread the address. The resulting paperwork had been a nightmare.

Twelve armored officers ensconced in military-style SWAT gear jumped out of the vehicles and onto the front lawn. They huddled around the sheriff, who called the play. Because drugs were involved, it was assumed that the occupants were armed and dangerous, so this would be a no-knock raid. That meant they would bust through the front door with a battering ram and toss flash bangs through the side windows. The thugs inside wouldn't know what hit them.

Everyone would lead with guns. In this case, the guns were AK-47s for some, M16s for others. More gifts from Homeland Security, so that neighborhoods would be safe.

Jake Finney had the honor of battering the ram and commanding the troops once they were inside the house. Sheriff Don, as always, would wait outside, explaining the operation to the press.

With a clap of hands, the team dispersed from a huddle and set their play into action. Finney ran to the front door carrying the ram, a thick, thirty-inch rod of epoxy and steel, by its two handles. He lifted it back and up and then rammed it forward into the front door, which popped open. "Let's go!" he shouted.

As they entered the house, flash bangs exploded in the rooms to the right and left of entry. A dog came around the corner, barking and jumping. Finney lifted his AK-47 and fired a series of shots at the dog until it was dead. It was a kind of terrier, and it lay still, dripping blood on the living-room carpet.

He pushed through to the kitchen, where an old woman stood at a stove covered in pots. A ladle lay on the floor; she'd dropped it. An officer pulled the woman's hands behind her back and cuffed them, then pushed her down to the floor. "Where is everyone?" he screamed at her.

The woman was in her seventies, thin and frail. She didn't answer. She only cried.

Feet clattered on the staircase, and Finney led the team to the bottom of the steps. A man stood halfway up the staircase, screaming, "What's happening?" He wore dress slacks and a button-down shirt. His hair was black and trim.

Finney grabbed him and threw him to the bottom of the steps, where another officer cuffed his hands and tossed him down next to the dead dog.

"Why are you doing this?" the man screamed.

Finney knelt down next to the man and screamed at him, "Is there anyone else here, sir?"

The man was crying. Finney grabbed his shoulder and shook it. "Answer me! Is there anyone else here?"

"No!" he yelled. "Why are you doing this?"

"Where are the drugs, sir?"

"Why did you kill my dog?" He was sobbing. "There are no drugs. You have the wrong address. Why did you kill my dog?"

"Where are the drugs, sir?"

The man collapsed in tears. Two officers pulled him up from the floor and walked him outside. Another two officers escorted the old woman out. Finney motioned for his men to tear apart the house.

Every drawer was dumped. Every mattress was sliced. Drywall was punctured. Floorboards were torn. Toilets were opened, and tubs were smashed. The team knew how to look for drugs. They had done this many times.

After fifteen minutes of destruction, an officer handed him an envelope. "It was in the man's desk." He smiled. "Cash."

Finney opened the envelope and counted its contents. Sixty-three dollars. He flipped the envelope over and saw hand-printed words: *Yard Sale Proceeds*. "Keep looking."

When they were finished, they'd torn apart every room and punctured every wall. There were no drugs. Their target had cleaned it out. Perhaps he knew they were coming for him.

Finney stepped out to the front porch, where Sheriff Don was speaking to the news camera. The sheriff smiled at him and continued talking: "About two weeks ago, we received a tip that an illegal migrant was selling marijuana to kids at the high school. After investigation, we determined that this dealer was employed by B&R Landscaping. We raided B&R two days ago and obtained their client list. To our surprise, Councilman Kepner was a frequent customer of the illegal landscaping operation. And the drug dealer had worked here, 1230 Homestead Drive, performing landscape work and who knows what else, on at least three different occasions."

All of this was a surprise. The good sheriff had never mentioned that Kepner was a councilman, and he had described him as a drug dealer, not a landscaping client.

"I am astonished by the brazenness of this crime," Marigold continued. "Mr. Kepner was elected by the good people of the city of Bilford to honor and protect the law, not to break it. There are good Americans who need jobs, and . . ." He shook his head and covered his eyes, shielding his tears from the camera. "I mean, the people here have suffered enough, in this economy, for goodness sake. That's all I have today."

He backed away from the microphone, and the news crew started packing up their equipment. Finney sidled up to the sheriff on the way back to the tank.

"Sheriff, I thought Mr. Kepner was a drug dealer."

"Well, we don't know exactly what he was up to. But he was putting money into a drug dealer's hands. Whether this was a laundering situation or not will unfold."

"But a councilman?"

Sheriff Don turned to Finney and put his hands on his shoulders. "In this righteous cause of justice, we are necessarily going to run into folks with power. We can't let their titles or politics get in the way of doing what's right. Councilman or not, we've got to treat him like any other law-breaking citizen."

There was enough sense in that to keep Jake Finney's faith.

CHAPTER 59

···

"He's the devil himself." Officer John Beamer grabbed the remote and turned off the television.

Dagny and Brent were sitting in the Bilford PD conference room, reviewing files concerning Jenkins's disappearance. They had taken a break to watch live feed of Sheriff Don's latest raid.

"Who is Councilman Kepner?" Dagny asked.

"He's a good man who was thinking about running against the sheriff in the next election," Beamer replied.

Brent looked up from the files. "Why would Sheriff Don think he could get away with such a crass, political move?"

Beamer sighed. "Because he always does. People here like when law enforcement enforces. They're going to say that Kepner never should have hired illegals and that he's getting what he deserved."

"You really should run against him, John," Dagny said. "I'm serious about that."

He shook his head. "I couldn't."

"Yes, you could."

"I wouldn't stand a chance, Dagny."

"You're a bright, young officer with a strong moral compass. A local boy. Handsome and articulate."

"Yeah, well . . ." He paused.

"What?"

"I wouldn't win."

"Give me one reason why you couldn't."

"Because . . ."

"Because why?"

Beamer threw up his hands, shook his head, and finally closed the door to the conference room. In hushed tones, he whispered, "Because I'm gay, okay?"

It hadn't crossed her mind that he might be. "I had no idea."

"Well, I don't advertise it."

"I mean, you live like a slob, and all that *Star Wars* stuff at your house."

"We're not all flamboyant."

"Does the rest of your force know?" Brent asked.

"A few do. I don't talk about it. It doesn't go over well in Bilford. Which is why it's silly to talk about running against Sheriff Don. You'd have to be a war hero or something to overcome being gay in an election in Bilford."

"Well, that's a shame," Dagny said. "Bilford's loss."

"It's just the way it is." He sighed again. "I've got to go brief the chief. Track me down if you need anything."

After he left, Brent popped a DVD into Dagny's computer, and they watched video feed from the lobby of the Hampton Inn on the morning of Jenkins's disappearance. At 5:31, Jenkins appeared on screen, pulling her suitcase through the lobby and out the automatic doors. There was no camera outside the hotel to capture what had happened next.

"How was she going to get to the Hoover farm?" Dagny asked. "Did she have a rental car?"

"No," he said. "It's a mystery. We figured she must have called for a cab, but we got her cell phone records, and there were no calls to a taxi company."

"Maybe she had the hotel call for her?"

"We checked the call log for the hotel front desk and for her hotel room. Again, no calls to taxi companies from either."

"Uber?"

"No Uber service out here, or Lyft."

"Well, she wasn't going to walk from New Bilford to the Hoover farm. Someone had to be picking her up."

She played the video footage from the hotel lobby again. "No clerk at the desk?"

"He was in the restroom when she left," Brent said. "We talked to him. Says he never saw her or talked to her."

"What about the clerk who worked the night before?"

"We haven't gotten to him yet."

"Why not?"

"Because we've had a lot on our plate, and we're prioritizing."

"Maybe Jenkins had him call for a cab the night before."

"He didn't. Remember? We checked the hotel call logs."

"He could have used his cell phone."

"Why would he do that?"

"Maybe he had the number of a cab company programmed in his cell, and it was easier to hit the call button than to dial all those digits in the hotel phone."

Brent seemed to be searching for a counterargument but came up empty. "Okay, you're right. Let's go talk to the guy."

CHAPTER 60

The thin man tried to screw the video camera onto the tripod, but it wasn't working. "Never done this before," he said to Allison.

It was good that he hadn't done it before, she figured. It meant that he didn't get off on filming his murders, so maybe he had something else in store for her. Her mouth was muzzled, so she couldn't tell him that he was spinning it the wrong way.

Finally, he tried turning the camera the opposite way, and it attached. "Rookie mistake," he said. "I'm told this is a good camera and will get us good footage. Good enough for all the news stations, I hope." He walked over to her and untied the scarf that covered her mouth. "You're going to be famous, Ally. Famous all around the world." After a moment, he added, "Almost as famous as me."

Her arms, torso, and legs were still tied to her chair. "Want to undo the rest, too?" she asked.

He smiled, ran his hand through his greasy hair, and smacked her in the face. The blow stung her cheek. "There are a hundred ways this story could go, and you end up alive in only one of them. You should do your best to stay in my good graces."

She studied him as he fiddled with the camera, pushing buttons and adjusting the zoom on the lens. Who was this man? In her short career as a journalist, she'd had the chance to cover a few murders, but all of them involved family disputes or business deals gone wrong. This was her first serial killer. He was wearing a human body, but she was having trouble finding anything else human about him. "You know, I don't even know your name," she said.

He smiled. "I like that you stay in reporter mode. That will work fine." He pushed the "Record" button on the video camera, and a red light came on. Allison smiled—an involuntary reflex to a live camera. "I'm trying to get it so that we're both in the frame. What do you call that?"

"A two-shot," Allison said. "I need to use the restroom again." She hated to ask, because each time he watched her on the toilet.

"After we're done, if you do a good job."

"A good job at what?"

"Making the world like me."

Tall order, she thought.

He tore three sheets of lined paper from a pad and placed them on her lap. A series of questions had been scratched in childlike print. He had scripted an interview.

"I need to test the sound," he said. "Give me an introduction."

She took a deep breath and looked at the camera. "This is Allison Jenkins, live at the home of—"

"Cut!" he shouted. "You need to bring the energy, Ally, or this isn't going to work. I want this to feel like a real newscast."

She forced a smile and tried again with feigned enthusiasm. "This is Allison Jenkins, live at the home of the silo killer."

"Better," he said. "I like the silo-killer thing." He rewound the tape and played it back. Seemingly satisfied, he flipped the camera's monitor around so that it faced Jenkins. "What do you think?"

She looked terrible. Her hair was stringy and oily. There were bags under her eyes. Her cheek was still red where he had hit her. If she got out alive, it would make great footage for her reel. "Looks fine," she said.

He grabbed the remote for the camera, sat across from her, and scooted the seat forward so that he was within the frame of the shot. "I've written your questions," he said. "They'll take me through the whole story."

"I can't turn the pages with my hands tied."

"I'll turn them for you." He smiled and tilted his head as he craned it closer to look down at the notes. "This is going to be great." He pressed a button on the remote, and the red light came on. "Okay, Allison. Let's start."

She looked into the camera and imagined that she was talking to the world. This time, she didn't need to feign the enthusiasm. "This is Allison Jenkins, live at the home of the silo killer, with an exclusive interview."

It took a half hour for him to tell his story. He gave long answers to each of the questions she read, and though his words seemed rehearsed, they also seemed genuine. The first part of the story—the part before the murders—was heart-wrenching and powerful; at one point, he began crying, and, lost in the moment, so did she. This man had been wounded in an unimaginable way. The press should have reported what happened to him, but the press didn't; it was one of those silent tragedies that no one ever knows, or at least it would have been if the man hadn't started killing people.

Any sympathy she felt for him disappeared as he described his descent into murder, which he portrayed alternatively as accidental, involuntary, necessary, impulsive, premeditated, cathartic, and never anything less than genius and poetic. He doted on the details of each gruesome death with a sickening pride. By the time he had answered the last question he had written, she was filled with such disgust and contempt for the man that she wanted to spit on him.

The thin man smiled at her. "That was perfect, don't you think? Now, everyone will understand why I had to do this."

She stared at him. "You didn't have to do any of this." The words bubbled out from the most human, least ambitious part of her soul.

He leaned toward her, and his face filled with rage. "I just explained it as clearly as I can. You still don't understand?"

She'd made a mistake and had to undo it. "No, I understand. It does make sense."

"You just said it didn't."

"I was wrong. It does."

The man froze for a moment, and then his body began to shake. "You know what? You've been a silly distraction, and this has been a waste of time." He raised his voice. "I've given you all this attention, and the gift of my story, and all you've done is deceive with your beauty and your manner. I opened my heart to you!"

He went to the closet and pulled a thick, coiled rope from the shelf.

"Please, don't. Please! I understand your story. I appreciate your gift."

He walked toward her with the rope. "It's too late, Allison. We were having a wonderful moment, and you ruined it."

He looped the rope around her neck and pulled it right. It hurt her for a moment, and then it was over.

....

CHAPTER 61

"Okay, so how does this work?" Matthew Darrow wiped the sweat from his forehead. "Do I need a lawyer or something? Or do we just talk?"

"We're asking everyone at the hotel questions," Brent said, patting the boy's arm with a collegial charm that Dagny never attempted. "Just listen and tell us what you remember. It's easy."

It frustrated her that Darrow hadn't been interviewed yet. Anyone working at the hotel during Allison Jenkins's stay should have been questioned immediately. Even in the largest investigations, things fell through the cracks.

"You were working at the front desk the night before Allison Jenkins disappeared?" Dagny asked.

"I was, yes."

"Did you see her that evening?"

"She had trouble with her key card, so I had to recode it."

"Do you remember what time that was?"

"No. Not too late."

"After dinner?"

"I think so. I'm not sure."

"Can you remember what she said?"

"The whole conversation?"

"Yes," Brent said.

"As well as you can," Dagny added.

"She came up and had her card in her hand and said something like, 'I seem to be having trouble with the key card.' I explained that this happens sometimes, and that I would be glad to recode it.' And then I did and gave it back to her."

She knew there was more detail to be had. "How did you know what room to recode it for? Did you ask her name?"

"I didn't have to. She's on TV."

"Did you look up her room number?"

He paused. "I don't remember. I must have. Maybe I asked her."

"And then what?"

"She went back to her room, I guess."

"Nothing else?"

He shook his head, but then stopped. "Actually, she asked me to call her a cab for the next morning."

There it was. "What time in the morning?"

Darrow folded his top lip under his bottom. "I'm not sure. Early, I know. Maybe four thirty."

"And then what happened?" Dagny asked.

"She went back to her room, I guess."

"And did you reserve a cab?"

"I must have."

"But you didn't use the hotel phone," Brent said.

The boy shrugged. "I don't know."

"Could you have used your cell?" Dagny asked.

The boy pulled his phone from his pocket and scrolled through his call history. "I don't see it here." He handed it to Dagny. The only calls on the night in question were to "Mom" and "Tony."

"Who's Tony?"

"He's a friend from high school. We met up at Steak 'n Shake when I got off that night."

"So you didn't call a cab for Ms. Jenkins?" Brent asked.

"I could have sworn that I . . ." There was a flicker of cognition in his eyes. "No, I didn't call because there was a guy in the lobby who worked for a cab company. He said he'd make the reservation."

No one ever remembered the important stuff right away. "Who was this guy?" Dagny asked. "Had you seen him before?"

"No, never."

"Did he say his name?"

"No."

"The company he worked for?"

"I don't think so."

"What did he look like?"

The boy scratched his head. "The only thing I remember is that he was real thin."

"Clothes? Height? Facial hair? Accent?"

"I'm sorry. I just don't remember."

This is okay, Dagny thought. "Where's the security feed from that night?"

"We boxed up their whole system and took it back to the high school," Brent replied.

It took them twenty minutes to drive back to Bilford High, and then another ten to sift through the file index to find the box that held the hard-drive recording of the Hampton Inn security feed. Brent pulled it down from the shelf, and they hooked it up to Dagny's laptop in the gym teacher's office.

The camera showed the top and back of the clerk's head and a clear shot of everyone who approached the counter. The time slider at the bottom of the video showed the length of the recording: nine and a half hours. Dagny wished the kid had a better recollection of the time he had talked to Jenkins. She toggled the playback speed until it reached 16x.

At 8:11, a young, attractive woman approached the counter, followed by a man in a suit. "That's Allison Jenkins and her producer, Jack McDaniel," Brent said.

Dagny paused the video and pointed to a man sitting in a chair in the lobby. His face was hidden behind a newspaper. "That's the guy the kid was talking about." She hit "Play" again, and they watched the clerk recode keys for Jenkins and McDaniel. When they left the frame, the seated man tugged down the bill of his Reds cap, folded his newspaper, and walked to the desk. The cap obscured all but his mouth and chin.

"He's thin, all right," Brent said. "That's the unsub."

When the thin man walked out of frame, she rewound the video until she found him entering the hotel lobby. They watched him grab a newspaper and head for a chair.

Dagny scrolled slowly through the sequence again and found a frame where the thin man had tipped his head up a bit so that the bottom of his nose was visible. "Sadly, that's as good as we're going to do." She took a screen capture and e-mailed it to the Professor.

Brent rubbed his fingers on his chin. "So the unsub's at home, watching coverage of his crime. Sees her on the news, develops a little crush. Follows her to the hotel, and then arranges to pick her up the next morning?"

"He'd need to steal a taxi," Dagny said. "He'd want her to get in the car willingly, so there wouldn't be an altercation that a clerk might see."

"Maybe he's a taxi driver. If he stole a cab, wouldn't a taxi company report it to the police?"

She tried to think of a scenario when it wouldn't. The gruff voice of an octogenarian called out a possible answer. "Perhaps the driver owns his own car and was set to go on vacation."

They turned around to see the Professor standing in the doorway. "The NSA is still sifting through its data, trying to isolate calls from Diablo Rico to Ohio," he said. "In the meantime, that taxi is our next-best bet. There are six taxi companies that service Bilford. Split up and find the taxi that's missing."

CHAPTER 62

The thin man had carried a lot of bodies over the past few months, but none were as light as Allison Jenkins. He tossed her over his shoulder and took her down the stairs of his house, scanned his front yard through the window, and carried her out the door to the back of the stolen taxi. Sliding the key into the lock, he popped the trunk, only to be overcome by the stink of a rotting body. The stench was so pungent that he dropped Allison to the ground.

"Jesus Christ," he muttered. He'd forgotten about the driver. It was a stupid and dangerous mistake. The thin man lifted the suitcases out of the trunk, reached into the cabbie's pocket, and fished out his cell phone. The battery was dead. What did that mean? Could they still trace the phone to his home? That Snowden kid said they could track just about anything.

The dead cabbie's skin had developed a greenish hue, and his face looked bloated and grotesque. "You deserve this for what you've done to me," the thin man said. Picking up Jenkins, he tossed her on top of the old man's body and slammed the trunk shut.

He jogged over to the front passenger door of his pickup, pulled a gun from the glove compartment, and holstered it under his arm. Bounding back to the taxi, he climbed into the driver's seat and started the engine.

His mind was spinning, and he lay his head on the steering wheel. Was the old man's phone a problem? The government traced phones— he knew that. Were they tracing the taxi driver's phone to his house? Were they coming for him right now? He turned off the engine and ran back into his house, flipped on the television, and sat down.

A reporter was standing in front of the Hampton Inn, talking about Allison Jenkins's abduction. The station flashed to a video still of the thin man standing at the hotel's registration counter.

"Shit," he muttered. "Shit, shit." They knew about the taxi, and they'd be looking for it.

It was time to move. The banks foreclosed houses ten times faster than they could sell them, and he knew of at least a hundred vacant houses in the county. Cycling through them in his mind, he narrowed the list to the most secluded.

He ran upstairs and stuffed a duffel bag with clothes and supplies. That goddamn Dagny Gray was making him leave his house. It was the only thing left in his life, and now he had to leave it for good. She'd taken something important from him, and he was going to take something important from her. Seething with rage, he ran down the steps and out the front door, tossed the duffel in the back of his pickup, hopped into the truck, and set off to kill a man.

CHAPTER 63

The first two taxi companies were dead ends. No missing taxicabs, no thin drivers. Now it was dark. Dagny glanced at the dashboard clock. It was half past nine. Another day was almost gone. She checked her Weight Watchers app and saw that her point tally for the day was zero. Scrolling back, she saw that yesterday's was zero also. Perhaps this system of weight management wasn't built to last.

She drove through a Wendy's drive-through and ordered a Double with the works. She parked in the restaurant lot and ate it while flipping through e-mails and text messages. One text from her mother said simply: **Call me.**

Dagny had texted her mom before, but this was the first time her mom had sent one. Something had to be wrong. She dialed her mother.

"Dagny, I'm so glad you called. I figured your phone was broken, it's been so long."

"What's wrong, Mom?"

"What do you mean?"

"You texted me."

"Oh, yes. I can do that now. I got an iPhone."

"You bought an iPhone?"

"Yes, and it's a really good one. It has a Microsoft logo on it."

"That's not an iPhone."

"It is. You touch the screen to do things. It says it was made by HP."

"You got a smartphone. Not every smartphone is an iPhone."

"Well, I'm pretty sure it is. How are you?"

"I'm fine."

"Healthy?"

"Yes." Dagny looked at her half-eaten double cheeseburger.

"I saw you on the news, you know, but I didn't call because I know how much you hate that. Talking always seems to make you angry."

That made her angry, because it was true. "Is there anything else, Mom?"

"Are you in danger?"

"No."

"Are you going to catch the guy?"

"Yes."

"Good."

It was only one word, but it was so supportive and unconditional that it took Dagny by surprise. She needed a moment to respond, and then managed to say, "Thank you, Mom."

"I love you, Dagny."

"I love you, too."

For the second time in two weeks, she sat in a Wendy's parking lot in Bilford, eating a burger and crying.

There was a Red Top Cab company near Dagny's home in Virginia; its headquarters had four garage bays for servicing its fleet of taxies, gas pumps to fuel them, and thirty or forty red taxis sitting on the depot lot at any given time. The Red Top Cab company in Bilford, Ohio, by contrast, was located behind a strip mall in New Bilford and had neither garage bays nor fuel tanks. There were only two cabs parked in front. Dagny parked next to one of them and walked into the one-room office building.

The man sitting behind the counter was reading the newspaper. "I didn't know that people still read print," Dagny said.

He lowered the paper. "How else do you get your coupons?" He was middle-aged, mustached, and round in most places. The cap on his head hid what was likely a receding hairline. "You looking for a cab, ma'am?" Even in Ohio, taxi dispatchers sounded like New Yorkers.

"Kind of." She pulled out her creds and set them on the counter. "I'm Special Agent Dagny Gray."

"Marcus Wells," he said, glancing at her credentials and then sliding them back. "This about the silo thing?"

"It is."

"How can I help you?"

"How many drivers do you have?"

"Ten."

"You have photos of them?"

"You think one of them did it?"

"No idea, Mr. Wells. Merely trying to fill in some gaps."

"I've got copies of their licenses in their personnel files."

"That will do."

He ducked down and opened a cabinet drawer, pulled a stack of files, and set them on the counter. Leafing through them, Dagny counted six nationalities and seven sideburns among them. None could be described as anything approaching thin.

"Any cab missing, Mr. Wells?"

"No."

"I only saw two cabs in the lot. Is that all you have?"

"No, ma'am. We've got twelve. Drivers lease them from us, take them home at night. Company's got two extra in case we're overbooked and need more coverage."

"Do your drivers use their cabs for personal use?"

"Yes, ma'am."

"And none of them are missing?"

"I talked to all of them today. All except Arthur Mavis. He's on vacation."

"Vacation?

A review of the drivers' schedules showed that Mavis began his vacation the morning that Allison Jenkins disappeared. A call to Mavis's cell phone went straight to his voice mail. His son, listed as his emergency contact, said that he hadn't heard from his father since he left for vacation and gave Dagny the address of his father's cabin in Petoskey, Michigan. Dagny called the Petoskey Police Department and asked them to check out the cabin. Twenty minutes later, they reported there were no signs of recent entry. Mavis had never made it to the cabin. He had never made it out of Bilford, most likely.

Dagny called the Professor, explained the situation, and gave him Mavis's cell phone number so that the NSA could find the last recorded location of his phone. "Between Mavis's phone and Diablo Rico, I think the NSA has some promising leads to work," Dagny said.

"Unfortunately, they're working more slowly than I had hoped."

"Why is that?"

He waited a moment before answering. "They insist upon getting warrants for each search."

"I think a smart person suggested that we needed a warrant for this."

"That's funny. I don't know any smart people."

"I guess the winks expired. You need me to swear out a declaration?"

"I swore one for you. Imitated that chicken scrawl you call a signature."

"Thanks." After hanging up, she called Brent and Victor to update them on what she'd found. The case was almost over. She was sure of it.

Exhausted and spent, Dagny drove back to the Bilford Motor Inn. She grabbed her backpack, climbed the stairs to the second-floor landing, and found Diego's dead body lying in front of her motel-room door.

CHAPTER 64

Dagny dropped her backpack and ran toward his body. "Diego!" she shouted, but he didn't move. She kneeled at his side and held her hand in front of his nose. No breath. She started to cry. Placing two fingers on his wrist, she felt for a pulse that wasn't there. There was a bullet hole in his forehead. His eyes were open. His hands were cold. "Diego," she cried softly.

She fell back against the balcony rail and crumbled to the floor. He was dead because of her. She had allowed him to become too involved in the investigation. He was a priest—he had no business climbing silos and gathering intelligence on Diablo Rico.

Diablo Rico. Perhaps they had tipped off the thin man. Perhaps that was why Diego was dead.

Closing her eyes, she took a deep breath. There wasn't time to fall apart. She pulled her phone from her pocket and texted Beamer, the Professor, Brent, and Victor: **Diego dead at Bilford Motor Inn—Hurry!**

Looking over at Diego's body, she noticed there was no blood on the concrete around him. Maybe it was just hard to see under the dim fluorescent lights under the motel overhang. Waving her iPhone flashlight along the floor, she searched again. No blood. He'd been shot elsewhere and had been dumped here as a message.

Dagny steeled herself. This was a crime scene, and she had to investigate. She walked back to the top of the stairs to get her gloves from her backpack, but the backpack was missing. If the thin man had waited for her to find Diego, he could have grabbed her backpack when she ran to his body. If that's what happened, he couldn't have gotten very far. She sprinted down the steps and circled the perimeter of the motel lot. There was no sign of anyone. He was gone.

She ran back to Diego's body to protect it from tampering. Kneeling over him, she studied the lines of his face. The soft whine of distant sirens built to a cacophony as a fleet of police cars and ambulances flooded the motel lot.

Beamer led the troops up the stairs. When he saw the body, he muttered, "Dear God," loud enough that Dagny could hear it.

Beamer walked over to her and kneeled beside her. "I'm sorry, Dagny."

There was nothing to say except business. "Establish search points at roadways three, five, and ten miles from here," she said. "Request neighboring police departments assist on the outer perimeters. As for the motel property, no one enters or exits. All guests must stay in their rooms for now. We don't want them contaminating the crime scene. Your men need to limit their own pathways. They can't gallop up and down the stairs as they like. Everyone hug the left side so that most of the stairway remains untouched. We'll need witness statements. Hopefully, the Professor is bringing agents to conduct interviews, but we may need to augment them with your men. After witness interviews, we want to evacuate guests through the rear windows of their rooms so that we limit contamination of the landing and parking lot. I assume that the Professor has notified the Bureau forensics team that we'll need them to collect physical evidence. However, if your men could establish custody over any surveillance feed the motel has, that would be appreciated."

"Okay," he said. "I'll rally my troops."

"And after that," Dagny said, "you'll need to take my statement, so that we get down everything I remember before I forget it." Then, thinking it over, she said, "Forget that. I'll do my statement now."

She pulled out her iPhone, activated the voice recorder, and began dictating. There wasn't much to record, but she had to stop twice because she was crying. As she put the phone back in her pocket, her eyes settled on Diego.

He wasn't wearing his clerical collar, just tattered jeans and a T-shirt. She wondered if that's why he stayed in Dayton—to unburden himself of priestly duties. His hair seemed shorter. He'd gotten a haircut. Right when he was ready for a rebirth, life had been taken away. She reached out to run her fingers across his face but stopped short. He wasn't the man she had kissed two days ago. He was evidence now.

And so she sat against the wall in front of her room at the Bilford Motor Inn, oscillating between catatonic numbness and convulsing sobs. Father Diego Vega hadn't only been a good man. He had been a genuine saint in every sense of the word, the kind whose quiet acts of sacrifice and heroism made him too good for canonization.

The gentle touch of Victor's hand on her shoulder woke her from these thoughts. She stood and accepted his embrace. Hugs were doled out only in times of tragedy in her work, and they occurred with all too great a regularity. "He was a great guy," Victor said.

Brent followed with his own embrace. "I'm sorry, Dagny," he whispered in her ear.

When he pulled away, the Professor was standing behind him. "The evidence-response team is on its way," he said. "We need to establish perimeter points and take witness statements."

"Beamer is setting up perimeter points," she said.

"I've also arranged for four drones to surveil from the skies. We'll have them up in minutes. With respect to metadata, warrants have been approved. The NSA is searching through the data. I expect us to have coordinates for the unsub's home base within the hour. I've ordered SWAT equipment, and I would like you to lead the team, Dagny, if you are emotionally able."

This was the Professor's version of a hug, she supposed.

She nodded. If she'd learned anything in the Bureau, it was how to postpone grief. "I thought we didn't use SWAT teams, Professor. What happened to the theory that a small team is better?"

"I don't mind SWAT teams if they do what I say." He smiled. "When we catch him, things are going to change quickly for us. This isn't about the bodies in the silo or the girl from the news. This is about an opportunity to change the way we police the country."

For years, the Professor had been marginalized within the Bureau, so the promotion would be validation of his efforts and victory over his opponents. He'd be the oldest Director in the history of the organization, mostly likely the smartest, almost certainly the least corrupt. Like every Director before him, he suffered from the personal flaw of wanting the position. And he wanted it so badly that he couldn't parcel a thought to the dead man on the landing who had brought him the case. It made her sick.

They had to surrender their perch on the motel landing when twelve members of the Bureau's Evidence Response Team arrived on the scene to begin their forensic analysis. Dagny slowly stepped away from Diego. She knew he'd look like a stranger the next time she saw him. Crime science had a way of sucking the soul from a body.

As they walked down the steps to the motel parking lot, she thought about her backpack and the fact that her iPad was in it. She'd collected and saved most of her notes on it. The unsub was likely to inspect it, and if he turned it on, its location would be logged to her iCloud account. She pulled out her iPhone and opened the Find iPhone app. Her iPad showed up under her account as "offline." She clicked "Notify When Found" so that she would receive an alert if the unsub turned it on.

Six white vans parked adjacent to the motel, and additional teams of FBI agents swarmed into the lot. John Beamer walked over to Dagny. "I see your cavalry is here," he said. "What do you want us to do?"

"Brief them on what your men have done, and offer to assist as needed."

He nodded. "How are you doing?"

"I'm okay," she said with a quiver that undermined the declaration. She gestured to the commotion around them. "It only becomes real when this is gone."

Victor tugged at her shoulder. "We're meeting at the high school to plan the raid."

CHAPTER 65

There were six new trucks parked in the lot behind the high school gymnasium. One was a tank. The others were armored vehicles disguised as two FedEx trucks, two mail trucks, and a moving van for a company called Helping Hands. Dagny wondered how the Professor had been able to pull these resources together so quickly. No matter how much she thought she was running the investigation, he was the one who pulled the strings in the end.

She parked Diego's Corvette next to a faux mail truck, flashed her creds to the guard, and went inside. Dozens of technicians and agents were still processing the evidence from the silo. She realized that she didn't know any of them by name. Victor had done an incredible job organizing the effort. It was something she couldn't have done. With any luck, though, their work would be moot.

Brent was standing in front of the men's locker room. He motioned for her to come.

"The Professor got those vehicles pretty fast," she said.

"You haven't seen anything yet. Follow me."

Dagny had never been inside a men's locker room, and she wasn't sure she was entering one now, since it looked more like an armory. All of the lockers had been pushed aside to accommodate a dozen racks of weapons and gear. She surveyed the collection of machine guns, pistols, shotguns, flash grenades, Kevlar vests, belts, helmets, visors, gas masks, canisters, camouflage, boots, and infrared cameras. "Good Lord, Brent. Is this Bilford or Fallujah?"

He smiled. "I think the official policy is better safe than sorry."

"Who are we getting to wear this stuff?"

"CIRG is sending its national team." CIRG was the Critical Incident Response Group. The Professor was bringing in the best and brightest. "They should be here within the hour."

"And who's in charge of them?"

Brent laughed. "The Professor says you are."

"Why, exactly?" It sounded funny when she said it, but it was an honest question.

"I guess you're the only person he really trusts."

That was a lot of weight to carry. Her phone buzzed, and she looked down, hoping to find an alert as to her iPad's location. Instead she found a text from her mother that read: **What is HDMI?** She slipped the phone back in her pocket.

They sat in silence, waiting for the Professor to arrive. She spent the downtime thinking about Diego and her increasing sense of culpability for his death.

There was a loud boom as the door to the locker room flew open. The Professor hobbled in with a stack of paper in hand. "We have the coordinates!"

Victor followed behind him.

The Professor handed the stack to Dagny. She leafed through it, trying to make sense of page after page of inscrutable data. "Does this come with a glossary?"

Victor walked over and took the papers from her hands, flipped through them, and explained. "There were dozens of calls from Diablo Rico to various locations in Ohio, but only one of them matches the last location of Arthur Mavis's cell phone." Two matching locations had been circled on the page—both showed 39.48747 longitude and 84.595838 latitude. "You overlay this on a map and you get the unsub's house: 4587 Kiggens Way, in Rhodes, Ohio, just north of New Bilford. Owned by a man named Harold Fisher."

"What do we know about him?"

"Ex-navy," the Professor said. "No real career. Floats from job to job. Last reported income was for a foreclosure outfit that helps banks manage vacant properties."

"I spoke to his last boss on the phone," Victor said. "Fisher quit a few months ago and wouldn't say why. I asked him to describe Fisher, and he said, 'Real thin.' First thing he said, honest to God."

"As soon as the CIRG team arrives, we're raiding the house on Kiggens," the Professor said. "Allison Jenkins may be alive, so it will be a tricky operation. I want snipers in the trees, and I want them to take Fisher out if they have a shot. I will station myself in the moving van, which is outfitted with monitors that will receive video transmissions from cameras embedded in each of the helmets worn in the raid. I'll be able to speak to Dagny's earpiece and direct the action."

That's why she was to lead the raid. It wasn't that he trusted her to head the operation; it was that he trusted her to be at his command. "Seriously?" she said.

He smiled. "My brain will be in your body."

"It's like I'm a drone."

"Exactly," he replied, missing her sarcasm or choosing to ignore it.

She might have pressed him further on this, but the CIRG team arrived—twenty-two men and six women, every one of them an expert in tactical maneuvers. Victor borrowed a projector from the high school AV closet, hooked it to his laptop, and projected a satellite image of

Fisher's property onto the white locker-room wall. The Professor stood in front of the screen and barked instructions like George C. Scott's Patton.

The house was located in a clearing in the woods. Taking any of their trucks close to the house would draw attention, so they would have to park out of sight and approach by foot. Flipping among satellite views, the Professor identified the most climbable trees for the snipers, who would take their places first. Then the others would advance from the west side of the property, because there were no windows on that side of the house. After the team reached the west wall, half would run along the front of the house, half along the back, and both would smash windows and toss flash and teargas grenades into the house.

"And most important, if you have a clear shot at Fisher, shoot to kill! Allison Jenkins may still be alive, and we can't give Fisher a chance to harm her. Special Agent Dagny Gray is in charge, and you should all obey her commands. Now, let's do this!"

Everyone picked through the fatigues on the racks to find the best fit. The women took theirs to the girls' locker room. A flat-screen television hung on the wall. CNN was still broadcasting live from Bilford, even in the middle of the night.

As they changed, one of the women asked Dagny, "You ever do anything like this before?"

"I've been part of SWAT raids."

"No, I mean have you been a part of anything *like this* before?"

"Not like this."

As she dressed, her phone buzzed again. Another text from her mother: **Never mind, I did the Google on it.**

"But you're going to be in charge out there?" It wasn't really a question; it was a judgment.

"Actually, the frail ninety-year-old in the other room is going to be in charge," Dagny said. "He'll be relaying his commands to me."

The woman rolled her eyes. Wait until he's Director, Dagny thought.

The bulbous figure of Sheriff Don Marigold flashed on the flat screen and caught Dagny's eye. CNN was replaying footage from a press conference on the courthouse steps earlier that day. The bottom banner read: *Sheriff Don Announces Arrests.*

Dagny walked over to the set and turned up the sound.

"And that's why," the sheriff said, "I'm happy to announce that we have arrested Juan Sanchez, owner of Bilford Ford, for his employment of illegal-migrant labor, which renders him complicit in the recent massacre and in the disappearance of Allison Jenkins. Had Mr. Sanchez not enticed and exploited the young illegals, they never would have moved here and would likely be alive today. Without a massacre, Ms. Jenkins would be safe and well. And that is my message to the rest of Bilford's business community: If you hired illegal workers, I will get you, and you will be held accountable for what has transpired. We in Bilford have sinned. It is time to do the Lord's bidding. And I will continue to do it, no matter what the heretics might say about me. I love America. I love the people of Bilford. I will not stop this crusade."

Someone has to stop the crusade, Dagny thought. Her phone buzzed.

Harold Fisher had turned on her iPad. She opened the Find My iPhone app and found his location. She smiled. They were going to catch him.

She looked back up to the blustering sheriff on the television. If Diego's sacrifice was going to mean anything, it wouldn't be enough to catch Fisher. She had to bring down Sheriff Don, too.

In a flash, she knew how to do it. Immediately, she wished it had not occurred to her. It was reckless and stupid, entirely inappropriate, and probably illegal.

It was also the right thing to do.

She called John Beamer. He took some persuading.

CHAPTER 66

Dagny climbed into the fake moving van with Brent, Victor, and the Professor while the CIRG team filled the other trucks. Taking a seat across from Victor, she noticed for the first time that he was wearing civilian clothes. "You're not joining the raid?"

"I know my strengths."

"Tech support," the Professor said. "Lord knows we don't want a gun in his hand."

As they rode, Dagny studied the faces of the team, wondering what they would think of her when it was all over. The Professor was smiling in silent satisfaction, certain, it seemed, that victory would deliver to him control over the entirety of the FBI. Until Brent had mentioned it, it hadn't occurred to her that the Professor would want to be Director. She felt silly now for having missed it. He was an elderly man with no children. The Bureau had been his life's obsession. It was his identity, and it would be his legacy.

Brent was thumbing through the ammo on his belt pocket. He was right, of course—she had been unfair to him. There was no reason for it. Dagny had repeatedly flouted the FBI's rules in ways small and big. Brent, by contrast, was the model special agent, loyal to the Bureau and its rules. For perhaps the first time, she saw this as a virtue. A Bureau full of lone wolves could never function. The world needed more Brents than Dagnys.

Victor, laptop open, was studying the geography of the raid. He was a great kid and fiercely loyal to her, having risked his career to join her in Bilford. Without his efforts, they never would have found the silo or the bodies inside it, and they never would have made the connection to Diablo Rico. She hoped he and his bride-to-be would have children, and that he'd find joy in them. She hoped he would never make the Bureau his life.

Dagny rode with a pit in her stomach, eager to bring this all to a close and afraid of what that would mean.

The convoy parked out of sight of the house. Everyone exited the vehicles and huddled around the Professor, who reviewed the plan for the final time. The snipers were dispatched to their stations, while the Professor and Victor retired to the inside of the van so they could watch their progress unfold through the magic of the helmet-cam. Dagny and the others huddled low, waiting for authorization to move on the house.

After a few minutes, the Professor's voice rang in her ear. "Snipers are in place. Begin ground operation."

She scanned the assembled team, all outfitted in fatigues, armed for combat. Their eyes were trained on her, waiting for instruction. Brent, usually dapper in a suit, smiled at her. He looked at home in his war clothes. It seemed wrong that battle wear was so comfortable while law enforcement clothing was stiff and stifling.

"Let's go," Dagny said.

She led the team on a crawl toward the house. There was a palpable energy from the collective adrenaline of the group. Brent sidled up next to her. "These are the moments we live for, right?" he said. She was too filled with dread to respond.

The team split at the west wall of the house. She led her half around the front, while Brent took his around the back. One of the CIRG members bashed in windows with a Hallagan tool, while another tossed flash grenades and teargas into the home. The Professor continued to bark instructions in her ear, but she couldn't hear him over the noise. Everyone donned their masks, and the strongest man in the group knocked down the front door. She entered the house with her pistol drawn, and the others followed.

"Fan out!" she shouted, but the CIRG team was ahead of her; they'd done this before, many times.

Dagny walked through the entry toward the kitchen. "Check the closet!" the Professor yelled, and she opened the coat closet in the foyer and rifled through the coats. It was empty. She continued into the kitchen.

"Where is everyone else?" the Professor said. "I can't see them. Check the pantry."

A CIRG agent came around from the dining room and beat her to the pantry door. Empty. He opened another door to the basement, and two more CIRG agents followed him down. "Spin around; I can't see what's behind you," the Professor barked, and Dagny complied, turning toward the family room. The television was on—more cable news about Bilford. She walked into the room and moved the curtains that hung at the window.

"The garage! Try the garage!" She spun around, opened the door to the garage, and peered in. It was empty. There were cabinets lining one of the walls; CIRG agents had already opened them.

"What's upstairs?"

Dagny walked back through the kitchen to the foyer, and the steps that went upstairs. Brent was walking down them.

"What did you find?" she asked.

"Evidence of confinement. Ropes, chains, tape. A video camera on a tripod."

The Professor shouted in her ear. "I don't care about any of that. I want Fisher!"

"No Fisher?" she said.

"Nobody," Brent replied.

The Professor shouted, "What about the basement!" She circled around to the kitchen. A CIRG agent was coming up the steps from the basement.

"Anything?" Dagny asked.

"No," she said.

One of the snipers came running up to her. "We found the driver and the newsgirl in the trunk of the taxi outside." She followed her outside to the taxi and peered into the open trunk. Jenkins's body lay on top of the dead cabbie's. The newswoman's neck was bruised and abraded, and there were rope burns on her wrists, but there was no decomposition—her death was recent. The cabbie's body was in worse shape, green and bloated, with bloody foam leaking from his nose and mouth. Dagny filled with sadness. They'd come close but hadn't managed to save anyone. Not the boy in the silo, who managed to scream for help moments before the silo's explosion. And now not Allison Jenkins, who had probably been killed only hours ago. If she'd been only a little bit better at her job, both might have been saved.

"I don't care about this," the Professor said. "I want Fisher. Has anyone checked to see if there is an attic, for Christ's sake?"

CHAPTER 67

Harold Fisher sat on an old wood trunk, listening to the sounds below. Boots clattering on the floor and stairs. Glass shattering, doors breaking. Flash grenades exploding. People yelling.

His right hand held his gun, a Springfield XD-S, with seven rounds of 9mm Luger. It was enough to take down a small team but not a whole army, and from the sounds of it, an army was coming.

The attic was maybe twenty by fifteen; it was eight feet tall in the middle but only two feet tall at the sides. Wood crossbeams rose from the middle of the floor to support the roof at forty-five-degree angles in both directions. If the army came for him, these beams would slow them. There was a small closet in the far wall, six feet high but only a foot wide. He tiptoed to it, opened the door, and looked inside. There was a broom and nothing else. He withdrew the broom and leaned it against the wall, then stepped inside the closet. If he hadn't been so thin, he never would have fit.

Fisher pulled the door nearly shut, leaving a small crack so he could see what was coming. His chest began to heave. For a long time, he'd wanted this final confrontation. Now that Dagny Gray and her army were just below his feet, it was too much. There was always the chance, he supposed, that they might miss him—that they wouldn't check the attic, or if they did, that they would overlook the closet. He closed his eyes and prayed to God, asking forgiveness for what he had done and what he would do if they found him.

The frenzy of noise below continued. How had they found him? Maybe when he had turned on the iPad? Could she have tracked it? His own curiosity had done him in. If only he had left that backpack on the motel landing.

He heard them pop the ceiling panel that led to the attic. A hand reached up and tossed a small black object into the room. It exploded with a bang that shook the closet door; the thin man held it to keep it from flying open. Smoke filled the attic. Another grenade landed closer to the closet. The thin man held the door tight and felt it shake when the grenade exploded. Now the attic was filled with smoke.

Fisher heard the smattering of steps on the ladder. He couldn't see through the smoke and guessed that they couldn't see him, either. As the smoke dissipated, he saw three officers covered in fatigues and helmets. He wondered whether one of them was Dagny. She'd been lucky his key no longer worked at the Bilford Motor Inn. He figured she wouldn't be so lucky today.

Opening the closet just an inch wider, he stuck the barrel of his gun out the door and peered over the scope. There were five officers now, and one was walking toward the closet. He squeezed his finger on the trigger and fired off a shot.

CHAPTER 68

When Dagny got back to the house, Brent was standing at the door. "The Professor wants to know if anyone checked the attic," she said.

He shook his head. "You need to see this." She followed him inside to the family room, where CIRG agents were huddled around the television set. Channel 2 was broadcasting live from a house in Bilford. One of the agents turned up the sound.

On the screen, John Beamer stood on the steps of the house, dressed in full tactical gear, speaking into a microphone held by a reporter and reading from his phone. "Approximately thirty minutes ago, we began an operation to capture Harold Fisher, the suspected perpetrator of the massacre in Bilford." Dagny heard the Professor swear through her earpiece. He was watching the report through the camera in her helmet.

"As expected," Beamer continued, "Mr. Fisher resisted our efforts to capture him and fired at our men. Fortunately, he missed. Mr. Fisher's actions, however, required counterfire, which killed him. We are processing the scene now. Our preference would have been for Mr. Fisher to stand trial for his crimes against our community, but the most important thing is that his spree is over."

She heard the Professor swear some more.

"None of this would have been possible without the assistance of the Federal Bureau of Investigation, which deserves the bulk of the credit for what happened here today. In particular, Timothy McDougal is singularly responsible for the success of our operation. Without his genius, we would not have found the bodies at the silo, we would not have identified Mr. Fisher as the perpetrator, and Mr. Fisher would still be free today. I think I can speak on behalf of all of Bilford in thanking Mr. McDougal for what he has done for this community."

The Professor let out a string of archaic expletives that Dagny had never heard.

Someone turned off the television, and the agents began to filter outside. "Wait!" Dagny called. "This is still a crime scene. We need to log the evidence."

"He's dead," Brent said. "There's not going to be a trial."

"But it's still protocol."

"Nobody cares about protocol," he said. "Nobody cares about anything. We lost."

CHAPTER 69

Dagny sat with the Professor, Brent, and Victor at the corner table at the New Bilford Chili's. Brent ordered a coffee; Victor, a slice of apple pie; Dagny, a cheeseburger with extra cheese. The Professor ordered nothing and stared at her, seething in silence. He knew, she decided.

"I don't understand it," Victor said. "How did Beamer find him? And why didn't he involve us in the raid? I thought he was a good guy."

"Sometimes," the Professor said, still staring at Dagny, "people have their own agendas, and they're willing to be disloyal to achieve them."

It hurt to hear him say this. There was nothing she could say in response.

"He's a jerk," Brent said. "Not only was he disloyal, but it was bad judgment. This was way too hot for the Bilford PD. They have no expertise for this. If we had led the raid, we would have captured him alive. I guarantee it."

The Professor continued to stare straight into Dagny. "I cannot fathom how Beamer knew where he was," he said. "Any idea, Dagny?"

"I don't know," she lied.

"I would ask him, but I doubt he'd tell me," the Professor said. "Convenient that Fisher was killed. If there were a trial, Beamer would have to explain how he found Fisher. But now, he doesn't have to."

Dagny took a bite from her burger. "No one else is going to eat?"

The Professor rose from the table. "Of course not."

Brent stood, too. "I can't take this, either. I'm going back to the hotel."

They stormed away, leaving Victor alone with Dagny. He turned to her. "What just happened?"

"The Professor is mad at me."

"Why?"

She thought about dodging the question, but Victor deserved the truth. "I gave Beamer the coordinates for the raid and told him to lead it without us."

He leaned back in his seat. "And the Professor knows this?"

"Apparently, he suspects."

"How did you get the coordinates?"

"Fisher stole my backpack at the motel."

"And you tracked your iPad?"

She nodded. "You mad at me?"

He tilted his head in contemplation. "No." Pulling his pie plate closer, he lifted a bite with his fork and ate it.

"Why not?"

"Dagny, I don't care who gets credit. A terrible murderer isn't going to kill again. That's all that matters. Everything else is politics. If you want Beamer to beat Sheriff Don in the next election, that seems noble enough to me, I guess."

He was always more perceptive than she expected him to be.

"You had to know that it would enrage the Professor and possibly damage his quest to be Director," he continued. "So I assume you texted

Beamer the speech he read, thanking the Professor for his help with the investigation. Trying to mitigate the damage."

"Whether it mitigated it or not, we'll see."

"It was super reckless, of course. Gambling on Bilford PD to pull this off. They've got no training for something like this. Imagine if it hadn't worked."

"I know." It was the most reckless thing she'd done as a special agent, and she'd done a lot of reckless things.

"I'm surprised Beamer went along with it."

"It gave him a way to defeat Sheriff Don. It was the only way someone would. You're really not mad at me?"

"No," he said, eating another scoop of pie. "All that matters is the harm we stopped, I figure. I know you think I'm naive about all of this."

"No," she said. "I'm pretty sure you're the wisest of all of us about this kind of stuff." She took another bite of the burger and studied Victor. At twenty-five years old, he was as far away from the Professor's Machiavellian ways as a kid could ever be. "Be careful, Victor. Everything about this job is designed to change you. I pray that it won't." The Bureau needed more Brents than Dagnys, but it needed Victors most of all.

Her phone buzzed. She picked it up and saw Diego's number flash on the screen.

CHAPTER 70

....

She pressed the button to answer the call.

"I saw the news. You said we'd get him, and you did it. I cannot adequately express my gratitude."

It sounded just like him. "Who is this?"

"It's Diego, Dagny."

"This isn't funny. Who is this?"

"It's Diego. Is this a bad connection? I'm headed back to Bilford."

It didn't make any sense. "Meet me at the high school." She hung up the phone.

"Who was it?" Victor asked.

"I'm not sure," she said. "But he says he's Diego." She flagged down the waiter and paid the bill while Victor shoveled down the rest of his pie.

Ten minutes later, they were back at the high school lot. Dagny blew past the guard at the door and stormed into the gymnasium, with

Victor following behind. She grabbed the first technician she found by the arm to catch his attention.

"Where is Father Vega?" she demanded.

The man led them to a stainless-steel gurney. The corpse on top of it was covered with a white sheet. "Take it off," Dagny said. The man removed the sheet, revealing Diego's naked, lifeless body. "Turn him over."

"I'm sorry," he said, not understanding her request.

"Turn the body over. I need to see his back."

He seemed puzzled, but he obliged. When she saw that the man's back was bare, she began to cry.

"What's wrong?" Victor said.

"Diego has a tattoo. This isn't Diego. This isn't him." She brushed away her tears. "He's really alive." She hugged Victor, who seemed surprised but reciprocated the gesture.

"If that's not Diego," he said, "then who is it?"

"I don't know."

"It looks exactly like him. The man could be his twin."

Her phone rang. She pulled back from the hug and answered her phone. "I'm waiting outside," Diego said. "What's going on?"

"We'll be right out."

Dagny ran through the gymnasium with Victor jogging behind her. She pushed open the doors, searched the lot for Diego, and sprinted toward him. Throwing her arms around him, she nearly knocked him down.

"You sounded angry on the phone," he said.

"Thank God you're alive."

"What happened?"

She pulled away from the embrace. "We thought you were dead. I found your body in front of my motel door."

"My body?"

"He looks just like you," Victor said.

"Who does?"

"A dead man on a gurney in there," she said, hiking her thumb toward the school. "Where have you been?"

"I resigned from the church, and then I went to see Katrina."

Dagny was surprised that it hurt to hear this. They had shared a fleeting moment in the middle of the excitement of the case. To the extent it seemed like there was something more to it, it had been an illusion. "How did it go?"

He shook his head. "She refused to see me."

"I'm sorry, Diego. Wait, did you say you resigned from the church?"

"Yes."

"Why?"

He laughed. "If anyone should understand why I don't belong in the church, it should be you."

She shook her head. "I can't think of anyone who belongs there more."

"That's a nice thing to say, but there's a different life for me out there." He paused for a moment, then said, "Did you say you saw a dead body that looked like me? I don't understand."

"I don't, either."

"May I see the body?"

Dagny didn't want to look at it again. "Can you take him, Victor?"

"Sure," Victor said. As they started toward the school, he turned to Diego and asked, "Who is Katrina?"

CHAPTER 71

The cold air startled Diego. "I forgot how it felt in here," he said, survey-ing the sea of gurneys in the gymnasium, searching for his doppelgänger.

"Who is Katrina?" Victor repeated.

There wasn't an easy way to answer the question. "She's one of the reasons I want to leave the priesthood."

"You love her?"

"I do."

"But she wouldn't see you?"

"She wouldn't."

"So, what are you going to do?"

"I don't know." If Katrina didn't love him anymore, he needed to hear her say it in person. That was the only way he could know it was real.

Victor stopped and turned to him. "Everyone has to do what they have to do, I guess. It's a shame, though, about you resigning from the

ACKNOWLEDGMENTS

....

If you thought I wasn't going to thank my wife first, you're crazy. Kate Miller is a brilliant, loving, and supportive spouse, the only person I trust with early drafts, and a tremendous partner for life. I would be lost without her.

My sons, Freeman and Calvin, bring me joy, make me laugh, and give me purpose every day. They better not read this book for at least ten years, though.

My parents, Joel and Linda Miller, can rightfully claim responsibility for anything good about me. They are my biggest fans, and I can't thank them enough for it. Stephanie Sellers is probably responsible for half of my sales in Texas. I am beyond fortunate to be her brother.

I sought out friends and fans of *The Bubble Gum Thief* to serve as beta readers for a draft of this book, and they provided incredible feedback. Thank you, Jill Sopko, Brian Mason, Brad Monton, Aimee Landis, David Mortman, Michael Rich, Lynn Wagner, Jeb Brack, Gail Anderson, Kate Craig, Matt Tauber, Vickie Krevatin, Jordan

Lusink, Stephanie Wakeman, Deborah Cochrane, Carol Gibbs, Lori Parr, Mikhael Shor, Michael Bronson, Vipul Vyas, Lisa Stewart, Jory Lockwood, Jim Bates, and Heather Har-Zvi. I am grateful for all of your time and efforts. The great author Michael J. Sullivan and his wife, Robin, provided excellent advice about the beta-read process.

The Arlington Writers Group, led by Michael Klein, will always be my home, even in absentia.

My agent, the lovely Victoria Skurnick, waited patiently for this book, helped make it better, and sold it. I'll do my best to write the next one faster, Victoria.

Thank you JoVon Sotak, Jacque Ben-Zekry, and everyone else at Thomas & Mercer for your support, and for doing so much to bring writers to readers. And thank you to my fellow Thomas & Mercer writers, many of whom have provided advice and support. It's wonderful to be part of such a community.

My developmental editor, Bryon Quertermous, provided excellent suggestions that improved and tightened the book, and reminded me that not everything is precious. Valerie Kalfrin not only fixed story problems and caught hundreds of typos in her copyedit but also kept me from naming three different characters Davis. Proofreader Stacy Abrams fixed things I never would have caught in a million years.

I try to find inspiration in the real world, and I'm helped immensely by those who write about it. Radley Balko always does terrific reporting, and his book *Rise of the Warrior Cop: The Militarization of America's Police Forces* is fantastic. Terry Sterling's *Illegal: Life and Death in Arizona's Immigration War Zone* was a great and illuminating resource. Eileen Kelley and the *Cincinnati Enquirer* did a wonderful series on immigrants in Southwestern Ohio.

There are surely countless other people I should be thanking, and I beg their forgiveness for the oversight.

ABOUT THE AUTHOR

 Jeff Miller started plotting stories as a boy on an Apple IIc personal computer, and he's been writing ever since. His first novel, *The Bubble Gum Thief*, kicked off his Dagny Gray series. Jeff lives in Cincinnati with his wife and their two young sons in a house littered with Legos. Visit him online at www.jeffmillerwrites.com.

priesthood. I'm not very religious, but if there were more priests like you, I might be."

"Thank you. That's a really nice thing to say."

"You sure you want to see this body?"

He didn't want to see it, but he knew he had to. "Yes."

Victor led him through the maze of people, tables, and gurneys. "It's this one," he said, reaching for the corners of the white sheet covering the body. "This is going to be weird for you." He slipped the sheet down to the waist.

The body was not merely of similar shape and size. It did not simply resemble him or bear an uncanny resemblance to him. Diego was staring at his own form, lying dead before him. "There was no identification on him?"

"None."

"I don't understand."

"Is it possible that you had a twin brother?" Victor asked.

"No," he said. "It's not possible. My parents would have . . ." He stopped. Would they have told him? Could he have been adopted?

Victor walked over to one of the technicians and came back with a pad of paper and an ink pad. "Let's try something," he said. "Give me your thumb."

Diego held his right hand out. Victor rolled his thumb in ink and then pressed it on the paper. He lifted the corpse's right hand and did the same. He held the prints close to his eyes and studied them.

"Are they the same?"

"Identical twins don't have the exact same fingerprints, but they're usually similar. They might have the same general peaks and curves. The same kind of pattern." Victor handed Diego the paper. "I'm no expert, but these are pretty close if you ask me."

The lines swirled and crested in similar ways. So similar as to mean something? He didn't know. "What about DNA? Is that definitive?"

"Yes."

"Can you do that for me? Is that something you could do, maybe as part of identifying the body?"

"Absolutely," Victor said. He called over a technician and explained the situation to her.

She rolled up Diego's sleeves and tied a rubber band around his arm. He looked at his possible twin while she stuck him with the needle and thought about the great loneliness he had felt his entire life.

She pulled out the needle and transferred the blood into two vials. "I need to swab you. Open your mouth." He obliged, and she scraped the inside of his cheeks. "All done," she said.

Diego turned to Victor. "You'll let me know the results?"

"As soon as I get them."

"Thanks, Victor."

"Sure." He started to cover the body.

"Wait," Diego said. "Can I have a minute?"

"Of course." Victor set down the sheet and backed away.

Diego leaned over the body. If this were his brother, why didn't he know this? Why had this man come to Bilford? Was he looking for Diego? He reached out to touch the cheek of his likeness.

"You can't touch—" a technician called out, but Victor raised his hand and stopped her.

Diego leaned closer to the body and whispered, "When Rebekah was pregnant with Isaac's twins, the babies jostled with her. She asked the Lord why this was happening, and he said, 'Two nations are in your womb, and two peoples within you will be separated. One people will be stronger than the other, and the older will serve the younger.' I don't know if you're my twin, but if you are, I promise I will serve you, and whatever you have left behind."

No matter how far Diego drifted from the church, the Bible would always be his vernacular. He grabbed the white sheet and pulled it over the body's head.

He felt Victor's hand on his shoulder and turned to him. "Thank you."

Victor nodded. They started toward the door. "You know, I'm surprised to hear about Katrina," Victor said. "I actually thought there might be something between you and Dagny."

Diego smiled. There was something. He thought about how to explain it. "She's an incredible woman, but being with her mostly just reminded me of the way I felt about Katrina. That probably doesn't make any sense."

"No, I get it," Victor said. "I called my fiancée last night and called off our wedding."

"Seriously? Why?"

"The more time I spent with her, the more I started to have feelings for someone else. That can't be good."

"Are you going to go after that someone else?"

Victor shook his head. "No. It wouldn't work, for all kinds of reasons. But the fact that I was thinking about her told me that my engagement was a mistake."

Diego stopped at the gymnasium door and put a hand on his shoulder. "I've spent years running away from love, and it's left me miserable and lonely. Don't let pride get in the way of your happiness. Don't give up just because it's hard. Whatever obstacles you face can't be bigger than the obstacles between a priest and a nun. Now let's get out of this place. It's freezing in here."

CHAPTER 72

....

Dagny was leaning against the hood of Diego's Corvette when the men came out of the school. She tried to decipher Diego's expression. Was it sadness or confusion?

He walked up to her. "I don't understand what I've seen."

"I don't understand it, either," she said.

"Either this is an astonishing coincidence, or I don't know anything about where I came from."

"Sounds like that might be something worth investigating." She pulled his car keys from her pocket and handed them to Diego. "Hate to give it up. I got used to the ride."

He reached into his pocket, pulled out his rental-car keys. "Take my rental."

She took the keys. "Thanks, Diego."

"It's nothing."

"No," she said. "Thanks for everything. You're the reason we stopped Fisher. It wouldn't have happened without you."

He blushed. "That's not true," he said, but even he had to know it was. "So, what happens now? You head back to DC, I guess?"

"It will take a few days to wind this down."

"And then what?"

"And then we look for another case."

"I can't imagine living like this all of the time."

"I was going to suggest that you try it. You'd be a good agent, Diego."

He shook his head. "Once is enough for me."

"So, what are you going to do? If you're really not going to be a priest anymore."

"I have no idea."

"Well, maybe you ought to give Katrina one more try," Dagny said. The girl might not have deserved another chance with Diego, but he sure deserved another chance with her.

"I might." Diego looked into her eyes. "So, I guess this is good-bye." He leaned forward and embraced her. "Thank you," he whispered. "I can't say that enough."

"I'm going to miss you, Diego."

"And I, you." He pulled away from her, climbed into his Corvette, and started the engine. Victor put his arm around Dagny.

"He seems like a great guy," he said.

"He might be the best man I have ever known."

They watched him drive away. When he was gone, Victor turned to Dagny. "How are you on your points?"

"Behind." She couldn't remember the last time she had logged them. "I might need a better system."

They spent the next several days closing down the shop. Bodies that were identified and claimed were released for funerals. They cremated the rest. Technicians were released from duty. Gurneys were collapsed. Equipment was returned. Dagny and Victor spent most of their time sifting through evidence, determining what needed to be saved and what could be pitched.

Bilford PD delivered four boxes of evidence that had been collected from the raid that killed Fisher. Dagny found her backpack among the contents.

Victor found a video camera in the collection. They took it to the gym teacher's office and plugged the television's HDMI cable into the camera. Dagny changed the input on the television and hit "Play."

Allison Jenkins sat, tied in a chair opposite from Fisher. Her hair was unkempt, and there were bags under her eyes. The bright-red handprint on her cheek suggested that she'd been slapped hard. "This is Allison Jenkins, live at the home of the silo killer, with an exclusive interview." She said it with surprising vigor, considering her circumstance. "Would you please tell the country who you are?"

"My name is Harold Fisher," the thin man said. "And I'm an American."

Jenkins glanced down at papers on her lap and read, "Where are you from?"

"I was born here in Bilford."

"What did your father do?"

"My daddy worked at the Dakota Ironworks." The thin man turned toward the camera. "Most of you are too young to have heard of it. It was a different country then. A time when men worked with their hands and knew how to build things. My daddy welded iron from six to five every day, and then came home and beat me for my transgressions.

"Most of the time, I deserved it." He pulled a sheet of paper from the floor and studied it, then set it back down and continued. "The heavy hand of my father's discipline made me into a man. We don't make many of those anymore, and it's because the whole country has gone soft. My daddy taught me to defend myself. He taught me that life wasn't easy, and that every day of pain is another day of life. He showed me that justice was order, and that being a man means standing for something.

"It took me a long time to learn these things. As a teenager, I drank and smoked pot. I shoplifted sometimes. Booze or magazines. My daddy always found out, and he bloodied me until I couldn't speak. I'd run to my mama afterward. She'd clean me up and beg me to be good. When I was sixteen, she told me she was going to leave my father. I asked if I could go with her, but she said no. She said I needed my father's guidance, and she was right." He turned to Allison and signaled for her to ask the next question.

"What happened after your mother left?"

"Daddy became violent. I took a knife in the leg one night. The next night, I put one in his while he was sleeping. Old man pulled it from his leg and smiled. 'Finally,' he said. 'Finally, you're a man.'

"After that, he didn't beat me no more. I graduated from high school and joined the navy. Best decision I ever made. It taught me the importance of structure and routine. It gave me a sense of responsibility." He gestured to Allison again.

"When did you fall in love?"

"When we were stationed in the Philippines, I met a girl named Malaya. She was beautiful and fragile and loving. We didn't plan on her getting pregnant, but I stuck with her. I was there when she gave birth to the boy we named David, and I took them both back to the States when my stint was over. We got married here in Bilford, and I took a job at the Dakota plant like my dad."

"What happened next?"

"Malaya died when David was eight years old, and I was left to raise the boy on my own. I gave that boy all of my wisdom and all of my heart. When the Dakota closed down, I found odd jobs here and there, anything to put food on the table.

"David was a good kid. Graduated from Bilford High with better grades than me. Worked at the Olive Garden for a while and did just fine. Was saving money for college. Met some college kids, and when the cops busted them for smoking pot, they busted David, too. Sent him to jail for a month. On the day of the release, INS showed up and said they were going to deport him to the Philippines, and they took him away."

"How could they do such an injustice?" Jenkins dutifully read.

"They said I wasn't his daddy. They said his mother was a whore, and that she whored around. Said David's birth date and weight suggested he was conceived before my ship arrived in the Philippines." His voice grew louder, angry. "They said that this boy who I had raised was not an American citizen, even though he had been raised in America by a man who had served his country with honor."

"What did you do?"

"I hired a lawyer, and she got David a conditional release and a nine-month stay of deportation. And I took this boy back into my home. But when I looked at him, I didn't see me anymore. And when I pictured his mother, I didn't see a woman who was beautiful and fragile and loving. I saw a woman who slept around. I saw filth and deception.

"And this boy who had been released to my care," he continued, "was just a lie. I had devoted my life to this lie. There was none of me in him. This made me angry, and in this anger, I struck him and killed him."

Allison Jenkins stared at him. He looked at her and motioned for her to ask the next question. She looked down at her list. "Why did you kill him?"

"I didn't kill him. This country did. This country that I'd served. It made me kill him. David was my boy until the INS showed up. Malaya was my love until the INS showed up. No one would have cared about David if immigration weren't an issue in this country. And it's only an issue because so many Mexicans have poured over our borders.

"And to be fair, I helped it happen. I had hired those Mexicans to tend the properties we had foreclosed, and I had placed them in other jobs, too. You can see the irony, Allison, right? I had helped make this problem, and if I hadn't, David would be my son, and Malaya would be my love, and everything would be all right. I had to undo what I had done. And so I started killing them."

He spent several minutes describing his murders in sadistic detail and with obvious pride. "But then I realized that none of you cared, and that I didn't matter to you," he said, looking into the camera. "So I blew a fireball into the sky, and suddenly, you noticed. You sent all the pretty people to Bilford with their cameras and their theories. And yet, you still don't get it. This story isn't about the murder of some Mexicans. It's about what you all did to me. You're all monsters out there. You all deserve to die.

"If you kill, I shall rise like Christ and smite you all." His voice, rising, began to shake with fury. "You shall ravage in the bowels of hell for what you have done. You shall rot in the stink of your filth. My hands are clean. The blood is on yours. And now you shall live with this knowledge, just like you gave me knowledge to live with."

He turned back to Allison and smiled. "That was perfect, don't you think? Now everyone will understand why I had to do this."

Allison stared at him intently. "You didn't have to do any of this."

The thin man leaned toward her, and his face filled with rage. "I just explained it as clearly as I can. You still don't understand?"

"No, I understand," she said, backtracking. "It does make sense."

"You just said it didn't."

"I was wrong. It does."

Fisher froze for a moment, and then his body began to shake. "You know what? You've been a silly distraction, and this has been a waste of time." He raised his voice. "I've given you all this attention, and the gift of my story, and all you've done is deceive with your beauty and your manner. I opened my heart to you!"

He disappeared off screen and came back with a rope. Dagny stopped the playback.

"What do we do with this?" Victor said.

"Bury it in the file."

"Won't people want to see it?"

"That's why we bury it. You don't grant the wishes of murderers."

They put the camera in the last numbered box of the file. The next day, trucks came to take everything away. The morgue was converted back to a gymnasium; the armories were returned to locker rooms. She welcomed the coach back to his office, thanked Principal Geathers for her hospitality, and sent Victor back to DC.

Dagny stayed in Bilford for three more days. It took that long to help John Beamer reassemble his train set.

CHAPTER 73

Diego performed a final and unauthorized sermon to a packed crowd in the back of Barrio Burrito. He riffed a bit on Ecclesiastes 3, and then told them it was time for him to leave. They loaded him with food and gifts and buried him in hugs.

Back home, he loaded his last possessions into a suitcase and tossed the house key on the counter so the landlord could find it. He'd given most of his things away through Craigslist. They wouldn't have fetched much if he had tried to sell them.

He tossed his suitcase into the trunk of the Corvette and drove one last time to Dayton. Every few minutes, he fiddled with the envelope inside his coat pocket to make sure it was there.

McPherson Convent was both colonial and gothic—a brick-and-wood melding of American and Renaissance styles. He parked across the street from the front entrance, wishing, once again, that he drove a less conspicuous car.

The entrance to the convent was blocked by a tall iron gate. An intercom allowed visitors to request admittance. Last time, he had buzzed it enough to wear out his welcome.

He watched as sisters filtered in and out of the convent. One of them was Katrina, but he knew better than to try to approach her. Instead, he waited for Sister Cathy, because she had always been kind to him, and because she was a little rebellious.

When he spied Cathy returning from an outing, Diego rushed from his car and ran up beside her.

She turned to him and jumped. "Well, *you* shouldn't be here."

"I know," he said. "But I need a favor."

"I can't let you in."

"I don't need you to. I just need you to take this." He pushed the envelope toward her hand, but she refused to take it. "Please?" he begged.

"I'm sure this is a mistake," she said, grabbing it and taking it inside.

Diego went back to his car and watched. He watched the kids walk home from school. He watched the rush-hour traffic clog the streets. He watched the streetlights come on. He watched until he fell asleep, and he slept until Katrina knocked on the passenger window the next morning and woke him up.

He reached over and unlocked the door. She opened it and climbed into the passenger seat.

"You read the letter?" he said.

She said nothing and nodded. Finally, she turned to him. "Why do you have to make everything so hard?"

"I love you, Katrina."

"I know that, Diego."

"I know you love me, too."

"I love God."

"You could love us both."

"God's love is better. He never left me."

"I never left you, either. Not really. That's why you're here."

"What do you want me to do?"

"Come with me to Texas."

She shook her head. "You have things to work out with your family. Go and come back. We can talk then."

Diego shook his head. "I want you to come. I *need* you to come."

Katrina kept shaking her head. "It was a good letter, but it wasn't that good." She sighed. "They're sure he's your brother?"

"He's my twin. That's what the DNA test said."

"How did he end up in Bilford?"

"I think he was looking for me. I think a coyote helped him cross the border."

"So, he was from Mexico?"

"It would seem."

"But you're American?"

"I don't know. I feel like I don't know anything right now. Except that I love you. Please come with me."

"Diego . . ."

"Do you love me?"

"That's not a fair question."

"Do you?"

"The last time I told you, you broke my heart."

"I won't this time."

"You're asking me to give up my dream."

"I'm asking you to start a new one." He felt the window closing. "You've been in the convent awhile now. Are you happy?"

"I'm content."

"God wants more for you."

"Diego, you don't even believe in God."

"I do."

"You're just saying that."

"No, I mean it. I've done things recently where it felt like someone was guiding me."

"Of course, he is guiding you, Diego."

"And he has guided me here, sitting with you, asking you to come to Texas."

"You went to Bilford because you didn't trust me to make my own choice. Do you understand how angry that made me?"

"I do. I didn't back then, but I do now."

"I don't want you to ever do that again."

"I won't."

She shook her head, then tilted it and gave a hint of a smile. "Okay. I'll come with you."

Diego leaned forward and kissed her. "I'll wait here while you pack."

She opened the passenger door and reached for a suitcase on the curb.

"You already knew you were going to come?"

"It was actually a very good letter," she said.

CHAPTER 74

They convened at the Professor's home in Arlington. The Professor sat behind a desk that looked larger than it had before. Or maybe the Professor just looked smaller.

Brent and Victor sat on the sofa opposite her. Victor was waving a file in the air. "Henderson Equity is a hedge fund out of Short Hills, New Jersey. Its portfolio is diversified, but when you look at the breakdown, you'll see—"

"This sounds like a case with no bodies," the Professor said.

"No bodies, but there are—"

"I want bodies." He turned to Brent. "What do you have?"

"Missing girl in Jackson, Wyoming. Seven years old—"

"Are her parents divorced?"

"No."

"No custody issues?"

"No."

"When was the abduction?"

"Three days ago."

"Then it's probably too late."

"To save her, maybe. Not to catch the guy."

"Why should we take it? What makes this case special?"

"The girl is black," Brent said. "And poor. Not a lot of poor black girls in Jackson. Low media coverage. Local police aren't giving it a full-court press. It's a chance to do something right."

The Professor sighed. "I suppose there is value in that. It's too small a case for us, though—"

"We could wrap it in a week," Brent said. "Get the headlines and move on to something new."

"Perhaps."

"I have a case," Dagny said. "Four murders in Lexington, Kentucky, all within the last three months. Two students and two other college-age women. One of them—"

"You're not picking this time," the Professor said. "We've done enough of your cases for a while."

"It's a good case."

"I said no." He stood. "Brent, you can fly out to Jackson today. You have forty-eight hours to make some progress with it. Otherwise, we'll do Victor's stupid money case, I suppose."

"I can go with Brent," Dagny said.

The Professor shook his head. "This is Brent's case. If you're needed, we'll pull you in."

Victor glanced at Dagny. She nodded. This was her punishment. They had wondered what form it would take.

The Professor saw them to the door but asked Dagny to stay behind. After Victor and Brent left, he turned to her and said, "I'll make you a deal."

"What is it?"

"Tell me how you knew where Fisher was."

She knew it was killing him not to know. "Will it buy forgiveness?"

"Absolutely not. But I'll let you fly to Lexington and poke around, see if your case can beat Brent's little-girl case."

That was as close to forgiveness as she could expect. "Fisher stole my backpack when he dumped the body at the motel. When he turned on my iPad, I was able to track it."

"You must be kidding."

"I'm not."

He smiled. "I'm glad to hear that."

"Why?"

"Because it means it was dumb luck. If you'd outsmarted me, I would have been worried."

"So, I can go to Lexington?"

"You can leave *tomorrow*. It's only fair to give Brent a head start. Same deadline for both of you."

"Thanks."

The Professor frowned. "Things will never be the same between us, you understand. I don't trust you anymore. I don't know that I even like you anymore."

"I understand." She walked out on to the front porch and looked back at the Professor. He stood in the doorway, shaking his head.

"You've hurt me, Dagny," he said, closing the door.

As she drove home, those last words bounced around her head. They rattled inside her while she packed her bag for the next day's trip and while she made herself a salad for a late lunch.

She picked at the salad while sifting through bills and junk mail, and returning calls and e-mails from acquaintances who had seen her press conference in Bilford. When she finished, she felt bored and sad.

She grabbed a DSW coupon from her pile of junk mail and headed to Pentagon City, where she treated herself to three new pairs of sneakers. When she returned home, she laced up a new pair and went for a run.

The Mount Vernon trail was packed with people, bikes, and strollers. She treated them like video-game obstacles. Passing a runner got her two points. A bicyclist was five, unless it was a tandem bike, and then it was twelve. Strollers were worth twenty points. At one point, Dagny passed a woman juggling on a unicycle; Dagny gave herself one hundred points for that one.

By the time she got to Thomas Jefferson Island, Dagny had racked up 682 points. The run back home got her another 421. A twenty-minute shower let her map out a strategy for the next day's trip to Lexington. She turned off the water, grabbed a towel, and dried. Stepping onto the bathroom rug, she stared for a moment at the bathroom scale. Every instinct told her to ignore it, but she knew those instincts were bad. She dropped the towel to the floor and stepped on.

One hundred and eighteen. Seven pounds less than her target. It could have been worse, but it should have been better.

She wrapped the towel back around her body, walked to her bedroom, and dialed her phone. "I'd like to make an appointment," she said.

"Can I have your name?"

"Dagny Gray."

"Are you currently a patient of Dr. Childs?"

"I am."

"How is Friday at eight a.m.?"

She would be back from Lexington by then. "Perfect."

Hanging up the phone, Dagny glanced at the clock. It was 7:15 p.m. She dressed quickly, grabbed her keys, and drove to the Target at Potomac Yard. Grabbing a cart, she darted back to the toy aisles. Superhero costumes, *Star Wars* Legos, Elsa dresses—none of it seemed right. A shelf full of Nerf guns caught Dagny's eye. She grabbed the biggest one and tossed it in her cart, then added Scotch tape, a birthday card, and a roll of wrapping paper to her haul on the way to the checkout counter.

"Who's the lucky boy?" the clerk asked as he rang her up.

"Girl," Dagny said.

She wheeled her cart to her car, popped the hatch, rolled out the paper, and set the toy on it. Tearing the paper by hand and applying a good amount of tape gave her a passably wrapped present. She dug through her glove box, found a pen, scribbled a message on the card, and sealed it in its envelope.

It was only five minutes to Old Town. Dagny pulled into a cobblestone alley and parked in front of a three-story brownstone. Present and card in hand, she jogged up the steps and knocked on the door. She heard the clatter of feet and the turn of the latch. When the door opened, Julia Bremmer was standing there, holding a phone to her ear.

"Hey," she said into the phone. "I'm going to have to call you back."

"I'm sorry I missed Emily's birthday," Dagny said.

Julia smiled and threw her arms around Dagny. "I've missed you."

"I've missed you, too."

"Come on in."

EPILOGUE

··

Two months later . . .

"It's ten thirty-five, and you're listening to *The Hank Frank Show*. Let's go to Ted on line three. Ted, how's it going?"

"Permission to speak frankly, Hank?"

"Permission granted."

"I like this Beamer kid as much as anyone, but I'm hearing rumors that this kid is gay."

"Ted, there hasn't been a bigger supporter of Sheriff Don Marigold than Hank Frank. Anyone who has listened to me over the years knows that. Don is a great man and a great American. But the primary job of a sheriff is to keep the county safe, and it might be a good time for some young blood with the energy to do it. Now, I'm not a big fan of the gay agenda, as you all know. I don't know if John Beamer is gay or not, but I do know that Sheriff Don didn't find Harry Fisher, and the FBI didn't, either. If another maniac were on the loose in Bilford, I'd want a sheriff who could find him, not someone who will make a few grandstanding arrests that have nothing to do with anything. Whatever John Beamer does in the privacy of his own home is his business. Keeping this county safe is the business of the office, and he's shown us he can do that. So, if Beamer can get enough signatures for a recall election in the spring, he's got my vote."

Frank pushed a button to release the call. "Now, folks, I've got to tell you that this morning, I was a big Hank Frank crank when I read in the paper that there are folks in the statehouse who want to institute a property tax on our cars like they have in Kentucky. So, let me get this straight—we're going to pay a sales tax when we buy the car, and then more tax every year on the car until its value dwindles down to nothing? I call this a perpetual tax, and you can bet I'm going to do my best to stop it. One of my allies is State Senator Max Winger, and we'll check with him after this break."